Each Alone, Across A Vast Unknown

A Scottish Family's Lives and Solo Journeys to America

Sally Eccleston

Strategic Book Publishing and Rights Co.

Strategic Book Publishing and Rights Co., LLC
USA | Singapore
www.sbpra.net

ISBN: 978-1-68235-485-8

This book is dedicated to my beloved grandchildren, Gracelyn and Hudson Sylvester, who have lent to me delightful insight into the enchanted imaginations of children. They are the basis for my portrayal of the Baird family children of Scotland, with their endearing conversations, creative interactions, and energetic activities, as they learn to navigate their complex and thrilling environment. At times, children must steer through a scary and unpredictable world, but extract unlimited magic from the universal source to aid them – their innocent minds are much closer to this source and more receptive by way of their imaginations to the wonder of it all. My grandchildren have rekindled in me a sense of what it was like to be a child, as well as having bestowed in me an understanding, from an adult perspective, of the fathomless optimism, joys, creativity, and unlimited energy of childhood. What I would give to have such energy and optimism once again! I also would like to dedicate this book to my son, Bret, who inherited from me a penchant for literature and writing, particularly as it relates to the natural environment. Having studied literature and writing in college in Nevada, he has enthusiastically aided me in my book endeavors. Above all, I would like to thank the historian, raconteur, and preserver of our family records, letters, and photographs, my mother Jean Erwin Eccleston.

TABLE OF CONTENTS

Chapter Two

Chapter Three

Chapter Four

Chapter Five

Chapter Three

BOOK TEN

THOSE REMAINING IN SCOTLAND **485**

Chapter One

Chapter Two

EPILOGUE

ADAM, HENRY, AND CATHERINE IN FRESNO — LATER YEARS **503**

PREFACE

Each Alone, Across A Vast Unknown is a fictional depiction of the lives of my four great-grandparents, three of whom voyaged solely from Scotland to America by steamer ship in the 1860s and 1870s. A fourth great-grandparent, Sarah Weir Baird, a widow in her late thirties, was already living in the San Joaquin Valley of California when she met my maternal great-grandfather, Henry Baird.

Two of my great-grandparents, Adam and Henry Baird, were siblings from a berry ranch (Drumdruils) in Bridge of Allan, Scotland. Adam was my father's grandfather and Henry my mother's grandfather, which made my two grandmothers first cousins, though of different generations.

Adam Baird was romantically involved with a church and school friend, Ruthie Malcolm of Helensburgh, for several years during his adolescence in Bridge of Allan. The entire Malcolm family was by all accounts close friends with the Baird family and belonged to the same church. Adam most likely would have married Ruthie Malcolm if his urge to follow his dream to America had not taken precedence. Perhaps Adam had plans to send for Ruthie to join him in America later on, but, sadly, Ruthie died while he was crossing the Atlantic on the *S.S. Will-o-the-Wisp*. Eventually, Adam sought out Catherine Malcolm, Ruthie's younger sister, after establishing himself as a carpenter in the Caledonia mines of Virginia City, Nevada. Adam courted Catherine Malcolm, a Helensburgh schoolteacher, through letter writing (an erratic, frustrating way to relay his sound character and personality, and to justify his qualifications and desirability as a marriage partner, due to the extremely slow mail service across the vast American frontier). Adam eventually enticed Catherine to travel from Helensburgh, Scotland, to Virginia City, Nevada, to be his wife (perhaps by the wit and charm of his missives) after her mother died, although Catherine could hardly have known what to expect in Adam's appearance or persona, as she was a young adolescent when he left for America.

Henry Baird, Adam's younger brother, had an illegitimate child in Scotland by a lassie who died in childbirth. (In the book I invented a marriage for Henry and his girlfriend Annie that is fictional, but that union might have occurred if Annie MacGivens (a fictional name) had not died giving birth.) After coming to America more than five years after Adam, Henry lived in Virginia City near Catherine and Adam, and worked for the Caledonia mines as an accountant. He eventually moved to the San Joaquin Valley in California to be a ranch manager, where he met his wife, Sarah Weir, in the small valley town of Armona. This late union produced a second daughter, Katherine Baird, my maternal grandmother, as Henry would have been in his early fifties by then, and Sarah Weir in her forties.

The senior Bairds raised Henry's first daughter, Mary Baird, along with the younger siblings of Henry and Adam, on the Bairds' ranch of Drumdruils. Several of the Baird siblings stayed on the ranch their entire lives, as did Mary. Sadly, Henry never went back to Scotland and never saw his daughter again, but supported her and the other Baird siblings through college years after becoming affluent. Mary became a schoolteacher in Bridge of Allan, and was a spinster.

A rancher's wife in St. Louis, Missouri, Sarah Weir Baird, Henry's later-in-life wife, had a young daughter and two grown sons when widowed. Sarah and her daughter came to live with her brother, John Weir, in Armona, California. The Weir family had arrived from Scotland much earlier, dating back to the earliest American settlers. Her family had traveled from an eastern part of America to the Missouri area by wagon train when Sarah was 10 years of age.

Sarah and Henry lived in Armona wherein they had their daughter, Katherine. Unfortunately, Sarah died from complications of childbirth when my grandmother, Katherine, was only fourteen months old, leaving poor Henry with two motherless daughters, one in Scotland and one in America. Henry was certainly unlucky in love, but from all accounts a handsome, charismatic, very generous, and overall wonderful man. He financed the educations of many of his Baird siblings back in Scotland, as well as children of family friends and relatives in California.

Although this is a fictional story of my ancestors, most of the happenings are surprisingly true, having been taken from diaries of Catherine Malcolm and Adam Baird, and from stories told to me by my parents and grandparents. Adam chronicled his journey across America, working on the railway as well as his carpentry work in the mines of Nevada. All of the stories of Adam's journey to Nevada are true (save for involvement of Wee Ones and his best friend, Adrian), and came from his journal.

Catherine Malcolm Baird left an autobiography of her perilous steamer journey to America on the *S.S. Alabama*, given to me as a present by my paternal grandmother, Ethel Baird Eccleston. Catherine came perilously close to death when a giant iceberg struck the *S.S. Alabama*. She stayed in St. John's, Newfoundland, for three months awaiting repair of the ship and, it appears by all accounts, had a marvelous time. Catherine did have a romance with the Scottish captain on the ship and in St. John's, but the intricacies of this romance have been left to my fertile imagination. Why she decided against the captain and ventured on to Nevada is left to conjecture.

Of course, the Wee Ones are fictional characters, but I cannot imagine all my ancestors surviving such perilous voyages without a wee bit of interventional magic. The Scottish people, on the whole, revere the Wee Ones in their folklore, and a fair percentage of them prefer to hold onto their childhood beliefs that these incredible magical creatures really do exist in the dun-shis of Scotland, coming out to aid them in times of dire need.

ACKNOWLEDGEMENTS

I am grateful to my ancestors, those I have known and those who came before me, for lending me a rich tapestry of information which has enabled me to relay the stories of their lives. Without their fearlessness, I would not be alive and living in America in the twenty-first century, a technologically rich life that they would find incomprehensible, although the beginnings of the technological age were taking root in their homeland in their time; and, in fact, Scotland was at the center of it all.

In looking back at the lives of these amazing people, I am struck by the notion that they were far braver and their lives far more interesting and colorful than my own. I can only say that I am proud to be a descendent of these adventurous Scottish people, who left a beloved homeland not out of necessity but by a mysterious inner drive to fulfill their destinies in a wild land. In giving these characters life, I have used some of the personality traits of myself and my family members, for it must be said that descendants inherit vestiges of personality (temperament, predilections, energy, intro/extroversion, humor, etc.) from those that came before them; also, it must be that families pass down from generation to generation their moral beliefs and modes of ethical behavior, as well as lenses through which to interpret and respond to the iniquities and mistreatment of their fellow human beings while encountering the world at large.

I would also like to thank my parents and grandparents for passing on letters and stories of their grandparents and great-grandparents. My father knew his grandfather, Adam Baird, and my grandmother, Katherine Baird, told me many stories of her beloved father, Henry Baird, who died when she was twenty-one years of age and a mother to a one-year-old baby, my mother, Jean Erwin.

Adam Baird and Catherine Malcolm Baird raised my paternal grandmother, Ethel Baird Eccleston, along with her five siblings. I can imagine what Adam and Catherine were like as parents, in having known well my Victorian grandmother until her death in her nineties. She was strict, kind, and loving, and I inherited many of her physical attributes as well as, most likely, some of her personality traits. I would love to have known all my great-grandparents and to have heard their stories firsthand. I am amazed that in these time of longevity of life, my own grandchildren have had the privilege of knowing well some of their great-grandparents.

I'd like to thank the editors at Strategic Publishing for their editorial assistance.

All of the poetical quotes at the beginning of some chapters come from the nineteenth century book *Complete Dictionary of Poetical Quotations: Comprising the Most Excellent and Appropriate Passages in the Old British Poets; With Choice and Copious Selections From the Best Modern British and American Poets.* Philadelphia, Claxton, Remsen and Haffelfinger, author: Hale, Sarah Josepha Buell, 1788-1879; Addington, John F. {from old catalog}; Susan B. Anthony Collection {Library of Congress} DLC {old catalog}

Subject: Quotations, English
Publisher: Philadelphia, Lippincott, Grambo & Co.
Year: 1855
Possible copyright status: NOT IN COPYRIGHT
Language: English
Book contributor: Harvard University
Collection: Americana

PROLOGUE

"If you want your children to be intelligent, read them fairy tales. If you want them to be more intelligent, read them more fairy tales."

– Albert Einstein

"I shall once more lie in bed, and see the little sandy isle in Allan Water, as it is in nature, and the child (that once was me) wading there in butterburs; and wonder at the instancy and virgin freshness of that memory; and be pricked again, in season and out of season, by the desire to weave it into art."

– Robert Lewis Stevenson speaking of his summer vacations as a child in Bridge of Allan

A living, breathing magic existed in our homeland of Scotland, magic that resides in all its living creatures, its mountains, lochs, rivers, hillocks, woodlands, and sky. Remembering Drumdruils farm in Bridge o' Allan and the magic o' Scotland soothed my loneliness in America. I carried my homeland in my heart wherever I went!

– Reminiscences of Adam Baird (imagined by the author). Adam died in Oakland, California, at age eighty-five in 1931.

I pray someday to come home and die in Scotland at a very ripe old age – singing, dancing, and drinking to me heart's content amongst the Wee Ones on a fairy hill, thanking them for igniting my spirit with enchantment. The ancient Good People taught me from an early age o' the extraordinary powers that exist in the human spirit and mind, the power of imagination. They possess a tad more of this in their beings due to their close relationship with the heavenly angels. With an imaginative spirit one can overcome all obstacles, because the power o' this magic in our beings connects us to all universal powers and our true selves. There's a need to stay connected with this part of oneself in times of strife.

– Reminiscences of Henry Baird in 1905 (imagined by the author) after the tragic loss of his wife, Sarah Weir Baird, from childbirth. Henry died in Armona, California, in the San Joaquin Valley at age seventy-three in 1925.

BOOK ONE

CATHERINE MALCOLM — 10 APRIL 1869 — AGE 20

Chapter One

I. Catherine Malcolm's Life in Helensburgh, Scotland

Catherine Malcolm sits outside on the veranda swing perusing the *Helensburgh Gazette* while savoring a peaceful, sparkling spring afternoon on her own. She had taken off and tossed, in a gesture of defiance, her straw bonnet atop a white wicker table, allowing the mild warmth of the Scottish sun to play soothingly on her fair, prone-to-freckling skin without reprimand from her mother. A sea breeze wafts moisture that dances ever-so-gently over her face, which she likens to the feel of being brushed by a dewy petal. Pausing momentarily from her reading to sigh aloud, she weighs in on the immutable fact that life on some days can be so perfect, yet on other days unbearably harsh. Despite the perfection, even on a splendid day as this one, there arises, from a reservoir of emotion at her core, an uninvited niggling of woe. *What's disturbin' my peace? Today, life seems perfect and imperfect at the same time; I must pinpoint the reason why. For heaven's sake! My blessed time in the sun is becomin' unblessed!*

Her fluctuating mood, she analyzes, could possibly be caused by forces in the universe she has no control over. Perhaps movements o' the sun and moon, or high winds and fog o'er seas cause changeable moods.

Catherine looks back down at her newspaper with furrowed brows. Her attention is drawn to an interesting article concerning prostitution in the tenements of Edinburgh, in which she becomes completely absorbed. *Why are women obliged to perform such demeaning acts?* she wonders. *Could this be happening in Helensburgh as well?* Catherine's natural bent of curiosity is ignited. She would love to do some fieldwork and find out what's going on in other portions of society that co-exist in close proximity to her own, women in poorer circumstances behaving disparately on issues of morality. Destitute women are not that much different from herself in physical, emotional, and moral makeup, she estimates. Having befriended the mothers of her poorer students, some so poor as to not eat or dress well, she has found most of them to be intelligent, well-intentioned, and in possession of pure Christian values. So what is going on? In trying to understand and be empathetic towards members of her own sex, she considers the circumstances under which a woman might sell her body. It couldn't be just for the money. The degradation to a woman's spirit wouldn't be worth any amount of money. Maybe if her life or the life of someone she loved depended on it? Catherine's certain she'd never sell her body. *But, then again, maybe I would if I could get Ruthie back. I would sell my body just one time if my sister could come back to life, no matter how unpleasant!*

After a few more articles, Catherine looks up from the *Gazette* to rest her eyes on the stunning display of new spring growth bursting forth colorfully all around her. She sighs more deeply this time, in frustration at the glory she is seeing and her ungrateful reaction to it. The beauty is excruciatingly dazzling, so vibrant that she can't take it all in without experiencing a wee touch of melancholy. The perfection lends urgency in her to capture its essence: the nose-tingling scents, the array of color, the emerging new growth, the sensual sounds of insects and birds. The fresh air is exquisite, like an elixir. She is frustrated by this perfection, ashamed that she isn't feeling more grateful for God's gift of splendor.

An urge comes over her to run giddily across the moors as she did as a teenager. It was a rite of passage for her, a way to worship the glories of an emerging spring each year – that is, until she became a teacher and a role model for her students a couple of years ago. Her mother told her on many occasions, "Catherine, 'tis na dignified for a lady o' yer stature tae gallop aimlessly out-of-doors as a horse," but she still gallivants on occasion in total abandonment, whenever her spirit cannot be contained. It would be beyond refreshing, she thinks, and her mood becomes almost euphoric just imagining a romp across the wide-open moors.

Catherine's mood spirals downward abruptly. She wonders again why her emotions are wreaking havoc on her peace of mind on this fine day, as her analytical nature often nudges her to consciously search for reasons behind her feelings. *Of course, 'tis the spring beauty not lasting long enough*, she thinks despairingly. *Will likely be gone on the morrow as the sky opens up and it commences to pour again.*

Catherine challenges herself to go further in pinpointing her dismal mood. *Ah no, not again, so soon!* she despairs. It strikes an excruciating chord in her that this day is the anniversary of Ruthie's death. Catherine's sister died tragically in the spring four years ago to the day, 10 April, of an ear infection at the height of her youth and beauty. Ruthie was only eighteen. Catherine considers the prospect that she, too, could very well die at any time and miss out on the next spring, as her sister is missing out on this and every beautiful spring each year. She reasons that if it happened to Ruthie it could happen to her, for she considers herself far less deserving than Ruthie was. She counts the three springs that Ruthie has missed out on thus far, and this very lovely one that she is missing out on at this moment. An expanding guilt purveys her consciousness – like a stone forging larger and larger concentric ripples when thrown into a pond. Catherine is indulging in springtime's bliss when Ruthie is not. She yearns for a spring that does not provoke these irksome feelings that arise each year on the anniversary of her sister's death, as well as intrusive reminders that she shouldn't be squandering her blessed life with mediocrity. *After all, Ruthie didn't even get the chance to live a full life. I have to live twice as fully for the both of us!*

These prickly guilt-ridden irritations always come up as the spring season shows off its finery. If she remains like a piece of garden statuary in what constitutes her life now, she considers her existence will have been all for naught. Was Ruthie's short life all for naught? Quite the contrary, she decides. Catherine reflects that Ruthie in her short time on earth gave everyone so many gifts of joy merely by being sweet, affable Ruthie, unlike her own not as pleasing character. Catherine judges herself to be far from sweet and accepting of her lot in life, as she's always had far-reaching, perhaps inflated, expectations for what life should offer her. She views herself as not the popular, pleasing lassie that her sister was, but somewhat of an oddball, looking from the outside in, not always living up to the expected standards of behavior or aspiring to the goals of marriage and family as do her peers in Helensburgh. Catherine has always had an irrepressible desire for more out of life than the norm.

Why did Ruthie get so little time on earth when she had so much to offer, and so much to live for? Catherine proceeds to chastise herself for bringing such dismal thoughts on this fine day, and attempts to clear her mind of all negativity. She's lectured her students many times that to reach their goals they must have infinite patience and persistence, and above all optimism. *Practice what you preach*, she tells herself. Catherine chastises herself even further for not being stalwart and unflinching in times when negativity arises uninvited from within.

Looking away from the showy environment in disgust with herself, she resumes an article on the latest steamer ships being built on the Clyde River in Glasgow for the American war effort, not far from her home in Helensburgh, that transit passengers across the Atlantic to America. Lately, Catherine has had daydreams (she appraises these as fantastical musings) of boarding a ship without much ado and leaving the mediocrity of her life behind.

Being an unwed schoolteacher in the small township of Helensburgh has left her spirit quite uninspired and deflated. *Life is just too predictable*, she has thought many times recently, and the rapid march of years has been without any major accomplishments, thrills, or joys on her part. Only a few years ago she was a schoolgirl at Helensburgh Secondary, and presently, she's a teacher in a role of authority there, respected and admired by her students, presumed by her revering charges to have mature, worldly experiences under her belt, of which she has none.

Catherine glances up from her reading to look at the sky, to wonder where the squawking free-flying gulls are so intent on heading once they get out o'er the water. She conjures up fretful thoughts of her youth passing by all too swiftly, without substantial highlights to her existence – flying by as quickly as the progression of these creatures soaring overhead on their way out to sea, she reflects. *There flies my life on the wings of a gull to be smothered in a pillow of clouds o'er the sea! How humorously poetic something as fleeting as my life can be*, she thinks while chuckling softly at the absurdity of feeling sorry for herself, a young woman of means and education, one with potential to have a fine life. *I'm only twenty*, she thinks. *Perhaps fate will take me by the hand and lead me, a lass who can't seem to get it right and needs to be led.*

The birds are so very purposeful in getting to where they plan to go, communicating back and forth with visceral screeches as to their proper course, formation, and destination. Perhaps they'll land on a fishing trawler and scavenge scraps left by fishermen, then fly back closer to shore as the air is cooled by the soupy evening fog moving inland. *Not such a bad life. They have freedom to see and experience so much*, she muses. The puffy clouds are scudding rapidly in a northerly direction as if they, too, were on an important mission.

Clouds are racing fast across the open sky to exciting places; and here I remain fixed and immobile like a piece of garden marble! How wonderful it would be to fly out o'er the water and experience the sensation of being high up looking down o'er the world.

Catherine reflects on the notion that birds are very fortunate creatures in their perspective from on high. If only humans could fly like that! Catherine wonders if gulls are only of this world or transit to other planes of existence as well. The Wee Ones, of whom she has intimate knowledge, are known to fly, and their scope is far-reaching and spectacular. She is well aware that they are not creatures of this world alone, but of other dimensions.

II. Catherine Struggles with Her Perceived Uniqueness

Once again, her perceived shortcomings in her life come to the forefront: her lack of significant milestones or major accomplishments; her lack of inertia and wherewithal to set forth on anything relevant for her happiness and future wellbeing. Thus far, she considers her existence to have been commonplace, like that of so many of the lassies of Helensburgh who live and die in one place, sometimes even the same home. She acknowledges she's different from many of her peers because of her second-sight, and has assessed that her gift to see Wee Ones from different planes of existence is most likely the culprit behind her abnormal longings to gain greater spiritual and intellectual growth from otherworldly experiences.

Maybe 'tis not a gift to see these wee creatures; mebbe 'tis what makes me vulnerable to wantin' things I can't have, she thinks. *To see creatures that others can't see could be a mere aberration o' my mind, an ongoing daydream, like someone who imagines they can see the Holy Spirit. Aye, I could be in a dream state in the daytime when I see otherworldly beings. Mebbe 'tis acause my imagination tends to run wild in the same way my body desires to run wild out on the moors.*

Yet with this prescience, Catherine has had confounding visions of her life in the future that she has found preposterous and unlikely to pan out, having had glimpses of three lovers in store for her! The first gentleman in her otherworldly daydreams she's felt the closest to. This kindly lover, she hopes, if such visions bear fruition, will become a permanent fixture in her life some day when the time is right. The second vision is a love interest she feels a glorious synchronicity of spirit to, a splendidly attractive member of the opposite sex with whom she'll be completely enamored; the connection will be, she senses – trying to find a metaphor for what she feels during this vision – like being swept away on a wild but comforting and exalting tempestuous sea. The third envisioned fellow, a kindred spirit, captures Catherine's heart unconditionally and forever. The existence of three makes her even more dubious of their credibility. *Can visions of three lovers possibly be true when I'm a grown woman and thus far have had zero lovers in my life, and there are so few eligible men in Helensburgh? Mebbe I'm aimlessly reaching for the stars!* She wonders if these foresights are merely manifestations of wishful thinking whilst in an aberrant state of mind. *Do I have a slight mental illness along with unfulfilled sexual matters, or am I just a run-of-the-mill oddball?*

No one in her family was ever aware of Catherine's aberrant mind – she was the stalwart family pragmatist, the one who was intolerant of and made fun of the silly illogical notions and outlandish thinking of her zany mother. Catherine and her father were allies in practicality, and brushed off her mum's zaniness as ludicrous and endearingly off the beaten path, though at times terribly witty and funny. Her father and Ruthie are now deceased. Her mum is her only remaining family. Catherine loves her mother dearly, but still views her as a wee bit eccentric, so contrary to the intelligent and highly respected matronly woman that she represents in Helensburgh society as chair of the Helensburgh Women's Club. Her mum comes up periodically with humorous but outlandish quips that she loves to dish out to her club friends.

"'Twas ordained by the god o' the golden gavel for me to be

elected president o' the Helensburgh Women's Club, as I hiv the required gumption to administer judiciously and mightily a joltin' pummel atop the heads o' errant town officials"; or another nerve-jarring quip that Catherine takes as personally directed at her, "'Twas in the stars for me to hiv birthed two fine daughters acause I'm adept at handlin' the fluctuatin' emotions and wild mannerisms o' the zestful female spirit."

Catherine wonders if she should have revealed to her father that it was she, not Mum, who was the zany one, that she has been communing with Wee People since a young child. Now, to top all else, she's having other fantastical, recurring visions of enticing gentlemen whom she'll love in the future. *'Tis anither aberration o' my wayward mind! Dear Lord, something is na quite right wi' me heid!*

Catherine is doubtful that any of her dream-state visions will come to pass. So far, no major marks on her life's record of experiences have been crossed off. She's never had a significant romantic relationship, nor has she been outside the County of Perth, except to Edinburgh and Glasgow. There is no prince knocking at her door with a glass slipper, no eligible bachelors bidding for her hand, save for several rogue farmers who have been courting her for the last few years – out o' the question to marry an uneducated and rough-around-the-edges farmer is Catherine's verdict on the matter. Yet she doesn't have the heart to be rude or hurt the feelings of those inspired with a hopeful eagerness to court her, and so without a blatant rebuff they continue to visit and bear gifts like worshipful followers of an exalted princess. Her mother encourages these "country gentlemen" to keep trying, as she foresees that "diamond-in-the-rough laddies," as she refers to them, will someday inherit their fathers' lands and be wealthy.

Ahead of the pack, due to his cunning, is Catherine's most determined pursuer, Mr. Leeds, principal of Helensburgh Secondary School, who has been irritatingly demonstrative in his affection towards her from the time he started coming around the house and befriending her mother. Mrs. Malcolm finds him most worthy of her daughter because of his education and respected standing in society. Catherine cringes at the thought of being stroked by Mr. Leeds's stubby little fingers, or hugged with those short, bulbous arms. At forty years of age, Mr. Leeds has a small stature, a chunky, slightly obese build, a receding hairline, overpowering tobacco breath, and irritatingly exudes an air of officiousness when visiting the Malcolm home, as he if he were her superior outside school premises. Catherine is kind-hearted and polite and tries to see the best in him. It is difficult for her to hurt men with delicate egos, as she found out when she turned down a proposal from one of the farmer lads. He was utterly devastated and teary-eyed! She is now ashamed of herself for keeping his hopes up for too long. Catherine almost burst into tears when she saw the hurt in his eyes after she turned down his proposal. She had to make up a wee fib on the spot, telling him she'd been diagnosed with a serious female malady that would take years to overcome, and because of her condition he mustn't wait for her. In retrospect, she wonders if she should settle for someone like Mr. Leeds. Maybe life is too short to wait for one's prince who may exist only in fairy tales.

If Catherine could have her druthers she'd have a special partner in life, a counterpart to herself, someone with a vibrant personality she'd feel comfortable being touched by, performing those romantic and exotic acts that married people perform, which she and her girlhood chums had spent many hours in their adolescence pondering over with fascination and amusement.

Her friend Holly once told her, "I heard that certain men when they touch a lass can make her swoon and faint. 'Tis what happened to Rosie MacCready when Chad MacCady put his arm around her waist verra seductively. Rosie told me that she quivered and then fainted in his arms in ecstasy!"

Catherine's empirical mind had demanded clarification. "Does this happen all the time when certain men come close? Is that what happens to married women? Do they become ecstatic and faint? What's the point o' that? How do they manage a household when they're continually on the ground?" she had joked. Her friends had all laughed with her, and Holly was put on the spot to explain this phenomenon.

"Well, only certain gallant men have that power o'er women," Holly had clarified. "Most ordinary laddies daena possess this, 'specially if they're run-of-the-mill fellows. Most women are sae accustomed to their husbands that they daena react to them at all."

Catherine's reverie of her girlfriends' fantasies is interrupted abruptly.

"Yoo-hoo, Catherine, come quickly, me dear," calls out her mother, Mrs. Abigail Malcolm, breathless as she bustles at a fast pace, in a state of high animation, into the house, back from high tea at the Helensburgh Women's Club on Main Street. Her mother is attired in her silky white and magenta floral tea dress, topped off by a wide, flouncy, dark-pink feathered hat that reminds Catherine of plumage displayed during a bird's courting ritual. As a member of a civic-minded women's group in town, Mrs. Malcolm is an elected leader who tends to her duties with intelligence, assertive flair, and persistence, much to the dismay of the mayor and City Council members. The club's latest project calls for cleanup and beautification of the downtown's storefronts along the main street. The specifics: 1) Windows of stores are to be kept clean inside and out by owners (many members of the City Council are storekeepers); 2) Sidewalk plants and window planters are to be tended to year-round; 3) All trees in front of stores are to be pruned; 4) Streets and sidewalks in front of stores are to be swept clean of unsightly debris (bird droppings, leaves on sidewalks, and horse droppings in the street); and 5) No unsightly ads or stand-up placards are to be outside stores.

The mayor made no promises, but had hesitantly agreed to address the council on the subject matter. Thus far, no timeframe has been set, and that was a month ago. The council's bi-weekly meeting has come and gone. The women's club will be devising a timeframe to push things along and present this to the City Council at its next meeting.

The women's club's stern officialdom is offset by plump softness, pearls, flowery-scented perfumes, and frilly attire, full-to-the-brim gossiping, a tendency for insider jokes and puns, and unwavering camaraderie amongst its members. Not to downplay their good works, the ladies do have loads of fun – their official motto was voted to be "A social club that gets down to the enjoyment o' serious business." The Helensburgh Women's Club is a mainstay of the small Scottish community of Helensburgh. The ladies take pride in their community role and are certain that without their organization "not an iota of good work would be accomplished in Helensburgh – our community would be entirely at a loss without our efforts!"

"I bear delightful news, Cattie! Postman Moore just dropped off a letter from Jean Dawson Baird whilst I was uptown. Aye, indeed, that he did! He dropped off the most intriguing correspondence." She reiterates Postman Moore's delivery as if Catherine is questioning the validity of her statement. Catherine raises her eyes to the ceiling with impatience. Awaiting a longwinded flurry of words that oftentimes are circuitous to the intended point of the matter, Catherine holds in her breath rather than sighing. Mrs. Malcolm's large sky blue eyes are twinkling, her voice musically uplifted, as if she were to break into an operatic aria. The tell-all indication of her excitement is that her rouged cheeks are highly florid and glistening with perspiration.

"The letter pertains to your old school chum, Adam Baird, the gist of the news being that the poor dear laddie is very lonely out in the West. Poor, dear laddie!" she repeats.

"A pity with so much beauty to take in," responds Catherine sarcastically.

"Apparently, there are very few Scots in the new State of Nevada, and no proper women to speak o', that is to step out wi'," she whispers, as if she were speaking of an intimate bodily function. Mrs. Malcolm accomplishes her wholehearted sympathy for Adam's sorrowful plight with a look of feigned despair, her mouth and powdered fleshy cheeks drooping downward to a sorrowful pout.

"What a pity! His mum says he's quite dismayed that folks he encounters daena comprehend his dialect at first, even though he's speaking the Queen's English, mind ye! They view him as a foreigner from an obscure land, not a citizen o' the great British Empire! Can ye fathom the hypocrisy? Why, our empire houses the original speakers of the English language! People should follow suit and speak as we do," exclaims Mrs. Malcolm emphatically. "Adam has written o' the rude Western cowpokes along the way to Nevada that found him to be dimwitted. They thought he was speakin' gibberish or had a speech impediment. Can ye fathom anyone deridin' that bright laddie? Adam, Jean Baird writes, finds it imperative to speak the dialect o' an American cowpoke to be accepted," she declares in disgust.

"Cowpokes? Really, Mum? Is that what the prospectors in the West are called now?" Catherine inquires with sarcasm. "There must be lots o' different kinds o' people out across that large continent."

Mrs. Malcolm shushes her with a wave of her hand. She stands erect, clears her throat, and takes on the imperious expression that she dons in her women's club proceedings as she readies herself to convey the most tantalizing tidbits of Jean Baird's correspondence.

"Jean Baird does hiv a specific reason in writin' to us." There's a long, silent drum roll of pause by Mrs. Malcolm to clinch a dramatic effect. "Jean's much saddened by the fact that there's no female counterparts for her brilliant, handsome Adam, and she remembers his fondness o' the Malcolm girls."

"No women, Mum? Surely there are scores o' women out West," declares Catherine defiantly.

"Aye, there are women, per se, but no genteel women to speak o'," Abigail Malcolm clarifies. "Not the marrying kind, that is. Perhaps there's some lower class ladies of the night selling their goods." The latter qualification is whispered.

"Ladies of the night? Mother, really! Ye've been reading too many novellas!" Catherine is often exasperated by her mother's inanities pertaining to the world outside the premises of her limited surroundings that reach no farther than Edinburgh to the east and Glasgow to the west, and her tendency to draw sharp lines in classes, as if people of different classes were a different species altogether, with different kinds of thoughts, emotions, and needs. According to her mother, the upper and lower classes are as different as apples and oranges – different because o' ethics and inherited factors. The lower class has many more rogues and the upper class is generally a more honest people, according to her mother.

"He's written to his mum – aye, he has – to find out if you're still in Helensburgh and single."

"He does know o' Ruthie's fate, pray tell?" inquires Catherine, looking appalled. "Good Lord, we never received a letter o' condolence from him. She passed four years ago!" Catherine tears up at the reminder of her beloved sister's death.

"Aye, Jean Baird wrote and informed Adam o' our dear Ruthie's passing. He was still on the steamer to America when she died, but she wrote him at his boardinghouse in New York to the address that Adam gave her. Apparently, he'd already left New York for the frontier by the time the letter reached the boardinghouse, and he received our letter many months later in Ogden, Utah, where it had been forwarded. He wrote back to his mother indicatin' that he was very saddened by the news, and remorseful that he daedna bid Ruthie a proper farewell afore he left for America. He apparently wrote a letter o' condolence at that time, but it must've been lost, as mail service on the western frontier is sporadic and very unreliable. Jean did apologize for Adam not followin' up with anither letter, to assure his first was received. Aye, 'tis what transpired. He finally reached Nevada where the mail's regular and wrote back to his mum about gettin' in touch wi' ye once he was fully settled in his job and had a house. His younger brother, Henry, is living with him now. Ye remember that charming wee laddie? Henry, as I recall, was a handful as a child, but apparently very handsome now and sought efter by all the lassies. Henry, poor soul, tragically lost the love o' his life in childbirth, but has a darlin' daughter as a result. Jean relays that Adam desires to write to us o' his life out West, and hopes letters from you will be forthcomin' on your life in Helensburgh.

"From what he's relayed to his mother, he'd very much desire to correspond with ye, if you're obligin'," Mrs. Malcolm reiterates most emphatically. "He wrote he was very shocked and saddened when he heard about the death o' our dear Ruthie. He desires to hear from you and learn how you're doin' efter all this time."

Catherine is silent, her heart palpitating wildly, as occurs when she takes long romps across the moors. The entire color and texture of her tranquil afternoon has been transformed from peacefulness to ragged edges of uncertainty, with an inability to place her thoughts in orderly, sensible slots. Patches of color suffuse her face, and perspiration beads her forehead, so overwhelmed and flummoxed she is by her mother's news, though for the life of her she can't explain why she's reacting to news of Adam in this way. *I hardly know the laddie anymore!*

Catherine tries to hide her reaction from her mother, who can read her like a book. She rises quickly from her chair and runs to fetch glasses of lemonade for them both in the kitchen. Adam's been gone so long that she'd stopped thinking of his existence. *He's as dead to me as Ruthie is*, she reflects. Only a vague mental image of him comes to mind – a good-looking laddie with thick, dark auburn hair, very tall, and very shy and unsure of himself around people, especially lassies. Catherine imagines he's likely to have changed greatly in four to five years. She wonders if he still stutters when he's in a bind or nervous, as she had seen him do when talking to Ruthie. *What must it sound like when a Scottish gentleman talks like a Western cowboy and stutters?* she muses. Catherine smiles at the thought.

As an adolescent of thirteen years old, she had watched jealously as the romance between her sister Ruthie and Adam had blossomed. Catherine had revered Adam with all the fervor of a love-struck adolescent, and Ruthie had come between them because of her beauty and charm. Adam was seventeen when they'd last seen him, when he'd abruptly stopped coming to see Ruthie due to his work at the wheelwright shop in Bridge of Allan, and then his eventual move to Glasgow to work as a carpenter on the steamers.

Catherine admits that she and Adam had been great chums with an easy rapport at one time, sharing a mutual love of the outdoors and an almost uncanny ability for reading each other's minds and finding humor in the same things – that is, before his infatuation with Ruthie set in like a magic spell cast upon him. He became hopelessly besotted as Ruthie blossomed into an enticing young woman. Catherine recalls Shakespeare's play, *A Midsummer Night's Dream*, wherein the lovers are sprinkled with magic dust by the sprite Puck to make them adore one another. *'Tis what happened to Adam and Ruthie*, she thinks.

Catherine was the tomboyish younger sister that Adam gravitated to for church-sponsored sports and nature hikes, as Ruthie did not partake in outdoor activities. He was one of the church leaders of the adolescent nature group. As Adam reached his late teens, he began walking out with Ruthie and showed less interest in spending time as volunteer leader of their group.

Ruthie was the same age as Adam, outgoing and popular, with her own set of friends, a circle of friends Catherine was not privileged to belong to. Ruthie was the more cerebral of the two sisters, three years older than Catherine, more inclined to indoor activities – playing the piano, painting, reading, writing, poetry, and knitting – and many laddies from Helensburgh and Bridge of Allan had been drawn to her soft femininity and charm. Ruthie's death from sepsis brought on by an ear infection was so sudden that Catherine sometimes forgets that her sister is gone. Catherine often pretends Ruthie is away at the University of Edinburgh, the college she had applied to and had been accepted by the year she'd died.

After all this time, Adam's looking for a replacement for Ruthie. I'm second in line, second fiddle! How should I respond to this but to be genuinely insulted?

Catherine was upset with Adam for his neglect of her. To this day, she retains a touch of residual anger when reminded that he was in love with Ruthie, which left her, as she now reflects, out in the cold like a pathetic waif looking in through a window at their joyful togetherness.

When Adam dropped out of his role as a group leader of the church nature outings, Catherine was devastated, as there was no one else that could replace Adam's leadership and knowledge of the outdoors. Catherine soon dropped out of the youth club as well.

Before Adam had left for Glasgow and then the New World, Ruthie and Adam had enjoyed each other's company at many church-sponsored events. He'd escorted her to church and community dances. At the Spring Blossom Dance, they'd been voted "The Most Perfect Couple." Ruthie had confided to Catherine, a year before her death, that Adam had professed his love for her, and they had talked of marriage, which Catherine had had a hard time accepting. This was before their falling out had occurred, which was not long before Adam left for work in Glasgow.

The Baird and Malcolm families both belonged to the Church of Scotland, with services held at the grand cathedral in Dunblane, a township adjacent to Bridge of Allan. The families were well acquainted with one another, as Jean Dawson Baird and Abigail Rutherford Malcolm had gone to school together in Bridge of Allan. The Malcolms attended services at the cathedral only in the summer months, as they lived in Helensburgh the rest of the year. When back in Helensburgh after the summer, they often took the train to Bridge of Allan to spend weekends at their second home, particularly on holidays and when there was a visiting vicar giving a special sermon at the cathedral.

The relationship between Ruthie and Adam had started to show some strain when Adam dropped out of school to work on his grandfather's farm and at the wheelwright shop in Bridge of Allan, which gave him less time to spend with Ruthie. He did see her in church every week in the summer months when she was living in town, spending the rest of the day with her after church, and made a point of taking the train to Helensburgh to see her at least once a month during the times her family was abiding at their Helensburgh home. He'd explained to Ruthie before starting his full-time work in Glasgow as a ship builder that he was going to be very busy, but she'd had no idea that this meant seeing one another so infrequently. By train it wasn't hard to reach Helensburgh from Glasgow – a little over an hour's time. Ruthie had become increasingly upset by Adam's long absences. He hadn't tried or hadn't been able to come to Helensburgh to mend fences with her before he left for America.

Catherine recalls that Adam and Ruthie had been having problems long before the time he had left for work in Glasgow. Something had happened to make Ruthie question Adam's affection for her, something to do with another love interest. When Adam had come to the Malcolm home to bid them farewell while on his way to his carpentry job in Glasgow, Catherine had been instructed by Ruthie to let her have some time alone with Adam. Catherine had stood outside the parlor door trying to pick up on what was being said, but she could make out little of the conversation. When she'd finally been invited back into the parlor for Adam to bid her farewell, he had kissed her hand gently, smiling with difficulty. Catherine had sensed a dark cloud hanging over the room. Whatever had transpired had obviously caused relations to be very strained between her sister and Adam. Ruthie had been very subdued and teary-eyed, and Adam had stuttered terribly, trying to find words to keep the conversation going. She would later find out details of their troubles from the gossip mill. As Adam took his leave, he had promised them he would visit again before leaving for America, but that had never come to pass. Ruthie had been heartbroken when she'd learned he'd gone off on a steamer without bidding her a final farewell. Her sister had told her that Adam had changed a great deal since he'd started working in Glasgow, that he'd lost interest in their friendship because his life had taken a completely different course, one which she did not fit into.

Ruthie died in the spring of 1864, close to the time Adam left for America, stricken by an earache that turned into an infection that crossed into her brain. Catherine wonders if she hadn't died of a broken heart. She finds it hard to believe that her sister's been gone for four years.

"Cat, please respond. Cat, cat got your tongue? Ha-ha! I'm gettin' clever in me auld age. Yer father used to accuse me o' malapropisms, as if I possessed a malady as stuttering, that silly man, the love o' me life, who loved to tease me. 'Tis wonderful news! Perhaps Adam's in search o' a wife! Ye two were verra compatible and had great times thegither. I always thought he was more your type than Ruthie's, but you were so very young at the time – he certainly daedna have any idea you'd turn into a very bonnie young woman, but I always knew you'd be very lovely, a wee bit lovelier than Ruthie, in my estimation," Mrs. Malcolm says with pride, as she appraises her daughter's looks as one would appraise a fine garment, which makes Catherine fume and blush self-consciously.

"Adam's a fine, well-mannered and nice-looking laddie," continues Mrs. Malcolm. "The entire Baird family's verra intelligent. Think o' future children! He'd be a perfect match, though me heart will break into a thousand wee pieces if ye leave me to go off to

America. Always your happiness comes first with me. If 'tis what God wills then I willna stand in your way."

"Poppycock, Mum," replies Catherine, annoyed at her mother's blatant attempts at matchmaking, which are pushed on her all too frequently with disheartening results. "Aren't you jumping ahead o' yourself? Adam and I haven't seen one another in four years or more. He didn't bother to inform us he was leaving for America. He was in love with Ruthie, not me. Ruthie said he told her as much, that he loved her, before he left for Glasgow to work, but something happened between them – I think they'd a very serious falling out. 'Tis the primary reason behind him not comin' to bid us a proper farewell. They were struggling wi' a major problem – anither lass had caught Adam's fancy. I heard rumors o' a tryst wi' his teacher. I suspected as much. Ruthie seemed very hurt by what Adam had done, but she woudna confide in me. Adam niver came back to bid us farewell for a silly rumor that could have been resolved, and we niver saw him again. What kind o' man is so heartless as to not bid a devoted, longtime friend farewell?"

"Jean Baird's relayed to me that when Adam was in Glasgow, he had planned on returning to say his goodbyes to everyone afore boarding the ship, but 'twas difficult emotionally for him to leave on a long journey, knowin' he might not return for a very long time, if iver. 'Twas easier for him just to leave without thinkin' o' what he was leavin' behind. He did write to Ruthie when he reached New York, Jean does relay, but apparently the letter was lost. 'Tis water o'er the bridge, as presently he's very interested in you now, me dear!"

"Under the bridge, Mum, na ower!" Catherine tends to resort to Scots colloquialism when under duress, but as a school marm has been trained to converse strictly in the Queen's tongue. "Why, we're practically strangers after this length o' time. He's not a laddie – must be mid-twenties, and sophisticated in the ways o' the world with his experiences out West. What in heaven's name would we correspond about?"

"Och, Catherine. Nonsense! Yer students can testify to yer ability as a storyteller. Write Adam regardin' your students and teachin' experiences, and the Bridge o' Allan townspeople. Regale him wi' the Wild West show that came to Glasgow. I'm certain Adam has many excitin' tales o' the West to tell."

Catherine's initial reticence changes the more she thinks about it, a flicker of excitement overtaking her initial reservations. After all, it would be fun to be a pen pal to someone leading such an exciting life, the next best thing to traveling to a foreign country.

"Well, I'd love to hear tales o' the Wild West – of Indians and miners, and the railroad being built across the continent, educating facts on America to pass on to my students. Did Jean Baird send his address? I'll write him, I suppose, as soon I can think o' somethin' worthwhile to say," she responds with burgeoning enthusiasm. Much to her dismay, she's been infected by her mother's eagerness. Catherine chastises herself for feeling like a giddy teenager.

"Aye, get to it straightaway, me dear." Catherine is taken aback by what sounds like a command, and chuckles good-naturedly at her mother's audacity.

"Mum, I do believe you're tryin' to get rid o' me," says Catherine teasingly. "Mind ye, if I agree to marry Adam, I'll go out West and leave you all alone."

"Aye, well, that'll be a hardship," Mrs. Malcolm replies with a sigh. "We'll hop o'er that hurdle when we come to it," she says, a look of divine acceptance on her face.

"You mean jump o'er that hurdle, Mum," corrects Catherine in a half-hearted way, not anticipating a change in her mother's lexis in this lifetime. Mrs. Malcolm ignores the correction, as she loves to experiment with all sorts of expressions that no one else uses, a badge of pride that her language is colored with creative idioms that fit the bill, far more expressive than what she considers pompous intellectuals to have mandated as correct usage.

"I may jolly well come with ye. I do have some spirit o' adventure left in me auld bones. Mind ye, I'm not that auld. Aye, indeed, I do see in the stars a future trip o' some order for me," she spouts enthusiastically.

The next day Catherine writes to Adam for the first time, with Mrs. Malcolm hovering over her shoulder, offering ineffectual suggestions of what to include, reminding her twice to add a picture of herself. The correspondence continued regularly. As a teacher, Catherine is aware that what her students write are often mirrors to their souls. Adam's letters have been quite revealing of the man he has become. He, she recalls, was intelligent and kind, and well-bred with the highest of ethical values, and by his eloquent way of expressing his thoughts and emotions he's not changed. Catherine does wonder if there will be any romantic attraction.

"If he's lonely, Catherine, it indicates that he's desperate to find a wife soon and will be exploring all possible avenues. Ye might lose his interest in a wink o' the eye if ye don't act promptly and enthusiastically."

Catherine's aware that her mother is trying to convince her to respond to the overtures of Adam, even before a proposal, using Adam's extreme loneliness that Jean Baird has written about as a way to get at her soft-heartedness, a weakness of hers that her mother is well aware of. Catherine secretly admits to herself that Adam might look elsewhere, as her mother has pointedly suggested, if he gets the idea that their long-distance relationship is going nowhere.

"Mum, no man is so desperate to find a wife that he'll not take the time to find someone he thinks he'd be truly compatible with. 'Tis the reason Adam is spending the time writing me."

"Ye niver know, me dear," she responds shrilly. "Some men are quite the fools! Case in point: recall that poor laddie we read about in the *Edinburgh Gazette* who married the lassie because he thought he'd be very happy wi' someone to provide him wi' nourishing meals – she was a renowned cook. He later poisoned her acause it turns out she was an abominable shrew," she recounts matter-of-factly. "This demonstrates that he did not wait to evaluate her character afore he married her acause he was lonely and hungry for fine food and needed a wife. That could very well happen with Adam, to not wait and to marry the wrong lass. Aye, a vixen or worse he could end up with! Adam could be in danger of directing his heart to a very dark soul!"

"Really, Mum, I wouldn't call that man a poor lad if he committed murder! A murderer is a ruthless character. This has no bearing on Adam at all!"

When Jean Baird wrote to her friend Abigail Malcolm, conveying that Adam desired Catherine to correspond with him, Catherine had feared that their correspondence would be strained, as they hardly knew one another after so many years. These fears proved to be unfounded. Over the last six months, they've written each week. These heartfelt letters have been creative, free flowing, humorous, and intimate, as if they're old friends taking up from whence they left off years ago. Adam wrote that he hoped Catherine hadn't changed in the least because he recalled she'd been such an engaging, energetic, and fun-to-be-with wee lassie, and he would love to hike with her in the New World, as they had once enjoyed doing in Scotland. Catherine responded that she hoped Adam was the same sensitive laddie who had a knack for instilling self-esteem and self-sufficiency in adolescents by teaching them how to fend for themselves in the wild. Their correspondence takes a month or more to cross the Atlantic, and sometimes comes in bunches of twos or threes at a time. Adam's letters are packed full of the exciting adventures he'd experienced traveling across the country. His letters contain delightful and colorful descriptions of his first encounters with Indians working for the federal government.

From Adam's letters, Catherine detects a maturity and wisdom in him that pleases and excites her. He wrote that he was doing well as a carpenter in the Caledonia mines of Virginia City, Nevada, located approximately 150 miles east of Sacramento, California, near where gold was first discovered at Sutter's Mill. Virginia City, with nearly 7,000 residents, he wrote, is situated in very lovely, high altitude terrain in the foothills of the Sierras. He has confided to her in his letters that he is lacking in any feminine companionship, as there are very few proper single women.

"Virginia City does have a sizeable population," Adam wrote, "but I never meet single, genteel women available to step out with due to me shy nature and the scarcity of those o' marriageable age. Well, I take that back – there's a bunch o' maidens that hover o'er me like vultures ready to devour me on rare social occasions that I'm out on the town with my friend Adrian and his wife, as if I were prey to be caught for supper. They're quite unappealing by the very nature o' their competitiveness with one another."

Catherine had laughed out loud, envisioning Adam being pecked by a flock of bird-women. His letter continued to describe his social life.

"I don't partake regularly in theater, opera, or club meetings, though I did attend quite a few city civic functions when first coming to Virginia City. Civic meetings, I've found, are rather stilted, the participants longwinded and self-promoting. Needless to say, I'm truly exhausted after working in the mines for up to ten hours a day. On days off from work, I take delight in exploring the beautiful territory and viewing land to purchase, on which I'll eventually build a house. I have no desire to participate in clubs and organizations at this time."

Catherine begins to conjure up renewed reservations about Adam, brought forth by her skeptical nature, not totally accepting all of his words as truthful representations of what is really going on in his life. She finds that he shares too much information about his social life, in particular his relations with other women. A well-bred gentleman should be more discreet and never mention to a woman friend the extent of other unwed ladies being attracted to him, many vying for his affection, even if it is true! Is he trying to sell himself by making it seem that he has a flock of ladies hovering over him, and that he is above them all? Catherine wavers between being cynical and being admiring of Adam's desirability.

"Mum, what if he's a bag o' wind attemptin' to make himself appear desirable? Adam, in conveying himself a sought-after man, could be mouthing complete hogwash. He could be entirely different than from what we recall o' him, likely burly and coarse from his years in a rugged territory. Seriously speaking, this is a man I'll be obliged to sleep in the same bed come nigh, if I one day marry him. What a frightening prospect! Mum, what if he wants to touch me and I don't want him anywhere near me? What then, pray tell?"

Catherine takes pride in the fact that she's always had sound reasoning and has never been as fickle as some of her schoolmates in Helensburgh.

"Cat, don't be a silly, naïve child," replies Mrs. Malcolm. "You're goin' to love that laddie. I can feel it in me auld bones. If only ye knew the strength o' the bond betwixt a man and woman. The love will send ye to the moon and stars and back again, that I can assure ye."

"Mum, really! Love's not all that grand as to be equated to the enchantment o' the universe."

"Love's all part o' the grandeur o' the universe, ye'll see, me dear. Take me word for it."

"Mum, how can ye be so positive? Adam's been on the wild frontier for years. He could be quite coarse looking wi' abominable manners and actions, like the miners pictured in the newspapers panning for gold with ragged beards running down their chests, down to their blubbery bellies."

"Dear, ye forget that Adam was raised by the Bairds. Once raised properly, men do not change their stripes. 'Tis like a pussycat takin' to water."

"Mum, cats are not changeable like people."

"Och, then a cow galloping the range with the horses neighing in the wind."

"Mum, your analogies are ridiculously obtuse! People can change dramatically, but animals never do. A fine, respectable man may one day, given the right circumstances, turn into a ruffian."

Catherine is having a difficult time picturing Adam's face in her mind after so many years. She had sent him a picture of herself straightaway. To her chagrin, he has neglected to enclose a picture with any of his letters, which she regards as a deliberate omission, perhaps hiding undesirable alterations to his looks since his Scotland days due to his harsh living experiences. She pictures a weathered mountain man with a beard down to his chest and a potbelly.

Catherine was a teenager when she saw him last in 1864. She reflects that a young adolescent lassie might find a man attractive who is hideously unattractive to a grown woman, as the impressionable minds of the young have totally different perspectives than mature adults. She recalls having had a major crush on a male teacher, Mr. Hendricks, in her primary school years, thought him to be terribly handsome, but ten years on she perceived him to be quite homely and wizened.

Traits of Adam come to mind: his shy, kind, and gentle nature, and his adventuresome spirit in the outdoors. She recalls he was fine looking with reddish hair and a tall stature. Much to her dismay, many fond memories of their past times on hiking trips burgeon forth in her mind like uninvited guests at a party – hiking and swimming, bird watching, rock collecting, tree and plant identification, naming cloud shapes in the sky, all the wonderful things in nature to perceive and hold in one's heart. She recalls carving her initials in a tree and Adam carving his beside hers. Catherine does not share her memories of Adam with her mother, nor let on that she greatly respects him for having the courage to leave his close-knit family in Bridge of Allan, which she knew he loved, to travel all the way to Nevada to seek his fortune to help his family out financially. She finds this the mark of a man with fortitude.

Catherine considers with care the implications of a continued correspondence with Adam. It crosses her mind that their intimacy through words will most certainly lead to a marriage proposal. Catherine is not sure she desires a proposal, for if she decides against Adam, turns him down flatly as she might, she'd be hurting his feelings greatly. This would be unbearable for her, to quash the hopes of a poor laddie alone on the frontier without a family to give him emotional support, though she wonders if she's even cut out for marriage due to her aberrant nature. *What does a woman actually get out of marriage but financial support and the job o' taking care o' a man and his children? No one has ever explained to me the benefits for someone like me, who enjoys her independence and sees Wee Ones.*

The Malcolms are a well-to-do family with an estate in Helensburgh as well as a Tudor house in the spa town of Bridge of Allan, where they had spent four months of the year before Catherine's father had passed away. This had enabled the Malcolms and Bairds to maintain a close friendship. Over 30,000 people per year come to Bridge of Allan to indulge in the restorative properties of the water, much like health seekers partake in the healthful waters in Bath, England. There are spas to soak in and mineral waters to drink, to get rid of every malady under the sun (or so it is advertised in the papers to draw in tourists).

The Bairds have been friends with the Malcolm family for years. While the women of the Malcolm family stayed in their Tudor house in Bridge of Allan for the entire summer, Mr. Malcolm, a banker in Glasgow, rode the Scottish Central Railway line (which has since 1862 become the North British Railway) from the Dunblane station, a couple of miles from Bridge of Allan, to Glasgow for work at the end of each weekend and stayed alone in the Helensburgh house on weekdays. He commuted for many years to Bridge of Allan for long summer weekends, until he died in 1862 of a heart condition, two years before Ruthie's death in 1864.

Catherine and her mother now spend the summers in Bridge of Allan, as soon as Catherine's school term ends, and stay until the beginning of September when school re-opens. During their childhood and adolescence, Catherine and Ruthie, being full-time residents of Bridge of Allan a third of the year, joined the church and community events, and subsequently Catherine spent a lot of time in the youth groups sponsored by the Dunblane Cathedral, thus coming to spend time with Adam.

Loyalty to the past ties of their families, as well as her childhood/adolescent friendship with Adam, are factors in Catherine continuing their correspondence. The idea of becoming Adam's wife and being trapped in a nightmarish situation in the West often jars Catherine's equanimity to bouts of anxiousness. Catherine continues to voice her doubts about Adam's character just to annoy her mother. Mrs. Malcolm pesters her almost daily to write to Adam. Catherine tells her mother that writing too often would make her look overly eager. This would surely precipitate a proposal that she's not sure she wants to receive.

In the autumn of 1869, unbeknownst to Catherine, Mrs. Malcolm wrote to Jean Baird of her "upmost approval" of a marital union of her daughter with Adam. And so it was after only six months and twenty-five letters that Catherine received a marriage proposal on fine-grained, cream-toned paper from a fancy stationer in Reno. It was an invitation to join Adam in America, as soon she was able to make the journey, to be married at the Virginia City Presbyterian Church soon thereafter.

When the proposal arrived, Catherine found herself surprisingly thrilled and honored, as she had convinced herself she didn't desire any such thing. *Oh well,* she thought, *I was lying to myself about my true feelings! I had a reason to avoid my true feelings because Adam broke my heart many years ago.*

She'd decided, on the spot, that she would take the ultimate leap into marriage despite the risks of not having seen Adam for years. How many opportunities come to one in a lifetime? To be in Helensburgh her entire life would be squandering a chance for a vibrant, fulfilling future, she'd decided. Catherine wrote back her consent to marry in Nevada on the condition that her mother could come with her and live with them for as long as she desired. Since her acceptance of the proposal, she has been working on getting her mother to accompany her.

Mrs. Malcolm has been torn about leaving her beloved home and community in Scotland, but she has no intention of letting her only living daughter venture to "a savage land," as she called it, on her own. Her plan is to accompany Catherine to Nevada, and then make a decision after Catherine is happily settled as to whether she prefers to live in the West or desires to return to Scotland. Adam has sent money for both of their passages, and has made reservations for them to travel in May when the weather on the open sea is favorable. Catherine feels more secure in her decision to travel in her mother's presence on the voyage. If a union with Adam isn't suitable to her when she meets him – he might be totally unsuitable – she and her mother will be together as a unified team and will take the train back to New York, spend some enjoyable days of sightseeing, and return to Scotland on the next available steamer.

Chapter Two

I. Unexpected Illness of Abigail Malcolm — Autumn 1869 to January 1870

Mrs. Malcolm lay in bed throughout the bitterly cold, clammy months of November and December of 1869, with a bad head cold and cough that turned into bronchitis, which subsequently fulminated into pneumonia. Catherine took a leave of absence from her teaching position, spending long days and nights ministering to her mother's persistent congestion by applying hot mustard packs to her neck and chest, and steamy cloths soaked in menthol liniment under her nostrils. Catherine desired the house to remain toasty all night long to combat her mother's constant chills. She kept a constant fire of peat and kindling blazing in the bedroom by dozing in a chaise lounge in her mother's room, getting up every few hours to tend to it.

The cold spell that autumn and winter was unprecedented, so frigid that icicles remained hanging from trees, breaking off limbs from dormant trees, and decorated window frames and roof overhangs for days on end. The grounds were coated with a thick layer of frost, a visual winter wonderland that Catherine could not revel in. Farmers failed to keep most of their prized Angus livestock alive, but for a few that could be housed in their barns, and even their houses.

During her mother's illness, Catherine did not go to town, or anywhere else beyond the porch, becoming stir-crazy by not partaking in her customary treks on the moors. The grocer delivered food and milk, and kind neighbors and ladies from the women's club brought offerings of meat pies, casseroles, and treats of fruit cakes, plum puddings, and shortbreads.

Before her mother's sickness, Catherine had accepted Adam's proposal in marriage, counting on and thankful for the security and companionship of traveling to Nevada with her mother. Mrs. Malcolm had made a decision to accompany Catherine, fearing that her beautiful daughter might be a target for lecherous and unsavory ruffians and cowpokes, and above all the unbridled savages on the American plains. "They could kill ye or kidnap, Cat! Ye might end up an Indian concubine," Mrs. Malcolm had warned. Abigail had informed the women's club she would be resigning and that she would set up a special election for a new leader before she left. The club was left in tears by the news and could picture no one else to lead them.

Indoors while nursing her mother, Catherine spent hours daydreaming of their impending voyage, picturing the beautiful sea they would be crossing once her mother was well enough. She was cognizant of the great distance to Nevada, but imagined the journey going by quickly with so much breathtaking beauty to see. This voyage would be the culmination of her dream to nourish her spirit, to step outside the limitations for growth in a small Scottish community and find self-fulfillment. Catherine was so excited about their impending voyage across the Atlantic and train trip across the continent that she rarely thought about the final outcome – marrying Adam.

As days went on with no imminent signs of recovery from her mother, she found herself extremely worried, but at no time did she ever think of her mother as mortally ill, only that she would be very weakened and have a long recuperation. More than likely, it will take months for her to be strong enough for travel, Catherine had thought. After Christmas, when her mother had not thrown off the illness, she concluded that the journey would probably have to be put off until mid-summer. She wrote Adam to advise him of the delay.

Mrs. Malcolm was a cheery, optimistic patient. Each morning when her breakfast tray was brought in she drank her tea and sipped meager spoonfuls of bone marrow broth, and relayed to Catherine she was feeling much better and was definitely on the mend. Right after breakfast, she would fall asleep for the rest of the day. She seldom woke up for supper. Their neighbor, Dr. Mathias, came every afternoon and checked her vital signs and praised Catherine for her the vigilance in keeping Abigail's airways open, though her mother's throat was continually raspy when she spoke. Dr. Mathias said her lungs were not yet clear, but he offered no prognosis and tended to be optimistic, as his patient exuded a presence of vitality as she slumbered.

II. Death

Death is a privilege of human nature;
And life without it is not worth our taking.

– Nicholas Rowe's Fair Penitent

It was an absolute shock to Catherine that her mother took a sudden turn for the worse and died during the night of the third of January. Mrs. Malcolm was only forty-four years old. Catherine had been certain her mother was showing signs of recovery. Mrs. Malcolm had always been strong as an ox, exhibiting the stamina and robustness of a farmer's daughter, although her family, the Rutherfords, had been part of upper class society. When Catherine went to wake her in the morning, she knew immediately on rising from her sleeping lounge that something was amiss – there was a feeling of emptiness in the room as if the furniture, lamps, and rugs, which usually gave off color and warmth, had gone flat; everything was dimensionless. She approached her mother's bed. Even in slumber and in sickness, her mother ordinarily exuded a presence of warmth and vitality. Catherine could only sense emptiness in the room.

Catherine called out, beseeching her mother to wake, but got no response. She put her hand on her mother's chest and felt only stillness. For over a minute, she continued frantically to feel for the up and down movement of her mother's diaphragm, holding her own breath as if to spare more air for her mother. Mrs. Malcolm's vibrancy in life had ceased; she was now as inanimate as the furniture. Catherine looked up to the ceiling and wailed in desperation, ordering her mother to come back to her body. Catherine stood for a short while over the bed in a state of stone-cold shock, breathing rapidly. Taking control of her senses, she did the only thing she could think of in a medical emergency – she put on her cloak and boots and ran as fast as she'd ever run in her life to fetch Dr. Mathias.

Since her mother's passing, Catherine continues to go in to check on her, and is disappointed each time by a barren, totally lackluster bedroom, as if her mother took the charm, elegance, and vitality of the room with her. Each morning after a restless night wherein sleep is choppily interspersed by rude awakenings of sorrow, leaving her by first light in a groggy, trance-like state, Catherine's mind, in total upheaval, anticipates the sight of her mother in bed convalescing. The remembrance of loss sets in as she takes in the sterile void of the room without her mother. She longs for her father to get her through the heartbreak with his strong, reassuring, accepting presence. It was he who helped her come to terms with death by consoling her with the notion that each individual chooses the length of his or her life, and then they go forward on other quests that earthly humans in their limited vision cannot comprehend. Whether her father believed this or not, it was this philosophy that helped Catherine through losses of close friends and relatives, and even pets. Her father died before Ruthie, though, and it was Ruthie who helped her through that horrendous sorrow. Ruthie's presence is now sorely missed to lend to her a sympathetic and compassionate presence, to share the loss with her. After all, she concluded, children should grieve together for their parents' deaths.

Catherine envisions her father, mother, and Ruthie abiding in the same heavenly order, joined together in their love as a family unit but without her, which adds to her feeling of total aloneness. Since there are three of them up there in the heavens, she mentally beckons them to come to her aid, to reach out to her, to comfort her in a team effort that has power in unity.

III. All Alone

Catherine is taking tea in the parlor one week after her mother's death, a floral, blue and white porcelain demitasse sunk in her lap, staring listlessly at the velvet borders of the French wallpaper design. She is very tired from so many sleepless nights. Solitude and immobility are what she craves, for her mind to float on a plane of oblivion, to be at peace with no thoughts whatsoever. Becoming conscious of goose bumps on her arms, she focuses on the embers of coal smoldering in the yellow flagstone fireplace with an awareness of the uncomfortable chilliness of the room, but she has no energy to get up and remedy the situation.

I shan't get up ever again. If folks I hardly know call to offer their condolences, I'll refrain from answering the door, she decides. *I simply can't bear to talk to anyone about a loss so personal.*

An interminable procession of visitors came yesterday, some of whom she hardly knew, with an onslaught of well-meaning condolences that Catherine accepted graciously, but which left her drained both physically and emotionally. To be convincing to her mother's closest friends and to her own that she was perfectly well, not lonely or depressed in such a large house all alone, and to say this in an upbeat way, was a test of her patience and endurance. Today her tired mind is imagining places where she can find perfect peace.

Wouldn't it be nice to simply exist, she reflects, *to be a granite boulder, solidly grounded and sculpted by the elements into a smooth, beautiful shape, perched at a grand vantage point overlooking the water, or a verdant leafy tree that stands stoically, flaunting leafy limbs to the sky, raining leaves randomly to the ground when a cold wind rustles – to live without the exigencies o' being human?*

The drawing room of the house in which Catherine sits is large and airy, with 12-foot-high, rustic-beamed ceilings darkened by the burning of coal. The room is beautifully furnished with a dark russet mohair settee stuffed with down, three damask armchairs in gold, navy, and lavender tones, and mahogany end tables with lace coverlets. Her mother's beautiful ivory porcelain figurines and Limoges china plates glow on the mantle alongside her father's pipe collection that still retains the precious scent of her father. The dwindling fire fails to combat the sharp dampness in the air. Catherine throws a navy-green wool afghan, outlined with black and red, over her shoulder, the plaid of the Malcolm clan, and stares off into space.

The final week since her mother's passing, subsequent church service, and then burial the next day, with the harrowing experience of offering her mother's body back to earth from whence it came, as Reverend Greene coined it, have imposed on her a cocoon of numb mindlessness in the daytime. Alternately, at night, during recurrent bouts of insomnia, her mind is launched into tangents of philosophical thought. Her reveries pertain to how fleeting the days of one's life are, and the inequity of joy and peace doled out to individuals in this world, the question of why some people have enjoyable lives and others suffer terribly. She reflects that no one escapes life without suffering in some way, but some suffer much more than others. Abigail Malcolm had been a content person despite the loss of her beloved husband and daughter, admired greatly for her happy-go-lucky, charming personality. Her mother didn't grieve outwardly or seem spiritually defeated by the death of her father and Ruthie; she adjusted nobly to these losses with a tender, stalwart acceptance, busying herself with her club duties and friends. Her mother's life became even more remarkably purposeful after her losses. She continued to entertain and enlighten others on how to live well by being her totally delightful self, whimsical and quirky up to the last few weeks of her life. So many loved her, and she kept on with her witty sense of humor, malapropisms, and deliberate, over-the-top, and surprisingly profound and intelligent comments that brought laughter to those who knew her well, and stunned to speechlessness those that were her adversaries (mostly town officials). They were flabbergasted by her zany intellect. Catherine wonders why a larger-than-life woman lending so much to the betterment of those around her, and one so well suited to life on this earth, would be taken away and cease to exist in Helensburgh.

In solitude by the weak fire, Catherine reflects on whether she'll ever be the same person again, or be forevermore as she feels now, an empty shell housing a listless soul. *Will I ever laugh or smile, enjoy eating and reading, the company of others, running across the moors, be my happy, confident self, one desiring to travel afar?*

Catherine wonders if her own zest for life has disappeared permanently with the loss of her family. She sits upright, trying to regain a semblance of strength and normality. The answer comes to her like the sun gliding out from behind a cloud.

There exists universal wisdom to channel when I seek answers, she tells herself. *Of course I'll find happiness again in life! Just follow closely what your heart and mind are dictating to you.*

She wonders if perhaps her mum and father, and Ruthie too, are directing her from above. She'd like to think that they are helping her. *I need all the love I can get from up on high, wherever up on high is!* She looks out the window and up to the sky in a gesture of connection with the mystical universe.

Catherine is grateful that she hadn't broken down during the service. She sat stoically in the Gothic Cathedral of Dunblane, a stuffy, overpoweringly perfumed environment of floral bouquets and sweet-smelling, sweaty ladies festooned in colorful feathered hats like her mother's collection, matching their Sunday go-to-meeting ensembles. At first, the packed pews had given her a sense of community, as Reverend Greene had delivered a flattering eulogy to her mother. Catherine had kept her mind focused on the rustlings of hymnbook pages, soft breathing, whispers, nose blowing, and occasional baby cries from the congregation as a way to forget the solemnity of the occasion, and to enjoy the splendid tribute to her mother and the camaraderie with all attendees. Eventually her mind had segued to a meditative state, a zone where she had felt peaceful and safe, where she could feel her mother's presence. *Mum wouldn't miss her own service for anything*, she had thought.

Outside on the church lawn after the service, it seemed that the entire community had shown up en masse to offer their condolences, hugging and shaking her hand solemnly, voicing their concerns for her wellbeing now that she was alone in the world. Doubts of her belongingness in this community of kindhearted souls, as well as guilt and embarrassment for not being more grateful, had washed over her. Catherine acknowledged that she desired to grieve alone and not in a group.

Catherine continues to sit by a cold fireplace, whose embers died away more than an hour ago. She rises from her chair without being consciously aware of getting up. Finding that she is on her feet, she decides to take in some fresh air. *Perhaps*, she thinks, *a hike around the small loch on the fringe of our property will shake off my ennui.*

Outdoors she relishes being in the bracing cold of late morning, and sets out for the nearest loch that she long ago named Blue Mirror, walking briskly the ten-minute trek from the house. She breathes in the aromatic, earthy scent of peat moss that grows along the loch's edge, which elicits in her an atavistic connection to the aliveness of everything in nature. The aroma is sensual and sacred, she reflects, a reminder that we are all earthly creatures, and everything is broken down to dust and dirt in the end, including her mother in her grave, a thought that she does not back off from because she knows that her mother would love being part of these beautiful environs. Abigail Malcolm is buried at the Chapel of Helensburgh in the family plot, located near the town square, and Catherine wonders if that is the best place for her.

Perhaps Mother should've been buried out here in this lovely spot in lieu o' the churchyard in Helensburgh – granted, the chapel itself is lovely, but the graveyard surrounding it on three sides is dreary and unkempt from centuries of existence, she thinks. Catherine was too distraught to make the necessary plans and let others take the lead in the service and burial of her mother. Besides that, Ruthie and her father are buried in the derelict Helensburgh Chapel churchyard, and she is certain her mother would want to be with them.

The winter landscape is a beautiful, solitary, slate grey expanse, with patches of leafy greenish-grey ground covering. The low mountains far off to the south have received a dusting of white sugary powder. The trees are leafless quill-like sticks, and if it were not for the soft springy moss of chartreuse and reddish-brown growing on the rocks along the loch, or vivid green ferns and holly berry bushes, or the milky blue sky and pale sun, the winter environs would be quite drab.

Catherine has lived in the town of Helensburgh on the River Clyde, a port township, her entire life, teaching at the local secondary school for the past several years. After her beloved father's death six years ago, she and her mother and Ruthie continued to live in the large ochre-colored stone house on the expansive Malcolm acreage. After Ruthie's death, it was just the two of them to solider on. Catherine is aware that life is going to change drastically now that her mother is gone, and she prays for courage to face what's to come. Thoughts of the unknown quicken her heartbeat, causing her to flush. A few butterflies flit lightly in her stomach, but the insecurity lasts only briefly, as she valiantly gains strength by taking deep breaths in the crisp, cold air.

Catherine has come to the conclusion that if she doesn't muster up the courage to venture into the vast unknown and journey to America to marry Adam Baird, nothing momentous in life will ever come her way. And what does she have to lose? There is no one left of her family. The worst calamity that could occur would be being captured by Indians and becoming a captive squaw, as her mother so feared – the thought of which she tries to view in a romantic light – or to go down in a ship in a violent storm at sea, to drown on a bed of plankton and jeweled sand – also quite romantic, as she envisions a heroine in a novel succumbing to death as ordained by God.

If that happens I'll join Mum and Father and Ruthie wherever they reside. I hope I can be with them someday – maybe soon, if the Good Lord ordains it.

She doesn't really know Adam, but considers that marrying an unknown silver miner/carpenter of either deplorable or delightful character traits, one or the other, is a courageous undertaking.

I'm prone to be adventuresome due to my high-spirited nature, "full of spirit like the highland winds," as Father would say. Perhaps this is why I'm going so far away from Scotland to a destination I know nothing of. I've a wandering spirit in me. The fact that I can see Wee Ones means there's something out of the ordinary in my nature that might lead me to seek the vast unknown.

Teaching has been rewarding, but not enough to keep Catherine in Helensburgh, as any routine job has a way of stagnating. Her future in Helensburgh is as dreary as the blandness of winter, though she doesn't find fault with the town itself, or her wonderful students, as much as the ordinariness of each and every day. Life in her close-knit, charming, small community is quite pleasant but always the same; the townsfolk are like relatives, who know (or think they know) everything about her. *But do they really know me? How could they? I hardly know myself, and what I'm truly capable of. They know what they perceive on the outside of me, but that is only part o' me.*

Since her mother's death she made a point to visit the graves of her ancestors often, including her parents, who are all located in the family plot by the Chapel of Helensburgh.

Catherine's torn about leaving Mother and Father and Ruthie alone in their cold, desolate plots with no one to visit, though the Wee Ones have informed her in subtle, nonverbal communications – by tidying and placing wildflowers on her family's graves – that they will watch over her family, thus indicating to her that she's free to leave. *They are giving me their blessing to fulfill my destiny.* Her parents and Ruthie are fine in another heavenly realm, she has intuitively picked up from the Wee Ones. Catherine hopes her loneliness will diminish and she'll become more positive in her outlook on life once she's away. There will be so many challenges to face getting to her destination. There will be scant time to dwell on her past or to be lonely, and little time to miss Scotland, though Adam will remind her of her homeland once she sees him. It will be particularly hard for her to leave her family's gravesites for the last time. Catherine is aware that she won't be coming back for a very long time, if ever. She thinks she can perhaps worship them in their heavenly place by looking at the stars and moon. Surely, the same stars and moon fall o'er Nevada as Scotland.

It has been only a month since Abigail Malcolm's death, and Catherine plans to travel by steamship next week on the *S.S. Alabama* from Glasgow to New York, and then on the Transcontinental Railway to Reno, Nevada, to be met by Adam. Adam wrote that he would meet her in Reno with his buggy, and take her up the mountainside to Virginia City, which he explained was in the Sierra foothills at over 1,800 meters. After her mother's death Catherine decided to leave earlier than had been previously planned. Next month, on 28 February, her ship will be setting off.

Catherine braces herself against the sadness of leaving Scotland, the only land she has ever known. Despite the fact that her parents and sister are gone from this earthly domain, she likes to imagine their spirits residing o'er the land forever. Catherine wonders if her family's spirits might travel with her to the New World, but this is sentimental thinking on her part, she admits, and quite a departure from her wavering skepticism of specters of the deceased sticking around on earth at all. She wonders what kind of spirits could be hovering in the air o'er the American frontier, which she has heard is composed of vast miles of uninhabited territory, with buffalo thundering over endless grassy plains, a land that the Indians fight to protect with a vengeance. Perhaps the spirits of the Indians' ancestors in America are roaming in the cusp between land and heaven, and look down from above on the white people with disdain.

Catherine's Celtic ancestors carved out a place in the Old World and passed on their outward and inner traits to her. She will carry with her these inherited traits, as well as their customs and ethics, and their perseverance and courage to forge better lives in new lands. Catherine will also carry with her the Scots' great fondness for literature and poetry, philosophy, and music. Will there be Wee People flitting o'er the new land? That she doubts as well, for they are as much part of the Old World as the moors and lochs. The little dun-shis where they abide are their homes forever.

"Departure"
I travel all the irksome night,
By ways to me unknown;
I travel, like a bird of flight
Onward, and all alone

– James Montgomery

One week after her twenty-first birthday, Catherine travels to Glasgow to board the *S.S. Alabama*, a steamer ship headed for New York Harbor. Her neighbor, Frank McGowan, offered to drive her to the ship in his little surrey, a thirty-three-mile distance to the docks, which will take them over two hours. Her wooden trunk is packed to the brim with her possessions and placed in the rear of the wagon. She is bringing a few items that her mother had left her – a beautiful linen tablecloth, the embroidered pillowcases sewn for her dowry, some jewelry, and her mother's wedding dress that had been fitted to her figure by a tailor in town. Catherine left all the porcelain and china with her friends. She also brought along pictures of her mother and father and Ruthie, and a present for Adam in honor of their marriage (her father's carving of the Scottish Angus cow and his best pipes of carved wood and ivory), for he has written that they will be married the very day that she arrives in Reno. Adam plans for them to ride up to Virginia City where they will be married in the Presbyterian church and have their reception at his friend Adrian's house that evening. As newlyweds, they will settle in the small two-bedroom cottage on the hill that Adam and Henry are presently building with their own hands, which, he has written, is near completion.

BOOK TWO

SIX YEARS EARLIER — 1863

A Tragedy Comes to Bridge o' Allan

The wee lassies lie down in the pasture next to the soft, fleecy sheep. They are lost, very cold, and too weary to go on. How in the world they got lost is puzzling to them, as they travel the same way to collect eggs every other day, and know the route by heart. Somehow they got turned around after leaving the Davidsons' farm, their last stop before heading for home. When the storm blew in, it got dark earlier than Janet thought it was supposed to. The land became distorted like a puzzle that had come apart and couldn't be put back together. *Sort o' like Humpty Dumpty*, she thought. *All full o' cracks.* Trees that were landmarks were no longer there, and fields that they knew well by sight were darkened with a low, damp fog and looked all the same. It became a foreign land, seeming to be a place they'd never been to before. *Like walking on the crumpled face of the moon*, thought Janet. The moon was visible only for a short time before it disappeared completely behind dark clouds, much to her dismay. She looked for the moon's familiar, friendly face, hoping it would come back out through the dark swirls of cloud to give them a wee bit of guiding light, and some companionship.

They had tried to find their way back to Mary's house for about an hour until it became totally dark and they realized they'd never find the farm at night without light. Now resting in a sheep pasture, the lassies are reassured by the fact that someone will come looking for them when they don't show up for supper at the MacLaines'. Janet soon realizes the sky is devoid of any guiding light for anyone to find them, even if they were to try. Until there is enough light,

Mary and Janet are comforted by the warm, woolly creatures huddling close to the ground for protection against the howling wind and stony ice that has started to come down hard and strike them mercilessly. Confident the woolly beasts know exactly how to act in a storm, as sheep live outdoors in all kinds of weather, the lassies follow their lead as to the best way to brave a tempest. A continual bombardment of hail pings rudely down on them, as if deliberately trying to sting their faces and gloveless hands with tiny, white rocks. The sheep nuzzle their faces to the ground, so the lassies put their faces down on the soft, soggy hayfield as well. Janet loves the smell of dry, summery hay, but not so much the wet dog scent of the ground when it has been showered upon and becomes all mushy.

Mary and Janet had just finished their egg collecting from five neighboring farms when the storm blew in quickly without warning. They were headed back home to Mary's farm with their baskets full, where they had planned to have a special sleepover. Janet had come from the Baird family farm, a twenty-minute walk from the MacLaines', to help with the egg collecting, as she customarily does. *The eggs will probably freeze*, thinks Janet, *but they'll be thawed in the morning sun by the time we wake, if no one comes for us before then.* Janet is very sleepy and finds a mother ewe to huddle close to. She had owned a pet ewe once that she had loved dearly, and this warm, fuzzy, taupe-and-black sheep looks like her Meredith, who had disappeared one day out of the blue. No one knew what had happened to Meredith, not even her brother Henry, who is second-sighted, which means he can see things other people can't. Mary lies down on the other side of Janet, and her best friend reaches out to hold her cold hand. Mary is a very small child for her age, and one of the most intelligent children that Bridge of Allan has ever produced. Presently, Mary is wet and shaking uncontrollably, unable to think of anything other than wanting her warm bed and her mother. Janet tries to cover Mary's body with her wool cape to shield her from the onslaught of the cold ice, but it doesn't cover her head or her thin limbs completely.

Chapter One

I. Adam Baird's Early Loves

A great urgency to depart for America has arisen recently for seventeen-year-old Adam Baird, and this pertains to the imbroglio with Miss Carroway, his teacher for the last twelve years, as well as his long-term relationship with Ruthie Malcolm of Helensburgh, his close friend and love interest from church, whom he's been courting for several years. In all fairness, he has to tell Ruthie the truth about his dealings with Miss Carroway. As it is, rumors have been flying off the handle that he's in love with his teacher, and Ruthie has already been made privy to scandalous gossip, according to what her school friends have relayed to others, which has gotten back to him. Their expressions convey wide-eyed incredulity that shy, introspective Adam Baird, of all people, would be involved in a love triangle! Adam wonders why people are so interested in his love life. He views himself, as he thinks others must, as an uninteresting, mediocre fellow. The fact that Ruthie's friends found out about him and Miss Carroway is difficult to fathom. Someone must have seen him with his teacher, though he can't think of when or how, as he's only visited Miss Carroway once in her cottage after school hours. There was no one around, and her cottage is well hidden in the back of the school in a densely wooded area. Perhaps, he thinks, people are capable of picking up vibrations from the air about intimate goings-on. Could it be a dead giveaway by the way Miss Carroway looks at him in class? Adam, on further reflection of the matter, is glad that Ruthie found out, as the proper words to tell her would not have been eloquently relayed by him. Indeed, it would have been an awkward grasping for the right words, with incomprehensible stuttering and stammering. Better for Ruthie to be angry with him than emotionally crushed by his having to tell her out of the blue that he had an intimate, unplanned coming-together with his teacher, and on top of this shocking divulgence, relay the life-altering news to her – the lass who has plans to marry him – that he's quitting school to work full-time. Accordingly, he'll have to tell her that he'll have little time to visit her. On top of all these shocking revelations, Adam has to relay to Ruthie, as gently as possible, that in a few months' time, he'll be leaving for Glasgow for work, and eventually voyaging on a steamer to America to seek his fortune. Adam plans to visit Ruthie in Helensburgh as soon as time permits to get things sorted out, at which time he will explain what happened between himself and Miss Carroway. Perhaps by telling Ruthie the truth, she'll find it in her heart to understand, though in all likelihood she'll never want to see him again, which saddens him greatly.

His imagination for the dramatic, from all the novels he's read, has positioned the two heroines in his life, Ruthie and Miss Carroway, in a love triangle of operatic proportions, with himself at the apex. He finds it mindboggling that he, Adam Baird Jr., a shy, tongue-twisted, intellectual laddie, can have stirred up so much drama, wherein gossip is rampant about a presumed torrid affair with his teacher. Ruthie and Adam represent a respected couple in the small community of Bridge of Allan. Folks have assumed that marriage between them is on the horizon. Adam cringes with remorse when he thinks of letting Ruthie down, breaking her trusting heart. And now he has to inform her he's leaving for good and won't be marrying her. He'll get things straightened out, and swear on the Bible to her that he's not in love with Miss Carroway.

Adam does possess strong feelings for Ruthie, and did at one time have honorable intentions to marry her, but after a lot of soul searching his ardent dream to travel has taken center stage. Presently, he is deeply entrenched in plans to seek out his fortune in the New World, and this leaves his plans to settle down with a local Scottish lassie on an untenable plane. Marriage would keep him tied to Scotland for the rest of his life, the thought of which lends to him the caged-in frenzied feeling of a trapped bird. Adam acknowledges that Ruthie, as fine as she is, would make an excellent wife for any man, an uncommonly bonnie lassie, and so very considerate and intelligent. She's a talented musician, seamstress, and poet, traits that are conducive to Adam's intellectual bent. When he tells her his plans, he could ask her to go with him, but he already knows the answer would be an emphatic "No." Ruthie is a homespun sort, not an adventuresome, outdoor soul, who is happiest indoors enjoying the comforts of her family and friends, and pleasures from her music, sewing, reading and writing of poems, cooking, and, above all, her beloved cats.

On this day, before the daunting task of confronting Ruthie and crushing her dream, Adam has to contend with the third leg of the untenable love triangle, his revered teacher Miss Carroway. He plans to pay a visit to Miss Carroway after school hours, which he isn't looking forward to. He must convey to her his news of leaving school immediately, and of his upcoming plan to travel to America. This surreptitious meeting must be handled very tactfully. As with Ruthie, he is saddened to break Miss Carroway's heart, as he will certainly be doing. He must inform her of his intention to work full-time at MacDuffy's Wheelwright Shop, and explain to her the importance of his going to America to help his family out financially.

II. First Love of Henry Baird — October 1863

Adam's brother, sixteen-year-old Henry Baird, lies on the grass gazing dreamily up to the clouds, extracting blissful thoughts of Annie's essence from their lofty plumes as they parade across the infinite deep sea of blue sky. His daydream transports him to the blue of a spritely waterfall trickling steadfastly over rocks, resounding in breeze-kissed musical notes before toppling delicately into a babbling pool, the site where he had first learned the wondrous news. The dazzling blue water chiming on slick rock is an exquisite promulgation of his everlasting love for Annie, the kind of true love Henry did not believe in until it sought him out. Only a couple of years ago – he is soon to be seventeen – he found a couple's display of affection, so-called ardent love, particularly by his slightly older friends, as ridiculously maudlin and showing off, the lovers play-acting as though it was a necessary step to earn the rite of passage into adulthood.

"Daes onybody really fall madly in love so early in life," he had asked Adam before his falling for Annie, "or are our friends merely feigning ardent love? What are the odds o' finding one's true love that soon in life? Astronomical!" he had declared. "'Tis unlikely to hiv so many true loves coming thegither like honey to bread, when a soulmate could be o'er on the ither side o' the world. I ken ye really adore yer lassie, but is she the one and only true love o' yer life?" He's referring to Adam's Ruthie.

The look and feel of love – this newly found love of Henry's – is very different from what he'd expected. He is humbled by the realization that the universe actually had a masterful design for the jig-spirited Henry Baird, an extraordinary complementation to his unique, zany self with an angel like Annie, she being the epitome of all that is good, feminine, and pure. To Henry, being around Annie is like being at the end of a rainbow where the colors fuse to ultimate gold perfection. The myriad blessings in life are synonymous to the delightfulness that is his Annie – the feel o' soft summer breezes and winter morning mists on his face, the taste of ice cream topped with caramel, long swigs o' cool spring water, moonlit paths o'er water, shooting stars, harvest moons, and on and on and on infinitely.

When Henry first received the news of the impending birth from Annie, the two of them had been hiking in the woods above Drumdruils, on a path that wended along a stream leading to a lovely waterfall trickling down o'er a colorful backdrop of reddish-yellow moss covering blue-grey granite. As Annie stopped to admire the view of the waterfall up above, she suddenly lost her footing and tried desperately to regain her balance, but to no avail. Henry was able to catch her fall with only seconds to spare; she stumbled and collapsed awkwardly like a rag doll into his arms, looking pale as milk. Yet she recovered quickly and was soon chuckling at her clumsiness to mask her embarrassment. Her face began to lose its pallor, and her skin adopted an abnormally flushed peachy hue that Henry likened to a sunset color. Henry was alarmed, thinking she was coming down with a serious ailment, but a healthy glow and color soon returned to her skin within a minute of collapsing that relieved his concern a bit.

"I lost me footing, felt faint acause I've not breakfasted, 'tis all."

"Ye positive yer alright, Annie? It appeared you were goin' to pass out. You're still very flushed. Are ye feverish?"

"Oh, Henry, I'm perfectly alright, though I must speak openly with ye. I'm certain 'tis going to be the absolute shock o' your life. I might have come to be with child," she stammers. "Truthfully, I'm confident with surety o' the fact. I've been feeling sickly for two months on now with no sign o' me regular monthly times. Do ye recall when we made love under the cottonwoods down by the river following the concert on that blissful night in September?" asks Annie, blushing to a healthy rosy hue, remembering the blissful event. "I know 'tis the time the bairn's life came into being."

"My dear, dear Annie, 'tis wonderful news!" Henry responds with little hesitation, quickly recovering from his initial shock. "'Tis hard for me to fathom that a wisp o' girl like ye, so young, could be with child." He looks at her midriff for signs of any weight gain, and admires her remarkably slender and delicate form.

"Henry, 'tis too early for me to show evidence o' a bairn."

"Aye," replies Henry, recovered and emotionally grounded, "this firmly establishes that our lives are foriver entwined. We'll depart for America efter our bairn is born and commence a life far away from the insanity that bears down o'er us, that tries to tear us asunder."

"Aye," agrees Annie. "I canna fathom having a good life in Bridge o' Allan wi' me parents opposed to ye. A fresh start in a new country with our bairn will be best for us, and a grand adventure to look forward to."

A week after Henry's learning of Annie's condition, she informed her parents. The news prompted a visit to Drumdruils by a pugnacious Hank MacGivens – his intent being to bash Henry over the head, but luckily Henry had hidden himself away in the outer pasture. MacGivens's volatility could not be lessened with attempts at appeasement by Adam Sr. MacGivens voiced ardently to Adam Baird Sr. that the vulgar rogue Henry had raped his innocent daughter and should be hanged. He threatened to round up willing townsmen and tie Henry up to a tree. He boasted there were a good many in the town that would take pleasure in the punishing of a cad like Henry. Thus far, his attempts to form a lynching party have failed, as Henry is a very popular chap, and the town is well aware of the romance of Henry and Annie, which is regarded as a fairy tale love story.

Since the revelation of Annie's pregnancy and a wrathful confrontation by MacGivens with Adam Sr., the reins on Annie's freedom have been tightened – she's been confined to her home with the exception of school hours. She and Henry relish the short times together in the schoolyard, but always with schoolmates lingering close by, who try to catch snatches of their intimate conservation for purposes of gossip. The school is abuzz with rumors of Annie's pregnancy, but Annie and Henry do not talk of it with others. The antics of her father have been enough to seed rumors throughout town. Townsfolk are aware of Henry being in hot water – it doesn't take too much imagination to figure out what Henry has done to infuriate the ol' sot MacGivens. Annie has informed Henry that her parents plan to send her away to a maiden aunt's house in Glasgow when she starts to blossom. MacGivens has ordered Annie to never associate with Henry again, telling her he is a "lecherous Don Juan who takes advantage o' young lassies' vulnerabilities." Annie's parents refuse to accept Henry as a suitable future son-in-law, because of his roguish nature and the fact of the Baird family's membership in the Free Church of Scotland – the MacGivens are papists of the Old Anglican Church. Despite the roadblocks, Annie's pregnancy is all that Henry can think about, and he is constantly devising ways to meet secretly with her so they can plan their future lives with their bairn.

III. Different as Night and Day — Brothers Adam and Henry

As Adam watches his younger siblings play on the lawn, he reflects on the distance and cost of his forthcoming journey to America. He directs an inquisitive sidelong glance at Henry, who is calling out outlandish directives to the laddies, with the aim of giving the lassies an advantage in the game. Henry casts a very handsome picture with his smooth porcelain skin and jet-black hair, thick and straight with glints of mahogany, sweeping gracefully over his forehead and behind his ears, as if directed by nature to grace his face in a ruffled, flowing symmetry, even when windblown. His frame is narrower and he's less muscular-looking than Adam, giving him the appearance of not being a physically active sort, more of an aristocratic class; in actuality, he works the land with as much exertion each day as Adam, and has calloused hands to show for it.

Henry's countenance expresses positivity and thorough contentment to everything in life, void of any inner doubts or dark-sidedness to his nature, as if a heavenly grace illuminates the entirety of his being. His eyes are bluish-green, as bright as a loch on a clear day, and show a slightly amused twinkle at all times, as if he is privy to a treasure trove of jokes. This twinkle remains even when he's in trouble at school or being reprimanded by his father. Henry is one of those rare individuals with admirable fluency with words, expressing his thoughts and ideas simply, wittingly, and beautifully, almost lyrically. He is able to transfer his assurance that life is good to others, which has the effect of drawing many admirers to him.

Henry has told Adam that he definitely plans to follow him to America after the birth of his child. Annie being pregnant is causing scandal for the Baird family but not perturbing Henry in the least, which doesn't surprise Adam. It is in his brother's nature not to be worried about anything. Adam wonders what Henry really thinks about his leaving for America without him. Henry's been so tied up with his own affairs, with the impending birth and Annie's drunken father on the rampage, that it probably hasn't registered that he will be departing before long. *Mebbe he doesn't have the time for onything but wadin' in the muddle he's in. Henry always has a way o' weathering storms*, Adam thinks.

Adam estimates that Henry will have major responsibilities in helping to care for their younger brothers and sisters and fulfilling his duties on the ranch, added to the major responsibility of caring for his own bairn and Annie. *Can he handle the load efter I'm gone?* Adam shakes his head in a gesture to dispel the weight of monumental tasks he feels will bear down on Henry. The two brothers have been a good, dependable team, working the farm side by side next to the three ranch hands, Roy, Mac, and Guy, since early adolescence. Soon, he will be gone and an extra load of the work will pass to Henry.

Adam has been meticulous in the planning of his journey, down to how many pairs of socks and undergarments to pack, to the amount of weight he'll be carrying in his tattered leather satchel that his grandfather gave him for his seventeenth birthday. The serious-minded older brother wonders if Henry is capable of the tremendous amount of strategizing required for travel to America, especially with travails swarming around Henry like angry bees. Even if he didn't have his burgeoning difficulties, Adam believes that Henry's lackadaisical nature would hinder his readiness for boarding a steamer on time, especially with Annie and a bairn.

Adam and his brother are as different as night and day, though Adam wishes he had inherited some of Henry's more personable traits – maybe they go hand-in-hand with Henry's articulateness, his insight into human nature, and his ability to recount tales. His brother is outgoing and witty, and admirably carefree, while Adam thinks of himself as quite the opposite. Violet, the Bairds' housekeeper, attributes Henry's spunk to his second-sightedness, but it's got to be more than that, Adam has often thought, because all of the siblings had or still have second sight and they're not like Henry at all.

Henry is drawn to all sorts – he doesn't discriminate by class, gender, or even nice versus obnoxious personality types. He listens sympathetically to peoples' stories, which, in turn, he recounts to others in delightful spins, accentuating what he finds humorous in the actions of others. He once remarked to Adam that the tales folks tell are open books to their souls. Adam has concluded that as his brother listens raptly to the recitations of peoples' foibles, adventures, and emotional situations, particularly their humorous stories, he is given a spiritual lift. Adam has observed that Henry is drawn viscerally to God-given qualities he sees in human beings, as a sculptor is drawn to physical qualities in his subject matter, able to siphon as an art form the divine essence of spirit at the depth of humanness, which he translates into fascinating tales of life. Adam, on the other hand, prefers to study people from afar, an unattached observer, as one would observe a play or read about characters in a book, desiring to grasp esoterically the *raison d'être* in the circumstances of peoples' lives, but gladly leaving his characters behind in their far-off worlds when he closes a book, not desiring to meet any of his complicated book characters in real life.

People listen raptly to Henry's jokes and stories as if he were an older, worldly man who has experienced an exotic, exciting life. Adam reflects that Henry has experienced less of life than he has. He's never traveled more than fifty miles from Bridge o' Allan. Folks are entranced by his presence just the same, like he's a revered holy man who can perform miracles, thinks Adam with a wee bit of envy.

Adam is not incapable of forming strong attachments with others. He does have a select number of good friends that he grew up with, particularly Ruthie Malcolm and his best mate, Larry, but because of his dreamy nature he's often deep in tangential thought and not in the limelight as Henry. Adam is often perturbed that people don't respond to him as they do his younger brother, especially folks they meet for the first time. Even people he knows well, those in the small village of Bridge of Allan, have a tendency to gravitate to Henry when the two brothers are out together, which gives Adam the notion that he is perceived as a bit of a cold fish. Adam's standoffishness is largely due to his being uncomfortable in social situations and not understanding people who display boisterousness, crudeness, drunkenness, or other unsavory human characteristics. *Henry respects all people, and isn't annoyed by their faults as I am,* reflects Adam. Adam acknowledges that Henry is not put off by human foibles and conflicts, and people respond to him like bees to flowers because of his natural warmth.

Violet has proudly stated that Henry is inordinately possessed by the jig-spirit of the Wee Ones, and, accordingly, has one foot on another plane, wherein he can see the entire picture from a superior vantage point. As Adam recalls, his own connection to the world of the Wee Ones waned little by little to eventually become a figment of his imagination. Henry claims Wee Ones are still with him, and that he has never completely lost his second-sight. When his mind is in a receptive mode, Henry says Wee People come in clearly to him, particularly his pesky sidekick, Punt, who comes to him all the time, even when he doesn't want him to. Adam tells Henry that it is childish for a grown man to hold onto such fantasies from childhood, but he is secretly envious of the magical world of the Wee Ones, wishing he could've retained a wee dose of the jig-spirit to make his life richer and merrier and his persona more attractive to others.

IV. Likeness of Adam and Henry

Adam, of late, is aware that there is indeed a wee similarity between himself and the jig-spirited Henry. He considers the odds of anyone ever having suspected him of possessing a womanizing nature to be very miniscule before the "incident" with Miss Carroway came about. Now that he's gotten himself into a wee bit o' a situation with a woman, Adam is secretly pleased with himself for being a tad like Henry when it comes to the opposite sex, though he can't fathom why getting into a serious jam with a woman would boost his morale. He admits to himself that he feels a wee bit manly. At the same time, he is embarrassed and mortified that this imbroglio happened to him in the first place. He reflects that he is definitely capable of a wee bit of recklessness like his brother, despite his shy nature. Adam's romantic troubles are not as mortifying as Henry's – the whole township is whispering about the pregnancy of Henry's

Annie, but Adam's problem is a "gentleman's complication" with the fairer sex.

Adam's predicament arose quite unexpectedly in his dealings with his longtime teacher, Miss Carroway. Never in a thousand years would he have guessed what Miss Carroway was really like, or that she was capable of unseemly acts. He wishes he possessed more of Henry's ability to remedy a tight spot with a clever word, a humorous gesture, a wink of the eye, or a jaunty smile. Presently, Adam has to face Miss Carroway after the embarrassing incident, and his courage is jumping to and fro like his brother Malkie's frogs. One of his primary reasons for leaving for America without delay is that he cannot be a student any longer, not with Miss Carroway as his teacher.

So unfortunate that the full blown vision left me when I was a wee laddie, unlike Henry, who can call on his imaginary Wee Person when desperately in need of a wee bit o' aid.

Henry says that Wee Ones can remedy a situation by changing the thoughts of a person with a magic dusting – like casting a spell – thereby changing the way Miss Carroway feels about him, which would make it easier to extricate himself from this imbroglio, though Adam doesn't buy into this fantastical remedy.

The situation in question goes back to the fateful day when he sought out his beloved teacher after class for help with a perplexing math problem. He now wonders how an algebraic question could segue into so much trouble. The rigors and discipline of maths certainly aren't conducive with what went on that day. Adam has relived that incredulous time over and over again in his head.

Chapter Two

I. In the Woodland Above Bridge o' Allan

Did you ever hear of the frolic Fairies, dear?
They're a little blessed race,
Peeping up in Fancy's face,
In the valley, on the hill,
By the fountain and the rill;
Laughing out between the leaves
That the loving summer weaves.

– Mrs. Frances Sargent Osgood

Morning of the Great Storm, 23 October 1863

There is a flurry of activity in the dun-shis, the conical, green fairy hills, as beautiful luminous creatures with astral changeable bodies fly hither and yon, soaring out from subterranean tunnels and fortified dens of hillocks, their superb, gilded bodies glistening and iridescent in the sunlight. When they are present, there is a magical chiming sound in the air, so soft as to be almost imperceptible, yet the stalwart guardian trees respond with a gentle rustling of their leaves, and the woodland creatures tense up with alertness and look around with widening, glassy eyes. A life-and-death situation is moving stealthily towards the human population, necessitating quick-wittedness by these magical creatures called Good People or Wee Ones. An innocent child is predicted to die in the evening storm. They step up their pace and put their contingency plan into action. No time to linger in the gloriousness of this exceptionally fine autumn morning. Periodically, they swoop down to suck spiritous liquid nectar from plants and flowers, sustenance to fuel their fast-paced flights.

By their size, these spunky little creatures might be taken for iridescent dragonflies or very small hummingbirds, if they were visible to humans. In reality they are charmed creatures of a higher order, between man and angel, and in possession of extraordinary intelligence. Viewed on land by select humans with second-sight who have the ability to see them, these charming creatures appear much larger when not airborne, ranging from two to three feet tall. They are finely proportioned and strikingly good-looking, with gleaming flaxen hair hanging at shoulder length. These semi-angels are morphologically equipped to magically transform into smaller hummingbird-sized creatures in flight. Being affectionate and caring creatures, with no envy, malice, or hatred, and possessing utmost compassion, they are protectors of all living things on earth, coming to the aid of the human race quite regularly.

Called Good People or Wee Ones by grown humans who have second-sight, as well as by those possessing the gift as children, these magical creatures teach moral lessons, are courteous, respectful, and humble towards all, and have a blessed reverence of nature, whether it be flora or fauna. Because of their voracious energy requirement, they find it necessary to borrow food from their human friends in times of short supply (mostly in winter months) by invisibly entering human kitchens and deftly taking a smidgeon here or smidgeon there of meal, flour, barley, oats, or other staples, always reciprocating a favor from their host with a task of labor – cleaning, sweeping, or dusting with the rotary action of their incredibly fast wings, and with presents of medicinal herbs, mushrooms, and cooking spices.

The fervent picture of all-out industry to aid in a foreseeable human tragedy coming to Bridge of Allan is at odds with the behavior of one Wee Sprite lingering in the woods, taking more than his fair share of nectar from the plants and chasing insects away by rotating his wings at an astronomical speed. Rest assured, he is not of the norm – fairies are playful, but this Wee One takes loafing around to another level, making it habitually a prominent part of his day. This dynamic wee fey is a fine example of a harmless merry prankster who plays in the woods amongst his industrious peers. He is fittingly named Punt because of his layback habit of blithely kicking bits of stone and bark into ponds. Punt is a beautiful male creature with flaxen hair and gorgeous chiseled features, who has yet to heed the orders of his father, clan leader Elor, directed by telepathic means to all members of the clan, to come to action immediately. Punt is flitting about in the woodland, enjoying the morning sun while imbibing delectable flower nectar and berries, some varieties that have the mind-altering effects of very potent aged wine. He is oblivious to the urgent messages from his father that would alert him to the impending disaster. Punt is needed back at headquarters to track the imminent storm with his superb scientific expertise. He periodically indulges in short naps under the shady fronds of a large fern to recover from his wine-induced stupor.

After waking from his nap, Punt decides to seek out his very favorite human, sixteen-year-old Henry Baird of Drumdruils Ranch, to see what the good ol' laddie is up to – hopefully something to entertain him. Punt adores Henry, and has hung around with him since his best friend was a wee bairn. Henry is very accustomed to Punt's presence, as the merry sprite has a tendency to ride on his shoulder and whisper witticisms in his ear at unexpected times of the day. Henry is very vulnerable to the playful suggestions given by Punt because of Henry's jig-spirited nature, which means Henry is fun-loving, full of life, and sometimes mischievous. Punt often puts outlandish schemes into Henry's head, which Henry sometimes carries out, though he acts on his own volition and is in no way controlled by Punt. Nevertheless, Punt has an ingenious way of getting Henry to buy into some of his escapades by telepathic suggestion, though Henry will often nix schemes if they are beyond his better judgment. Punt's promptings are usually on the order of having Henry spout out an uproarious witticism to someone or by suggesting a playful prank for him to carry out, which are in no way destructive or mean-spirited.

Punt was the instigator behind the idea, which Henry put into action, of spraying his mother's best French perfume onto dried English bluebells and placing the fragrant blooms in hymnbooks. On Sunday, an elected altar boy passed the tomes out to the lassies as they entered the church for service, to lend them a special sensual treat, and particularly to ease them through the reverend's long and tortuous, often disjointed sermon. The fragrant hymnbooks were meant only for the young lassies of marriageable age, but as it happened a few of the matrons and even one gentleman received the gift inadvertently. Mr. MacRae, a widower, took the flower out and pinned it to his lapel and looked quite dapper, attracting a few older women to his sensual scent. The recipients learned that Henry, whom the lassies in town all revere as a god, was behind the gift of romantic flowers, which enamored them even more to the extremely handsome laddie's personable self. Being very popular with the young lassies already, he now regrets bringing more attention to himself, as he cannot handle too much adulation from so many at one time. After church, Henry had to make a hasty departure before the onslaught of admiring lassies came vying for his attention.

"Henry," teased Punt, "the lassies treat ye like royalty. It must be goin' to your head being so high and mighty."

"Aye," replied Henry, "I'm true royalty. Me heid's continually on the chopping block, just as Mary Queen o' Scots."

Henry finds wondrous, unique qualities inherent in everyone he meets, qualities that, most often, the possessors of such are not aware of in themselves. Once people sense that Henry has unfolded greatness or remarkable qualities unbeknownst to them in their beings, they are likely to reciprocate by being Henry's friend for life. In Henry, Punt has a perfect match of wits. Indeed, Henry is the only human Punt knows who is highly spiritually evolved (a few steps away from semi-angel status) and who possesses jig-spiritedness to an infinite degree – that is, Henry's full of life and fun and periodically gets himself into messes due to his well-intentioned, curious, friendly, and loving nature. This endears him greatly to his wee friend, who is a sprite after all, and is prone to the same kind of entanglements.

Punt has been visible to Henry as long as he can remember, as Henry has retained his second-sight of Wee Ones, whereas most people lose their ability to see these wondrous beings after the age of seven. Punt accompanies Henry whenever he has the whim, perching on his shoulder, singing off-the-cuff nonsensical tunes, and whispering silly anecdotes and observations in his ear. Perhaps this is the reason that Henry has developed his sense of humor, and a wondrous spark to his being, fully alive in each and every moment. He approaches life with awe and eagerness, and with much mirth, as if each day has brought new wonders he has never experienced before. Henry is a rare human being who has never become inured to the glory of being alive, which is in accord with the Wee Ones' way of life.

Punt comes upon Henry out in the field tending to the grazing sheep. It is a fine patch of green pasture and a bucolic setting for enjoying oneself amongst the gentle creatures. Henry has his eye on a little lamb that seems to be slightly lame and has been rejected by his mother. On further examination, the lamb looks to have been cut by the barbed wire of the fencing. He will carry the little fellow back to the barn, feed him by bottle, and tend to his cut.

"Good day, me fine friend," calls out Punt exuberantly.

"Hallo, Wee Man," replies Henry looking about guardedly, as Punt tends to have a prank or two up his sleeve at any given moment.

"I've a wonderful joke for ye, Henry, about the ladies – me favorite topic, ye know. I'm on me way to the village to view the ladies, and thinking o' jokes to go along with their fickle natures. The older ladies, and some o' the young'uns, are an extremely humorous lot indeed."

"Punt, don't bother the poor gentlewomen, I beg o' ye. Ye must refrain from this idle pastime. Don't ye hiv better things to do with your time?"

"Och, Henry, coincidentally I've a bonnie joke for ye regarding time, to fill yer day wi' merriment."

"Alright, but it better be humorous to the hilt," replies Henry in jest, painfully aware that Punt's jokes are often excruciatingly lame. He goes along patiently with the game, knowing full well that his harebrained friend will not cease from pestering him until he's able to spill his silly joke.

"Which herb's most injurious to a lady's beauty?" inquires Punt.

"Which herb?" asks Henry, on cue, obliged to answer or face the consequences.

"Thyme!" replies Punt. Henry laughs superficially as he assesses the joke.

"Och, 'tis no very funny. Really lame, Punt! I've got to get back to work and tend to this poor wee lamb and do not desire ye travelin' on me shoulder whilst I'm working. Will ye grant me the favor o' gettin' back to your dun-shi? Surely your faither has a task for ye. How can ye have fun all day long? Aren't ye iver serious, me wee friend?" inquires Henry.

"Och, I'm not a merry soul all the time, Henry me friend. There are two sides to ivery nature, including me own. I sincerely relish fun and laughs, but 'tis to counteract me serious side whilst working on what needs to be done."

"What serious side is that, and what needs to be done?" inquires Henry skeptically. He tries not to laugh at what he concludes is a rather mock display of sincerity. "I've niver seen yer serious side. Ye certain ye have one?" he inquires jocularly.

"How do I explain to ye, Henry me fine lad? My fun-loving side puts me more in touch with the human condition? 'Tis acause I love humans greatly that I'm amenable to being around them for jest. This lends to me a specific touch o' knowledge on how to aid folks."

"Is that a fact?" chuckles Henry, dubious that this is the true motive behind what he considers Punt's mischief.

"Whilst I'm observing folks, I'm actually pointing out their follies to them, making them truly see the reality of their ways. For instance, when a drunk appears foolish in public and he's made aware o' how he appears to ithers for a few seconds, he may change his tune. I take away his drunken state with fey dust for a wee bit in order that the drunk can see the reality of his behavior."

Henry looks at Punt incredulously. "Why did ye niver tell me this afore, Punt? Are ye joshin' me?"

"Nay, Henry, there's a time and place for everything. You're growin' up, a man now, and will be out o' me clutches soon enough, so I will not be able to look efter ye."

"Och," replies Henry, feeling a wee bit of sadness in the prospect of not having his mischievous friend around his entire life. "Why won't ye be here, Punt? Whaur ye headed?"

"Henry," replies Punt soberly, "I'll be here – you'll be gone!"

Henry looks at him incredulously, wondering where he might be going. "Hopefully, I willna be dyin' anytime in the near future?" responds Henry jokingly.

"No, me friend, ye'll be carried away by the river o' life to meet your fate. And, Henry, life willna always be easy for ye acause you're workin' from a higher plane. Your powers are being developed to someday be a higher spirit in the universal scheme o' things."

"What do ye mean, Punt? I'm just an ordinary chap with second-sight, which means I can see your silly face. A lot of ither Scottish folks see the Wee Ones. Why should that make me life difficult?"

"Henry," replies Punt, "let me tell ye some things in advance so you won't be crippled by what's coming. Ye need to prepare yourself. Suffice it to say, ye'll have many challenges coming, but with tremendous joy and despair to enlighten and test your spirit. Ye'll have three great romances in your life, ye lover-boy ye," says Punt jokingly. "I'll not reveal the particulars of all of this, but there'll be wondrous, rewarding experiences from these relationships. And ye'll have beautiful children. I'll not reveal to ye their sexes. And, to top it all, ye'll not stay in Scotland, but travel to a beautiful, faraway land to live out your life. Sadly, ye'll suffer two great losses, Henry, but you must keep your sense o' humor and strong moral compass, even in the face o' despair and adversity, and particularly when you're tested to the greatest degree by difficult people and circumstances. And Henry, you'll be a respected member o' your community and become a wealthy man some day, and help ithers reach their goals acause o' your generosity and need to help ithers. Henry, ye'll live a tryin' but awesome and worthwhile life, and in the end ye'll have earned an exalted status and greater universal power in the heavens."

Henry has never heard Punt talk of serious things his entire life and holds his breath waiting for the punch line, but nothing more is said by the wee sprite. Punt flits off into the air looking like a large dragonfly that rules the sky.

II. Violet Shaw, the Baird Family Housekeeper

Fairies are visible to only a minority of grown humans, one being Henry. Another individual belonging to this select group of second-sighters is the housekeeper to the Baird family, Violet Rose Shaw, who helped raise all of the Baird children from infancy. The captivating Violet of Drumdruils Ranch will soon be strolling down the woodland path with the younger Baird children. Violet is a short, stout, buxom woman in her late fifties, with coarse hair the color of nickel, swept back in an attractive chignon. Her visage is sanguine, truly pleasing in its equanimity, with a comforting round regularity to her features, and brilliant blue, luminous eyes that are an open window to her soul. Looking into Violet's intelligent eyes, sparkling with hints of humor and wit, one gets the impression of her being on the edge of a "grand knowing," venturing ever so close to a revelation of the meaning of life but falling short as happens with a divine fleeting disclosure, or beholding a star of an awe-inspiring majesty, but alas looking away for a mere instant and losing it forever to the nighttime sky.

Violet has been blessed, as long as she can remember, with the ability to view Wee Ones at will. These blessed creatures are also visible to children under eight years of age, but most inhabitants of rural areas of Scotland are secondhand believers – many Scots are so besotted by their early childhood memories of fairies that they are disposed to be heartfelt believers throughout their lives.

The fairies are thought by believers to be highly magical creatures, given their enhanced ability to fly and to become invisible at will. The rural inhabitants of Scotland believe the Good People to be God-given, divine creatures and accept them as an integral part of the fauna of the land, just as they accept birds, bees, and insects as parts of earthly life. As adults, indoctrinated Scots integrate, quite readily, their inherent magical beliefs with the doctrines of their Sunday Christian sermons. As a result, they have indelibly imprinted in their psyches a hodgepodge of archetypal pagan and Christian lore, which lends, in part, to Scots being a rare composite of highly creative, inventive, mystical-believing, and ethical people.

The siths are called *sleagh maith*, or Wee Ones, Good People, wraiths, elves, brownies, pixies, fairies, sprites, feys, hobgoblins, elves, gnomes, etc. Scots have innumerable descriptive names for these small flying creatures. They dwell on earth in a similar manner to humans in that they procreate, fight wars against those who try to harm them, and form families, clans, and larger communities that lend them companionship and protection. Wee Ones are known to fashion spears out of a light flexible substance composed of elements not known to humans, which are very lethal in their effect, especially when dabbed with hemlock. The Wee Ones exist all over Asia and Europe, and their origins are unknown, but in Scotland it is speculated by a few scholars that they might be related to the indigenous ancient tribes called the Picts (Pechs) or Calendonii, a people of small stature who are known to be the earliest human inhabitants of Scotland. Most scholars on the subject disavow the idea of Picts being related to Wee People. The handful of scholars who theorize that the Wee People were indeed Picts theorize that Wee Ones/Picts might have played a part in the building of the beautiful cathedrals in Glasgow, but most historians date the Pict tribes to being extinct long before the time that the cathedrals were built in the thirteenth, fourteenth and fifteenth centuries.

Written accounts as well as fairy tales describe unfavorably-viewed fairies notorious for foul play, those being a capricious and mischievous lot, as imps or sprites or hobgoblins. As in the human race, there are miscreants amongst Wee People, but these comprise a very small minority. Tales abound in the literature of Wee People acting evilly, maliciously, or as ruthless pranksters. On closer investigation, many of these acts constitute counterattacks against those who have struck out against them, either by physical or immoral acts. The hobgoblins, closely related to brownies, are known to delight in practical jokes, but are entirely harmless, and at times these jokesters have been known to exhibit acts of goodness as well.

Wee People are acutely in tune with the synchrony of the universe and its mysteries and work ardently to promote the health of the earth for all living creatures. The Wee Ones keep tabs on all earthly happenings, particularly the interactions of humans with their neighboring clans (wars, famine, agriculture, etc.). They follow the expansion of human development pertaining to the scope of human knowledge, spiritual growth, and creativity. Wee Ones abound on earth to aid in the evolution of their human counterparts, so that earthlings will someday advance to a higher order, and in future centuries ascend to the level of "enlightened" beings. Wee Ones strive to become further evolved themselves, for they have not yet reached the total enlightenment of pure angels, though being semi-angels is much closer to the purity of angels than humans. These delightful, multidimensional fairy creatures live for eons, and due to their longevity have acquired a vast store of historical knowledge from having been acquainted with all preceding generations of earthly inhabitants. Being multidimensional creatures, they are also privy to the future, which lends to them great scientific knowledge.

The Wee People, being of the universal order of semi-angels, whose presence on earth is for the purpose of guiding humans towards the unlimited possibilities of creativity, spark the imaginations of children under eight years of age by lending them a glimpse of the multidimensional forms of reality, including the magic abounding in the universe. In the world of fairies, creative possibilities are unlimited. Children view the magical flight of the delightful, spunky creatures and develop aspirations to soar high like majestic birds in the sky. They hear Wee Ones communicating with animals and thus commence to mimic and befriend lower life forms. The Wee Ones magically create objects out of thin air, which spark in a small child's imagination the unlimited possibilities of invention. Children are imprinted to perceive, from a very early age, a three-dimensional world of objects, but are endowed as the Wee Ones to see beyond these perceptions to the unlimited dimensions in the universe, to where other realms of reality exist. The development of a magical fantasy world of children carries over into adulthood long after a belief in fairies has vanished. The fantasy remains in subconscious minds as archetypes that materialize during dreamtime. Seeds of unlimited possibilities spark human creations through scientific inventions and creative works in art, literature, and philosophy. Creative individuals have robust fantasy lives, and most likely were intimately connected to fairies as youngsters, or are have retained possession of second-sight as adults.

The Wee People live physically in the earthly dimension and non-physically in other realms as spiritual beings that are egoless and eternal with a predominantly higher consciousness. They are ethereal, energetic spirits, as are the angels. Humans are fixed in the physical world, living primarily within the realm of their physical selves, and are prone to be ego-oriented. Wee People enjoy the physical realm because they love to interact with humans, and to help them, but don't reside altogether in the human dimension. In their dun-shis, they are focused primarily on the nonphysical world, and communicate amongst themselves as nonphysical, multidimensional, ethereal spirits (precisely as angels do).

The ancient clan of Wee Ones, known to humans with second-sight as Elor's People, has dwelled for eons in the lower highlands of Scotland in the County of Perth, near the township of Bridge of Allan. This verdant land is very accommodating to their comfortable lifestyle. Green hillocks descend into sequestered cave-like labyrinthine dens that stretch underground for endless miles, and the surrounding woodlands of thick copses of alder wood, scrub oak, and Scotch fir, as well as bountiful, bubbly streams, provide excellent hunting and fishing grounds. The country is alive with the musical sound of rocks being pummeled by the spray of lively waterfalls, whose waters enter small inland streams progressing towards larger bodies of water, the rivers and lochs, and eventually to the lovely firths to the sea, such as the Firth of Clyde near Helensburgh and the Firth of Forth near Edinburgh.

III. A Fine Day for a Stroll — Catching Up with Wee Friends

23 October 1863

On this warm, sunny autumnal morning, Violet, after tending to the children's breakfast, gathers the accoutrements for their customary two-mile morning walk: jackets should they need them later; morning snacks, as the children will be ravenous by eleven-ish; hats for protection from the elements of sun, damp fog, rain, and the like; bandanas, a good article to wipe faces and clean hands in the streams; and woolen scarves to wear around the neck for warmth. Violet comes out of the main house to view the morning sky. She assesses the day to be a clear one with no clouds over the horizon, and proceeds to call inside to the youngsters, shrilly beckoning them out by calling, "Daena dawdle, bairns!" She listens to the customary pandemonium coming from the breakfast-room table where Malkie and Telford are fighting over the last sourdough biscuit, and from the open upstairs window where Baby Susan is fussing as her mother puts on her shoes. She wonders what's keeping Janet and Emma, as they have a tendency to get involved with the dollhouse when they are supposed to be dressing. Violet sits down for a moment on the stoop of the Bairds' two-storied house for a peaceful moment and sighs in contentment. Her morning chores have been accomplished and she has a bit of alone time to relax before the children come storming out for their walk. The forthcoming outing will be enjoyably sunny, and hopefully precipitate a meeting with her special subterranean friends, Elor and Twixie, which she is very much looking forward to.

Violet sits on the stoop of the main house that is sturdily constructed of quarried regional limestone brick surrounded by an impressive garden. Ivy clings tenaciously to the exterior of the house in artful geometric patterns, and pink Lacecap and lavender Mop-ball hydrangeas, in shades of raspberry pink, bluish-purple, and white, surround the lawn in a festive pom-pom-like fashion. Bright purple/magenta fuchsias, colorful primroses, and jeweled white-and-pink variegated rhododendron grace the sides of the walkway and stoop leading up to the house, imbuing the abode with an inviting fairy tale charm. Violet takes pride in having planted this verdant masterpiece of a garden.

Small, rustic outbuildings are set off from the main house where two middle-aged bachelor farmhands, Roy and Mac, live, and a second bungalow houses the married chief farmhand and his wife, Guy and Ruth Cook. Ruth is known by the eponymous name of Cook, as she works alongside Violet in the kitchen. There are several other crude outbuildings that store farming equipment and supplies. A larger four-room bungalow comprises Violet's pleasant quarters, located on the western side close to the main house, though she spends most of her time when not sleeping in the main house.

The Drumdruils farm grows fine berry crops consisting of a variety of raspberries, red and black currants, gooseberries, and tayberries, made into delicious jams and jellies (with the secret ingredients of honey, lemon, and orange peels soaked in whiskey, and a smidgeon of rosemary and thyme) that are marketed the breadth of Scotland, Wales, Ireland, and England. The older Baird children also sell berry baskets in town as a supplement to their allowances. The Bairds raise sheep, Angus cattle, and handsome red and white Ayrshire cattle for milk that graze on the hilly, rocky terrain on the eastern slopes of their land. Alas, with many mouths to feed (seven Baird children, the senior Bairds, two part-time ranch hands, plus the Cooks and Violet), the fruit jam and sheep profits often fall short of a comfortable income.

As she waits restfully for the children, Violet notices that she has left the bedroom window to her bungalow wide open, and walks across the courtyard to shut it. She stops in her tracks when she sights a Wee One named Marvel through the window. He appears to be sweeping her floor by his back and forth movements. She is glad she remembered to leave a smidgeon of bread on the counter for a wee visitor. Marvel will shut the window when he's done, she is certain, so she doesn't bother. She returns to her place and plops down on the stoop again.

Violet reflects on the fact that she is turning sixty years old in December, and has lived in Bridge of Allan her entire life, with Wee People being a major part of her existence, a clan of individuals she feels as close to as her Baird family clan. There has been no physical travel to other places on earth for Violet, only mental telepathic journeys to other dimensions, though she's satisfied with the richness of her life thus far – the enlightenment to see remarkable vistas outside ordinary human perception. Violet views herself very fortunate to be in possession of second-sight, which has endowed her lifelong access to a broader understanding of the synergy of all living things on earth and their relationship to the universe.

The Wee Ones have taught her how to access the magic that exists in each and every aspect of aliveness, to reach deep down to the inner workings of one's spiritual self to find one's true identity that exists apart from physical form – the part of one's self that is infinite and lives on, the part that is magical and capable of wondrous imaginings, a vital element of being that can be accessed by humans but is often not developed. From early in their childhoods, Violet has imbued the Baird children with the ability to access magical realms for preservation of their vital spiritedness, inspiration, creativity, foresight, and forbearance – a backup reality that all humans can benefit from – to ease the harshness of earthly reality when tumultuous grays and blacks in life inevitably arise like storms in a surging sea. She has made it her primary mission to endow the children with the capacity to fall back on mindful, creative, spiritual activities as a way to find solace, solve problems, broaden their perspectives, and to remain open-minded to the multitudinous wonders of life, in the event that their second-sight dwindles.

Having second-sight has not always been blissful for Violet, for it renders her glimpses of future happenings that can be rather unsettling. Oftentimes, her premonitions are not accurate but mere archetypal images arising from her subconscious mind, as occurs in the dream state. If a valid premonition occurs, a current of energy quickens her spine like a mild electric shock, or a feathery tickling of her tailbone. At the present moment, this is precisely what she is experiencing as she waits patiently for the Baird children. While looking out to the west to a view over the colorful tile rooftops of the township of Bridge of Allan, a quickening in her spine is felt as an appalling image enters her mind – a small child is lying in a freezing pasture, and a small coffin is being lowered into the ground of the kirkyard of the Gothic Dunblane Cathedral. The vision flashes electrically like lightning and subsides abruptly. She brushes the disturbing image from her mind, somewhat appeased when she rationalizes that these unpleasant images have probably been triggered by this morning's newspaper story describing an increased incidence of children in the slums of Edinburgh succumbing to typhus and cholera. Yet she ponders over the fact that the image pertains to Dunblane, the adjoining town to Bridge of Allan, a short distance away.

Violet looks out to the north and is aware of her Wee Friends in the distance, flitting around in the woodland, adding to the orchestral humming, chirping, and buzzing of insects, plaintive calls of doves, and vociferous melodies of song thrushes. She is now more eager than ever to meet up with her Wee Friend, Elor, the clan chief, on her walk with the children, for he can confirm whether her unsettling premonition is real or imagined. She senses something has excited the Wee Ones, for they are exhibiting out-of-the-ordinary industriousness; in fact, all the creatures in the woodlands are stirred up in a flurry of sound and motion.

Wee People have been a part of Violet's world since early childhood. They are as natural to her environs as flying birds and insects, and she supposes people would find birds and insects flying around totally unbelievable, too, if they had not had them visibly present in the world they were born into. Why, she ponders, are there so many skeptics who, once they've grown out o' their belief in the existence o' Good People, find it untenable to believe in their existence in the aviary world along wi' birds and insects? Many insects are very tiny and invisible to humans like Wee People, and educated medical scholars and practitioners believe in the existence of invisible entities that carry disease.

Since Violet's world is governed by her unique insight – there are very few adults that see Wee People – she is able to enjoy the world in its full splendor and from a different perspective than most. The Wee People furnish to those adults who can see them the assurance of a well-orchestrated universe not destined to come tumbling down in a catastrophic doomsday scenario. The earth is part of a living energetic maze of wholeness on an infinite scale of balanced synchrony which the human mind is incapable of comprehending. Those with second-sight have comfort in the knowledge that human beings are not alone in their powers of reasoning and foresight – higher beings are guardian protectors of the earth and all of its inhabitants. A higher order of beings (the semi-angels) has been sent to earth as emissaries to offer knowledge and know-how on living life to its best advantage; to lend insight on the evolution of the earth and what is in store for the future; and, above all, to aid in the spiritual and creative development of humankind. From her perspective, Violet is dumbfounded by people's lack of the basic belief that Mother Earth is a blessed sanctuary that humans must protect, safe environs of a beautiful, living, self-sustaining entity. Life, she thinks, should be enjoyed and people should worship the Almichty with a perpetual sense of gratefulness, and not worship the Almichty out of fear of retribution, as many religions espouse. Despite her acute awareness, Violet is very protective of the children because she knows that Wee Ones cannot interfere in the Almichty's absolute directives on life, death, and adversity, but by their superior knowledge they can aid humans in avoiding calamities that are the makings of mankind and nature, and aid in the development of spiritual strength to overcome adversity. The Wee Ones can also teach humans the importance of work, study, relaxation, exercise, laughter, dance, courtship, love, and other beneficial rituals in life that have evolved with human spiritual development, to be passed down from generation to generation, all part of the wondrous experience of being human.

IV. Story Time at Drumdruils

Violet has an endless repertoire of magical fairy tales, ancient folklore of the Celts, and stories of the present-day Wee People inhabiting the woodlands and dun-shis of the hillocks, which she shares with the Baird family each evening during Story Hour. She takes pride in possessing second-sight and being intimately acquainted with the Wee People dwelling in the dun-shis of Dunblane and Bridge of Allan, particularly those dwelling on the Drumdruils ranch. She shares her knowledge of the fairies through the tales she recounts to the family. The Baird children love to hear the story of Violet's early life with the fairies. Eight-year-old second-sighted Emma, in particular, has soaked up, word for word, all of Violet's accounts of fairy goings-on, particularly their magical practices, lending her a vivid imagination and her extraordinary creative spark.

The children are particularly spellbound when they listen to Violet's darker fairy tales of mysterious castles, warlocks and witches, ghosts, devils, brownies, wraiths, apparitions, giants, dragons, and the associated dark notes that accompany tales of intrigue in regards to the aforesaid, but a good many of her stories deal with enchantment and love.

Violet has, many times, regaled the Baird family with her own thrilling personal story of having dwelled with the Wee People for a time in a woodland cave when she was five years old. This occurred after she had been accidently separated from her mother, who had been unduly preoccupied in picking blackberries for a summer solstice celebration. Wee Violet had wandered off to explore and had found herself hopelessly lost. The Wee People found the wandering child, entertained and fed her, and kept her safe in the den of their clan leader, Elor, who is still the clan leader of the Good People more than fifty years later. He has remained a very close friend of Violet's. Violet was returned to her family that very same day in only a few hours by earth time, but she was never quite the same from that day forward – in "fairy time" she had resided in the dun-shi for many months. Her ability to see the Wee People in adulthood was developed inordinately while in their company due to her young, impressionable mind.

Violet remembers that she and the Wee People had a spectacular time, and she was not afraid of them in the least, as they were about her size, enchanting, and very entertaining. She regarded them as friends to play and have fun with. The Wee Ones taught her how to dance the jig and play the fiddle, which she does expertly to this day. Many are skeptical that she had learned to play the fiddle in so little time, but Violet explains that time in the dun-shi is very concentrated. When she did return to her family, she had matured in her knowledge and in her physical appearance.

Violet claims to have inherited her second-sight from her maternal great-great-great-grandfather, the Reverend Robert Kirk, a scholarly reverend who was educated at St. Andrews and the University of Edinburgh, notably very proficient in Greek and Latin, and a greatly respected vicar due to his intellect and wonderfully insightful, easily understood sermons.

The reverend was a devout preacher of Christianity as well as a fairy believer, evidenced by the treatise that he wrote in the 1690s concerning the lives of elves, wraiths, and brownies that he had come to know. Later on in his long life, the reverend was said to have met an untimely death on a fairy hill (dun-shi) in Aberdoyle near his parish when he suffered a swooning episode and fell into a fairy turret. The reverend sent word to a good friend with second-sight that he was very much alive and well living with the Wee People. He indicated that he would be attending his grandchild's christening, and that he could be brought back to the human world if his friend would tap him on his shoulder during the christening. As per his word, his second-sighted friend saw Reverend Kirk at the ceremony, but unfortunately the good-intentioned friend was so taken aback by seeing the reverend in full-form that he failed to tap his shoulder to break the spell of his sojourn in fairyland. As a result, Reverend Kirk remained with the Wee Ones, albeit happily, and lived for eons with them. The reverend was often seen about Bridge of Allan by second-sighters, looking in on his relatives and past parishioners, and gained the ability to change to the minute form of a dragonfly and zoom o'er the land.

It was common practice for the parishioners in the days of Robert Kirk to adhere to their pagan fairy beliefs after Christianity became a dominant force in their religious lives. They were brought up with fairy lore, and had a natural inclination to retain fairies in their belief system. According to Violet, Wee Ones are extraordinary astral creatures, part angel, but related to mankind on earth. The siths or fairies are said to reside in a middle dimension between man and angel, and are intelligent, fluid spirits, with light astral bodies (somewhat of the nature of a condensed cloud best seen in twilight). Their bodies are incredibly pliable from the subtlety of the spiritual realm they are attached to, and they are able to make themselves appear or disappear at will. Even some adults with second-sight cannot see Wee Ones that have deliberately transformed to an invisible spectrum, but most children ages seven and below can see them in both visible and non-visible light spectrums.

"Me Wee Friends are always near," Violet often relays to the Baird children. "They whisper in me ear when they've anything important to relay, or when they're in need. Oft times, they come to me in the kitchen in want o' tidbits o' breads and cakes, but bring goods to trade in the form o' their wonderful medicinal salves brewed from woodland herbs. They're expert healers o' many o' the afflictions besetting mankind."

The Wee People have been known to entertain human visitors in their homes with song and dancing of jigs that last the entire night, but Violet has warned those whom she knows never to go with the fairies to their homes. Since human time is very different than fey time, some poor souls have gone in for an evening of dance and drink to come back months, weeks, or even years, later; in some ill-fated instances, poor souls are gone for what they think is a few days, but this turns out to be a lifetime on earth. They find out on their return to human time that everyone known to them has died; soon after coming back, these unfortunates entering back into the earthly world crumble to dust from the extremes of old age. On the contrary, and in a more ideal situation in time travel in the dunshis, some visitors are with the Wee People for months and come back to earth only a few hours later in earthly time, as Violet did as a child, though she had matured by a few years. Whether the loss of a few hours or the loss of years, this all depends on the dimension that humans find themselves in once inhabiting the multitudinous realms of fairies.

The Baird children have been raised with an abundance of fairy lore due to Violet's influence, and all have been befriended by Wee People as young children. The Wee People visit Violet frequently when she's out and about with the Baird crew on walks – feys are keen on frolic and play, delighting in the Baird children's innocence, spunkiness, imagination, and vitality, which is totally in accord with the traits they possess. The older Baird siblings have grown out of their ability to see the Wee People, and have, for the most part, abandoned their childhood beliefs – with the exceptions of Henry and Emma. Reflecting back on their younger years, the siblings who can no longer view the fairy presence regard their memories of them as figments of their childhood imaginations, although the fey magic is tucked away deep down in their psyches. Adam, nearing eighteen years of age and no longer possessing second-sight, still calls on the Wee People, as he did as a child, for "fey good luck," to send him money he needs, to overcome a sickness, or to help him unravel a bind he's gotten himself into, just as nonbelievers of any society superstitiously have lucky totems and icons like rabbit foots. Of course, Henry, who has retained his second-sight, calls on the fairies often, as he has a tendency to get himself into a lot of jams. When feeling low, Adam and Henry both call on fey dust to lighten their moods. The Good People, messengers of the divine spirit, love to help out their human counterparts, and go out of their way to seek out those in need, even though the recipients of their kindly acts are unaware of the generosity that has been bestowed on them.

With Henry's second-sight very much intact, he sees his Wee Friends often, but doesn't talk about his gift to others in the family. Violet is quite aware that her Henry is special and has retained his ability to see Wee Ones. She often giggles when she views Punt riding on Henry's shoulder.

Violet, being a talented raconteur, loves to recount to the Baird family tales of the Wee People, and thus the children have been instilled since bairns with stories of the Scottish fairies. They have also memorized by heart most of the fables of fairies of other worlds that have been relayed to them over and over through the years. All the same, they love to hear them again and again. Violet has recounted one of her stories at the nightly Baird Story Hour many times: "This is a tale of a poor servant girl wi' second-sight who was a good worker and swept the house every day. She emptied her sweepings on the great heap at the side o' the house. One morning when she was starting back to her work, she found a letter on this heap, but as she could not read, she took the letter to her employer efter she had finished her day's work. The employer read the letter out loud to her and she found it to be an invitation from the elves, who asked the girl to hold a child for them at its christening. The girl didn't really know these elves well, although she'd been cordial to them when passing by on her way to work each day. At length, efter much persuasion, as she was told that it was no good manners to refuse an invitation o' this kind, she consented. Then three elves came and escorted her to a hollowed-out mountain whaur the Wee Folks lived. Everything there was small, but elegant and more beautiful than can be described. The baby's mother lay in a bed of black ebony ornamented with pearls, embroidered with gold. A cradle was adorned in ivory, and there was a font o' gold whaur the baby was to be dunked for the christening. The girl stood up at the christening as the godmother. Efter the christening, the girl requested to be escorted home, but the wee elves persuaded her to be their guest for a few days, and so she stayed on for three days, passing the time in pleasure and gaiety, learning to dance and partaking in a wee bit o' their nectar drink, which was fermented, a very strong alcoholic concoction. The Wee Folks did all they could to entertain her in style, and the time passed by quickly. Finally, on the third day she set out for home. The Wee People gave her a thank you offering, filling her pockets full of gold, and then they led her out of the mountain turret to a path that led her to her home. When she got home, she wanted to begin her work promptly, as she'd been gone so long and did not wish to upset her employer, and so she picked up the broom that was still standing in the corner, and began to sweep their kitchen. Then some strangers came out of anither room in the house, and asked her who she was, and why she was intruding in their house. They thought she was trying to steal their broom. As it turned out, she had been gone not three days with the Wee Ones in the mountains, as she thought, but seven years in earthly time. In the interim time, her former masters had died. She was out o' a job, but with her pockets full o' gold she was quite a wealthy woman. No longer a girl at all, she was a woman of twenty-one. She bought her own house in a nearby village and lived very well, and eventually married a local boy, and always greeted the Wee People she met very cordially as very good friends do, but niver again consented to join them in their dun-shis."

Violet also has recounted stories of fairies that can cause harm to humans, though she emphasizes that these miscreants are a very small minority of the Good People population. The practice of surreptitiously exchanging babies (called changelings) for human babies is a well-known practice in folklore.

"A dark side of fairies unfortunately can exist," says Violet soberly, "but a dark side to some human beings can also exist as well. Fairies are part human and part angel, and therefore can possess an evil or destructive element to their makeup. Some fairies have had children born with defects, as happens in the human population, and have been known to exchange their babies for a perfect human baby; that is, they leave a changeling that is abhorrent in appearance in place of a beautiful human baby that is verra enticing. It takes a lot o' cunning to get the human bairn back from the elves, as the fairy mother grows very fond of it and comes to regard the child as her own.

"I'll tell a tale now o' such a happening, wherein an unfortunate human bairn was switched at birth for a changeling.

"A mother had her child kidnapped out of its cradle by elves, and a changeling wi' a large head and protruding, staring eyes was put in the place of the babe, so in the mind o' the elves it was not really stealing. This grotesque-looking babe with huge-looking monstrous eyes that were askew and a lopsided head would do nothing but eat and drink, and lay in its cradle, not developing day-to-day like a normal human babe. In her grief, the mother went to her neighbor and asked her advice, for she thought this was her child that had contracted some terrible disease. The neighbor told her it was not her child at all, but a reject from the Wee People. The neighbor said that she should carry the changeling into the kitchen, set it down by the hearth, light a fire, and boil some water in two eggshells, which would make the changeling laugh. If the changeling laughed, all would end for the best, for the elves would respond to the laughter of one of their own and think the changeling had recovered from its grotesqueness. The woman did everything that her neighbor bade her to do. When she put the eggshells wi' water on the fire to boil, the goggle-eyed babe declared, 'I'm as old now as the western forest, but niver yet have I seen anyone boil anything in an eggshell.' And he began to laugh hysterically. Whilst he was laughing, there came suddenly a host o' little elves who brought the human child back, set it down on the hearth, and took the changeling away with them. The human child was no longer a newborn, though, but a babe of one year."

As to the subject of changelings, the entire Baird family gathers around the hearth during Story Time to hear a short introduction to Shakespeare's *A Midsummer Night's Dream*, pertaining to the changeling in the play that Violet had told them about, which they have heard many times before but never tire of. Adam Sr. is an avid Shakespeare fan and insists that all the children be exposed to the literary giant. Violet, as usual, recounts the play little by little, mindful of the younger children's ability to comprehend too much at a time. The family are re-introduced to the basic plot and the major characters in the story, particularly the royal Wee Ones, King

Oberon and his Queen Titania, who continually battle over the beautiful human baby that the queen stole from India. The queen is very much in love with the baby, while the king is very jealous, and connives to take it away from the queen, for he wants the boy to join his army.

Shakespeare, in his fertile imagination, with one foot in the supernatural, was enchanted by and well versed in Wee People lore, and perhaps had second-sight in adulthood, as many creative poets and writers are suspected by believers of having been blessed with supernatural gifts; or an alternative explanation, espoused by many eminent scholars, is that Wee People have been immortalized in European folklore and that has made a monumental impression on their creative human talents.

Violet has explained to the Baird family that the Wee Ones run the gamut of types of individuals, just as humans are very diverse in kinds. The majority of the Wee Ones are good citizens. There exists a cluster of nefarious individuals who practice thievery and worse acts of depravity, while there are a few lighthearted, inquisitive, merry souls like Robin Goodfellow in *A Midsummer Night's Dream* who are "full of the dickens," getting their kicks by playing tricks on people. In *A Midsummer Night's Dream*, Puck (also known as Robin Goodfellow) turns himself into crab and jumps out of a woman's porridge bowl to frighten her. In Bridge of Allan, Punt is a notorious trickster, goodhearted but full of chicanery, and falls into this category, though he is also very scientifically gifted and has the prospect of growing up and changing his ways. Violet has explained that many Wee Ones are scientific geniuses like Punt's father, Elor, who is chief of the Good People's clan in Bridge of Allan, and his daughter, Twixie, a co-leader and co-creator. They are eons ahead of the times; in fact, most Wee Ones have mystical, supernatural abilities and have the ability to transit to infinite past and future realms on a whim, but choose to exist in the present earthly realm to aid humans.

V. Awaiting the Children for Their Morning Stroll

Violet eases her mind out of its reflective state and begins to wonder, with a slight bit of irritation, what in the world is keeping the children! She calls out to them again, through the open front door, in her cheerful but commanding voice, to "come along posthaste." Violet has been intimately involved in the rearing of each of the Baird children since their first breaths of life, and has perfect insight into each child's individuality. On their daily morning walks, she aspires to teach them the wonders of the natural world, desiring for them to be in tune, at every level of awareness, to the glories of their earthly environment.

In due time, the rough and tumble troupe of four energetic youths, Telford, Malkie, Janet, and Emma, crowd out of the door all at once, limbs entangled as they compete for egress, shoving and poking their way through the impediment with their butterfly nets. Jean hands over Baby Susan to Violet to be put in her little red wagon. The children will take turns hauling Susan along the paths. They eventually make it through the doorway, though appear a bit disheveled, with their clothes and hair awry. Violet hands out their hats and wraps a kerchief around each little neck. The beginning of their walk resembles a race off a starting line. Violet calls to them to hold their horses and stay thegither.

The terrain on which Violet and the children hike is a haven for wildlife: a menagerie of buzzing airborne creatures – butterflies, dragonflies, and insects galore – that intersect over the gurgling streams in a melting pot of arthropods and other waterborne creatures. Surrounding the stream, bulrushes and thick alder copses and ferns grow in profusion. Wild water birds like geese and ducks waddle in and out from beneath the thick bulrush and reed. An occasional bellowing of a roe and clipped chirping of chaffinches herald a fine day to relish the activities of life on the ponds and streams. The children use their nets, designed and sewn by Violet, to catch their prey. Pollywogs and an assortment of amphibians skirt this way and that through the water, as well as a plentiful supply of trout that swim innately towards a prescribed destination; deer frequent the water's edge to quench their thirst; plump beavers plow through the water with their thick tails, busily intent on weaving their homes out of sticks, bulrush, and reeds. The Baird youngsters and Violet traipse merrily over hill and dale, along the many intersecting streams, covering more than two miles of dense woodsy flora that will eventually come out on the other side of the woods in Dunblane, though they will not go as far as the town today.

The children's myriad adventures in the "Land of Drums," as they call their home territory of Drumdruils, are wildly imaginative, strenuous, and rambunctious. When not accompanied by Violet, they have unfettered freedom to roam where they please o'er the woodsy land, as long as they play safely, take care of one another, and do no harm to the crops.

With their adult protector, they travel obligingly the paths she has chosen, knowing that Violet has an even greater sense of the landscape than they do, and will lead them eventually to the more plentiful streams where they can catch their tadpoles, pollywogs, and butterflies. Along the way, the lads and lassies snack on the wild blackberries that grow in abundance throughout the woodsy terrain, smudging their hands and lips with purple stain. They know well to stay clear of the poison oak, poison ivy, and the toxic holly berry plants.

Chapter Three

I. Storm of the Century Brewing — 23 October 1863

Since very early in the morning, on this lovely October day in 1863, the Wee Ones have been storing food and imbibing nectar in haste in preparation for the coming of a Great Storm, as they have foreseen significant devastation to follow in the wake of the upcoming volatile tempest. The Good People habitually warn their human friends possessed with second-sight of unfavorable conditions occurring in the atmosphere. A couple of subterranean Wee People, very close friends of Housekeeper Violet, are out and about on this fine morning and deliberately seek out her company as she and the children meander along the shores of a gurgling stream, its murky water a tangle of swaying reeds and moss, rising up from a colorfully pebbled mushy bottom. Tadpoles, pollywogs, and other grotesque-looking aqueous creatures that circulate through the waters are particularly enthralling to the curious eyes of the youngsters. Elor's clan of fairies has been intimately acquainted with the Bairds for innumerable generations – Wee People have resided for centuries in dun-shis located on the hillocks above Drumdruils.

The Good People adore the young, impressionable minds of human children, especially those children who haven't yet lost their ability to see them, and particularly those with second-sight for life. The Baird children under eight years of age come across their wee fairy friends as often as they come across birds and insects, particularly when close to the dun-shi hillocks; the young children are able to see Wee Ones well in their human-like forms, as well as in insect forms invisible to most second-sighted adults. A select group of older children and adults, who are beyond the age of innocence, are also blessed with the sight of these beautiful, luminous beings once they have landed on solid ground – these humans possess minds of super-plasticity and remain open and in tune with other levels of universal consciousness. These humans are less impressionable to dictates of societal norms and imprinting, and tend to be the great creative individuals of the human species, such as William Shakespeare, William Blake, and Leonardo da Vinci.

II. A Child Will Die Tonight?

Two Wee Ones, Elor and Twixie, swoop down on the Baird children of Drumdruils as they stroll alongside Violet down by the stream. This pair of fairies possesses the typical flaxen hair of pixies, some strands gathered attractively atop their heads by gold combs. The Baird children are carrying little packets of crumb cakes and pumpkin bread, offerings to the Wee People, as they have been eagerly anticipating running into their Wee Friends at some point along the path.

Elor, the clan chief, is a jaunty, winged wee gentleman dressed to the hilt in a green tartan blazer and finely styled green-and-blue woolen kilt, with a green beret atop his head. He is shod in fine silver felt, pointy-toed shoes. His movements are lightning quick, lithe, and bouncy, as though he might commence a lively jig on the spot. He greets the walkers cordially and jovially, exemplary of his gentlemanly, convivial nature. He sweeps down to hover close to Violet's ear, speaking in a low monotone, mindful of Violet's slight deafness, though respectful of not alarming the children with his message. Violet is not hearing well today, and so he proceeds to land next to her in a larger form, but still half the height of Violet, who is a short woman.

"Greetings, my dear Violet. Ye look enchantin' on this fine morn wi' yer violet eyes to match the verra blue color o' wildflowers. Indeed, a bonnie sight to rest me weary eyes on! Och, to spoil this scene o' tranquility! I do fear I've come to ye wi' tidings o' a most unfavorable nature."

"Pray tell, what do ye fear?" inquires Violet, a look of alarm lighting up her luminous blue eyes as she waits expectantly for Elor to divulge his news.

"Och, Violet, there's a horrendous swarmin' o' minute cosmic particles up in the northern skies. 'Tis o' a swirlin' hornet formation – a whoppin' purple and magenta circular configuration. Aye, verra majestic in shape, but appearin' to be wickedly spiteful in character. Yonder the swarmin' beehive formation is a monstrous conformation, the image o' an ice deevil, rantin' and ravin' his deevilish curses. Way afar, in the outermost reaches o' the ither world" – Elor stretches his little arms up to the blue sky – "there's a michty orange ball o' cosmic energy, twisting a' twirlin' round in circles, resemblin' bats gone rabid, gatherin' up swords o' light in an endless formation o' marchin' soldiers. I've a keen smell for a michty tempest from miles afar – me nose twitches wi' the dense metallic scent o' condensed air. Aye, skies'll open thair floodgates tonicht, and menacin' Auld Cluits will show off his tremendous forces soon efter. By the grace o' the Almichty, we must pray the tempest will cause only a wee bit o' damage and no bodily harm, but I duly fear for the safety o' residents o' Bridge o' Allan and Dunblane. I foresee a tragic happenin' to the community at large, a devastatin' occurrence due to the wrath o' deevils – not to alarm ye, but death's part o' the equation. I foresee a child in grave danger tonicht – a child's liken to succumb to the wrath o' the deevilish storm."

"A child could die tonicht? Lord Almichty," cries out Violet unabashedly, in utter horror and desperation, her already rosy complexion flooding with a profusion of high coloring as she recalls her premonition that morning of a child lying in a frozen pasture. It appears she might be succumbing to a stroke, but this is only a sign of her discomfiture, as she is a very fit individual. She fans her flushed, perspiring face with her sunbonnet brought down from her head.

"Och, Elor, I did indeed hiv a vision o' a poor child lyin' in a pasture!" She looks anxiously around for the children, though the laddies are nowhere in sight, having gone down a steep bank to the stream in search of pollywogs.

"Lord, might we be protected from forces o' nature beyond reason," beseeches Violet as she gazes up at the heavens, which appear at present remarkably sunny and cloudless. Violet strikes a stance of determination to retaliate against an egregious assaulter, as did the ancient queen Boudica, who readied her troops for a charge into battle.

"I must gather up all me children posthaste and warn Mr. and Mrs. Baird straightaway. By all means, we'll make a concerted effort to be safely inside by early eve, and stay put through the onslaught." Her visage and rapid eye tracking are testament to her thoughts spinning at automaton speed. "What'll become o' the Wee People?" she inquires. "Will ye be safe?"

"Rest assured, me dear friend, we'll be snug in our dens down in the solid ground. No flurries can breach our buttresses," exclaims Elor proudly. "Wi' an honest dose o' foreboding, I do unfortunately foresee the Bridge o' Allan community suffering a great catastrophe."

With the protectiveness of a mother hen, Violet takes inventory of her young charges. She walks over and looks down to the river's bank to catch sight of the laddies and Janet. Eleven-year-old Janet, who no longer sees the Wee Ones, joined her older brothers, Malkie and Telford, in play as soon as Violet started communing in her secretive language with what seems to them to be plants and insects. The children are throwing stones into the stream to stir up the tadpoles and pollywogs from their hiding places at the mucky bottom.

"Stay close, Malkie and Telford, and ye too, Janet," she calls out in a distressed tone to her flock of high-energy youth down by the stream. "Stay in one spot where I can see your location at all times, 'specially ye, Malkie. Don't wander downstream efter frogs. We're departing shortly for home."

"Why?" whines Malkie, protesting. "'Tis not time to leave!"

"Mind yer manners, laddie," yells Violet shrilly. "Ye'll be in bed afore nightfall if ye don't behave."

Elor describes in fuller detail his prognostications of the juggernaut that will sweep o'er Bridge o' Allan. Violet becomes more and more distressed with Elor's sobering account of the upcoming torrent.

"The brawny deevil in flux in our skies is o' a most intense magnitude, no to be seen for a century, but Wee Ones are on the alert!" Elor's lithe, muscular body stands postured, with his arms flexed at the elbow, as if he plans to bear the brunt of the storm on his shoulders with his brute strength.

Little Emma is blessed with second-sight, exhibiting a very strong proclivity in this regard, which indicates she will most likely retain her gift for life. She is holding onto Violet's hand, listening attentively with a wide-eyed, bewildered gaze. The full scope of Elor's whispered message is beyond her comprehension, though the excited demeanor of the Wee One, who is bouncing up and down with urgent gesticulations, prompts her to keep her big, blue eyes fixed intently on him. Emma wonders if his small size grants him permission for tantrums, as that's very near the manner in which she and her siblings act out when they feel that everyone is ganging up on them. Then again, she knows Elor well. He has never been prone to tantrums before. He's a very excitable Wee One, indeed, but never has been as demonstrative as at this time. Emma surmises that something serious must be happening to make him jump around with his eyes protruding like a sheep's, like an unlucky creature that's been caught in a wire fence. She'll learn more from Twixie soon. She thinks that maybe she'll be able to help, whatever the problem is. Emma is very glad that she has second-sight because Wee Ones make her feel special and are so much fun to be around. If the Wee Ones left her, who would make her wishes come true and send her on vision quests to faraway lands, farther away than the moon?

Janet no longer sees Wee People and doesn't seem to miss them. Her second-sight waned over a period of a year, and then entirely disappeared from her consciousness, as other things in childhood diminish or disappear, as do baby teeth and baby fat and imaginary friends. Emma thinks Janet doesn't need Wee People because her life has many other advantages. Their parents treat Janet almost like an adult now, providing her with grown-up activities – piano lessons, sewing, and knitting, and sometimes cooking – and have allowed her to do many things that Emma isn't allowed to do, like walking alone down the lane to visit her good friend, Mary MacLaine. None of her older brothers and sisters has second-sight any longer except for Henry. Henry is that way, as Emma sees it, because Henry is always going to be Henry, the happy-go-lucky brother who makes most everyone laugh out loud by his funny words and funny faces, or under their breaths for those trying hard not to laugh in front of their father. Emma is proud that her family still worships the Wee Ones; even her parents, who are non-believers, love to hear tales of the Wee People during Story Hour, and are known to call on the fairies for a wish come true, as when her mother asked the Wee Ones for a fancy dress for her birthday.

Our lives are happy acause o' Wee Ones, reflects wee Emma. *We're safe acause they live on our land, acause they look efter us.*

Violet ensures the children learn about the world of the Wee Ones through her storytelling, and in her songs, and even in the way she relates to the outdoors, particularly as they walk out in nature. The Wee Ones are all around them, very much a part of the natural world, and Violet points them out along the way. Oftentimes, Violet glances out the kitchen window of the main house and sees the Wee Ones. She will then open up the window wide and start a conversation with them, acting as a translator for the children. Soon enough, the siblings who are not second-sighters join in the conversation with the Wee People, despite their loss of second-sight. Emma thinks it is like talking to the Almichty in their nightly prayers. As long as her siblings are in the right frame of mind, the Wee People really exist for them, just like God when they really need him, even if they can't see him.

Oh, well, thinks Emma, sighing, *whitiver is the matter wi' the world, Twixie and Elor will make it awricht.* She adores her Wee People friends and believes they are responsible for most of the good happenings taking place around them.

On this fine day, Emma wears her new lavender and cream gingham dress with a baby blue/lavender-striped sash to show off to the Wee Ones, who have a penchant for fashion, and who are in their own right extraordinarily style-minded in their attire. To divert her attention from the high-pitched ranting and gesticulations of her father, Twixie beckons Emma over to her. Emma drops Violet's hand and runs over to greet her Wee Friend, who is the size of the smallest species of hummingbird and possesses the sparkling iridescence of a hummingbird as well. Twixie flies in circles playfully around Emma's head, whispering sweet nothings in her ear, exclaiming that Emma is one of their favorite lasses in all the land, the best dressed she's seen in many generations. Twixie lands next to Emma and now miraculously appears approximately the same height as the child.

"Emma, my sweet, ye've the prettiest dress I've iver had the privilege to view in a long while, which makes ye one o' Scotland's most fashionable beauties, as grand as the genteel women in royal salons o' Europe," exclaims Twixie after admiring Emma's dress.

Emma is bowled over with delight and pride by the compliment from the charismatic Twixie, whom she regards as her "fairy angel."

The other children are paying no attention to Violet's ranting over the upcoming storm, so intent are they in the examination of their fruitful catch of tadpoles and frogs. They are accustomed to Violet and Emma partaking in imaginary discourses with Wee People while on their daily walks out in nature, as much as they are accustomed to Violet's habitual prattle to unseen entities out the kitchen window while rolling her dough or stirring her pots of stews and soups. The older children have outgrown their intimate rapport with fairies, although somewhere embedded indelibly in their subconscious minds the Wee Ones persist, coming to the forefront in their nighttime slumbers, which comprise a compilation of infinite archetypes from places and things from infinite dimensions that the dreamer accesses and utilizes.

"Emma," says Twixie, "some o' our clan folks are planning to pay a visit to the Baird family in the eve, mebbe to borrow a smidgeon o' flour in exchange for a scrubbing o' the floor."

"Ah, Twix, it would be so merry an occasion for ye to visit. We'd love to hiv ye for teatime. Violet could prepare her sesame seed teacakes."

"Ah, regrettably, Emma, I'll be aiding Faither tonicht wi' the challenges o' the coming storm. But rest assured, I'll join ye in your time o' slumber and fly wi' ye on a magical journey in your dreams. I'll be close by to ensure that your mind's full o' soothing, blissful thoughts all through the nicht, and that you're not frightened by the storm."

A few yards off, Elor tries to placate Violet's trepidation over the family's safety by divulging more of the projected countermeasures he plans for the upcoming deluge.

"Violet, the Wee Ones will definitely be watching o'er the Baird family. Aye, we'll ensure that our friends are safe and snug in thair abodes afore the ither world weeps down its tears o' sorrow," exhorts Elor.

"We'll most seriously heed yer warning, Elor," says Violet. "I beg ye to take care of yourselves."

Elor and Twixie fly up into the air, gradually becoming smaller in size, as they go off o'er the grassland that is wet and shiny with dew, so aerodynamically smooth in the air that from a distance they look like beautiful dragonflies with iridescent wings in the bright morning sunlight.

III. Afternoon Before the Great Storm, Drumdruils Farm — 23 October 1863

"Run, Janet, run faster!" hollers Adam Baird at the top of his lungs. "They're coming round the bend." Adam alerts his sister Janet that the gang has spotted her and that she must touch home base promptly to avoid a clobbering. The lively sport takes place on the family's berry farm of Drumdruils, located in the hillocks above the River Allan, a great waterway cutting through the center of the town of Bridge of Allan. Drumdruils is a bucolic, picturesque farmland at the heart of the Bairds' world, a beautiful environ unparalleled in its verdant tranquility. The ranch is located high up in the hills above Bridge of Allan, the land rocky and persnickety to the growth of most kinds of crops, but excellent for berry growing and the grazing of sheep, and a great place for children to spread their wings in wild abandon.

Adam is refereeing a riveting game of hide-and-seek with his younger brothers and sisters. The air is crisp and energizing, and the sky a cloudless slate blue, with a deceptive feel of spring in the air, despite the approaching winter season. The sharp, cold winds that unfailingly roar in from the Highlands this time of year have yet to materialize, although it is late October. The seasonal tardiness of wintry weather lends credulity to the lackadaisical notion that winter has been cancelled from here on out by the powers that be in charge of weather, that mild climate is to be the norm for the small town of Bridge of Allan and its outlying ranches and dairy farms forevermore. Only Violet is on guard for a deluge. She's taken to heart Elor's prognostication of impending disaster. Safeguards have included promises by the Wee People for assistance if the family should need it, and lecturing the children about staying together and being on the alert at all times for sudden cloud movement.

Violet has warned the Baird children – in the shrill, commanding voice she uses to bring home a point – of a big storm coming, sounding more like a declaration of Armageddon on the horizon than a mere storm.

"Make haste in yer game playing. No lingering oot aboot past dusk," she has ordered with firmness.

The children don't quite buy into her dire forecast given the balmy weather outside, with no indication of foul weather on the horizon. As Elor had assured Violet that the storm would not hit until late evening, she has reluctantly granted permission for the children to play outside, so long as they promise to stay with Adam and Henry and not wander off. Violet reasons despite her forebodings that they will be cooped up inside for the next couple of days once the storm hits, and so it's best for them to let out their steam beforehand.

Adam and Henry lounge on the grass at the sidelines, soaking up the sun's meager warmth – two unusually large young men who provide a perfect climbing platform for the younger children. Adam has curly, dark auburn hair with blond highlights covering a well-shaped head, and the high coloring of some Scots, rosiness flooding his sharp, high-boned cheeks when animated. He has a gentleness to his visage that conveys sensitivity and the reflective intellect of a philosopher; in contrast to his gentle nature, he is in possession of the strong muscular frame of a Highland warrior that would be daunting to an enemy were his life or the life of his family to come under attack. Baby Susan is balanced atop Adam's shoulders, and Emma is sitting in Henry's lap. Rather than join in the game, the older boys assume a guardianship role over the younger kids, now and again calling out ineffectual reprimands or advice. The laddies and lassies revert to colloquial Scot dialect when roughing it outside, but the Queen's tongue is a requirement in the presence of their parents and teachers.

"Malc," Adam yells, "eneuch! Give the lassie a chance."

Malkie does not heed his older brother's directive. Janet runs with all her might, her spindly legs working like automatons – one sock up, one down, the sash of her dress untied and dangling at her ankles – but Malkie forges ahead to tag her with all the unabashed recklessness of a gawky prepubescent, prodding her roughly in the small of her back as she edges within centimeters of home. Janet lunges for the base, and propelled by Malkie's fierce shove, skids along on her side like a careening winter sled, the skin of her knees and elbows taking the brunt of the slide, a dusting of dirt going up her nose and into her mouth.

"Ye're tagged!" cries out Malcolm adamantly after the forceful tagging his sister's back, thus eliminating her from the game according to the rules.

Soft, airless gasps sound meekly from Janet's small lungs, segueing into full-blown high-pitched bawling as soon as she spots a smidgeon of blood on her arm. Adam hands Baby Sue to Henry and runs over to pick up his little sister, consoling her and dusting the grassy weeds off her blue-flowered cotton dress with the back of his hand, and cleaning off her dirt-streaked nose and mouth with his sleeve.

"Och," Janet yells disgustedly. "Me airm! Ye're in trouble, Malkie."

"Not me fault," responds Malkie.

"Come on, wee lass, ye're awricht," says Adam soothingly. "Just a smidgeon o' dust to the gills. Go in and hiv Violet clean up yer knee and airm."

Adam grimaces. Violet will have a conniption when she sees Janet's tattered dress, with ugly scratches and yellow bruises marking her tender legs and arms. An image of Violet's apron-draped chest heaving up and down distressfully comes to mind. Of course, she'll blame him and Henry for not keeping their wee sis out of harm's way. Thankfully, they won't be present for what Henry calls "one o' Violet's bantam theatrics." He holds Janet in his lap and tickles her until she bursts out involuntarily into bubbly giggles.

"You're a brave one, Janet, the best athlete we've got in the entire Baird clan. When bigger not onybody will dare to push ye down."

"All the same, I'm goin' to tell Faither," says Emma adamantly, standing up for her older sister. "Malc's not playing fair. He's a mean bully. Malkie, I'm going to hiv Punt throw bird droppings in yer hair when yer not looking. Mind ye watch the sky! Ha-ha."

Emma's referring to Henry's Little Friend, whom Emma can see very well with her second-sight, though lucky for Malkie Punt is not present at this time. Janet stands up abruptly and puts her small hands on her waist, adopting a pose of an authoritarian on matters of game rules and etiquette.

"The laddies hiv to learn they canna treat lassies harshly. We're divine," declares Janet.

Adam chuckles under his breath. "Divine, now? Lassie, daed I hear ye right? And whaur daed ye learn that exalted word?"

"Mary says it means we're blessed. We're sweeter, too. Made o' sugars and spices, and all things nice." She looks up reflectively at the sky as if trying to lasso a divine revelation from above to sort out the differences between boys and girls.

"We're smarter and not auld bullies. We're bonnier and finer, so the Almichty prefers us best," she says haughtily.

Janet shakes her bony shoulders, shrugging off the weight of her deep philosophical thought. To let Adam know that she's jesting, she displays her most endearing smile, wide with a slight gap between her two front teeth, transforming her beautiful, angelic face into endearing jagged imperfection. Little-girl rhythmic giggles, husky and deep-throated, rev up and gain amplitude as they feed upon themselves, and so it seems they could go on endlessly.

Janet is a very happy child, immensely content in her own skin, satisfied in being a very dominant member of her large family, reveling in a one-upmanship with her close-in-age brothers and holding her own very well. She is an equal amongst them, and won't let them forget it. Janet can run as fast, throw a ball as far, swim as well, and catch and race frogs with dexterity. She takes pride in the fact that her brothers and sisters look up to her as being the strong, smart one, a leader to follow, particularly Malkie and Telford. Janet has the tenacity to set in motion anything she puts her mind to accomplish, and oftentimes, she is successful. Due to her sensitive, perceptive nature, the deplorable conditions of the world outside her family disturb her greatly; simply put, her young, impressionable mind finds it unfair that many do not have what the Baird children have. Janet believes, with all her heart, that everyone is entitled to be happy, that no one should be dissatisfied with their lives, and that all wee boys and girls should be provided with basic wants and needs. Her tender heartstrings are tugged at constantly, as she often notices inequality amongst townsfolk, especially the poor, unkempt country children in town on Market Day, and in her schoolmates who don't have proper clothing and carry their meager meals to school in shoddy burlap sacks. She makes a point of sharing her food with her hungry classmates. Those children, she reflects, who are not as happy as she is are lacking in things that it would be easy for them to have if others would help out. Her little heart is tugged at constantly, and she vows to help everyone in the world when she is older, to put things right. *'Tis so simple. Make everybody equal. How cruel na to be generous!*

Adam lifts Janet over his head into the air, his large muscular arms admirably on display as they flex and extend. Being the eldest, strongest, and most mature of the siblings living at home, the youngsters often stage Adam in a frozen position to resemble a statue like the one of Rob Roy in Town Square, daring him not to flinch as the they grab hold of his dark, reddish curls for balance. He peers intently into Janet's green-blue eyes as he catches her, viewing a vista to her soul that reflects a sparkling intelligence and humor. He finds comfort in the fact that Janet has the spirit and gumption to fend for herself when he's away in America, which no one in his family has been made privy to but for Henry. And, of course, Emma will be fine as well with the Wee Ones for support; imaginary or not, they give her an edge in creativity and self-sufficiency.

Adam reflects on his upcoming journey with more than a few qualms. He strains to keep his rising anxiety from interfering with his painstaking plans for departure. On more anxious days, he thinks of his breaking away from the family as being a wee bit like dying – his loved ones will not be present in his physical reality for a long, long time, or, possibly, never again, depending on his circumstances; nor will he be in physical form to them – more the semblance of a wraith in their imaginations after days and days on end without seeing him. In a wink of the eye, he'll be traveling far from home in a rugged and inhospitable territory, an open target to those who find his presence on the frontier menacing, be it four-legged or human. Extreme danger will be lurking around every bend. Predominant in his thoughts is *There's a good bluidy chance o' me' being bludgeoned by savages or wild animals.*

What could be as bonnie as Scotland? He shudders in dismay when coming to grips with the abandonment of his country and his dear family – he'll not see Janet and Emma blossoming into fine, lovely lasses, or see them marry and have families of their own. Though with luck in making his fortune, he'll be able to send Janet and Emma to college at the University of Edinburgh, or to the great colleges of Glasgow. Successful, educated young ladies they'll become. Sadly, he thinks, Baby Susan is too young and will not remember him at all. He wonders about his decision to leave these precious children. Life is so blessed with the merry troupe, exuding their tender caring and warmth, soothing him like a cozy winter fire in the hearth.

After much agonizing over what he's to lose, he clears his mind to concentrate on the formidable task at hand. *'Tis time to break the news to Mum and Faither, give them time to adjust to me departure. At supper tonicht, I must inform them o' me agenda!*

The senior Bairds are completely in the dark as to Adam's plan to leave home in the next six months – his intention is to quit school immediately, work several more months at the wheelwright's shop, then move to Glasgow to work on the docks as a carpenter until he accumulates enough money for passage. When the necessary funds are earned, he plans to board one of the many cargo steamers being built on the River Clyde bound for the Americas, many being used in the American Civil War effort. Adam Sr. and Jean, for their own peace of mind – being inundated countless times with highfalutin tales – have tuned out the farfetched, mile-high, boisterous talk of their sons at the supper table, elaborate, nonstop discussions of the glories of their sons' forthcoming adventures out West. To the senior Bairds, these half-baked schemes are impractical, illogical prattle that will never materialize. Suppertime has been a time for the boys to amuse themselves by glorifying the wonders of the West, and their dreams of being in a world far more beautiful than their beloved Scotland. In the boys' estimation, reaching America is the equivalent to reaching paradise. The lads compete in a game of one-upmanship along the lines of who can best describe the great wonders of the West. Their dialogue, on a scale of the upmost grandeur, would top any sales campaign for Buffalo Bill's Wild West show that they saw in Edinburgh last year.

"The skies are clearer than Scotland's, the bluest o' blues, like the color o' bluebell; the air's so fresh 'tis like treading high up atop lofty clouds. Gold sits on the bottom o' streams in large clumps, sparkling like the Queen's jewels in the Tower o' London, catching the light o' the sun, just waiting for a hand to come down and swoop them up," exhorts Adam as he pantomimes a scooping up of imaginary gold with his hand.

"The animals, especially the buffalo, are so large and heavy that when they run the whole earth shakes like an earthquake, and from their speed and weight new rivers are carved into the land," exclaims Malkie loudly, with his mouth full of biscuit so that he sprays breadcrumbs on Telford as he talks. "If one of those beasts accidentally falls down from a high mountain, a lake is instantly created!"

"Och, Malkie, yer brain's stuck in the bottom o' a mucky stream. Heed yer uncouth mouth!" exhorts Telford good-humoredly, as he sets out to contribute his two bits to the discussion. "The Indian braves are verra strong and courageous. They charge thair ponies straight into a herd o' buffalo, and then put a spell o'er them so they become tame as lambs and lie down meekly at their feet," he exclaims with great admiration in his voice. "The mountains are verra high and it takes days to reach the summits. Aye, indeed, up so high one's verra close to the Almichty, and the answers to questions as to why we're alive, which are unobtainable down here, magically spring to mind when on high."

"Mebbe 'tis the intense perfume o' the thousands o' different types o' wildflowers growin' on the mountain slopes, with multitudes of colors, that give the mind a euphoric lift, up to the realm o' angels. So beautiful, 'tis like peering through a prism," adds Adam. "There's pure magic, but not as here. We've magic only in childhood. O'er there, magic lasts a lifetime. The magic's everywhere, in all things, the rocks, water, air, trees, and plants. No need for Good People to act as spiritual advisors – the spirits are embedded in nature, and the Almichty speaks to all through nature."

Topping it off, Henry rejoins with his own brand of embellishment. "The mountains blow their tops whaniver they're angry, and send boulders sliding down their slopes to unsuspecting animals, and sometimes people. They're kings o' the land and wear white crowns atop their heads in wintertime. Warning – niver iver say anything to make them angry, like saying 'that's an easy mountain to climb.' The streams gurgle and laugh aloud, whispering sweet nothings to Indian maidens peering down at their reflections, and the waterfalls call out 'down we go' as they spill from the mountains with glee." Everyone laughs but Adam Sr., as he gestures brusquely for an end to the nonsense.

Habitually, to stop the brag-fest, Adam Sr., who relishes his meals in peace and quiet – a room full of children is not conducive to this – takes his knife, spreads his arms out in wild abandon, holding them perpendicularly in the air much like a falcon taking off from a cliff or a symphony conductor with his baton, in a signal to faze out the sound. He is vying for a soft, pleasant easement to the incessant hum in the room (in this case, annoying chatter). Raucous noise usually continues by some of the inattentive conversationalists/orchestra, not aware of the conductor, at which time he pounds the table mightily with his fist. All eyes land on him immediately. The diners are thus shushed, whereby he can get a word in edgewise. At this point, he reminds them that they will not get dessert unless they cease their nonsensical babbling.

"Umph, lads," retorts Adam Sr., "talk the Queen's English at the table. Not good for the constitution to stray from rational thought with all these tall tales, for you'll be forever searching for the unreachable, never pleased with what's before you. You must have evidence and experience, and of that you have neither." Adam Sr. has been reading the philosophy of empiricism of the great John Locke, and has become a proponent of logic through scientific proof.

Chapter Four

I. Science Lab in the Bowels of the Earth, Before the Great Storm

Late that afternoon, after Violet and the kids are safely back at Drumdruils, Elor can be found in his study of the dun-shi headquarters, assuming a far more sophisticated demeanor than the country bumpkin persona he portrays around humans who are able see him. His earlier display of gaiety and jauntiness, as well as his exaggerated Scots colloquial dialect, has been exchanged for that of a pensive erudite – he sits at his desk, his tortoise-shell spectacles resting on his nose, scanning a computer screen that displays a large weather map plotted with values of temperature, humidity, wind direction, and the vertical height above sea level of the pressure surface of the atmosphere. The Wee People are multidimensional time and space travelers and privy to all twenty-first century advanced technologies and computerized scientific equipment to be created on earth in the future. Stored in Elor's dun-shi study is state-of-the-art electronic machinery that Scotland will not be privy to until the latter part of the twentieth century.

Humans with second-sight in the nineteenth century have gotten an earful from the Wee People, descriptions of innovative technologies to come in their lifetimes – the telephone, motorized vehicles, and airplane travel, to name a few advancements, though these sophisticated technologies are difficult to fathom by individuals living in an era of horse-drawn carriages and wagons. Most often, even outside-the-box thinkers with second-sight attribute the grandiose descriptions of future technology by Wee Ones to their whimsical nature – grand embellishments to offset their diminished statures. But visionaries like William Blake of the eighteenth and nineteenth centuries, whose poetry embraced otherworldliness, Leonardo da Vinci of the Renaissance era, or scientists like Albert Einstein of the twentieth century had minds that were blessed with creative intuition and the faculty to step beyond their earthly dimension with a mindset of otherworldly possibilities.

Intuition and creative thought laid the foundation to expand the mind and create extraordinary advancements on earth, promoting the creation of new, unheard of modern devices for the industrial age, advanced philosophical thinking, and the spread of the concept of equality for all mankind. Many visionaries are predisposed to second-sight, even if they've never had the good fortune of meeting Wee People. If Einstein had walked in the woods of Scotland in the early twentieth century, his eyes might have captured a Little Person alighting from a tree branch or lounging on a flower petal. Robert Louis Stevenson, who spent summers as a youth in his beloved Bridge of Allan, might have been influenced by the mystical world of the Wee People that he perhaps encountered as a child on his walks through the woodlands as he went past the dun-shis.

The Wee People engage in multidimensional travel. Their everyday existence is transitory between this world on earth and multitudinous dimensions. They interact with the souls of other dimensions just as easily as they interact with souls residing in human form on earth. The true reality of the universal realm is that each earthly soul is under the auspices of his or her own Master Soul that resides at a nexus from where all dimensions bifurcate. A Master Soul can manifest in more than one physical form on earth as well as in different physical forms in other dimensions, which means that a human life on earth is only one part of a complex interconnection of many diverse forms of a personality. Each diverse form of life carries out roles on earth and in other dimensions with predetermined learning experiences. Elor and his kind are privy to everything that goes on in the lives of the people they live side by side with in the Bridge of

Allan community. They have no need to predict the future – they see the present, the future, and the past as simultaneous temporal occurrences, as their consciousnesses dwell outside time and space. From this perspective of time, they can aid their human friends in disastrous times, though they cannot control what is destined to be, for this is under the auspices of the Master Soul of each individual.

The Wee People, highly advanced in technology, are able to see adverse weather patterns in the atmosphere and use their scientific knowhow to zero in on the focal point and magnitude of a storm. By relying on sophisticated satellites and Doppler mapping, these wee scientists routinely track storms through antennas on weather balloons sent high into the atmosphere. Precipitation and debris in the air (such as raindrops, snow crystals, hailstones, or even insects and dust) scatter or reflect radio waves sent out into the atmosphere back to the antennas situated at high altitudes. Weather radar electronically converts the reflected radio waves into pictures, including Doppler images. By measuring the strength of the waves that return to the radar and how long the roundtrip takes, forecasters can assess the location and intensity of precipitation. The Doppler radar also measures the frequency change in returning waves, which provides the direction and speed at which the precipitation is moving. This key information allows forecasters such as Elor to see rotation occurring inside thunderstorms before tornadoes form.

Elor communicates via computer with his brethren living up in the Black Cuillin on the Isle of Skye, a range of rugged mountains in the Highlands that collect sophisticated storm data. Elor's colleagues, with their access to advanced weather satellites, have forewarned him of a destructive storm brewing, and have calculated the time and eye of the target. Unbeknownst to their human friends in Bridge of Allan, the Wee People have come to their aid many times throughout history, with behind-the-scenes maneuvering via subtle forewarnings or hands-on measures to attenuate the effects of a calamitous situation.

Elor is eager to go over a plan of action and calls out to his daughter. Twixie, who is in the other room preparing their nighttime meal, picks up on the urgency in her father's voice and responds immediately to his beckoning by flying into his den.

"'Tis paramount to track the storm diligently," alerts Elor. "The huge front's heading in the direction of Bridge o' Allan. The eye o' the storm's centering on a half-mile radius along the river running from Town Square down to the train depot. Twelve inches o' rain or more will be coming in a period o' three hours – enough water to overflow the river. Unless the front veers off course, the river will flood the entire village and surrounding farmland. 'Tis necessary to set up a backup plan for the water surge and potential avalanche of mudslides that'll cascade down from the saturated hills into town buildings. We must draw out escape routes for the villagers who live along the river. Livestock in the lowland farms must be herded to higher ground afore the storm begins. Hiv our appointed rescue teams leave sandbags in the town square that can be distributed readily. Inform the second-sighted folks that there are boats to be used for evacuation tied up under the bridge in 'A' zone, in an area that hopefully will be protected from the water. We've calculated the water to rise and overflow the levies. Hiv demarcations mapped to show the whereabouts o' most likely places whaur the rise will flow to.

"Heaven forbid if the bridge comes down! Ascertain that our emergency teams are stocking the corners of Henderson Street with sandbags. Seek out humans wi' second-sight to urge the storekeepers to protect their stores wi' sandbags, and hiv those individuals fill as many sandbags as they can. The second-sighters must be informed o' the severity o' the situation and take on the role o' community leaders in directing ithers in storm preparedness."

The Wee People are also adept at suggestive thought, and relay information telepathically to impressionable humans who possess remnants of second-sight from childhood, those experiencing periodic glimpses of Wee Ones out in nature but not registering what they are seeing, thinking they are looking at dragonflies or hummingbirds.

"Aye, Father," replies Twixie, with a tremor in her voice, alarmed by her father's strict contingency plans that impress upon her the severity of the coming storm.

"Och, where's that numbskull?" inquires Elor emphatically, waving his short arms in frustration. He's referring to his fickle son, Punt. "I need him desperately. Now! See if ye can track him down, Twix. I need aid wi' the computer weather maps."

Punt, an extremely talented computer programmer, has the ability to analyze the weather data sent to them from the Highland headquarters with ease. Thus Elor is able to close in on the precise time that a weather system will be upon them – that is, if Punt can be located and is in the right frame of mind to concentrate. Fun-loving, lazy, and spending an inordinate amount of his time with humans, Elor rests assured that his son is not a malicious sprite and will eventually grow out of his fickle ways. The clan chief is aware that one of Punt's favorite pastimes is following his best human friend and idol, Henry Baird, around after school, especially when Henry's come to town for supplies and a drink in the pub.

"Check to see if he's wi' Henry Baird," he yells to his daughter. "That rascal is always wi' the boy."

A few minutes later Twixie comes across Punt with Henry, who is on his way to visit Annie MacGivens's household. She concludes that her brother is helping Henry deal with a debacle concerning Annie's father.

II. Brothers Discuss Their Futures

Henry lightly nudges Adam's shoulder and wakes him from his

reverie as he doles out coaching advice to his siblings.

"Laddie!" Henry calls out to Malkie. "Being that the Almichty made ye pigeon-toed, ye must raise yer eyes up to the clouds for balance. Emma, place yer foot to the back o' his knee and punt."

"Och, I'm not pigeon-toed, Henry," hollers Malkie, with attempted bravado, in the scratchy, high-pitched crackling contralto of adolescence.

"Telford, keep yer stomach tucked in and yer eyes o'er the ground so ithers daena see ye're out o' breath." Telford gives him a cutting look and breathes deeply to inflate his chest and show the power of his lungs.

"Malkie, yer heid's a magpie' s nest. What's crawling in yer hair?"

Though chuckling under their breath at Henry's witticisms, the lads scowl outwardly in annoyance and exasperation for Henry's benefit, all too accustomed to his playful comments.

Despite the joshing, Adam thinks of Henry as the kindest, most sensitive soul, lamenting again the fact that he's not more like his brother. Henry is charming, affable, and outgoing, and has a knack for becoming bosom buddies with most people from the outset. He goes out of his way to help everyone. Getting into scrapes is not really his fault. Adam has concluded that Henry's trusting nature is the root of his foibles, seeing only the best in folks and caring about their welfare. Adam wonders how Henry's going to make it on the American frontier with his gullible nature, particularly his inability to see danger coming. *A pity Henry cannot go with me in the summer so we could watch out for one anither. Henry could do all the talking, and I could cover his back in case o' trouble.*

The family is accustomed to Henry enlivening their lives with his off-the-top humor, providing a spark of levity to somber or boring occasions. His wry witticisms can be counted on to get a laugh, or at least a spontaneous smile, from just about anyone he encounters. His infectious laugh and charismatic personality touch even hard-core sourpusses.

According to Violet, his bent towards merriment "flew in on the wings of the stork," along with a propensity for mischievousness, though the outcome is a proneness for getting himself into jams by which he has to use his cunningness to dig his way out by humor. Violet fondly regales the family with stories of the incorrigible Henry, "the laddie who was born curious – the bairn's head stuck between the pickets o' a fence at age two; the laddie with his arm, from hand to elbow, up a beehive; the laddie who climbed atop the outhouse and jumped, with wings made o' reed and sheets!" Henry's jocular nature often stirs up discord with Violet, his favorite target for jests. Violet loves to put on a melodramatic show of being highly offended by Henry's remarks.

"Listen to this, me dearest Violet," he'd said just the other morn at breakfast. "I heard an intriguing tale in town last evening, not hearsay but from the horse's mouth. 'Twas written in the *Times*, but the delicious details were omitted for politeness's sake."

Henry clears his throat and looks around, his eyes twinkling gaily, as if he were in front of a large audience.

"A group o' fishermen were readying their boat in the first light on the River Clyde when one o' them spotted an apparition o' the Blessed Virgin Mary rising up above the water, appearing as a stark-naked wraith in the misty morning haze. The far-sighted fisherman pointed to the vision for the others to take a gander, and they indeed all caught an eyeful o' an unclothed Mary. One auld seasoned fisherman, more pious than the rest, disagreed with the interpretation o' the vision and proclaimed, 'Tis not the Virgin Mary, as Mary's always clothed in a modest gown befitting the mother o' Jesus, and this woman's stark naked.' The others studied, with careful attention, as birdwatchers do, the apparition closely for a long stretch o' time, and by-and-by they all came to agree with the more pious fisherman – 'This Virgin Mary who wears no clothes is a strumpet and not Mary.' The fisherman who'd first seen this apparition vehemently disagreed, not wanting his grand vision to be diminished, and proclaimed, 'Aye, 'tis indeed the Virgin Mary! She came to the River Clyde for a bath.' The other fishermen concurred that this was mebbe a likelihood acause the Mary they observed was blessed wi' an itherworldly physique. They'd decided not to invade her bathing privacy anymore."

Violet, a devout member of the Church of Scotland, despite her pagan/fairy beliefs, had feigned indignation at the sacrilegious remarks, just as she has always responded to Henry's high tales since he was a small laddie, her ample chest heaving up and down in synchrony with the pounding of her rolling pin on the oak kitchen table.

"You're an irreverent laddie, Henry Baird, wi' no respect for the sacredness o' the Almichty. Someday the deevil's goin' to swoop ye up and take ye down to Hades like they tried wi' poor Ol' Tam o' Shanter. And ye already hiv yourself in deep waters wi' yer lassie!"

"Och, Violet, whaur's yer sense o' humor?"

"Henry," replies Violet, "you're too clever and witty for yer own good. Daena think that ye'll always be able to free yourself from the scrapes ye constantly climb into. Ye willna always be so charming and witty. That tongue o' yers will become tied o' knots when ye're auld."

Henry clucked his tongue, chuckling under his breath as he left the room, satisfied that he'd gotten her goat. After he had departed, Violet broke out into a hearty chuckle as she rolled the pastry dough out with fervor, this humorous encounter with Henry lending a boost of energy to her day. Henry, as Violet is well aware, is blessed with a strong dose of Wee People's gumption. The Wee People call it jig-spirit, which means that Henry is bursting full with the dance o' aliveness. Violet is aware that Henry's possession of spirit has its drawbacks. She fears that to be blessed with such a power preordains him for a good many challenges and hardships in his life, though contrariwise, a good many people will benefit from knowing him. Violet, who adores him, believes with all her heart that her beloved Henry will continually come out on top and do a lot of beneficial deeds for the world. She has surety in this belief, as Elor has said as much, and Elor, who transits to many dimensions, can see into the future.

Adam's reverie is interrupted by the laughter of his brothers and sisters at play. He looks over to Henry with tenderness, lamenting the fact that they are nearing the end of their carefree boyhood days. He wonders again if Henry will be able to join him in the New World. What if he cannot journey to the West because o' the bairn? The predicament with Annie could complicate matters. Henry can't retreat from his responsibilities. *Why did Henry have to get himself into such a mess? Well, Henry was just bein' Henry. He always lands on his feet!*

Adam prays that his brother's winning personality and optimism will get him over the hurdles that he's going to encounter. *No one stays angry wi' Henry for verra long. He cares for folks and folks respond to him acause o' his carin'. Mebbe Annie's parents will come round to accept him as part o' their family, and they'll wish them well on thair departure to the New World.*

Adam often questions his own judgment in departing Scotland, self-doubts propelling to and fro like an out-of-control wind-up toy. He considers these uncalled-for doubts intrusive irritations to his well-thought-out plans. They most often come about when he's reminded of the possibility of not seeing his family again for years.

Adam wonders what stirs his soul to desire to travel thousands of miles to a foreign land, a land that might not measure up to Bonnie Ol' Scotland. Is he being wise, or risking his health, forfeiting his family, and gambling away his future contentment? If he stays, though, he'll never develop to his full potential, never delight in new sights, sounds, and places, never grow to be the kind of accomplished man he desires to be.

Adam envisions the future, viewing himself as a very old man having lived at Drumdruils for the entirety of his life with little of anything monumental to show for his years – a mediocre lifetime spent in a small community, confined to the dimensions of a township and farm. In spreading his wings in the New World, surrounded by majestic mountains, wide-open plains, fierce, roiling rivers, and the inevitable adventures that will arise, he hopes to expand that intangible, magical, mysterious part of his spirit that the Fairy Folk instilled in him when he was a wee laddie, though he's not cognizant of where this inner desire for an expansion of his spirit arises from.

Henry looks over to his brother wistfully, sensitive to the fact that Adam is mulling over something monumental, most likely juggling the pros and cons of his departure. Henry finds his older brother far too serious and stern. Occasionally, he tries to physically shake him out of his rigidness by challenging him to an impromptu wrestling match. *He never relaxes*, thinks Henry, *always looking for some dragon around the corner to slay.* Henry thinks that possibly Adam's this way because he's the eldest and has been entrusted with so much responsibility in watching over the family. *He's out of touch wi' the fairy magic o' childhood, and daesna know how wonderful 'tis to believe and trust in the wisdom o' Wee People.*

Henry socks Adam in the arm playfully, to stir up in his brother's overly serious nature, to make him aware of the innate joy that their siblings are displaying in their game. Adam's daydream is abruptly interrupted by Henry's fist in his arm. He gives his brother a grimace of quizzical annoyance, and looks out at the scene before him – energetic children playing in the bucolic setting of billowy grassland atop small hillocks, and farther beyond he sees the densely-wooded paths leading to Dunblane. Adam consciously makes an effort to take in the scene visually so as to remember it, as he won't be privy to these exquisite soft textures of beauty of his homeland in America.

"Whaur are ye, Adam? Yer heid's o'er the clouds," inquires Henry gently, with a mischievous twinkle in his eyes as they lounge in the glorious, sparkling sunshine. Adam lost once again in his deep thoughts fails to respond to Henry.

"If ye think too much yer heid will turn to stone, as Violet says."

"What, Henry? What daed ye say?"

"Penny for yer unsavory thoughts, unless they're too salacious for me tender ears. Are ye having visions o' bonnie naked lassies? If so, let me in on it." Henry lightly jabs Adam in the shoulder and chuckles aloud, reading in Adam's eyes a dazed awakening from some far-off dimension of the mind. Adam sits up abruptly.

"I'm just lamenting on the sad fact that we're growin' up verra quickly, departin' Drumdruils in a wink o' the eye. I'll be on anither continent soon. I canna fathom what it'll be like to reside in America. This land's all I've iver known." He sweeps his arm out towards the hills. "'Tis surreal just dwelling in my heid on the idea o' not living any longer in the place whaur I've lived since birth."

"We'll be thinkin' o' yer heid every day ye're away, praying for the safety o' yer scalp," says Henry in jest. "I hear that red hair is in great demand for wigs on the frontier. The Injuns use auburn scalps as totems, and red's a precious novelty for the brothel ladies as well. They desire wigs to liven up their business prospects. Best to keep yer hat on. Seriously, I pray more fervently ye willna get lost on the frontier wi' yer poor sense o' direction!"

"Och, my sense o' direction's far finer than yers. You're the dunce who gets lost in the woods."

"'Twas when I was seven years auld."

"Nevertheless, Henry, 'tis ye I'm concerned for."

"I'll be fine and dandy. I've the love o' me life at me side – Annie and I hiv our entire lives ahead o' us. We're verra suited for one anither. Soon, I'll hiv a bonnie family to accompany me to America. Granted, it willna be easy to depart, bid farewell to the laddies and lassies, Mum and Faither. They'll miss me terribly, being that I'm their favorite, but all o' the Bairds are composed o' tough fiber."

"If ye think you're their favorite, think anew. Their favorite eyesore, mebbe?" teases Adam.

"Aye, life's moving along like a fast-paced melody building up to a crescendo," expresses Henry eloquently.

"Or life's moving more to the tune o' a roiling river, overflowing and spreading us out o'er the world," replies Adam with some foreboding.

"Aye, the life and times in the Land of Drums is turning us topsy-turvy in wild ways, 'specially whaur I'm concerned," laments Henry. "Annie's a godsend. Our soon-to-be bairn will be cherished, but we've a bit o' hurdles to jump 'cross. Why canna her folks see the forest for the trees? Even Mum and Faither are humiliated by Annie's 'condition.'" Henry whispers "pregnant," mocking those who are embarrassed to say the word aloud. "They canna see the joy o' bringing a sweet wee bairn into the world, canna see past Ol' MacGivens's infantile lion's roar! Our laddie or lassie will be the bonniest, smartest Baird yet, wi' me beauty and Annie's intelligence," says Henry in jest.

"Ye mean to say with Annie's beauty and intelligence, and yer marvelous ability to talk yourself out o' muddles. Aye… they'll come round as the shock subsides," says Adam consolingly.

"Mr. MacGivens called on Faither yesterday, ranting like a blathering idiot, causing Faither's head to spin round like an unraveling spool of thread," responds Henry. "Ol' MacGivens's feathers were riled like a fuming rooster, declaring me a lecherous rapscallion. Faither, being a dignified gent, daedna voice a word in edgewise. 'Tis upsetting for Mum and Faither to be chastised for bringing up their son with 'moral turpitude.' Auld Man MacGivens was hollering at Faither all sorts o' curses 'bout me character."

"Och, Henry, 'tis just not right for that auld man to act ungentlemanly," says Adam sternly, a touch of anger in his voice. Anybody treating Henry poorly brings out Adam's need to defend his younger brother.

"MacGivens has the likeness o' a reddish prune when riled. Just the sight o' me makes him apoplectic, as if he's goin' to explode into millions o' pieces. The poor bastard's a drunk and reeks o' bloody spirits. 'Tis seeping out o' his pores when he's riled. I feel sorry for him at times, but question how Annie can bear to reside wi' that unstable crackpot."

"Ye've got to stay away from him," warns Adam.

"Aye, acause her folks are being hardnosed regarding this, Annie and I intend to depart in secrecy for America to start life anew. We'll be sailing right behind ye. Ye shall be our trailblazer."

"Och, Henry, ye must finish yer schooling first. Ye're only sixteen! 'Tis imperative to acquire a good education – mebbe a trade o' some sort to make a good wage out West."

"Aye, I'll finish me schooling but forgo university. Faither wants me to assist him wi' the farm and wi' accounts. I'm not as fine a craftsman as ye, but I possess fine mastery wi' numbers in managing the affairs of the Kingdom o' Drumdruils. For a wee bit longer, I'll reside in Scotland to work the land and continue schooling 'til graduation. Annie will be residing at her Aunt Ethie's house in Glasgow 'til her birthing time. We'll sail for America efter the bairn is auld enough for safe passage. I'll go to Glasgow to find employment near the time the bairn is to be born, which will be in seven months' time, and I'll hiv completed school by then. Mebbe we'll stay in Glasgow anither three to four months whilst the bairn matures. If all proceeds smoothly, we'll meet up wi' ye in America by the middle o' next year," replies Henry.

"I'll plan to hiv adequate room to accommodate ye. 'Tis jolly for family to join me out West," responds Adam enthusiastically. The prospect of having loved ones to join him in America washes contentment over his countenance.

The brothers look up at the game to find it wearing down, with overwrought, combative children at each other's throats. No one is willing to admit defeat. Henry gets up and yells, "Ollie, Ollie in free," and the game concludes. Sweaty-faced children charge wildly onto home base like a herd of horses let loose to pasture, yet the day's games are not over by a long shot. The energetic clan moves on to their next athletic endeavor – a lively game of catch gets underway. Malkie and Telford take the lead whilst Adam and Henry lay down the rules for good sportsmanship. The smaller youngsters relish running after the balls in the field.

III. Westward Ho!

Adam lies beside Henry in the grass, his back propped up against the sturdy trunk of an old birch tree, taking a respite while the children are hard at play. His thoughts, as do Henry's, stretch down a precipitous path of uncertainty to the future.

This might be one o' the final times I'll play wi' the children. I'm gettin' bleary-eyed from school and town work, and soon I'll be ten hours a day at the shop, thinks Adam as he watches Telford pitch a ball that spirals overhead to the outfield. His younger siblings eagerly run out to retrieve it.

Adam plans to leave the school that he loves and has excelled in – he has only one term to go before his graduation date – to work full-time at Mathew MacDuffy's Wheelwright and Undertakers Shop in the position of senior apprentice, a job he has worked at part-time after school for the past two years. Today, he plans to inform Miss Carroway, his beloved teacher, of his plans. He has very personal reasons for leaving school involving the aforementioned Miss Carroway, compounded by Grandfather Dawson's need for assistance on his farm. For the last six months, before school, he has spent early mornings helping Grandfaither, as the family has deemed the old gentleman too elderly at eighty years of age to farm alone. His grandfather is a dapper old gent with loads of energy and a remarkably strong and limber physique, but a severe chest cold took its toll on his health last winter, making him more frail than he's ever been. Adam has decided to quit school and continue helping Grandfaither in the morning, as well as working full-time for MacDuffy's as a carpenter to earn money for his planned departure for America. His parents have no inkling of his plans, and, as he anticipates with dread, they'll be saddened by his decision. His plan to work full-time at the shop and help his grandfather until he's ready to depart will take every bit of his energy.

"Ye goin' to miss yer family, Adam?" inquires Henry. "Yer goin' to leave us all outright in the blink o' an eye, wi' no remorse?"

"'Twill not be easy, but I'll be coming back now and again. Not a big ocean, really – only the first time across will seem like a verra long journey. When I've made me fortune, I'll travel back often."

"Aye," agrees Henry, with more optimism. "Ye willna be so verra far away; only a month-long trip back to visit will alleviate this. 'Tis the only way I'm goin' to hiv the courage to leave, to hiv a way back home when I desire. I might buy a two-way fare for us just to ensure this."

The laddies become quiet, swallowing reflexively, as they reflect on the uncertainties of a major life change, on the immensity of their decision to leave the only home they've ever known, the comfortable, safe world they've lived in since they were born. Their reflections of being gone for a very long time, if not forever, bring on a slight surge of adrenaline similar to that which they've experienced when jumping off the Bridge o' Allan into the cold river, not knowing for certain if they'd surface before being swept away to sea. The challenge and the excitement of the beauty and new experiences they plan to encounter in their travels in the new land of America override the fears of unknown danger that will certainly arise, as well as the immutable loneliness of being so far away from a loving family.

After the strenuous game of catch, Adam and Henry rise from

their resting place and beckon the children over with hilarious duck calls that sound more like frogs. By unanimous consensus, the children opt to wade downstream in a shallow rivulet, to float their miniature wood boats with colorful burlap sails sewn and dyed by Violet and crafted by the skilled hands of their older brothers. The children slush playfully along the edge of the stream, sinking their feet into the mushy silt bottom while splashing each other. This gentle stream, after fanning out in waterfalls, runs circuitously for miles downhill before reaching Bridge of Allan, where it empties into the River Allan. The River Allan, which divides the town from Dunblane, cuts a straight path through the town's center. In the spring, after the winter's heavy rains, the river's banks are brimming, and frequently on the verge of overflowing into the town. Stores have unfilled sandbags ready to prevent flood damage, which has occurred periodically with violent storms.

Adam and Henry watch the kids attentively in the water; the sharp sun playing off the water causes them to squint and see flashing sparks of golden and red light in their vision. They are well into the month of October, and the shallow stream is comfortably warmed from the sunlight, but the air is crisp and nippy. Adam and Henry plan for the children to wade not more than ten minutes, though these warm-blooded bundles of perpetual motion are comfortable in cold water. Henry has Baby Susan curled up on his lap asleep, and Adam stands close to the edge of the bank watching over the kids at play with attentiveness. The stream is only a eighth of a meter deep, but the youngsters can't be left unattended. Janet has a school chum over to play – her best friend, Mary MacLaine, from the closest neighboring farm. Janet has entirely recovered from her rough skid into home base, though she dons a white cloth bandage on her elbow. Her knees and arms are scraped from the skid, but she has no open wounds. She steps into ankle-deep water.

"The water feels stingy and cauld to me poor leg," Janet yells out to Adam, as a means of gaining his sympathy. She splashes her brothers playfully, administering Malkie a slog of water as payback for her injuries.

The lasses hold their dresses up and wade down the middle of the stream, the ruffles of their hems brushing the water. They prance like water nymphs, the sun sparkling in iridescence on their droplet-splattered skin, clasping their hands together while rotating in circles. The girls are excited because they have plans for a sleepover at Mary's house tonight.

"Mary," says Janet. "We're best friends. We're just like identical twins. Mebbe we could hiv our mums sew us alike dresses. Sisters, we'd be!"

"Aye," replies Mary. "D'ye desire to be sisters foriver? Best mathes, we'd be." She lisps due to the wide gap in her front teeth. "We'd play together 'til we're auld."

Says Janet, "Think o' us grown up. We'll do everything thegither and abide close by as neighbors. We'll hiv much gaiety in our lives acause we'll laugh and laugh thegither foriver."

"Aye," replies Mary, "we'll laugh and laugh, dance and dance, and sing and sing, thegither foriver." They join their little hands and dance in circles.

"Mebbe," spouts Janet, "we shall open a theatre whaur we can hiv our plays."

"Aye, that'll be jolly," replies Mary. "I canna wait 'til we're auld."

"Mebbe we could share bluid as the Injuns to be true sisters," responds Janet gleefully. "I read Injuns in the Americas do this to be blood brithers foriver and iver." The little girls jump up and down excitedly, and giggle merrily at their sisterly pact. They live on the cusp of reality and imagination, so anything is possible, and everything is exciting and new.

Mary is a bonnie, golden-haired child, very precocious with an adult's vocabulary and a precise, adult-like manner of articulating, except for a mild lisp. Janet informed her family that Mary has been reading since three years of age, and is now in an advanced learning group with the fourteen-year-olds at school, even though she's only eleven. The MacLaines are very proud of her. She's their only child, and they were blessed with her in their forties.

"But how are we goin' to get our bluids? Shall we retrieve a knife from the kitchen?" inquires Mary, her eyes widening in trepidation at the prospect of a painful cut.

"Aye, a big, sharp butcher's knife," answers Janet teasingly.

"Blessed are the weak," chants Mary, citing one of her Bible lessons. "Must we? We might be too weak to tolerate the hurt. Mebbe just a pinprick from a sewing box pin."

"Alright, but let's do this anither time." They both look relieved to put off the grim task for another day.

"Aye, we should hiv a ceremony. Mebbe down by the river when 'tis warmer water? Injuns in the Americas hiv a big ceremony," says Janet.

Violet's been reading the kids accounts of Buffalo Bill's Wild West traveling show, popular in Scotland and England at the time.

Janet remarks, "We can hiv Adam and Henry teach us to swim. They'd hiv to take us down to the River Allan in the warm weather whaur the waters are deep. We'll hiv a ceremony efter we dunk." The little lasses give exaggerated, wide-eyed looks of awe and dread at the prospect of swimming in deep water, even more concerning than the thought of drawing blood.

"Aye, perhaps anither time, mebbe in springtime when 'tis warmer," repeats Janet.

"What if we drown?" inquires Mary melodramatically, her eyes feigning fear, as she is in actuality a fearless wee soul.

Janet calls out to Adam. "Will ye save us from drowning, Adam, even if we're deep, deep, sunk beneath the water o' River Allan?" she cries out plaintively.

"Aye, Janet, dinna fash! I'll keep ye lasses afloat even if I hiv to turn me body into a human raft."

The girls giggle triumphantly, satisfied with this scenario, jumping up and down in the water with ecstatic vigor, causing their dresses to display large splash marks.

From Adam's vantage point, little Janet and Mary paint a fine picture as they frolic in the babbling stream, reminding him of beautiful cherub paintings he once saw in the Museum of Scotland in Edinburgh. He hates to end their merriment, but he'll get an earful from Violet and Mum if Janet comes in shaking with cold, with another dress to be laundered to boot.

"Lassies," calls out Adam in good humor, "daena go and get soaked. Attempt to stay a wee bit closer to the bank. The water isna deep and 'tis warmer. Ye'll catch yer death o' cauld, Mary. Yer mum will hiv me hide if ye get wet."

Last year, a child of Bridge of Allan died after swimming in the River Allan. The doctor attributed swimming in cold water and getting too chilled to be the cause of the child's grave pneumonia.

"We must get out now," announces Mary perfunctorily. "Time to fetch eggs," she murmurs shyly in her soft, raspy voice, her cheeks bearing bright red patches, cognizant that the older boys are interested in her grown-up duties. The MacLaines collect eggs from the neighboring farmers and take them to town every other morning with their own to save the farmers the time and trouble of going into town so often.

"Adam, ye know I'm goin' to Mary's?" inquires Janet. "Mary's mum says I can help her wi' chores and spend the nicht. I'll return to home efter breakfast. I've permission from Mum and Violet," she voices with conviction. Janet often stays over with Mary, who loves to have other kids at her house, and her parents enjoy the company of having two beautiful little lasses together.

"Right, lassies," replies Adam. "Violet apprised me o' the plans o' ye two and yer exclusive nighttime party. Janet, ye be good. Help out wi' the home chores and dishes at the MacLaines'."

"Och, why waesna I invited?" inquires Henry, his mouth curving down to show dismay. "Boo-hoo! I should've been invited," he whines teasingly. Henry's very fond of Mary and loves to jest with her. She has a precious look of feigned confusion on her face, only halfway certain that he's joking.

"Och, yer not comin', Henry," responds Janet firmly, knowing full well her big brother is joshing. "You're crazy, Henry, if ye think you're coming. A peculiar laddie, me brither, to want to come wi' lassies."

"Peculiar is me middle name. Aft times, I daena recognize myself acause I'm so dignified looking."

"You're the craziest brither I hiv," tops off Janet. "A loon and a dingbat," she spouts out, laughingly spraying water through the space in her front teeth at him.

"Ye insult me," replies Henry, holding his hand over his heart. "I'm wounded to me verra core."

Mary responds sympathetically, unaccustomed to sibling teasing, as it sounds to her seriously quarrelsome. "Henry, ye can come if ye desire. Me parents would love that acause ye tell so many good stories and they say ye're verra witty."

"Thank ye kindly, Mary," he replies. "I just remembered, though, I've some wee cow matters to tend to."

"Janet," calls out Adam, "make certain an adult accompanies ye home in the morn. Daena venture to come home alone. We'll come efter ye by mid-morning, if Mary's faither daesna bring ye. Violet says there's a storm coming. Daena try to meet us halfway. Stay in the house 'til we arrive for ye," he repeats. "Violet's in a perfect tizzy o'er a mighty downpour. I see no evidence o' it, but there's no convincing Violet when she's a bee in her bonnet."

Mary lives two kilometers down a winding country lane of high, rounded hillocks bordered by scrub oaks. Janet knows the route like the back of her hand, and wishes they wouldn't treat her as a wee child, but she nods in agreement not to come home alone. The lassies skip happily down the lane, twirling back around like ballerinas performing a *pas de deux*, a graceful feathery waving of their small cherubic hands before exiting off stage – in this case, out of sight around a twist in the road. After Mary and Janet are out of sight, the children go in and wash up for Story Time and then supper.

As he watches the lassies skip away, Henry says out of the blue, "They're the bonniest lassies in the world, 'specially when thegither, wi' a special quality verra upliftin' in thair natures like the heavens dusted them wi' cuteness and charm. Mary's verra intelligent. She'll be a verra special person when she's grown, and our Janet as well."

"Aye," agrees Adam reflectively. He has an unsettling feeling as he watches the young lassies skip down the lane by themselves, innocent and vulnerable, but it's only a blip of uneasiness that lifts as quickly as an insect is swatted away. Adam has an important matter to attend to before supper, one that is dominating his immediate thoughts to a greater degree.

The children, after the exhausting late afternoon games, tromp inside for a pre-supper snack before Story Time, their tiredness demonstrative by their willy-nilly, wound-up movements that tend to infringe on each other's personal spaces, which inevitably segues into slaps and kicks. Violet orders them to sit at the table and to keep their hands to themselves or face the consequence of no treats. The scent of cinnamon applesauce bubbling away on the stove is an enticement to mind their manners.

Chapter Five

I. Adam and Henry Tend to Personal Matters

After Adam and Henry have sent the children to the house, they go their separate ways, both with pressing tasks to get out of the way before supper. Henry heads towards town, jogging down the winding road towards Henderson Street. Adam traipses in a southerly direction for a kilometer on a gradual climb into the hills towards the old schoolhouse. As he climbs up into the hills from the Drumdruils farm, the terrain rises steeply through dense and lush woodsy vegetation. A babbling rivulet pours down through thickets of thistles, maidenhair ferns, thick bracken, and brush, fanning out over high vertically rising granite boulders, to create a waterfall splashing down on logs and pebbles into a shallow pool, in a play of mesmerizing sparkling showers. Lush four-foot-high ferns and snowdrop windflower, holly, and blackthorn shrubs grow in profusion among Scotch pines, rowan, elder, oak, and birch, making it almost impossible to walk without bare flesh being brushed or prickled by flora, which explains the perpetually marked-up legs and arms of the Baird children.

II. Miss Carroway — Bridge o' Allan Schoolmarm

23 October 1863

With great trepidation, Adam walks over to the little one-room, granite-stone Scoto-Grecian-style schoolhouse to inform his teacher, Miss Carroway, of his plans to quit school. He runs through his mind what he'll say, but even in his head he finds himself stuttering. The schoolhouse with its unattached teacher's cottage out in the back is set in the midst of a field of wildflowers and woods of sweet pine and Scotch firs. A babbling stream wends its way along the side of the two buildings, a calming and mesmerizing effect for the students after winter's thaw. There is a laddies' playground, and another for the lassies, both lined with pitch pine benches. The teacher's cottage is where Miss Carroway resides – Adam's been inside before, but only once, a couple of months ago, and cringes at the thought of what happened there. When he looks over at the quaint cottage, his heart begins to race and the base of his spine tingles. He breaks out in a cold sweat. Windows in the schoolhouse are left wide open in the spring, summer, and autumn to let in the cool breezes and keep students alert. In the winter the stream becomes a strong rivulet with a rapid flow that eventually freezes over. Many years ago, a couple of pupils fell through the ice and became hypothermic from the cold, although the water was only one meter deep. Fortunately, the little stove in the corner of the schoolroom, fed with peat all day during class time, was going strong. The students were warmed immediately, with no lasting harm done. Since that time, the rule is immediate suspension for walking on the ice of the stream.

Adam loves the schoolhouse with its wide-plank floors and wooden desks. Blackboards and walls are covered with maps and colorful art and diagrams. It has a lingering scent of waxed pine floors, chalk dust, art glue made from flour and water, oil soap, embers from the stove, and the scent of tin lunch boxes tinged of sour milk and apple.

To avoid the other students, Adam has made a point to drop by when school is out for a holiday. He is anxious, pleased, astonished, proud, dismayed, and embarrassed – all rolled into one – about the last encounter with Miss Carroway. He thinks of their time together as having been played out like a romance novel. He plods stiffly into the room, his feet feeling like dead weights, and eyes Miss Carroway sitting at her desk. Her posture, as always, is ramrod straight, as if a cord from the ceiling was attached to the top of her head by an invisible pulley apparatus. Sometimes she reminds him of a marionette with her dangly hands and arms. Miss Carroway is attired in her customary white-and-navy shirtwaist, her tawny-brown hair flattened by oiliness, severely parted down the middle and pinned up in a tight little bun at the back of her small, pointed head that emphasizes her elongated neck. She is wearing her customary round, wire-rimmed glasses with tiny lenses for shortsightedness. Adam realizes – perhaps he's always known but refused to consciously acknowledge it – that Miss Carroway is a woman, not just an educator, and not all that old. He admits to himself that he's taken pride in being the teacher's pet, her prized student, in her presence every day since the age of five, and that he's taken her for granted, viewing her as an ageless embodiment of knowledge. But lo and behold, he found out unexpectedly, and shockingly so, just recently, that her feelings for him go far beyond a student/teacher relationship, crossing the boundaries of normalcy. Today, as he walks into the school, it is extremely difficult for either of them to maintain composure because of their last encounter. They have not been alone since that time. Adam keeps his eyes on the maths equations on the blackboard behind Miss Carroway.

On a Thursday, a month back, after a long day of class, a situation arose that will be cast in Adam's mind as long as he lives. He becomes sweaty and tingly all over as he recalls the intricacies of their last encounter, which had unexpectedly occurred. It was not something he had imagined ever to happen, nor was it an unconscious or conscious desire. He wishes he had been more aware of the intricacies of their relationship. A month ago, Miss Carroway, the rail-thin, prim-and-proper, thirty-year-old schoolmistress of the thirty-five-student schoolhouse, had been sitting at her desk, grading papers. The students call her Madame Ostrich behind her back because of her unusually long, swan-like neck, owlish eyes magnified by the thick lenses of her tiny spectacles, and her mousy brown hair pulled back in a bun. Adam has always found her attractive with her ivory skin and bird-like bone structure. She's been a much-admired fixture in his life for as long as he can remember.

The meeting had started out innocently. He had gone to see her regarding a maths test question, and from that point on the teacher/pupil relationship had been altered dramatically, segueing to previously unexplored territory, a fantastical leap from that which is proper. Miss Carroway had become surprisingly amorous and had displayed her loving nature. She had instigated their closeness, though he feels blameworthy for reciprocating – he had leaned in and she had embraced him exuberantly after he had grasped a complex mathematical equation. Finding his personage in close in proximity to hers, and being enveloped by her warm body heat that emanated an enticing, sweet floral scent, Adam had spontaneously reciprocated with a quick friendly side hug. This innocent act had initiated a more passionate embrace from Miss Carroway. At that point, a dangerous intimate proximity had been established, whether intentional or not, which lent to the ease in which her arms next locked tightly around his waist, and her head found a resting place on his chest. The embrace progressed to a quick smooch, halting abruptly as Miss Carroway – that is, Edna – lifted her head to his face. A passionate, lingering kiss ensued. Adam had temporarily forgotten that this was Miss Carroway, his teacher, and not Ruthie, whom he was stepping out with, though he and Ruthie had never gotten this far in the game. Shocking to Adam, but excitingly so, Miss Carroway had displayed another side of her staid schoolmarm persona, completely abandoning her role as an educator – she had gone so far as to unbutton her shirtwaist to expose her plump, white bosom, then proceeded to lift up her skirt to expose her white, knobby knees.

Adam's more serious side caught up with him just in the nick of time – he'd remembered that this woman had been like a mother to him since he was a small boy, someone he'd revered as a saint. He'd immediately backed off, jumped up, and had rushed out the schoolhouse. His mind was numb for the rest of his day. Henry had asked him if he'd been imbibing whiskey because his speech was a mumble-jumble of inaudible words as they went about their chores after he got home.

"Adam, ye're acting a wee bit like a man who's wrestled wi' a wraith," he had commented. "What have ye been up to?"

Since that time – excluding the "climatic" event that transpired the very next day – he and Miss Carroway have never been alone together, and Adam has kept his head down in his books during class, and has been the first to exit the classroom at the clang of the bell. In Adam's mind, their relationship has been brushed aside, regarded as a dream-like fantasy, not having transpired in real life – a fictional chapter of a book they'd both partaken in.

III. No Way Out — The Verra Next Day

The very next day, Edna Carroway – he is now mindful of her first name – had passed him a note as he sat at his desk, which he immediately destroyed. She'd invited to him to her cottage for tea under the auspices that they should discuss the parameters of their student/teacher relationship as it applied to what had transpired between them the day before.

In her quaint cottage, she had laid out a tray of tea and blueberry scones on a beautiful display of red Staffordshire plates. They had conversed across a low marble-topped coffee table, Adam on the couch and Miss Carroway in a blue-velvet wingback armchair. The conversation had gone along very pleasantly, but quite stilted, regarding Adam's schoolwork and his college plans. There might have been a touch of cognac added to the Darjeeling tea – Adam's acute taste buds picked that out immediately. The tea tasted exotically spicy with a warm orange/caramel flavor. Adam had become very warm and relaxed, and had begun to feel very much at home in the beautifully furnished room of floral chintz-covered ottomans and solid wood accent pieces – a couch and chair covered in royal sapphire velvet upholstery and solid floor-to-ceiling mahogany bookcases with great classics that Adam had perused while Miss Carroway had gone to fetch more tea in the kitchen. When she returned, she had sat down on the couch next to him, which had caused Adam to blink his eyes rapidly and swallow hard. She then leaned in closer to Adam while reaching for her teacup on the table. Adam had picked up the scent of her violet perfume that reminded him of the freshness of the cool green grass in the spring. She had taken a sip of tea and her visage had transformed to a dreamy, trance-like look, as if she was remembering a faraway, exotic place. Coming out of her self-induced hypnotic state, Miss Carroway had set her teacup down and had scooted closer to Adam, crossing her arm around his back as she set her head with a strong pressure on his shoulder. She had begun to snuggle against him. Adam had blushed head to toe, his entire body on fire with desire. One thing had led to another, and he had begun to have no other thoughts in his head but of the utter pleasantness of the situation. Adam had pulled her into his arms and she had lain her head down on his lap. They ended up making love in Miss Carroway's quaint bedroom with its blue wildflower wallpaper. Miss Carroway had her hair down and looked completely different than in the classroom – a lot younger, more feminine, and sensual; her eyes, no longer magnified by glasses, were not owlish but vibrantly blue ovals that looked like sparkling sapphire jewels.

IV. Small Town Gossip — Secrets Inevitably Get Out

As Adam was sitting in Miss Carroway's parlor imbibing her excellent Darjeeling tea laced with honey liqueur and cognac, unbeknownst to Adam and Edna, two school laddies happened to come by to peep in the window, a favorite pastime of theirs. They had been playing in the stream coursing through the schoolyard and had come up, as was there usual routine, to catch a glimpse of their revered teacher through the window. As twelve-year-olds, Farley and Alexander had a fascination with their teacher's sexuality, and had hoped to catch her in a state of semi-undress, as they had once caught her in a revealing, low-cut silk robe. They had gathered enough knowledge about Miss Carroway's rather dull life to not expect any visitors, as she never had any, always tutoring students after hours in the schoolhouse, not in her cottage. Ordinarily, they would view Miss Carroway sitting alone in her parlor drinking tea while reading a book or grading papers. They observed that often she laced her cup with a dollop of alcohol. No matter how mundane Miss Carroway's life appeared to others from the outside, their vigilant watch over her was continually riveting.

What a revelation it was when they caught Adam Baird on the settee, and Miss Carroway kissing him passionately! The laddies were full to the brim with glee from their astounding observation, skipping back into the woods chanting "Love and kisses for Adam and Miss Carroway." They wrote this on the board the next day before Edna or Adam had entered the room, and quickly erased it after everyone had a chance to read it. Fortunately, they had left before Miss Carroway and Adam adjourned to the bedroom. Unfortunately, Farley's sister was a good church friend of Ruthie Malcolm's, and Farley was able to bribe his sister by offering her inside information about Adam in exchange for one of his sister's possessions that he coveted, a set of crystalline blue and green marbles. The next day Rosemary told Ruthie what Farley had relayed to her, word for word.

"Adam was kissin' Miss Carroway in her cottage. Farley saw it all wi' his own eyes. They must be verra much in love by what they were doin' on the sofa."

Ruthie didn't believe what she was hearing, thinking Rosemary's brother was pulling a practical joke on them. What she was being told went against everything she had ever known of Adam's character. Before she was able to discuss with Adam the outrageous rumor going around, she heard it again from another source besides Farley's sister. This time it was Adam, who wrote Ruthie a long missive explaining what had happened between him and Miss Carroway (he realized the gossip would reach her soon enough and he wanted to prepare her). He tried to convey emphatically to Ruthie that he had no romantic feelings for Miss Carroway, that the incident had just happened out of the blue because Miss Carroway was lonely, and he couldn't explain it to himself how he got so entangled with his teacher, only that he had drunk some "strange tea, probably spoiled" that had somehow left his judgment incapacitated.

In the next paragraph, he had written that she mustn't worry about Miss Carroway and him, as he wasn't going to be seeing her for much longer. He was quitting school in two months to work full-time at MacDuffy's. In the letter, Adam promised to ride out to Helensburgh so he and Ruthie could talk over the unfortunate situation. To her dismay, the letter informed her that he was going to be working really hard at the wheelwright's shop so did not have a specific date that he would be able to visit her, but assured her that he would definitely try to come to see her as soon as his schedule opened up. He also relayed to her that he had plans to tell Miss Carroway about quitting school before he came to see her. Ruthie felt like screaming after she had read the letter. She was thinking that two more months was a long time to be in the classroom with Miss Carroway. Anything could happen! Tearfully, she had tossed the letter on the table and left the room, leaving it for Catherine to pick up and peruse.

Today, on his important mission, two months after the climactic event, Adam enters the schoolhouse. Miss Carroway drops her stiltedness and becomes animated with an eager look in her eyes reserved only for lovers – that is, until he informs her of his intention to terminate his education and begin full-time work at MacDuffy's the following week.

"I'll be up at the crack o' dawn wi' morning chores for Grandfaither, then racing o'er to MacDuffy's at ten to spend rest o' the day 'til dusk," he explains.

Miss Carroway becomes misty-eyed, her long, thin, wiry lashes sparkling with dew. Her initial shock segues to an alarming pallor. Adam has been her pupil since five years of age and she'd never anticipated his leaving before graduation. Her outward emotion embarrasses him, as it brings their tryst to the forefront of his mind.

"Adam Baird, ye hiv promise o' becoming a great scholar," she says remorsefully while wiping her eyes with a hanky. "Please reconsider this. Daena let anything that's happened between us alter your future education," she pleads, looking guilty, as she thinks she is the cause of his sudden departure from schooling. Miss Carroway always speaks the proper Queen's English, and she insists all of her students drop the Scots vernacular when in the classroom, but this bombshell of Adam's has unnerved her and she resorts to her native way of speaking.

"Please be wary o' such a life-altering decision," she beseeches. "Ye could teach at the university level, if ye put yer mind to it. I truly understand the necessity o' comin' to the aid o' yer family, but Adam, ye must continue yer studies. Education will keep yer mind open to opportunities in life as they arise. I implore ye to complete yer term once yer able, and then further yer education at the University o'

Edinburgh. Please reconsider coming back to school in the spring."

"Grandfaither and the family need me, 'specially Grandfaither, Miss Carroway. He's auld and unwell, and the family requires extra money. Sorry to let ye down. 'Tis nothing related to me relationship wi' ye."

Miss Carroway replies sternly, her language more proper now. "Adam, you are not letting me down, only yourself. But when you're older, in a few years' time, you might reconsider having some sort of relationship with me. Not now, I understand, but perhaps in three or four years the prospect of a relationship with a woman will be more important to you. I'll be here, and I'm hopeful I might be viewed as a fair candidate."

Adam's pale face flinches and reddens in response to this painful interaction. He's always performed his best to keep up to Miss Carroway's standards of excellence. Doing well for Miss Carroway had always been a mark of pride to him.

Does she really think 'tis acause o' what happened betwixt us? Adam asks himself.

Miss Carroway must have read his thoughts.

"Adam, I understand you're acting for the benefit of your family, and not because of me, and I admire you for that, albeit I've always envisaged you as an academician in some field of higher learning that you aspire to. If you choose a trade like carpentry for a time, I know you'll be successful, as you'll be applying your maths skills. While taking a hiatus from schooling, I suggest you write down your experiences in a journal. This will aid you in maintaining an active mind and keeping your power of observation keen to help develop your writing skills. When you want to continue your education, you'll be prepared." Forlornly, she gives him a resigned look. Adam, finding it hard to relay the entirety of his news, swallows hard and clears his throat a number of times.

"Adam, in a few years' time, you'll be grown and maybe come back to visit me, and perhaps grasp the unlimited possibilities that such a love as ours can bring. I'll keep our love in my dreams, and hope that you see the beauty of our togetherness. I'll be waiting for you, Adam. With all my heart, I believe it could work out between us in a few years' time."

"Miss Carroway," he whispers, "I canna reflect on that now acause I've made a definite decision. This is to be kept betwixt ye and me – me folks hiv yet to be informed – but I'm departing for America efter I've saved eneuch money for passage. I intend to make me fortune in the mines to help support the family. I'm informing the family at suppertime tonicht."

"Oh, no, Adam," is all Miss Carroway is able to voice, in a sound of deflation, her eyes downcast. A long, awkward pause ensues as she brings her emotions under control. Her face flinches, as if she'd been dealt a severe blow.

"You're certain 'tis not on account o' what happened betwixt us? I pray not. I'll feel forever guilty. You're not leaving because of me, are you, Adam?" Miss Carroway is sounding very maudlin, and Adam cowers in humiliation and guilt.

"You know I love you with all my heart," she says. She comes over and embraces him, and tries to kiss his mouth. Adam backs off, not wanting the sweetness and allure of Miss Carroway to override his great plans.

"Nay," he stutters. "'Tis not acause o' anything ye've done. Acause o' me family's finances, and me dream to see the world. 'Tis the reason for me needing to leave."

"Aye, then ye've considered this life change carefully, have ye? There are other alternatives. I was hoping someday you'd come around to being a proper suitor to me and perhaps my future husband. I suppose that was a fantasy," she says wistfully. "That kind o' life is not in the stars for me, I fear," she states dejectedly.

"Aye, Miss Carroway, I've dwelled long and hard o'er this, and 'tis truly what resonates in me heart as bein' the proper course for me life."

"Very well, Adam, I'll not stand in your way, nor try to sway your mind. I wish you the best of luck, my dear. Then, 'tis a final fare-thee-well, my dear laddie." Miss Carroway appears to Adam totally devastated. "I'll be keeping you in my prayers. I do truly desire you come back home after you've had your grand adventure." Adam has the impression that Miss Carroway thinks he's going to the West on a short trip, and after his travel bug has been satiated he'll be home again.

"Thank ye wi' all me heart for bein' the finest teacher in all the world, Miss Carroway. I willna be remiss in correspondence to ye from the West."

"Adam, if ye could manage, I'd be so immensely pleased. I shall share your travel adventures wi' the class." They shake hands very formally, and Adam turns away from his dear teacher, whom he's revered most of his life. Her eyes are moist with unshed tears. He waits until he's out in the woods, homebound, to shed freely a tear or two in nostalgia and regret that his cherished education is at an end, a continuum that has been in his life almost as long as he can remember; he'd started his schooling at age five when Miss Carroway had been only a little older than his age now. On the other side of the coin, he's much relieved to be going to America, having found Miss Carroway's romantic visions for their future very uncomfortable and constraining and slightly maudlin, though his mind is rife with fantasies of their intimacies, which he will rely on in the future when he is lonely out West. After having become entangled romantically with Miss Carroway, Adam, in a newfound maturity, assesses that it would have been impossible to go back to their former teacher/student relationship.

Years later he will look back to his time of education at the little schoolhouse in Bridge of Allan with an emotional wellspring of soulful tenderness for Miss Carroway, grateful to her for being such a wonderful, caring teacher. As a mature man, he is able to view her from a different perspective. What he will feel for her after he learns of her death is a mingling of sympathy and sorrow, and a renewed love, the same untainted love he had for her as a wee laddie. In looking back, he assesses that she was the personification of a lonely spinster, unfulfilled in love, but magnificently gifted in her unlimited love for learning, which she in turn gifted to her students. He remembers her genuine spirited enthusiasm for teaching and eagerness to set high standards for him. The picture that Adam retains in his mind in later years is that of the Ugly Duckling, waiting to turn into a beautiful swan. As he later heard from his sisters, her life was never to progress beyond the one-room schoolhouse and little cottage. She developed cancer that changed her appearance abnormally from her string bean figure to a noticeably bloated, almost pregnant-looking woman, according to his sisters, who were her students at the time. She died at the age of forty-two. And so, he reflected, she didn't have time or advantage on earth to become a beautiful swan, but in his mind he imagines her floating away from her body as a beautiful bird. According to letters from his sisters, she remained unmarried, and was quite homely and unkempt towards the end of her life. Telling no one she was sick or in pain, she continued teaching up to a week before her death.

By quitting his completion of secondary school, Adam will not fulfill the mandatory requirements to enter the University of Edinburgh. As a consequence, if he returns to Scotland and desires to attend school at university level, he'll have to enroll in secondary school for another term. To his way of thinking, he'll benefit educationally from his experiences in the West and have no need of a formal university education if he returns. After his interaction with Miss Carroway, the thought of missing out on learning has placed a slight damper on his resolve to leave before finishing the term. Adam had always planned on attending the University of Edinburgh, until recently, when the needs of the family had come to the forefront in the form of mounting financial problems being put on his father. The slumping of his father's shoulders, the lines creasing his forehead, and the darkening under his eyes from burgeoning money problems affect Adam greatly. The price of stock feed has increased significantly, and food for the growing Baird family is at an all-time high. Dreaming of the splendor of the Western landscape and the wealth of the land has kept him focused on his goal, dreams that have been a panacea for overwhelming anxiety due to his family's problems, and the fact that he's going to be leaving soon. In his geography lessons, he's learned of the vast open lands in America, and newspapers have highlighted articles on the Silver Boom taking place in the newly formed state of Nevada, touting even more silver in the mines than the gold found in California. Front-page daily news of the making of great fortunes has helped spread the lust for easy fortune over Scotland. Glasgow newspapers have also been reporting news of the American Civil War, and recently of Confederate and Union boats being built along the riverbanks of the River Clyde. American sailors are coming over to help in the building of these steamers, navigating the prize ships across the Atlantic to the southern states and New York.

If I can strike it rich in the mines, I'll be able to support the entire Baird family, Adam reflects. *Perhaps steam back to visit the family ivery few months, and pay passage for the laddies and lassies desiring to come to America. Now that the hurdles of leaving have been jumped, 'tis time to tell the folks.* Adam heads to the Furry Beast Pub in town to meet Henry.

V. All the World Loves Henry Baird, Bar None?

As Adam heads for the schoolhouse to inform Miss Carroway of his plans of leaving school, Henry heads to town in the direction of Melville Place. He is greeted by a good many townspeople on the street, all seemingly aware by their rallying gestures of Henry's business and where he's headed. Henry is strikingly handsome in his youthful vigor, his black hair glazed with red highlights, and brilliant blue-green eyes twinkling good-humoredly when he engages in conversation. His friends and family often say that Henry is one of the happiest individuals in the world. Henry's trademark is his infectious laugh, wit, and ability to put people at ease in his presence. He casts a magical effect on others, lending them the notion that they, too, are in possession of extraordinary qualities like his own.

"Good afternoon, ma dear Henry," Mrs. Gertrude Fenton, a beauty of years gone by, in her late sixties now, greets him enthusiastically. She has a tendency to flirt with any man under the age of fifty. "Yer a fine-looking laddie, a sight for sore eyes in this godforsaken town. Aye, 'tis filled to the brim wi' auld sots wastin' thair lives away in the pubs." Henry tips his hat to her cordially and winks, with the outcome of her blushing like a schoolgirl.

"Stay true to yersel, let naebody tell ye whit's right," shouts an old coot, lounging on a wood bench in front of the general store.

Henry lifts his hat cordially and walks on. There is no other option but to meet with Annie at her house at this time, as a strict curfew has been laid down by Mr. MacGivens. Henry is planning to secretly (though not so secretly to the townsfolk now) rendezvous with Annie at the MacGivens residence, which is a block off of Henderson on Poplar Avenue. Having to call on Annie at home is risky, as there is a chance he'll be detected by Mr. MacGivens, who is out of work as a whiskey distillery bottler for a month due to a back injury. Annie has assured him that there is a way to avoid her father's watchdog scrutiny. He takes a nap every afternoon from four o'clock to five o'clock before supper. The plan is for Annie to be waiting in her bedroom, with the window ajar at the specified time of half past four, and to proceed downstairs and outside to the west side of the house when she hears Henry's characteristic duck call, a shrill unequivocal avian sound that won him first place in the annual duck calling contest two years in a row. Annie has assured Henry that her father in unable to see him on the west side of the house, as there are no upstairs windows on that side, and downstairs the dining room drapes are tightly drawn. His snoring will indicate to her that he is in a sound slumber, which is most certain, as he must be physically roused at six o'clock each evening for supper.

Punt makes his presence known to Henry by jumping up and down on his shoulder and playfully honking a duck call into his ear. The sound fortunately does not carry any farther than Henry, as Punt is the size of a large hummingbird when not on the ground.

"Punt, wee lord o' all that's lighthearted and fun in the world, I beg ye, please scram. I'm on an urgent mission. I implore ye to keep yer distance and yer silence for once in yer intrepid wee life. 'Tis imperative! I'll give ye the all-clear sign when me mission has a favorable outcome, and I'm out o' the woods from danger."

"Of course, Henry," promises Punt, locking his lips with an imaginary key. "I love these manly games o' valor." He smiles impishly and jumps lightly off Henry's shoulder, knowing full well that Henry is intending to meet his sweetheart. He disappears discreetly into the bushes.

As Henry stands with his hands over his puckered lips about to whistle, the door opens and his expression brightens. From behind him he hears the voice of Punt. His Wee Friend has not gone away as instructed, which irks Henry to no end. He is hoping against all odds for Punt not to interfere with his plan, as the wee fey is prone to outlandish acts of mischief to get his kicks and always runs at full tilt to protect Henry when he's in trouble. Henry doesn't desire his help this time.

"Watch yer back, Henry. Trouble's coming!" calls out Punt. Henry doesn't register Punt's warning, as Punt is cloistered in a hydrangea bush too far away to be heard very well. MacGivens, having charged out of the front door on a rampage, resembling a bull let loose into the ring, is now stomping over to the side of the house where Henry is standing facing the window. Punt giggles with delight at the inevitable confrontation in store for Henry, and makes punching gestures in the air. Henry looks around expectantly with a smile, thinking Annie has come down, but instead he comes nose to nose with MacGivens. The big Scot appears to him about ten feet tall; his nostrils flare like an angry bull out to kill the matador.

"Knock him dead, Henry," calls out Punt excitedly. Henry glances quickly over to see Punt sitting on a bush smoking his pipe, a stein of beer in his hand, an enthusiastic spectator for a big showdown.

"Ye could have given me an earlier warning, my Wee Friend. What's friendship for but to save the life o' yer friend?" sighs Henry under his breath.

"Niver show yer face here again, ye rapscallion, ye good-for-nothing scoundrel, violator o' innocent lassies." His foul breath of stale whiskey and tobacco is so close to Henry's face that Henry must cease breathing through his nose to avoid the noxious fumes. MacGivens punches Henry on his cheek below his left eye and pushes him down to the ground. Henry rolls backwards once down on the ground to avoid any more punches, and scoots back another five feet before rising shakily to his feet. Getting his distance from MacGivens pays off because as MacGivens charges towards him, he trips on a stump in the lawn and falls to the ground, remaining down on his on back on the grass where he's landed a few yards away from Henry, snorting heavily like a hog about to be slaughtered and cussing to high heaven.

"Ye're a lecherous and unsavory fool! Ye daena deserve to be wi' decent folk," he calls out as he tries to get back up. He rolls over, and while on all fours, not having the agility to stand up, yells vehemently, "I've heard o' yer reputation for gettin' into trouble, pulling pranks on folks who're not able to defend themselves from yer conniving."

"Faither!" screams Annie from her upstairs bedroom window.

"Leave him be. I love him dearly. Please daena harm him!"

"Hold yer horses, MacGivens, I daena plan to bail on yer daughter. We plan to be wed. I'm asking as I solemnly stand afore ye for Annie's hand in marriage."

"Nae, I'll never grant ye permission to marry me Annie, ye coot scumbag. Scram, or I'm comin' efter ye, and this time I'll show no mercy. The bairn will be put up for adoption, as we daena desire yer kind."

"Och, come on, ol' man, give me a chance. Ye know I'm the right one for yer daughter. I can make her laugh and bring love and laughter to her life. She'll hiv as many grand moments in her life as there are stars in the sky."

"Yer a half-wit, Henry Baird!" exclaims MacGivens, attempting to get himself off the ground. "Yer full o' yourself. And no one laughs at yer jokes acause they're lame."

Henry, trying in vain to stall from being hit again, tries to find common ground with MacGivens through humor. Gibberish spills out of him as he tries to gain control of the situation and quell his anxiety, as it is apparent that MacGivens is in attack mode. Henry looks at MacGivens, who remains immobile on all fours. Mr. MacGivens, he finds, is fuming like an overfed furnace, his face the deep ruby color of a beet.

"Yer a stupid ingrate!" he blasts.

"Och, na dinna fash. I'm no here to harm ye. Let me help ye up."

"Stay away from me, ye cad."

Punt, with all his jokes and pranks, is a semi-angel and has a few good words of advice for his best friend. "Henry, ye must make him feel guid about his relationship with his daughter. Tell him ye'll niver turn his daughter away from him. 'Tis what frightens him the most."

"Punt, we're goin' away to America acause o' his attitude."

"That's the point, Henry. He senses that and feels miserable acause o' that circumstance."

"Och, Punt, ye're right and wrong thegither. He willna change. He might desire to, but he willna."

"Perhaps ye're right, Henry. But ye must see his viewpoint and not act foolish, or ye'll niver be able to accomplish what ye desire. Ye must let him see that ye're a mature fellow."

"I'm na bein' foolish, Punt. Just actin' out me frustrations." He turns to the older man, still on the ground. "MacGivens," he calls out, "I'll niver turn yer Annie from ye. Ye must ken 'tis true."

"Get out o' here and niver show yer face again!" yells MacGivens.

Henry looks up to the window and sees Annie's pale face and troubled eyes, reading in them her desperate desire for him to get away before it's too late. Henry backs off gracefully, picks his hat up off the ground, tips it graciously towards MacGivens, and blows a kiss to Annie.

VI. The Furry Beast Pub

After his fight-and-flight surge of adrenaline abates, Henry walks nonchalantly back down Henderson Street, as if he'd merely stopped in at the MacGivens household for a spot of tea. He has a planned meeting at the pub with Adam to talk over the success or failure of their respective missions. Henry views his mission as being pitifully unsuccessful. He mulls over the encounter with Ol' Man MacGivens on his way to the pub, coming to grips with the fact that he'll never win over the man. *Hank MacGivens is surely afraid o' something*, he thinks. Henry ponders over the impenetrable cocoon of sadness and anger MacGivens lives within in order to keep happiness at bay.

Henry's in possession of great compassion for others and his sympathy extends even to Mr. MacGivens and the poor man's fearfulness in loving. He understands and forgives MacGivens for being foolishly afraid, as he forgives and understands everyone for their weaknesses. He only wishes MacGivens would come out of his self-imposed cocoon to bask in the light that shines in his world and through his own spirit. If the man were brave enough to shed his cocoon, he would be free to fly as a butterfly in the warmth of light and love offered by his beautiful daughter. Henry's God-given gift is to see the many manifestations of the blocked inner light of peoples' spirits, for it is a part of his jig-spiritedness. He sits on a rung close to the semi-angels who see all very clearly.

Henry walks into the Furry Beast Pub and spots the solitary figure of Adam sitting in repose at a table by the window close to the fireplace. His brother is staring out the window in that common reflective pose of his when out in public at a bar. The thought enters Henry's mind that Adam is more than happy to sit by himself and enjoy his aloneness than to socialize with the friendly, but noisy, patrons in the pub.

Haesna ordered a drink yet! Most folks feel foolish sittin' in a bar by thairsels minus a beverage in thair hand, thinks Henry. He loves this about his brother.

Henry also admires this introspective aspect of Adam. His shy, reserved brother is very content to live in his own world, carefree of the approval of others. Adam doesn't try to fit in, put on airs, or seek ego gratification from others. Henry is aware that, by nature, people are two-sided – part good and part evil, with a pendulum of movement towards one side or the other. Adam's pendulum swings far to the side of goodness, as opposed to Ol' Man MacGivens's pendulum that definitely swings towards the grey, muddled area of a lightless spirit, where it remains stuck like a broken clock. Perfect strangers will put their trust in Adam, sensing his kind nature, but he is content to stay in the background unobserved. Due to Adam's gentle character, people are attracted to him like magnets, though he tries to avoid bringing attention to himself. When people do approach him, he is open and willing to help anyone with any need. Henry observes his brother as he approaches him. He intuits that Adam's visit with Miss Carroway did not go any better than his own visit to Annie, as there is a dark and heavy clouding of his brother's countenance.

"How're ye faring?" Henry inquires. "Ye daena appear verra spritely."

"Had a bit o' a rocky road," replies Adam with a thick, dry tongue. "I attempted to let Miss Carroway down gently, but she's an extremely sensitive soul. She understands me need to travel the world, though is hopeful that I might return to Bridge o' Allan in a few years' time, a more mature man, mebbe to court her for eventual marriage."

"Let her possess hope to hold on to. Mebbe ye'll tire o' America and come to view Scotland as the bonniest place in the world. If ye come back wi' a wife and child, she'd see the light o' day."

"Quite unlikely, me brither, for I've no idea what I might encounter in the West, but 'tis certain I'll not find a bride in a rough and rugged territory."

"Hiv ye tauld Mum and Faither yet?"

"Tonight, if the mood's right. I canna dally. Mum and Faither need time to adjust to the idea afore me departure."

As soon as townsfolk on the street see Henry sitting in the bar in the window, they come in to pat him on the back playfully, offering raunchy comments about his messed-up face, alluding to the infamous "MacGivens fight," which has spread like wildfire throughout downtown area. Neighbors, having heard the commotion, had put their heads out of their windows to view the maelstrom. The men coming into the Furry Beast look riled up, on an adrenaline and testosterone high, as if they've been in a fight themselves. Seemingly, the desire to live vicariously through the complications of Henry's imbroglio has imbued them with secondhand manliness. Several friends join Adam and Henry at their table, slapping Henry on the back in a congratulatory gesture and buying him drinks.

Henry is in his element with the bar crowd and becomes increasingly animated, indulging in each round of drink bought for him. As the proclaimed winner of the so-called "duel," he does his best to play the part of a hero.

Adam sips at his whiskey, attempting to enliven his mood with the smooth amber liquor. He is keenly aware of his standoffishness, that he is not participating in or enjoying the liveliness of the conversations around him. He finds himself becoming increasingly drowsy from the whiskey. His thoughts continually fall back to his meeting with Miss Carroway, reliving in his mind what he had said and what she had said. Fortunately, his good friend Monte Bull comes in and sits down, finally drawing him into the fold of a conversation.

An inebriated customer, Mr. Hutch Ferguson, an old weatherworn sheep rancher with skin toughened to jerky, comes up and talks to Henry in slurs and spits, sloshing beverage on the floor as he sways from side to side. Adam is annoyed when Henry invites him to sit down and have a drink with them, and is uncomfortably ashamed that he is not as nice a person as his brother. Henry shows great compassion for the old rancher and inquires about his family and his farm, and proceeds to tell some farm animal jokes. He has everyone roaring in laughter. Adam and Monte sit quietly, imbibing slowly, chuckling politely at the lame jokes.

Ol' Ferguson, laughing the loudest, leans into Henry. "I hear ye got into a bit o' a scrape wi' MacGivens. Leave town immediately is me advice to ye. MacGivens is a hothead and will be coming efter ye for a kill. Appears that he tried by the looks o' ye. His lassie couldna be sane bein' brought up by the likes o' him. Would be advisable for ye to get away from that harpy."

Henry, surprisingly, doesn't look insulted by the inappropriate, insensitive comment. "Ah," he replies smoothly, "Annie's an angel. I'm verra much in love wi' the bonnie lass."

"She's na as sweet as she appears. Rumors are circulating she's wi' bairn, ye ken." Ferguson continues to insult Annie's reputation. Henry sweeps it under the carpet by offering Ferguson another drink and telling another joke. Henry is in no mood to be riled up with anger.

"Henry, we hiv to get back," implores Adam, drained by all the events of the day and the insults slung at Henry. "Only an hour until supper. Story Hour must've started…" Adam stops mid-sentence, embarrassed that he mentioned Story Hour, and blushes to a deep rosy hue. Henry gulps down his drink and smiles cheerfully at everyone.

"Thank ye for all yer support, me friends! I love ye for all yer kind words and offerin' o' drink; me spirit's lifted to lofty heights as I climb the mighty hills to home."

Ferguson slumps over sideways in his chair at that point, and Henry catches him before he falls off. Adam, Monte, and Henry ease the sodden drunk onto the floor and roll him over to the rug by the hearth. As they leave they see the innkeeper, Mr. Dodd, sprinkling water on Ferguson's face, a habitual christening which seems to do the trick of rousing old Ferguson from his drunken stupor. The lads head for home.

Chapter Six

I. Adam's Announcement to His Family

Gazing out over the hilly farmland as Adam and Henry climb the steep paths homeward to the Drumdruils ranch, Adam has a few moments to reflect while enjoying the approaching dusk. Suppertime will be called as soon as they reach home, at which time his dreaded pronouncement to his parents of his travel plans will take place. In the meantime, he is savoring the peace. He tries not to fret about the outcome, as he can only imagine the scene of angst that will ensue – a volatile outburst on the part o' Faither and a distressful whimpering on the part o' Mum. He has readied sound arguments in defense of his impending travel to America, all boiling down to the fact that the family's very survival depends on it. He plans to assert with conviction his rationale:

There are too many mouths to feed at Drumdruils, and times are gettin' harder and harder wi' Scotland's wretched economy. Money brought in from the berry crop and jam production has gone way down. He'll be mailing home to the family most o' the funds acquired.

Adam assures himself that once he presents these arguments in a mature manner, his parents will have no recourse but to agree with its merits. Methodically, he goes over the manner in which he will broach the subject. Should he stand up and chime his crystal drinking glass with his fork to get everyone's attention? *No a guid idea,* he thinks. Too much like Faither's unserious and comical gesticulations to modulate the children's loudness wherein everybody starts laughing. Adam wants to be taken seriously. He decides to stand up abruptly and clap his hands, and then start talking in a loud, authoritative voice to get everyone's attention.

Adam looks over to his brother, who is calm and reflective as well, and back to the velvety hills, startlingly greenish-yellowish in their vividness from the sun's low-casting rays, and then to the woodlands off to the north, glimmering in jeweled iridescence. Off to the south, he gazes at little hillocks rising up from the ground where the Wee People are said to live in their dun-shis. The mounds are, he surmises, natural hilly outcrops of the plains that were carved by antediluvian glacial floods, now devoid of anything but dense coverings of grass with insects and birds flitting atop – wild-life taking advantage of the profundity of organic matter.

A sense of nostalgia for his younger years besets Adam as he gazes at the irregular green and yellow outcrops in the land. He oftentimes sits on the mounds of hillocks where the Wee People are said to dwell while he's tending the sheep, legs crossed at his knees, back leaning against a lovely rowan tree. It has been his habitual spot throughout boyhood and early manhood. Sometimes sitting out beside the hillocks, Adam forgets he's a grown-up, for his life has remained unchanged for as long as he can remember. If not for the largeness of his body, he could very well be the wee laddie he was a decade ago sitting atop a mound. At that time, he believed ardently this area was the homeland of the Wee Ones. Many grown-up Scots revert back to these "wonder years" as a coping mechanism to escape the harsh realities of life, like imbibing a strong whiskey, smoking tobacco, or savoring a luscious childhood dessert, all ways to relieve stress. To fall back to imaginings of a magical world elevates Adam's spirit, makes him happy and care-free, comforted by the idea that wee creatures are indeed down in their dun-shis watching over his homeland. He half wishes they were part of his adulthood, for they brought him so much pleasure as a child – peace of mind, magical enchantment, curiosity, creativ-ity, the belief that anything is possible. A part of him will always be stirred emotionally by the magical connection to the world endowed by the folklore of Wee People. *It daes no harm to pretend to believe in what's not apparent, for 'tis what imagination and creativity are. None o' God's miracles have been proven. 'Tis certainly contrary to Faither's empirical beliefs, but Faither's possessed plenty o' belief systems o'er the years in accord wi' his readings.*

As they approach the farm, Adam takes in a deep breath of fresh, fragrant air infused with scents of heather, peat, and pine, and scans the expanse of land that belongs to the Bairds – he has an ideal vantage point to see for miles in every direction.

Drumdruils is set on a perfectly situated, picturesque site looking down over the quaint, charming village of Bridge of Allan. The land provides a wonderful playground for the Baird children, with ample room for roaming. The breadth of the land compensates for the full-to-the-brim house – nine members occupying two bedrooms – with the addition of a sun porch that serves as the bedroom for Malkie and Telford, and a cold cellar bedroom where Adam and Henry sleep under heavy quilts. It is a coveted space with the quiet and privacy it affords them. The bedrooms are equipped with wooden trundle beds beneath taller bed frames. Emma, Janet, and Baby Susan sleep upstairs next to the bedroom of their parents.

The family is a happy-go-lucky crew despite their cramped quarters. The household is run like a well-oiled machine – a necessity to accommodate a large family abiding under one roof. Everyone must complete assigned chores, without fail, to keep the household wheels turning smoothly. The large stone house (of yellowish cream-colored stone from a local quarry) is kept immaculately clean, with the walls and wood banisters buffed to a high shine through the diligent efforts of Housekeeper Violet. The large bedrooms are cozy with colorfully woven cotton rag rugs, and satin or silk quilts stuffed with layers of wool or chicken feathers. The kitchen, with its large stone hearth, is a napping haven for the family Airedale, Kipper, who is a constant fixture, slumbering as close to the hearth as he can get without torching his fur on damp or rainy days. On fair-weather days, however, Kip is out romping with the children, or catching fish in the shallow streams in the woodlands above. The large, high-ceilinged main rooms of the house, with thick exposed crossbeams painted a shiny mahogany, provide enticing gathering places, especially the warm, cheery kitchen with its the mouth-watering aroma of yeasty baked goods, coffee, and spices. The kitchen is where the laddies and lassies congregate around a large, round oak table for art projects and homework, and in anticipation of a tidbit from Violet, as she deftly rolls out dough for breads, berry pies, berry scones, and shortbread.

Adam Baird Sr., a widower, married Jean Dawson, the present-day matriarch of the family, after the death of his first wife. Adam Sr. and Jean have nine children, with seven siblings still living at home. The first two of the nine siblings, the eldest two sons, Edward and Rutherford, are grown. Edward left to seek his fortune in America over six years ago, and Rutherford is a successful businessman who has a large family estate in Dunblane.

Adam's plan to leave home, which he finds logical and an enticing solution to the Baird family's mounting financial burden, has been romantically inspired by his readings of the West and by fanciful bedtime chats with his brothers entailing the easy swooping up of gold and silver in Nevada and California. He has been methodically planning out his trip over the past year.

As soon as sufficient funds are acquired from his wheelwright's job in town, he'll be able to pay for his room and board in Glasgow, the bustling shipping city where he plans to seek out work as a carpenter to earn the necessary funds for his trip to America. He will be following in the steps of his older brother, Edward, although Edward is now situated in the Territory of Alaska.

After he departs for America, Adam fears his chances of getting back home will be slim, though there are ships steaming to and fro across the Atlantic continuously to aid the war effort in the States.

I could readily jump on anither schooner to home if I'm homesick, he concludes, to assuage his feeling of trepidation. *Mebbe efter I've accrued money, I'll purchase a return passage, or send for the family to live in America wi' me.* He plans to write often about the wonders of the great land.

II. Story Hour — Off with the Queen's Head — 23 October 1863

As Adam and Henry are walking home, the Baird family congregates before supper, as they customarily do, around the fire in the sitting room to be read to by Adam Sr. or Violet. By late afternoon, Violet has overseen the preparation of the family supper cooked by Mrs. Cook, which frees Violet up for Story Hour. Cook is a cantankerous, stubborn wisp of a woman, of a nondescript age, who often comes to near blows with Violet by overstepping her boundaries in the kitchen, but she is a fine chef. Violet calls her "Ol' Sourpuss" behind her back. In the ten years she has worked and resided at Drumdruils, she has never divulged anything, in the least, about herself, and has spoken very little about anything at all but food preparation. Violet has speculated injudiciously, due to her bias, that Cook's previous life must've involved a great sin. This would explain her being close-mouthed about her past. At present, Ol' Sourpuss's conversation sounds of grunts and mumbles, and sometimes a gratified purring noise as she samples her own cooking. Henry is the only one who's ever been able to reach her. Even Cook can't resist his enormous charisma, and has been known to flutter her eyelashes and to giggle like a silly young maiden in his presence. As Violet remarked, "Henry can charm the pants off onyone, even a feisty auld loon."

Cook is putting the finishing touches on the supper, and will keep it warm in the oven until the end of Story Hour, at which time she will start dishing out plates. This evening Janet, Adam, and Henry are the only family members not present. This is due to Janet's sleepover at Mary's, and the laddies attending to personal matters, which lead the senior Bairds to speculate with dread about their laddies' involvements in some sort of trouble.

During Story Hour, the children are not allowed to speak in Scots colloquialism around their father, but Violet does what she wants and gets away with it. Inevitably, colloquial words spring from the mouth of Adam Sr. as well.

"Now, children," says Violet, "the days are shorter, darkness comes o'er us earlier, and tonicht, in particular, the weather's verra inclement and threatening. The Wee Ones hiv warned us o' a harrowing storm gathering force oot in the universe. This time o' year instills a mysterious imbalance to the workings o' nature, aften bringing out unimaginable egregious behavior in people predisposed to deevilish acts."

Malkie asks unabashedly in his cracking, high-pitched voice, "Ye mean spookiness and evil in the air acause ghosts and deevils are coming out for All Hallow's Eve?"

"Aye, Malkie, 'tis the season o' the year for souls to transition betwixt this plane on earth and the Beyond, and to make a showing wi' one last evil act afore departing."

"Deevil is verra bad," declares Emma emphatically, giving a dire warning to her siblings.

"Aye, indeed, Emma. 'Tis verra evil, na human, a verra cruel, evil thing. There're myriad, interwoven forces at play in the universe," continues Violet. "Acause o' the occasional conflicts in balance, atrocious acts are committed wi'oot any sense, spurred on by the deevil hissel."

"Who daes this deevil resemble?" inquires Malkie. "'Tis aw red and black and spiky?"

"He takes on many forms, and can take on the appearance o' humans."

"Eneuch o' this mumbo-jumbo o' ghosts, goblins, and devils," exhorts Adam Sr. "You're scarin' the bairns, Violet. Let's get on wi' the story." Violet's countenance becomes focused, with a far-off look in her eyes, as if she is entering the world of spirits.

"This evening, I tell a sad tale of Queen Mary's unfortunate life, which abounds with murder and ends in her execution; 'tis in itself a verra evil act caused by unsavory, deevilish forces takin' possession o' minds." Violet directs a sidelong glance at Adam Sr., waiting for him to object to the word deevilish, but he lets it pass.

Violet is an expert on the lives of Scottish queens and kings of the monarchies of old. The tale of Mary Queen of Scots's life is one of the children's favorites, but they've never heard the story of her execution, as they were deemed too young. The children shudder and "ooh" and "ahh" their delight in anticipation of an entertaining, gruesome story. Violet begins to recount the events leading up to Queen Mary's demise.

Malkie, always the prankster, tempts his fate of being sent to his room by dropping a leaf down the back of Emma. She reacts for the amusement of all the kids with a startled scream, and a roll-over on the floor like she's on fire. Malkie has put living creatures down her back in the past so her reaction is a justifiable, well-conditioned response.

"Malkie, what have you done to Emma?" growls Adam Sr. in his most intimidating voice.

"Only a wee bit o' leaf down her back, Faither," barks Malkie in his pubescent hoarseness.

"Stop your clowning, laddie," reprimands Adam Sr., "or your brithers are goin' to be picking ye up and dumping ye in yer bed. Carry on, Violet, before we have more disruptions!"

Violet begins, without further ado, with a Robert Burns poem:

But as for thee, thou false woman!
My sister and my fae
Grim vengeance yet shall whet a sword
That thro' they soul shall gae!
The weeping blood in woman's breast
Was never known to thee;
Nor the balm that draps on wounds of woe
Frae woman's pitying e'e'

Violet commences to read: "Queen Mary's secretary, Riccio, was murdered at Holyrood House in Edinburgh at the hands of Mary's jealous husband, Lord Darnley (Henry Stuart). Darnley was very jealous of the working relationship between Riccio and the queen, and accused them of having a romantic affair. Lord Darnley was, in every sense of the word, a tyrant who wanted to control Mary's power, and was most likely construing mischief to weaken Mary by taking away her right-hand man. The story goes that Mary, seven months pregnant with child, was in the supper-room with Riccio when conspirators working for Darnley broke into the room, led Riccio away against his will, then proceeded to bludgeon him to death in an adjoining room.

"In subsequent months, Mary, out of misplaced loyalty for her husband, came to his rescue when he was accused of killing Riccio, most likely because she was pregnant with his child. Soon after, Mary gave birth to their son, James (who became James VI of Scotland, as well as being James I of England).

"Queen Mary had horrendous struggles throughout her life due to her rivalry with Elizabeth I of England, who didn't want Mary to succeed her on the throne, though it was Mary's birthright – she was a direct descendent to the throne on both sides of her family tree (the daughter of Henry VIII). Mary was captured by English soldiers working for Elizabeth and held in exile for a number of years. Elizabeth's minions continually threatened her life in subsequent years. At age forty-four, Mary was sentenced to death by beheading by Elizabeth, who had become increasingly threatened by her, as her right as a legitimate heir the English throne was becoming all too apparent. Finally, Mary was put to the guillotine at Fotheringhay on 8 February 1587, and her death was verra gruesome and not for children's eyes.

"It took two strikes to kill Mary: the first blow missed her neck and struck the back of her head. The second blow severed the neck, except for a small bit of sinew that the executioner cut through by using the axe as a saw. Afterward, the executioner held her head aloft and declared, 'God save the Queen.'"

"*Violet Rose Shaw*," Adam Sr. roars in a deep baritone, "the bairns will have nightmares if ye go on wi' sic bluidy language! Hold yer tongue, ye daft woman, if ye've any sense left in yer heid."

Some of the even more gory details are left out for the children's sake. Nevertheless, the riveting tales of Queen Mary's tumultuous life are a family favorite. Violet feels strongly that knowledge of Scotland's history will widen the children's scope of the world around them. She ends her story with a verse from Robert Burns's poem "Lament to Queen Mary on the Approach of Spring," regarding the execution of Mary Queen of Scots, which the children haven't heard before. She decides they are now all old enough to comprehend the essence of the poem. Robert Burns is the most revered author of Scotland, and Violet is an expert on his poems.

"I do apologize, Mr. Baird, but Queen Mary was a verra important historical figure that I desire the children to be familiar wi'." Violet doesn't seem apologetic or worried by the reprimand. She has relayed stories flavored with horror at Story Hour many times before, but is always sensitive to the fact that there are children present. She and Adam Sr. have an understanding of sorts – he's allowed to be vociferous in his condemnation of some topics, and she's allowed to promote some of her questionable philosophies and topics, within reason, to what's appropriate for the children's ages, as long as he's allowed to yell at her.

"Well, try to sugarcoat it next time when you tell of poor Mary getting the axe! The gory poem of a head chopping isn't necessary to relay a story we've all heard before and know the outcome of." Everyone laughs, including Adam Sr., as soon as he realizes he's not making matters any less macabre.

After Violet recounts her gruesome tale, it is time to pick out another book from the shelf to be read aloud. Adam Sr. has compiled a list of the children's names to take turns in the nightly book selection.

"Janet's turn!" he calls out loudly, as in a roll call. "Where's Janet?" he inquires, not having noticed her absence previously.

"She's wi' the MacLaines," responds Violet, "spending the night wi' Mary."

"I'm taking her turn," pipes up little Emma.

"Bluidy unfair," shouts Malkie. "Ye picked two nights ago. Not yer turn!"

"Let her be," says Adam Sr. sternly. "Emma, dear, go ahead and pick out your favorite – perhaps a fairy tale from the shelf, something suitable for wee bairns to enjoy."

Emma skips airily over to the built-in mahogany bookshelf covering the entire southern wall, taunting Malkie with a victory curtsy on the way over. She ceremoniously climbs a three-foot stepladder and selects a gilded leather-bound book which is too heavy for her to lift down. Adam Sr. rushes over and lifts her down off the stool as she holds the book tightly to her chest. Emma proudly carries it over to Violet, as if bearing a precious gift. She has chosen the family's favorite author again – Robert Burns.

"I choose 'Tam o' Shanter,'" declares Emma decisively. "'Tis the season that witches come out wi' the ither creatures o' the nicht," she says emphatically, reaching her arms to the sky.

"Awricht, but I daena desire ye children having nightmares tonight," says Violet. "We'll hiv hot cocoa drink wi' calming herbs efter the story. 'Tis agreeable?"

"Aye, wi' a smidgeon of brandy?" inquires Malkie.

"Malkie, hold yer tongue round the children," chastises Adam Sr.

In her beautiful melodic voice, Violet begins her version of the macabre Halloween tale of Tam o' Shanter, which she knows by heart, with no need for reading the beautiful, illustrated book that Emma has placed in front of her. She offers the following rendition of the famous story:

The good but reckless man, Ol' Tam, was inebriated from the taking of ale all day in town in the public house on Market Day, and lingered over his pints well into the evening when other chapmen and storekeepers had wisely long before left the gates of the city for home. A storm was brewing when Tam finally started out for his country home, where his wife, Ellen, frantically awaited him, knowing the vices of her husband all too well. It was well past midnight when Tam galloped merrily out of town towards home on his faithful mare, Meg, on a dark, moonless night into an unimaginably spooky, perilous environment. Indeed, the night brought out the most threatening underworld creatures. First of all, it was necessary that Tam cross the ford where other villagers had met their deaths – where the cairn of a murdered baby had been found; where ol' drunken Charlie had broken his neck; where Mungo's mother had hanged herself. Tam saw the old abandoned church light up as he approached. Lo and behold, Tam passed through the field by the kirkyard where he came upon open caskets. He spied warlocks and witches standing around the open coffins in a drug-induced ecstasy of sacrilegious fervor. Each coffin inhabitant was holding a light by which Tam could see two unchristened bairns and a thief newly cut for a rape, his expression cast indelibly o' his last gasp. He also saw five tomahawks covered in blood o' red-ruse, and five scimitars wi' crusted blood from a murder. Tam watched as the devil played the bagpipes, and warlocks and witches had a grand ol' time performing the unholy rituals of underworld worship.

Tam's frightened horse, Meg, got spooked and took off running, which was fine by Tam, who was equally terrified when the demons began to pursue them. It was imperative that Meg and Tam cross the River Doon in order na to be captured, as demons won't pass over running water. Poor ol' Meg got snatched up by the tail afore she could make it across the river. What was left on the poor creature was a mere tailless stump, and this left poor ol' Tam o' Shanter more at the mercy of the most evil o' adversaries. Meg, a different looking creature, made it to the crossing o' the river with petrified Tam clinging to her, with no time to spare. Poor Tam learned his lesson and never drank o' the ale past early afternoon, or ventured out at nicht to the kirkyard again.

The Bairds sit contentedly around the hearth, musing over the adventure of Tam and Meg. There is nothing more satisfying, or cozier, than sitting around a roaring fire, enjoying the company of loved ones. Adam Sr. regards his close-knit family as a small village, and often refers to them as such, perhaps because the financial burden of keeping his large clan afloat rests heavily on his shoulders, as does a mayor's responsibility to his village. Henry and Adam have reached home and have now joined the family circle at the end of Tam o' Shanter's tale.

"Where've the merry shenaniganers been and what've the merry shenaniganers gotten themselves into now?" Adam Sr. queries of Adam and Henry in jest.

The family is prone to animated, high-spirited frivolity at their family gatherings due to their sheer number, all with diverse, dynamic personalities, and not discounting the Celtic temperament in their genes. It is inevitable that occasional emotional outbursts erupt if one youngster pesters another, or if Adam Sr. becomes irritated when one of the youngsters interrupts the storytelling with giggles, squirms, fidgeting, or chatter, all of which is taken with good humor by the rest of the family. The children are encouraged to openly express their thoughts, to share with their family what they deem interesting, what they have learned in school, or what they would like to do with their futures, but Adam Sr. thinks that sometimes they get out of hand. *They often remind me of creatures in the zoo, the way they act*, he thinks. He chastises himself for such an unspeakable thought about his own children.

After the story, Telford declares proudly, "I found a five-legged frog today in the stream that could run faster wi' his five legs than any frog alive. We raced Mr. Five-Legs against a normal frog. Mr. Five-Legs won by a meter."

Malkie vocalizes with indignation, "Yer frog daedna win by a long shot. The reason that he went faster wis that ye kept swatting his back wi' a twig."

"Not so loud, Malkie," Adam Sr. interjects.

"Daedna," replies Telford with conviction. "Only thrice I struck him when he went off course."

"That's cruel, Telford," says Emma. "Right, Faither?"

"Faither, we whip our horses to make them go faster, daena we?" inquires Malkie, sticking up for his brother for a change.

"I suppose 'tis fine to race frogs minding no harm's done to them, and the creatures are placed back in the water afterwards," replies Adam Sr., looking up from his book and tapping his pipe against a wooden bowl. As an afterthought, he adds, "Prod them gently with reed, laddies. No whipping."

Says Malkie, his eyes dancing in jest, "Ye ken how to tell when a frog's laughing, daena ye? 'Tis when his eyes bug out!" Everyone starts to laugh.

"Not funny, Malkie," Emma responds. "Frogs' eyes are ayeweys bug-eyed; they're born that way."

"No, ye numskull, they're born as tadpoles," replies Malkie. "Daena ye ken onything?"

"Malkie, eneuch o' that insolence or off to bed you go wi'oot supper," reprimands Adam Sr., forgetting his proper speech. On that note, they are summoned to the table by Violet.

III. Suppertime at the Bairds'

"Time for supper," calls out Violet at full volume after being informed by Cook that supper is on its way to the dining room. Henry and Adam rush through the door and eagerly to the table, anxious to temper the emotional upheavals of their afternoon with a satisfying meal. Both are unusually quiet.

On this blustery autumn evening, in which the ionic energy of an upcoming storm is ramping up outside, and the wind is howling and screeching to announce its impending arrival, the family, all but Janet, gather around a large mahogany table, settling down noisily in their chairs in anticipation of a delicious meal. On the eastern wall, a huge fire blazes in the jagged limestone fireplace – a crude, rocky expanse of earthen hues that covers the entirety of the wall. While dishing out food for the smaller children, Violet glances up anxiously, and often, at the northern floor-to-ceiling window, viewing the periodic large droplets of rain drumming down on the glass. She appears quite unsettled when she sees the rain turning to hail with intrusive forceful pings on the window. Violet can't put her finger on the exact cause of her anxiety, but there is a niggling thought arising in her mind without her asking, laying claim to her emotional equilibrium. Perhaps, she thinks, it is what Elor said about the dangerous ferocity o' the storm and the death o' a child.

"Good grief, calm yourself, Violet," exhorts Adam Sr. irritably as he catches her looking one too many times towards the window. "A God-given act o' nature, for Heaven's sake! Storms equate to more water for the crops."

"The Wee Ones hiv predicted this to be a verra horrific storm,

Mr. Baird," warns Violet.

"Umph! Violet, your woodland gnomes conjure every storm to be the devil's work, and thus far the Scottish people have survived their doomsday predictions."

"I beg to differ, Mr. Baird, but the Wee Ones have guided us in the darkness from a myriad o' perilous times. Their behind-the-scenes efforts that ye are not privy to hiv often saved us."

"I'm very content to be kept in the dark, thank ye kindly!" declares Adam Sr.

Soon everyone relaxes with the pleasurable food, forgetting the outside world, as the savory aroma of roasted lamb and scented floral bouquets blend symbiotically with the atavistic warmth and piney aroma of the roaring fire, putting forth its soothing, crackling sounds. The overall effect is that inanimate objects have an extraordinary vividness and vitality from the electrified air, lending a buoyant sublimity to the room and its occupants. Were it not for sheer number of occupants in the room, with an element of restrained pandemonium, the setting would be otherworldly. An orchestra of sound and motion, from jumpy reflections and the high-pitched voices of squirming children, imparts cacophonous disharmony, imbuing visual and auditory phenomena more of the earthly than heavenly realm, sufficient to stir up dust mites and scare away the mice, if any dared to be present in this impeccably clean house.

Adam Jr. is preoccupied by his thoughts, oblivious to the suppertime hubbub. He exists as a large, silent, slightly slumped over bulk at his habitual place at the table, staring down at a labyrinthine white watermark on the table, as if to portend his future destiny in the splotchy stain of a long-ago spill of milk. He counts down the days to his departure and reflects on the time he'll no longer be the in the midst of his lively family – the lonely times he'll endure when he's gone away from his family for good. *I'll micht be a wee bit forlorn by lack o' companionship. I'm verra accustomed to support frae the family.* He subliminally registers the clink of crystal glasses, silver utensils being scraped along china plates by uncoordinated hands, and the bouncing propulsion of Malkie's rolling of a marble to Telford across the slick, polished mahogany table. As far as his awareness goes, the background racket could be coming from the middle of a war zone.

Adam has a difficult time warming up to new people, a hardship for someone who will be traveling by himself. He oftentimes feels slightly threatened and very uncomfortable by situations wherein he has to initiate or keep a conversation going with casual small talk. Folks find him rather standoffish and preoccupied when they first meet him, but nevertheless are drawn to him because of his striking handsomeness – tall, muscular build, fine features, and lovely auburn hair – as well as his kind spirit that shines through, without him having to voice a word. Once he's warmed up to people, they find him to be an extremely likeable lad, a caring person who would give the clothes off his back if it were necessary. Conversely, his affable, outgoing brother Henry delights in seeking out folk for lively, spontaneous chats on any subject matter, and draws attention and admiration from people wherever he goes, due to his charismatic personality and extraordinarily fine looks. Adam usually stands in the shadows of his brother until drawn out of his shell by Henry. As Adam eats, he reflects on the dismal possibility that he won't meet anyone out West for companionship, at least until he's settled. *Mebbe the West is only full o' ruthless fortune hunters I willna desire to ken*, he reflects. He pictures himself a loner, wandering through unknown, difficult terrain as a wraith that no one notices. People will be too busy looking for gold. He wonders if he should find himself in trouble, would there be anyone to help him? *If I get into any tribble whatsoever, I'll try to find me way back to Scotland.*

Henry sits at the table, toying with his food, mulling over the complications that have arisen inexplicably in his life. He keeps his head bent low, his hair over his face to cover his recent war wounds. He only wishes he could be with Annie at all times to protect her from the harshness of life in her disharmonious family. He is dismayed by her ignorant father, cruel and unsympathetic, treating her poorly as though a sinner, making her life miserable when it should be a joyful time, and threatening to give away their child. She is to be blessed with a beautiful bairn, his bairn, the mere thought of which sends shivers of elation down his spine. He reflects that he has no ability to change the mind of Annie's father, a man who is living in contradiction to his religious and moral beliefs. His only option is to leave for America with Annie and the bairn as soon as possible.

IV. Disturbing News Comes Knockin'

Tragically, the serenity of this evening will be short-lived. Something is building to disrupt the enviable togetherness of the Baird family. An unfathomable calamity, causing great emotional fervor, unlike that of any other to be bestowed upon a township, is unfolding on this bitterly cold and frosty October eve, in the year of Our Lord 1863, as the Wee Ones, Elor and Twixie, have predicted. The misfortune, marring the hearts of an entire Scottish community, will cause the Bairds great remorse and maximize their desire to cling to their close-knit and comforting family – at present, a loud, animated kinship, as the dishes are being cleared for dessert, hot tea, and cocoa.

A seemingly polite but persistent *tap, tap, tap* of windswept branches on the cloudy, floor-to-ceiling, diamond-mullioned paned window draws momentary attention to the temperamental winds at play, whipping and thrashing in wild abandonment, as the family enjoys a sense of snug separation from the intrusive elements of nature. The skies outside are intermittently luminous in depth from the dancing light of the moon and stars playing hide-and-seek through veils of drifting clouds. As if on a preordained itinerary, the clouds scud across the violet sky. The interplay of light with cloud is becoming increasingly sporadic with longer and longer interludes of complete dark shadowy cover and sudden flashes of light. A periodic maddening clamor can be heard from distant thunder.

To the large northern window that rises all the way to the ceiling, little Emma, sleepy and dreamy-eyed, whispers expectantly, "Come in," as she hears the persistent *tap, tap, tap*. She is anticipating her pixie friends coming – Twixie had mentioned that some of them might visit. She smiles wistfully when no one appears, continuing to gaze upward to view a low-slung crescent moon, resembling to her vivid imagination a lemon wedge sitting at the base of a shadowy circular picnic basket. To Emma, the wispy, illuminated clouds are the work of an angel's wand – the moon basket and the entire northern sky, an indigo hue of dusk, have been ceremoniously veiled with gauzy swirls of a purplish cloud cover in preparation of the arrival of her best friends, the Wee Folks. The orchestration in the sky is a show put on by heavenly beings. The angels are obviously behind the scenes, up above, making the clouds swirl around the moon, causing the crescent moon to jump up and down in its basket like a bouncing ball. Electric shivers travel up and down her spine. Emma is certain that the angels have a hand in the mystical display of heavenly magic that she is witnessing. Her friends, the Wee Ones, are working in concert with the angels to put on an exciting show, as she knows they are able to move around the skies at will and look down at the earth.

Were it not for the ethereal Wee Ones, astral spirits who fly about o'er hill and dale, guarding the land, Emma is convinced that the world would come to an end – there would be no one to hold vigil, especially at night. All creatures must slumber, she reflects, except for the nocturnal owls that she hears hoot-hooting in the wispy Scotch pine that scratches against her bedroom window; even dogs, sheep, and birds need to rest, and their wellbeing would be in peril without the Wee Ones to protect them.

The beautiful dreamscape that Emma rests her pensive eyes upon, in anticipation of a visit from her Wee Folks, is in reality one of the elemental volatile forces of nature, the harbinger of a cold winter ice storm brewing in the northern highlands, readying itself for an aggressive onslaught. In less than an hour's time, the icy tempest will flaunt its might with relentless fervor, dramatically and unabatedly, as it charges fiercely like a juggernaut of unconquerable Mongolian warriors over the quaint town of Bridge of Allan, leaving in its wake a frenzied, spiteful churning of icy waters in the River Allan. It will flow angrily under the bridge through the center of town, eddied in a pool of jagged broken trees limbs and other detritus that have been swept along. The aftermath of the storm will cause long-lived sorrow for all, and be a catalyst for dramatic change.

Malkie kicks Emma under the table, jarring her from her dream world and causing her glass of milk to topple over. White foamy liquid flows outward and downward onto the floor. Malkie watches it with glee – *a waterfall effect*, he thinks. Violet rushes over with a rag to beat the milk's flow to the floor.

"Ye numbskull, naebody's out thare but the bluidy wind!" croaks Malkie in an attempt to be authoritative, his voice wavering in fear.

"Ye cretin-heid, the Wee Folks said they're coming tonicht," sobs Emma. "The monsters o' the nicht are goin' to come and take ye away, and the Wee Folks willna protect ye," she taunts.

"Shush both o' ye, or to bed ye'll go," roars Adam Sr. "And speak the Queen's tongue or I'll whack ye bottoms." Though Adam Sr. has never whipped his children, the guttural threat of such an act is sufficient to gain order.

"Faither, you said ye instead o' you," corrects little Emma.

Adam Sr. clears his throat in resignation. "Emma, right you are. Thank *you*."

The family is clueless that this night, like any other night, will mark the beginning of dramatic changes to the family. Presently, parents Adam Sr. and Jean, the eldest children, and even more so Violet, the beloved housekeeper, have watched with unease the curtains being drawn incrementally on the Bairds' bucolic life. The large, growing brood – bursting at its seams – is stretching the family resources to the hilt.

A glaring indicator of change came the previous week with the unexpected and startling announcement by Adam Jr. of his intention to quit school a term before he graduates in order to take on an in-town carpentry apprenticeship at MacDuffy's Wheelwright Shop. This promulgation was not taken lightly by his parents, nor by doting Housekeeper Violet. Adam's mother took to her bed for an entire day with an unspecified malaise. Poor Violet's customary demonstrative displays of emotion became more erratic as she has juggled her domestic duties with lip-synched kitchen-chants throughout the next day, as if Adam's leaving school portended an evil omen, the beginning of the end of something that had to be eradicated. She took the children out for a walk in the woods with the hope of running into her spritely friends for some foresight regarding Adam's future, as they have known him since he was a bairn. The Wee Ones assured her that Adam was following his heart, which was an admirable thing, and that he'd be successful in his career choice.

Further rocking the boat and troublesome to the elders is the burgeoning talk amongst Adam, Henry, and Telford of their prospective travel to America. Back-and-forth pre-prandial dialogue of travel plans has segued to high-flying boasts of acquisitions of great wealth on the vast American frontier – the land of gold and silver – where jobs are aplenty in the mines, and railways are being laid down at an unstoppable rapid pace across the continent to provide easy access to the great territory. Unlike the economy of Scotland, which has been in a recession for many years, with jobs few and far between, the newspapers have reported that the West has an unprecedented record of great fortunes being made, which impressionable readers have translated to mean that most everyone is making good money who has the gumption to travel out to the newly opened territory. For the Baird family, the deadly destruction to come from the unprecedented storm in Bridge of Allan will set these half-gelled dreams into motion.

To top off all discomfitures – indeed a large, looming elephant in the room, an unnerving alteration to the family's status quo – is the humongous scandal of happy-go-lucky Henry. The Baird parents have been tight-lipped regarding their son's imbroglio, as they are understandably shocked and attempting to get their bearings, wading through a vast unchartered territory of their own. Their parenting skills have been put to the test in attempting to deal with this untenable dilemma so it will have a workable outcome to save their son, Annie MacGivens, and their future bairn from lives of hardship. There are times that Jean's fears for her son can't be held at bay – she is often awakened by nightmares of a young family ending up in one of those ghastly work houses in the Edinburgh slums. Adam Sr.'s even-minded, analytical nature, wherein he believes there is a solution to all matters arising in life, is put to the test when he observes Henry, only sixteen years of age, acting like the child that he regards him to be, as evidenced by his immature behavior in the handling of his pregnant girlfriend, saying he's taking her and the bairn to America. At more tranquil times, as tonight, when the family is all together enjoying a comforting meal, a more positive mindset emerges, a needed though temporary respite; the senior Bairds, relaxing over their claret wine, regard Henry in a better light. He is, after all, their lucky child, who has an uncanny knack for coming out on top, no matter what his foibles and the precarious situations he's always getting into. Henry is carrying on tonight with his usual good-natured affability, which helps maintain their positive outlook, a necessary equanimity that benefits the family as a whole.

"Adam, I take it you're content workin' at the shop longer hours?" inquires Adam Sr. "An admirable trade you've selected." Adam comes to attention abruptly, having to take his mind off a very pleasant daydream. He's galloping across the wide-open plains of the American frontier on a beautiful black stallion, with majestic purple mountains in the backdrop, as he approaches a beautiful crystalline blue lake. He decides that this might be a good time to make his announcement.

"Aye, Faither, 'tis a good trade, and I'll be makin' decent wages, but I willna remain in employment at the shop for long. For now, earning a fair wage is necessary for the family's wellbeing and wi' Grandfaither ailing," he responds hesitantly, annoyed that he's not saying what he meant to say regarding his departure.

"Adam, you must return to school as soon your Grandfaither's recovered," interjects his mother, with a concerned tone to her voice. "You're only to work at the shop and aid Grandfaither on the farm for a few months."

"Education's a luxury, Mum, not a necessity. Will I need further learnin' for the life I'm to lead on the frontier o' the West? I plan to depart for Glasgow to seek employment in a few months' time, and then off to America on a steamer, workin' me way West." The words rush out of his mouth freely in a surge of atypical fluency, uncharacteristic of him, as though a faucet's been turned on.

"Nonsense! What kind o' rubbish am I hearing? Most certainly, ye'll pursue your education, Adam!" exclaims Jean in a ragged voice, without her customary subtlety and diplomacy. "Ye need more education as ye need the Lord's Prayer, to keep ye on a righteous path, as a compass to a moral, productive life! This talk o' goin' out West is a harebrained, immature scheme. 'Tis a dangerous land o' ruffians looking for an easy way to gain riches without hard work, full o' savages that despise intruders," she exclaims vociferously.

This is the first time Adam has mentioned his intent to leave, and is appalled that the news is being taken by his mother with so much rancor.

"Mum, naething beats experience wi' varied cultures to teach me the ways o' the world. Aren't people from ither worlds God's children as well? I desire to go places, view extraordinary sights, and shake the hands o' people o' different cultures. In America, there're settlers from all o'er the world. The Western experience will educate me much regardin' the true reality o' life on this planet, and how to become the type o' man I aspire to be."

"Adam, ye canna be serious! 'Tis just idle talk, a wild fantasy at play in yer mind. Ye've ayeweys been verra imaginative but my most level-headed child." Jean doesn't regard any of her progeny as being anything but children, even though her eldest two are in their twenties and living away from home. "Ye belong in the fine, noble country ye're born into. Ye're a descendent of brave Scotsmen who shed thair blood so their children could dwell peacefully and prosper on thair land. Why on earth would God put ye down in Scotland only for ye to pick yersel up and put down yer roots somewhaur else eighteen years on? What a travesty o' a God-given path and an insult to yer ancestors!" Jean sighs, out of breath from her long diatribe. "And ye live on a beautiful ranch that'll someday be partly yours." Adam Sr. does not interject in this conversation, as his wife is saying in her own way everything that is necessary to get their son to see reason.

"Just reflect on this, Mum. I'll be makin' acquaintances wi' noble, red-blooded Indians. Will view them wi' me own two eyes, riding out on the plains on their beautiful horses. What a grand a picture that'll be!"

"He's verra likely to meet fancy sing-song lassies from Shanghai in America, or a fine-looking Indian squaw, or mebbe an Oriental concubine," japes Henry. "Or the prize o' the town, a voluptuous Madame Shangri-La, overseer o' one o' the trés posh establishments o' the West."

"Henry, my dear!" admonishes his mother, trying to hide her

amusement. "Hold yer tongue. Children are present!" Jean has a soft spot for her charming, extroverted son. She notices Henry's face for the first time, wincing in empathetic pain as she examines the swelling below his left eye, but does not remark on his injury. There is too much tumult going on around Henry to add fuel to the fire by bringing to attention another problem – probably dealing with Annie's father.

"What daes voluptuous mean?" inquires Malkie.

"What are sing-song girls?" inquires Emma. "Do they sing pretty bird songs like nightingales?"

"Henry!" calls out Adam Sr., as if beginning a roll call. "Under the taxing circumstances of your life, taxing to your parents and taken ever-so-lightly by you, I see, I'd lose that dafferie o' yours." Adam Sr. picks up his pipe as if it were a weapon. He's avoided the subject of Henry for far too long, and his son's comedic playfulness is a call to action.

"What's Faither talking of?" Malkie whispers to his mother sitting next to him, aware that he is crossing the line by insinuating himself in an adult conversation and will be sent to his room if his father hears.

"Aye, indeed, we've pressing business to discuss regardin' this dire predicament o' yours. After supper, we'll be meeting in my study. This debacle ye've climbed into tops every tomfoolery ye've iver set on us, lad, and ye've managed to lay down plenty of strife in your short lifetime. Time to face the music, laddie – life's not going to be fun and games for ye any longer. What's happened to yer face?" Adam Sr. notices Henry's appearance for the first time. "If I hear ye've been near MacGivens's, I'll have your hide. He's a man hell-bent on destroying ye for what ye've done."

"What on earth has Henry done this time?" inquires Emma. "Are ye in hot water again, Henry?" Emma looks over to Henry with a dismayed look as Malkie rolls his eyes and chuckles with glee. Henry winks back at her endearingly, at which time Emma notices that Henry's face is black and blue.

"Henry, what happened to yer face? Did ye fall down?"

"A private matter, my dears," responds Jean, with tears in her eyes. She looks over to Henry's wounds a second time, intently studying the extent of damage done to his cheek and eye.

"Why's Henry ayeweys in a tangle, Faither?" inquires Malkie. "He's grown up and we're wee children. We daena get into muddles as Henry," he spouts proudly in his squeaky prepubescent voice.

"Malkie, speak the Queen's English at this table, please, or to your room!" roars Adam Sr.

"A personal matter," reiterates Jean gently, looking at her young ones affectionately, glad that they are still innocent and protected from the dire complications in life coming from the world outside Drumdruils.

"Och, I know what's wrong wi' Henry," says Malkie. "Lassie problems! All the lassies are efter Henry acause he's so funny and flirts a lot, and he loves to show off!"

"Once again, Malkie," reprimands his father hotly, "'tis not your affair. Do I have to pound this into your noggin o'er and o'er to speak the Queen's English in this house? Mind your manners and keep your nose directed to the affairs that concern ye. Matters o' childhood, not grownup affairs, are your only concern!"

As the family sits at the large candlelit mahogany table after relishing one of Cook's culinary masterpieces – a roast lamb supper with mint jelly and gravy, mashed turnips and rutabaga, and tender sweet baby peas and tomato preserves from the garden – a frantic, loud banging on the front door resonates throughout the room, which sets everyone's nerves on edge. Emma imagines that the storm is on their doorstep asking to come in, for the Wee Ones would not enter through a door but magically appear in the kitchen in Violet's presence. Malkie jumps up spontaneously and starts for the foyer at a racing speed, braking just centimeters away from the door. He opens it to young Duncan Mackenzie's rain-swept, burly frame towering over him. Malkie has to bend his head back to take in the pudgy folds of Duncan's round, ruddy face crumpled up in distress. He ushers the leviathan twenty-year-old into the dining room, wherein Duncan divulges in slurred, choppy speech – the result of alcohol as well as his natural way with words – that he and the men from all over, some of whom he has been with at the local pub, were brought together to form a search party. Haltingly and in a circuitous way, he relays how many men and dogs have come together and where their team plans to start looking first. The family waits patiently for more forthcoming information, trying to piece together what is going on from his disjointed words. They gesture with their hands for Duncan to elaborate.

"The emergency system is in place. 'Tis a real emergency! Alarm bells are soundin' in town."

"What emergency, Duncan? Spit it out, please, lad!" blares Adam Sr., his patience and politeness wearing.

Duncan blurts out quickly in exasperation, "Wee Mary MacLaine and yer Janet are gone missin'!"

When the alarming news is taken in, the family is left stunned, momentarily in disbelief.

"What? Are ye sure?" Jean and Violet voice this simultaneously. The lasses should be at the MacLaines' at this hour and they can't for the life of them construe what could have happened to detain them. The girls are very accustomed to their egg-collecting chore and the route they take, and would have been finished long before dark.

The family learns from Duncan's rambling talk that Mary and Janet didn't return home after retrieving eggs. They were supposed to return from Davidson's farm, their last stop, but didn't make it home after picking up the Davidsons' eggs. The family becomes panic stricken, everyone rising from their seats.

"We've search parties rounded up and ready to go," repeats Duncan, as he gestures for the grown males in the family to come with him at once so they can begin.

Approximately ten men from nearby ranches, and four bloodhounds belonging to Mr. Galway, are shuffling their feet in nervous anticipation outside. Adam Sr., Henry, and Adam grab their coats and rush out to join in the search party. Malkie attempts to follow them out, but is held back by Adam Sr.

"You're too young, laddie," says his father sternly. "Ye and Telford help Violet get the bairns to their bedrooms."

It will be necessary for the search parties to cover a vast acreage of farms in Bridge of Allan as soon as possible, for the torrential storm is bearing down menacingly, rendering visibility poor. The girls have been missing for over an hour. Immediate action is of the upmost importance. From their bedrooms overhead, the younger children hear the urgent calls of the search teams as they split into smaller groups and go in various directions.

"Janet, Mary, are ye out there? Mary! Janet! Answer us if ye can," calls out Duncan as soon as he steps outside, prematurely, yet riling the men into action.

Anxious, frightened, wide-eyed, miniature silhouettes are pressed up against the paned bedroom windows, smudging and steaming up the windowpanes, appearing as wavering frosty wraiths from the outside, unwilling to get in their beds despite a stern coaxing from Violet. They gaze fixedly at the orange bobbing glows of the villagers' lanterns that dance like balls of fire.

The town's emergency system consisting of word of mouth conveyance – door-to-door in the town and ranch-to-ranch in the hinterland – has been put into immediate effect. Designated officials are responsible for the organization of parties and ensuring everyone has been made aware. The town's church bells can be heard clanging in the prescribed number of rings to indicate an emergency, a call for the on-call search teams, who practice every few months alongside Bridge of Allan Fire Department, to congregate in Town Square. Townspeople living up in the hills and on the outskirts of town, as well as on the ranches that cannot hear the bells, have been notified. Townspeople and farmers from the neighboring ranches as far as Dunblane have congregated at the designated meeting place. Men in the Town Square are being organized into smaller groups and sent out on this cold night to cover all the outlying woodlands, hillocks, and moors between Bridge of Allan and Dunblane, in the unlikely event that the lassies might have wandered way off their prescribed path, perhaps confused as to which way to go due to the poor visibility brought on by the storm. The ten men in the Baird search party have been designated to take the route that the girls would ordinarily travel on and fan out from there. The Bairds are to visit the farms that they collect from.

They learn that Mary and Janet walked initially to the MacLaines' house to pick up egg baskets before starting their journey. The girls are known to have set out for the neighboring farms at approximately two o'clock, but didn't return back to the MacLaines' at half past four as expected. Their customary route is collecting eggs from three adjoining farms, each less than a half mile apart, ending at the Davidson farm. They were possibly stopping by the Graham farm along the route for a treat, to return via the same path, a distance of one and a half miles each way. Mary has been retrieving eggs every other day since she turned eight years old, three years ago, and Janet has been with her on many occasions.

Mary's parents became alarmed and went out in search of the girls as signs of a strong storm moving in from the highlands to the north began materializing in the form of gusty turbulence at around five o'clock. By that time the lasses were tardy in their expected arrival time home by thirty minutes, and it was getting dark early. The MacLaines had first assumed that the lasses were late because they'd stopped for a visit at the Graham farm for cookies and milk and to play with their new puppies, as Mary had mentioned to Janet they could visit the new little pups after picking up eggs. The Grahams are an elderly couple who no longer farm and love to have young visitors. But the girls were not at the Grahams, had never been, nor at the Davidsons, where they had done their last pick-up of eggs, and no one had spotted them on the road. The fierce ice storm blew in quickly at around five, a juggernaut of blasting cold air and ice, with winds of unprecedented speed and force.

The men search throughout the night despite the freezing coldness of the storm, but to no avail. They persist in the intrepid conditions, risking frostbite to their noses and cheeks, though wrapped up like mummies with their wool scarves.

As dawn approaches, the search party with the Bairds sights the lassies in a tranquil scene of two slumbering figures in a pasture of sheep, only an eighth of a mile from the Davidsons' farm. At first glimpse, a sense of relief passes over the men, though fleetingly. The lasses appear to be resting peacefully like slumbering nymphs – their blonde, wispy locks of hair fanning out over the hay. They are cuddled up close against the sheep, their wooly coats offering them protection from the elements. Upon closer examination, a sense of alarm grips and squeezes the hearts of all, plummeting spirits. As they close in on the supine, golden-haired girls, it is painfully apparent the lasses succumbed to the frigid night temperature. Their sweet faces have the glossy alabaster cast of angelic statues in the cemetery, but with an aberrant bluish tinge to their lips and noses. Adam and Henry stare down at Mary and Janet in disbelief, for they had been playing with the lasses only hours before, then so vibrantly alive. *These alabaster statues in repose cannot possibly be our lasses*, thinks Adam. *We are dreaming this.* Adam starts to run over to rouse Janet to wakefulness, but Adam Sr., stone-faced and mortified, holds him back. The boys begin sobbing helplessly.

"Dumb, blithering eediot sheep," sobs Adam Jr., falling to the ground on his knees in despair. "Why daena the bluidy beasts keep them warm? Wi' any sense they'd hiv covered them wi' thair bodies." Henry reacts to the sight of the girls by fleeing the horrid scene; he runs aimlessly across the frosty fields as if being chased by a phantom ghost.

Adam Sr. orders Adam Jr. to follow his brother. Adam Jr. starts up after Henry, tears flooding his eyes being dispersed by the wind as he runs. Adam Sr. stays to tend to his dear daughter and Mary. The lasses will be taken to the mortuary for the night. Janet and Mary being best friends, who would have remained best friends for a lifetime in this close-knit township, are bound in death eternally. They will, in all probability, be buried side by side in the graveyard of the cathedral in Dunblane.

The boys are in shock, adrenaline spurring them on, but after a half-mile of sprinting they collapse to the ground exhausted. Finally catching their breath, they stand up and look back longingly in the direction of the sheep pasture, wanting to go back and stand vigil over Janet, but know they'd be unwelcome. There is nothing they can do but head for home and come to grips with the painful reality that peace and wellbeing in the lives of the Baird family have been obliterated permanently. Adam's throat is tight and aching, but he is resigned to act the part of a grown man in charge and inform those at home of the tragedy. Breaking the hearts of the family, especially Mum and Violet, is going to be excruciating. He'd sooner take the place of Janet and be the one lost to them than bear this news. Henry is having a hard time getting his legs to work properly, stumbling like a wayward drunkard, but Adam pushes him gently onward towards home. They find themselves at the front door all too soon. They hesitate, entering tentatively like uninvited interlopers, unwelcome messengers of unwanted news. The necessity to articulate is unnecessary, as the news of tragedy is expressed quite adequately on their faces. Adam utters only one word: "Frozen." Violet and Jean go down on their knees, as though the air has been sucked out of them, beseeching a higher power to help them. The boys guide them to the table in front of the fire, and they sit for a spell staring into space, saying nothing.

Jean stays slumped at the kitchen table, expressionless, numb, lost in utter desperation, staring at the fire. Violet, uncharacteristically quiet, gets up to prepare warm chocolate milk, with a tincture of herbs and whiskey for the children and Jean, to ease their shock and make them drowsy for sleep. As she stands over the fireplace, stirring the liquid balm, she launches into a meditation in an effort to communicate with her woodland friends for insight as to whether this was the horrible event Elor had portended. The Wee Ones are busy with the storm rescue, and she will not receive any knowledge of their whereabouts for the next couple of days. Violet elects to go upstairs to tell the children of the loss of their sister. Adam follows her up. Henry stays with his mother and tries to console her by rubbing her back gently.

Emma displays what's assumed to be denial when word of Janet's demise reaches her. She burrows her face into a pillow, her hands covering her ears, stowing herself away from the suffering around her, chanting a verse of good tidings repetitively. As the chocolate milk is passed around she pops up out of her self-imposed refuge to take refreshment.

"The Wee Ones saved Janet," declares Emma adamantly. "The Wee People, Twixie and Elor, came to me and told me that she was saved from the cauld. They knew the lassies were in trouble. A group of Wee People came out o' the hillocks when they realized they'd lost their way. They fed the lassies whiskey to warm them and rounded up the sheep to snuggle against them. Mary daedna wake up acause she was assigned a greater job, to be an angel. They saw her climb up in the sky towards the heavens. The Wee People bid her farewell and said she was happy to go. They say Janet's alive, but asleep acause o' whiskey, not acause o' the freeze."

"Emma, no, dear, they found Janet and Mary thegither. They were both lying next to the sheep in the pasture," says Adam gently.

"No, that canna be," replies Emma. "Janet's alive. Ye'll see. I know my sister. I feel her now. She's still down here." Emma points to the ground emphatically. "Mary's gone away to Heaven though."

Emma emphasizes her certainty by pointing to the sky. "The Wee People told me so." She folds her arms over the chest defiantly and says nothing more.

The children want to believe Emma, but Malkie and Telford are skeptical, though they do not tell Emma that she is being foolish, for then all hope would be lost. They fidget uncomfortably in their chairs as they drink their warm milk, waiting for Faither to return with news. Quickly the milk causes the desired effect – drowsy and heavy-lidded, Violet leads them to their beds.

Later that morning, Adam and Henry are down in their cellar bedroom, lying on their bunk beds, sleepless, crying into their pillows, when they hear Adam Sr.'s deep baritone voice upstairs talking to an individual with a soft, melodious voice they don't recognize. Adam and Henry leap up out of bed and climb the back stairs, two at a time, to find Dr. Crawford bent over a bundle of thick blankets on the davenport. On further inspection, and much to their consternation and horror, they discern a small form covered underneath. Dr. Crawford adjusts the blanket so the face of wee Janet appears.

"Is that Janet?" asks Henry incredulously. "Is she goin' to lie here for the day?" he spouts out in wonderment. Initially, he resists looking at his dead sister and facing the certainty that Janet lies in eternal sleep, but abruptly turns and stares at her. He is soothed a bit by the appearance of death having normalcy, a peaceful beauty to it.

"She looks to be moving a wee bit. Is that normal in death?" inquires Adam Jr.

"No," Adam Sr. exclaims excitedly, "she's verra much alive, laddies! Dr. Crawford found a slight pulse and a shallow breath when he examined her in the pasture. We warmed her immediately with a campfire made in the field. I carried her to the Davidsons' and soaked her in a verra hot bath. She'll need to stay by the fire all day and be tended to by Dr. Crawford, but the good doctor says she's going to make a full recovery. She's breathing well now, and there appears to be no chilblains – no fear of losing any fingers or toes," he clarifies. "Janet was lucky indeed. The mother ewe and her lambs huddled up against her, providing warmth to aid in her survival. Poor Mary was not so lucky. She was found lying a wee distance away, removed from the warmth of the creatures."

Late in the morning, the children come downstairs to find Janet on the couch, and Dr. Crawford snoozing in the blue velvet wing-backed chair next to her. Adam, Henry, and Jean are sitting on the couch snoozing as well.

"I knew the Wee People were right," proclaims Emma. "See! She's not deid. Her lips are moving. She's snoring!" Emma lets out a chuckle, but then she remembers Mary and looks up out the window to the sky. In a husky voice, she declares with stoicism, "Mary's wi' the angels, I'm certain."

"Perhaps this means that the Lord is rounding up bairns for special spots in Heaven? Might he be in search o' friends for Mary?" asks Telford inquisitively. Being of an analytical nature, Telford's looking for patterns and reasons for what has occurred.

"No, me dear, ye and yer brothers and sisters will be fine," replies Violet. "Mary's special. She was picked to be a special messenger o' God, an angel of sorts."

"But what if God needs more bairns?" inquires Malkie shakily. He is slumped over on the edge of his seat, his big blue eyes rounded gravely.

"Trust me, lads and lassies," replies Adam Jr. vehemently, "he'll not take more bairns. God's not going to be that cruel." Adam utters his remark with conviction, though in the near future, as a coffin maker at the wheelwright shop, he will, many times, in great despair, come face-to-face with the seemingly random, merciless workings of the Almichty when it comes to children. Malkie doesn't look convinced in the least. He cocks his head to one side, his silky, light brown hair covering one eye, trying to conceal his emotions. A sweet, sensitive lad who is very engaging and funny, pleasing to be around most of the time despite his rambunctiousness, Malkie's regarded by his family to have just a tad hantle o' spunk. Under all the nervous boyish energy is something else – an innate apprehensiveness. Violet and his mother have been aware of this from early on in his life. Malkie is the child who insists that his door be open at night to let in a wee bit o' light, and the closet door must remain shut at night, as there's bound to be a hidden monster lurking in the dark. He'll never ever enter a dark room without a candle to light his way and someone to go before him. As a bairn he was scared of the wind if it blew too hard, and as a toddler, the ordinary creaks and groans of the old house would cause him to cower in a torrent of tears under the sofa. Violet and Jean, in observing his sensitive nature, could never figure out why Malkie was timid of the everything in the world, while his siblings were so fearless, taking on life with wild abandon, as if every new, daunting unknown lurking in their environment, however scary or dangerous, was to be challenged with gusto and conquered. Adam, Henry, and Telford had a contest as youngsters, wherein the one who could stay in a dark closet the longest with the door shut at night would be proclaimed the "Bravest Baird," and the winner could select a prized marble from each of their treasured collections. It was a toss-up as they all, on consecutive nights, had fallen asleep in the closet and had to be awakened in the morning.

"Daed the lassies get caught in deevil's field like Tam o' Shanter?" inquires Telford, looking for a theory as to why a youngster would die so young. "Did Mary and Janet cross a field full o' witches, warlocks, and murderers?"

"Aye," replies Malkie, "they must've walked into a deevil's field." He looks around for concurrence, as if this fact might definitely explain all evil happenings in the world and limit bad happenings to a particular area to avoid.

"No," answers Emma with certainty. "'Twas not what happened. Elor said they walked through a sheep pasture acause o' bein' lost.

Cauld's what caused them to lie down wi' the sheep and go to sleep. So cauld they weren't scared. Elor says it wasn't the deevil."

"Why daedna Elor save Mary?" inquires Telford. "Why daedna he find them soon enough? He's a magical fairy who's supposed to aid people." Telford doesn't see fairies any longer but remembers them well from when he was small.

"The Almichty works in mysterious ways," replies Violet solemnly.

"I daena understand at all," says Malkie resignedly. "We must live verra carefully from now on. I want to sleep down in the cellar wi' Henry and Adam for protection. Telford canna protect me by himself if the deevil comes."

"Malkie," says Adam, "ye've to be brave! Stay wi' Telford. He'll protect ye. If ye're awakened in the night and really scared, go sleep wi' the lassies."

"The lassies canna protect me if I call out. They're verra weak!"

"Deevil isna coming efter the lassies, Malkie," says Emma with bravado. "We're safer than the laddies acause the deevil fears our powers. We're stronger than the laddies."

"All the same, I desire to sleep downstairs wi' Adam and Henry." Malkie is ordered to stay in his own room, for they know he'll be just as scared in the cold, dark cellar.

The first couple of weeks after Mary's death, the children are listless, bowled over with grief, and stay close to the house, fearing they, too, will die at the whim of the Almichty. The resilience and optimism of youth take over, as if they've been sprinkled with magic fey dust by the Wee Ones. Eventually, the children – all but Malkie – come to the view death as a celestial happening, circling outside of their lives, like the rising of the sun and moon, or transiting stars, something magical to be in awe of. Through imaginary play and fantasy, the children cope with the loss of Mary, creating an alter world where she exists, somewhere up in a celestial wonderland, a place where it is conceivable that she's riding atop a star, or living in a doll mansion made of star prisms. They continue to mourn for Mary, though, and are fearful of death at night when readying themselves for sleep, for this is a time when children's imaginations tend to visualize devilish monsters coming up from the fiery interior of the earth, to hide in closets and under beds, in anticipation of an opportunity to pounce. Malkie has a hard time sleeping in his own bed, and sneaks from the sunroom he shares with Telford into the room of his sisters after they are asleep, often climbing into bed with Emma. Apparently, he believed his sisters when they assured him that they were a force to be reckoned with against the devil. Emma takes pity on him and lets him sleep with her when he is frightened.

"I wanna visit Mary, but I daena want to go up to Heaven. Mary must come to Drumdruils to visit us. I know she shall," says Emma.

"Emma, Mary willna no come back," replies Adam, bowing his head as he gets up from the table and walks towards the door on his way to work. "But Janet will be back to her ol' self soon. We're verra lucky she survived."

"Aye, Mary will come," says Emma. "Mary canna stay away foriver. There's naebody to play wi' her in Heaven. Only ither angels, and they're too busy to play wi' while doin' their angel work."

"Och," says Telford. "Daena ye know? Scores o' children get sent up there. Hiv ye na viewed graves in the kirkyard? She'll hiv plenty o' ithers to play wi'."

"Are there ither children in the graveyard whaur Mary will be buried?" inquires Emma.

"Aye! Scores and scores o' them," replies Malkie, his hands outstretched. "Telford and I explored the graveyard on All Hallow's Eve. Creepy! We saw will-o'-wisps in the grasses outside the kirkyard lit up from the colored glass o' the church windows. 'Tis whaur the ghosts and goblins tread a' night. Right efter Violet read us Robert Burns's Hallowe'en Tale, we went looking and spied ghosts floatin' o'er the air like hobby lanterns, flying low amongst the graves," says Malkie with bravado. He fails to tell them he was so scared that he will never go back again, and the only reason he went was to protect his older brother, Telford, whom he didn't want to die alone in a graveyard full of ghosts.

Emma brushes aside macabre thoughts from her mind and turns back to her tea table.

"Will ye come down for tea, Mary?" she inquires, ignoring her brothers and looking up to the sky through the large window. She sits patiently at her little table with her miniature blue and white china tea set laid out on the yellow oak table, as a hostess waiting for her guest of honor to arrive.

"Mary's coming," says Emma adamantly. "The Wee Ones tauld me she's just a hair's breadth away, and I heard her sweet wee voice o'er the wind." Emma has a place set for Janet next to Scruffy Bear. Scruffy Bear has been Janet's companion since toddler years, and he lives up to his name.

"She's not comin'," croaks Malkie. "She's gone to whaur the sky ends, and canna get back to us iver. Her body's gone so 'tis like thare's naething to wear, like a featherless bird." Malkie is on the verge of tears and throws Scruffy Bear across the room to divert his pain.

"She could come wi' her angel's wings," insists Emma. "Her spirit's alive. The Wee Ones tauld me she's fine and dandy, and verra happy in a bonnie place whaur she loves to be. Malkie, there's more out there than ye can fathom, daena ye ken? So much ye daena understand acause you're an eediot."

"Ye mean to greet her ghost? Ye desire her ghost to come down here?" inquires Malkie incredulously, his face blanching at the thought. "A ghost will scare the living daylights oot o' ye."

"No, 'tis not her ghost. The whole o' Mary will come, wi' a new body just like her auld one. God will make her a new body, but wi' wings, like a new set o' clothes." Emma pours the tea for Ol' Scruffy Bear, retrieves him from the floor, and becomes ensconced in her make-believe world. Malkie and Telford give up on talk so they can munch the biscuits that Violet brought up for the tea party.

BOOK THREE

AFTERMATH OF THE GREAT STORM

Chapter One

I. Janet's Recovery

Janet is very weak the first couple of weeks after the ice storm. The children hover over her protectively, taking turns standing vigil at her bedside on the couch in the drawing room by the fire during the day to ensure she stays covered and warm. Malkie fears she will turn back into an ice statue. She sleeps a lot, and when she's awake, she has a far-off look in her eyes like a mummy. As days pass, she becomes stronger and her natural spontaneity returns, as evidenced by her teasing Malkie, pretending to be a frozen ballerina doing a pirouette. She can stay in this position for up to 10 minutes without tiring. Malkie is perturbed and usually shakes her out of her posture, causing her to fall to the floor giggling. She plays with the kittens, her dolls, or stuffed animals that are placed on her bed for her amusement. The children are assured she will be back to her old self in no time at all.

In many ways, Janet has dealt with the death of her friend far better than Malkie, who feels the menace of death lurking about him at all times. When Janet first found out that Mary had died, she had been consumed with the question of why she hadn't died alongside Mary, for they had planned so much fun together, and if she'd died alongside Mary, they could be doing all those things they planned to do in Heaven. She really had wanted to go with Mary and, early on, had felt a little jilted that she had been left behind, for she saw Heaven as a grand palace in the sky, far better than earth. One day after Janet has made a full recovery, Malkie asks her what it was like to be dead.

"I waesna deid, ye numbskull!" exclaims Janet, exasperated. "I was asleep."

"How do ye know ye waesna deid?" inquires Malkie.

"If I was deid, Malkie, I wadna be here right now talkin', ye eejit!"

Emma tells Janet that Mary will always be an angel, and this is how Janet views her deceased friend, and will view Mary for the rest of her life. In the years that follow, as Janet matures, being of a very pragmatic nature, she comes to believe that she was saved for a reason, that she is needed on earth for a mission (otherwise she would have been sent with Mary), which has made her intent on finding that purpose. She very often poses the question to Angel Mary as to what her role in life should be. She thinks in terms of the virtuous qualities of Mary and tries to emulate them. In this way, she has come up with an answer, through meditative reflections and inquiries to Mary, that her role is to help others less fortunate than herself. Her heart goes out to the infirm, the poor, and the hungry. This is what Mary would have wanted her to do, she is certain. In her own personal struggles in life, whenever Janet has a difficult challenge, she doesn't hesitate to ask of herself "What wad Angel Mary dae?"

The community will mourn Mary for months, and Janet will be without her best friend for the rest of her long life, always yearning to share her experiences with her best mate, especially on monumental occasions like her graduation and her wedding. Mary MacLaine will become the town's icon for the many innocent bairns not reaching adulthood. A little statue of her carrying an egg basket will be erected in Town Square next to Rob Roy's statue.

The story of the Baird boys' beloved farm, Drumdruils, and the miraculous survival of their sister, Janet, in an ice storm will travel with them to America and be passed down to their children and their children's children. Many of their descendants will visit Drumdruils and think of little Mary MacLaine. Some will look for her grave in the kirkyard of the beautiful Gothic cathedral in Dunblane amongst the many other children's graves, and wonder what it was like for parents to lose so many of their children to what are now viewed as minor ailments.

II. Fear Not, Malkie!

Malkie, more sensitive and fearful of the unknown than his siblings, is the child his parents and older brothers watch over protectively. He tends to lose his natural spunk when life gets unpredictable and scary. The death of a pet, as when their kitten, Paws, died last year, caused him to sob in his bed at night for a week. When Little Mary freezes in the sheep pasture, he does not cope well at all. His younger female siblings, Janet and Emma, come to terms with Mary's death through imaginative ways, inventing plays under the direction of Emma, highlighting Mary's daily existence as an angel's apprentice and holding many teas in her honor. Emma has talks with her Wee People friends about Mary, and learns that she is doing well and is very happy. She relays this to the other children, who halfway accept her word, especially Janet, who really wants to believe this. Everyone believes except Malkie. Telford adapts through the use of his rational mind, telling himself that no one knows what happens when one dies, and therefore Mary could be somewhere else in some other realm. Perhaps it was God's plan for her to live a short life and become nonexistent in bodily form, but perhaps she's still alive in spirit; or she might even be a ghost now, living by their sides but just invisible to them, or a bird in the sky, or even a tree. That life is a grand mystery gives him hope by not definitively pinning an absolute on Mary's demise. But poor Malkie, normally entertainingly zestful in his approach to life, a rough and tumble adventurous lad, becomes overly boisterous and wild around his siblings to cover up for his emotional turmoil after Mary's death. He refuses to accept that Mary is doing well in Heaven, or that her spirit is in a higher realm, which irritates Emma to no end.

"She's gone foriver, lassies!" he exclaims. "The deevil's taken her! Ye better watch oot."

To Malkie, death lurks everywhere, and it could be any time that the Grim Reaper will come and take them all away. The other children understand that Malkie is a little different in how he processes his world, yet as children they tend to act on whim, and find it irresistible to press his fear buttons just for the fun of it.

"You're the one that deevil's goin' to get, Malkie, acause you're the eejit who's in mischief most o' the time like Tam o' Shanter," declares Janet.

"Aye," teases Telford. "The deevil looks out for the verra bad laddies acause they're the easiest to catch acause they're in the wrong place at the wrong time." Malkie starts to squirm like an animal caught in a trap, and Telford tries to placate him by amending his prognosis. "I'm just joshing, Malkie. Deevil's not goin' to bother wi' ye. Yer basically a good laddie, most o' the time."

"Aye, the deevil's not goin' to bother us at all," quips Emma, "but Malkie, ye should try to be good acause God may desire ye for his special work like Mary."

This sets Malkie off in a tirade to cover his fear that he may die sooner than later. He throws dolls and stuffed animals around the room, turns over the table where Janet and Emma are having an imaginary tea party for Mary, and storms out of the room.

The children cease their baiting of Malkie after that. They sense that Malkie is never going to come to terms with the loss of their childhood friend.

Confides Emma to Violet, "He's na acting himself. Malkie thinks he's goin' to die soon. What if Malkie niver is himself again?"

"Och, dinna fash. Ye must giv him plenty o' love. Help him to see that life's a beautiful gift, no somethin' to be lived in fear," says Violet. "Mebbe take more o' an interest in his frog and insect collections and talk to him in a gentle, understanding manner about his concerns."

Malkie, when the sun is bright and all in the world seems calm and glorious, when he feels safe from harm, will often set off by himself to visit Mary's grave in the kirkyard of the church and try to make sense out of what has happened, even praying to the Almichty to save him from a fate like Mary's.

III. Telford Baird, a Carefree Soul

Telford lives in the shadows of his two older brothers, Henry and Adam, and that's perfectly fine with him. Not being the focus of attention as a middle child gives him leeway to do what he wants. No one worries about even-keeled Telford, or even misses him when he goes off by himself to hike in the woods for hours on end, as he is doing today, enjoying the beauty and tranquility that the land provides. He sees death all around him in the natural world, and his analytical mind wonders if humans just cease to exist after death, as animals that decay in the ground and contribute richness to the soil. He has thought about this often, and has given consideration to the idea that humans could be different than other animals, that there might be an afterlife for them because they have advanced, complex minds and spirits. He reflects on all of this as he buries a young sparrow that he has found lying on the path. *Better giv him a proper burial, just in case there is a heaven for wee birds. Daena want him to be eaten up by vultures.*

Being younger than Adam and Henry by three and four years, respectively, and a thirteen-year-old, he is not given major responsibilities on the ranch as his older brothers are. He is the bridge between Henry and Adam and his younger siblings, Janet, Emma, and Malkie, the mediator of family quarrels due to his ability to placate emotions with positive, empathetic words and a kind, generous spirit. No one but Violet and Jean are aware of these fine qualities in Telford, as he is very subtle – the laddie who is taken for granted by his siblings, owing to his noncompetitive and unassuming presence. He possesses a mixture of his older brothers' traits, Adam's pragmatism and love of books and learning and Henry's love of people, though he lacks the wit and charm of Henry, and does not focus on intellectual pursuits as much as Adam, owing to his love of nature and the time he spends outdoors hiking. Telford reveres his older brothers and will continue to admire them his entire life, even after their deaths. With the development of his adult character, he sets a life path that will create a fine legacy for the Bairds by becoming the family historian. He will live the longest and pass down the diaries, letters, and pictures of his brothers, sisters, and their families to the next generation. He is also the Baird with a writer's bent. He will be a rancher for a short time, and then find his true calling as a journalist and writer of the natural world.

Chapter Two

I. The Coffin Maker — 25 October 1863

She's gone! forever, gone! The King of terrors
Lays his rude hands upon her lovely limbs
And blasts her beauties with his icy breath

– John Webster's poem from *Appius and Virginia*

Two days after Mary's death, Adam rubs the sawdust from his eyes and bends into his woodworking project. His craft as an apprentice casket maker/wheelwright at Thomas MacDuffy's Woodshop and Undertaking Shop, where the construction of wheels, carts, and coffins takes place, is a backbreaking business that requires precision and manual dexterity. To keep up with daily work assignments, Adam must push himself to near exhaustion. By the end of each day his back is a ball of knots and he is bent over like an arthritic old man. This has been a prized afterschool, part-time job for the past three years, but today he's started a nine-hour day at MacDuffy's on top of the couple of pre-dawn hours he puts in on his grandfather's farm. It's been two days since Mary's death and the meeting with Miss Carroway to inform her of his intentions to withdraw from school. Ambivalent feelings about his choice to drop his education come to the surface as he thinks of his younger brothers and sisters trooping back to the little stone schoolhouse without him. He has made a loose promise to his parents that he will restart school in the autumn, though he plans to be on his way to America by then.

The mood in the town of Bridge of Allan is very somber. The storm, like an evil phantom, passed through quickly in a mere night, leaving a heavy run-off of water on the roads, messy piles of downed trees, flooding to some of the businesses downtown, and destruction of livestock and crops. The river has finally begun to recede. The devastation from the storm will take many weeks to clean up completely. Adam grieves in his own way – holding his emotions at bay until he lies down to a fitful night's sleep. The world through his eyes is dull, flat, and colorless. Nature in its bleak grey-and-white wintry tones complies with his perception, casting a dreary backdrop to his sullen mood. Since finding little Mary and Janet in the sheep pasture, life has returned to a semi-normal rhythm, but has left in its wake the residual effects of the storm: death, destruction, and uncertainty of life's goodness.

Adam puts on a brave face at work, pretending that all is well, but, internally, he is emotionally crippled by the aftershock of the tragedy – his little sister, Janet, was only a hair's breadth from death, which makes him question the certainty of anyone staying alive in such a cruel world. The randomness and thoughtlessness of death in its striking down a beautiful child like wee Mary, who was not able to be saved in time but should have been, isn't lost on Adam. The wood he uses to make coffins, a medium he once loved to work with, is now a harsh reminder of death; he equates the sweet, musty redolence of pine with what is to lie inside. Adam is stricken with numbing thoughts of what decay does to a human body.

"Niver shoud o' happened in the first place. The wee lassies shoud hiv been supervised more carefully and na hiv been traipsing round the countryside at twilight," he murmurs while he works. "What kind o' Almichty lets a sweet child freeze to death?" he inquires under his breath as he looks down at the lathe.

He has turned away from acknowledging the existence of God. The Almighty he worships in church every Sunday is a figurehead with no spiritual significance to his life. Whistling under his breath helps calm his shattered nerves and steadies his mind to concentrate. Adam has been assigned the grim task of building Mary's coffin. His foremost desire is for the lass to have a beautiful wooden coffin to rest in for an eternity. Even though the town is in mourning for the entire week – the schoolhouse and most businesses are closed either for repair or out of respect for the death of Mary and three others killed in the storm – the business of building coffins is brisk. The shops that have stayed open are meeting places for townspeople to hash over the sad events from the storm. To keep his mind off the wee lass to be placed in the box that he is building, he pretends that he's making a cedar chest. Ordinarily, Adam enjoys his craft and has a true talent for it. Lathing wood to exact dimensions requires precise calculations for which he has an aptitude, and the joining of wood with nails, nuts, and bolts is a learned skill that takes great dexterity and concentration. He normally loves the smell of freshly milled wood, and the velvety feel of smooth-grained pine boards on his fingertips, but today the scent of wood and sawdust conjures up morbid thoughts, and he is having trouble concentrating on the measurements.

As soon as Adam has completed Mary's coffin, Mr. MacDuffy asks him to deliver the coffin to the undertaker's and pick up the body of Mary, and then ride out to the MacLaines' farm for the wake being held that afternoon. Mr. MacLaine has requested that Mary in her spirit be present at her wake. "The MacLaines," MacDuffy tells Adam, "want their child to spend one more night with their family before offering her back to the Almighty. Mr. Watson, the undertaker, will then pick up the coffin tomorrow at the MacLaines' house for the funeral service at the cathedral."

Adam hitches the old Bay horse, Jackie, to the shop wagon and rides out to the MacLaines' farm at two o'clock. He goes at a slow pace so as to not jar Mary around in her eternal resting place. He finds himself in a one-man, one-horse procession. The townspeople on Henderson Street stop to solemnly wave or salute Mary's casket. Gentlemen take off their hats, and some pay their respects with the sign of the cross as the wagon passes by. The old horse, Jackie, now and then raises his head regally; seemingly, he senses that this is a solemn ceremonial occasion. He maintains a steady clip-clop, not lingering along the path for bits of delectable weedy greens, as is his custom, which usually requires a stern pulling up on the reins.

After a time, the wagon turns down a long country road lined with grand old elms that give comfort to Adam in their graceful solidness. He proceeds slowly, still in processional mode, to the front of the MacLaines' house. Mason MacLaine opens the door of the large clapboard farmhouse expectantly as Adam pulls up to the front. He comes out and eyes the coffin in the back gravely. Adam steps out of the wagon hesitantly, at loss for words, and so greets Mason with a solemn nod, as though he is about to pray. Mason's eyes are red and puffy, and his overpowering whiskey-breath causes Adam to reflexively take a step back. Mason does not look like the rugged, muscled farmer of last week, but like an old man in declining years, now dressed up in the finery of his red and green plaid kilt for this somber occasion. Adam musters up enough courage to tell the grieving farmer in a hushed tone that Mary rests in the back of his wagon, in a wording that could be misconstrued to indicate that the child is napping after a long journey, if the raw facts were not known. Several younger men come out of the house soberly, their eyes averted to the ground, as if on cue, to retrieve Mary – not really Mary at all, but just a wooden box. The men are all dressed in their church-going kilts, as this shows respect for the family to be decked out to the hilt in their clan attire. The casket is carried into the house and placed gently on a makeshift pulpit in the parlor by the hearth, a candelabra housing white blazing candles and a silver cross set to the side. Juniper cuttings with blue berries, and holly with wine-colored berries, are draped along the wall backing the pulpit. The coffin is covered with a wool damask plaid cloth of predominantly reds, with blue and green stripes, a weave of the MacLaine clan by an elderly woman who appears to be in charge of the guests and food.

"Thank ye kindly for comin'," says Mr. MacLaine to Adam, shaking his hand vigorously, after the task at hand is completed, as if Adam had surmounted an impossible feat. Mason's hand is shaking as he brings out a schilling. Adam politely declines the token, but Mr. MacLaine insists by taking his hand and folding the coin into his palm.

"Laddie, stay for a wee bit o' refreshment. The neighbors have been so kind in bringing food and drink, enough for a holiday feast for the entire village. Ye'll have to excuse Mrs. MacLaine's absence. She's lyin' down in her room, verra exhausted from the grief. She can visit wi' guests for only a few minutes o' time." His eyes show despair as he explains the condition of his wife, and then a questioning look, as if wondering if she'll survive her only child's death at all. They also convey that he truly desires Adam to be a part of this somber get-together.

"Thank ye – 'tis a verra kind offer, but I have to get the wagon back to the shop afore MacDuffy docks me pay," replies Adam.

"Aye, but just for a wee bit," pleads Mr. MacLaine, looking sorely rebuffed. He gestures towards the dining room. "This magnificent feast, provided by so many kind folks, is worth bein' tardy for."

Adam reddens as he realizes his faux pas in mentioning that he's getting paid for the chore of bringing home Mary. He shrugs, then enters the house promptly. MacLaine escorts him over to the dining room table, which is laden with hams, mutton, vegetable dishes, breads, and an assortment of whiskies and wines, all tenderhearted offerings from friends and neighbors. Adam takes a cut-glass cup of apple cider and an oatmeal cookie, standing awkwardly between Mr. MacLaine and Mr. MacAfee, an old farmer, weathered and crotchety, whose teeth are a sieve for crumbs that fly out as he converses.

"The clime is warmin' some," says Adam, attempting to engage in light conversation, but immediately regrets his inappropriate remark about the past ice storm. "I meant to say, perhaps we'll have a mild winter."

"Aye," agrees Mr. MacLaine, "mild weather would suit me fancy. I certainly desire to put the comin' winter behind us. Mrs. MacLaine needs to have a respite from the cauld. There must be wee pleasures left in life for us, the Almichty willing, despite all the sorrow we must bear from now on, though it daesna seem that way," says MacLaine philosophically. "Death o' a wee one feels like bein' buried alive in an avalanche. Sunshine warms the spirit and soothes the soul, even in the worst o' times. Aye, we'll have to try moving out o' this bleary, and if the Lord be willing, make it past the storm. And how's yer family holdin' up? I canna dwell on just me family."

"The children are workin' their way through the grief. Mary's passing is foremost on their minds." Adam is, once again, embarrassingly aware that he has mentioned Mary's death, and stops talking abruptly.

Mr. MacLaine becomes teary-eyed. A neighbor comes up and pats him on the back and pours him another whiskey. MacLaine doesn't seem perturbed by Adam's remark, though, and seems genuinely interested in the wellbeing of the other children that were close to Mary.

"Aye, I pray wee Janet's well as can be expected efter her terrible ordeal?"

"She's doin' as well as can be expected, recovering from the freeze by sleeping a lot," replies Adam.

"Aye, I'm so thankful anither child wasn't lost to us. Janet's verra dear to us, bein' she spent many occasions wi' our Mary. I hope she'll come to visit us when she's recovered."

"She'll certainly desire to come visit ye when she's strong," replies Adam half-heartedly, though he's not sure if he wants Janet to be exposed to the sadness at the MacLaines'. Nothing more is said, and Adam stands awkwardly, remaining silent, stuffing cookies in his mouth, aware of his large, clumsy hands grabbing for more. He finds an opportunity to slip out the door when Mr. and Mrs. Avery knock, bearing a great quantity of food and gifts for the family, which requires Mr. MacLaine to escort his guests to the table.

Adam's return home goes much faster – the regal manners that the horse exhibited on the way to the farmhouse with the coffin have been shed, all pomp gone by the wayside in a quest to reach the barn for food. By late afternoon, Adam is back at the shop. He works on his lathing chores for about an hour, and then throws in the towel due to his inability to concentrate. He decides to leave work for the day even if it means losing a few hours of pay. Mr. MacDuffy ushers him out the door, assuring him that he'll be paid for a full day because of his special errand.

The wheelwright shop is situated along the riverbank, one block from the train station at the far western edge of town. Heading out from the shop, Adam walks glumly along the River Allan promenade for a quarter mile, heading east until reaching the Bridge of Allan Hotel. He stares down into the river's rushing waters, mesmerized by the lively, dancing current that emanates a cool misty breeze, imagining its perennial coursing to the Atlantic sea, the same mighty sea that he'll embark to America on. He walks across the bridge, crossing the River Allan and entering the township of Dunblane on the other side. After a ten-minute walk, he reaches his intended destination, the magnificent Gothic cathedral, built between the eleventh and fifteenth centuries of regional quarried granite and limestone. The ancient edifice is the pride of the community, with its grand arched vaults and buttresses, and its beautiful stained glass windows at the northern façade soaring up into the sky, reaching high above the tallest elm trees on the grounds. The front of the cathedral faces south, with a large grassy open space in front called "The Cross" because of its intersecting patchwork of lawns, a special gathering place for public ceremonies, bazaars, and weddings.

The beautiful stone structure has consoled people since medieval times. Adam wonders if it brings to people a state of mind where true belief in an afterlife overrides tremendous grief. He supposes its magnificent beauty could quench some of the pain of loss. An awe-inspiring cathedral, he senses momentarily a beautiful spiritual presence housed within. Sunday will be a sad sermon for Wee Mary, who did not get a chance to live past childhood. The cathedral will bring together most of the town and absorb all the pain, fears, and sorrows of the townsfolk. Adam hopes that everyone will walk away comforted, believing in an afterlife, assured that Mary's fine wherever she has gone, and the people of Bridge of Allan will soon recover from this tragedy and get back to some normalcy.

Three sides of the cloister are surrounded by a grassy graveyard mottled with weeds and headstones in evolving stages of decrepitude – generations of the townspeople's ancestors are buried here: young mothers who died in childbirth; babies and children who succumbed to communicable diseases; even strong young men brought down mercilessly by devastating diseases such as influenza, cholera, or diphtheria; and, not long ago, the wounds inflicted to young lads in the Crimean War. *All the beautiful children I've built coffins for durin' the years o' employment were as dear to their parents as Mary was to hers,* Adam reflects.

With this thought in mind, he segues to the conclusion that his leaving Bridge of Allan is perhaps for the best – he doesn't want to see any more children die, especially those he knows, which will happen sooner or later. All it takes is another nasty flu to take hold and overpower like a relentless army. He reflects that there are far too many innocents buried in this little plot of land surrounding the church who didn't get a proper chance at life. His eyes wander to a freshly dug grave showing damp, black soil. This is where little Mary will be laid to rest, alongside her grandparents and her baby brother, who died in infancy. He wonders about life and death, why some people live to be so old as Grandfaither, who is four score and five years, and others are swept up when they are mere children; why some trees live longer than people, like the beautiful redwood forests in the California mountains he has read about from writings of men who have trekked to the gold fields of the Sierras. Even the elm trees he stands under will last longer than most humans alive now.

There must be reason behind the Almichty's plan. Mebbe Wee Mary, wise beyond her years, was needed somewhaur up in the Heavens just as Emma insists, he reflects. *Perhaps she's an angel wi' wings by now, sent down to earth temporarily to lend joy to her family and friends for a short time, as Violet tells the children to console them. Mebbe there're ither places in this grand universe to abide, ither lives that need Mary's love and intelligence. The universe's a vast place and must hiv billions o' souls inhabiting a multitude o' places. Surely God daesna plan to waste Mary's brilliance and sweetness. Or mebbe I'm tryin' to console me grief by sugarcoatin' the raw reality o' this happenin' – a tragic permanent end to a lassie so tender and sweet. Life's a mystery!* He wonders if, when he's old, he'll have figured out at least a wee bit of the Grand Mystery. He concludes that life is sad for those left behind, and that life on earth is fragile. *I pray the rest o' me family stays safe when I'm away in America, when I canna watch o'er them.*

Adam listens to the church choir practicing inside, a tune he has known since he was a child, and whistles along:

Blessing, glory, and wisdom, and thanks
Blessing, glory, and wisdom, and thanks
Power and might, power and might
Power and might to the Lord our God, be unto our God
Forever more, forever more

He stops abruptly, ashamed of himself for being irreverent to the memory of Mary by whistling out loud. He prays silently, looking to the vast sky where he imagines the grand workings of the universe occur.

Dear Lord, bless and take care o' all the young ones lost to the world whom ye call back prematurely, and especially our dear Mary, who has so much to offer yer Kingdom in Heaven. Mary'll be buried on Sunday in this verra spot. Janet, her verra best friend, will come often to stand by her restin' place. Please watch o'er Mary in Heaven and her best mate, Janet, down on earth. Amen.

Crossing over from the riverbank, and heading back toward the train station, Adam walks west along the quaint, oak- and pine-lined Henderson Street, where shopkeepers sell their wares from sunrise to sunset. To reach Drumdruils Farm, he walks to the train station, then turns ninety degrees north to start up a moderate grade into the hills for a distance of a mile and a half. Once in the hillocks, the terrain is thick and woodsy with the invigorating minty and savory fragrance of fern and pine. The walk is peaceful, and the beauty of the countryside never more appreciated by Adam, as he reflects on the sobering reality of being away from his home turf for a very long time in the coming year. He does not let his mind linger on the possibility. His mind is for a short time diverted away from the depressing thought of Mary's death. Within twenty minutes, he arrives home to Drumdruils, greeted warmly by his comforting family. He promptly sits down to a hearty supper with his uncharacteristically somber family.

II. Story Time to Ease the Sorrow

Story Hour has been postponed to after supper this evening due to Cook being off due to a minor malady, and Violet being hands-on in the kitchen for its preparation. The family has been cast into a deep despondency over Mary's death. Janet is still recovering from her near-death experience; tired and listless and never warm enough, she is bundled in a blanket by the fire, displaying none of her usual spunk. Her meals are brought to her in the drawing room on a tray, but she eats little. The children are not themselves; that is, not as lively and rambunctious. They go through the motions of being children, who run, skip, hop, and jump, tease one another unmercifully, and they continue to explore the countryside, catching butterflies and frogs on their daily walks with Violet, but much more of their time is spent on indoor imaginary games wherein they go into themselves in less active aloneness periods. Nothing has bolstered them to their prior state of wondrous vigorous joy in life. Story Time is a needed imaginary break to bring out their great curiosity and imaginations. After supper, the family listens to Violet's rendering of a tale about the fairies and elves of Scotland, the Wee Folks that Emma loves and has requested to hear. Violet decides to go further into *A Midsummer Night's Dream*, as the children have already been introduced to the characters and some of the plot in earlier Story Hours. Emma skips to the bookshelf and picks out the play of Shakespeare's that deals with royal Wee People. The children never cease to be enamored by the little changeling that Queen Titania has adopted as her own, whom she considers to be her own flesh and blood. The other characters in the play have been introduced gradually, and now Violet decides to recount some more of the play.

"Children, I'm goin' to tell ye the first part o' Shakespeare's *A Midsummer Night's Dream*, a delightful comedy about the rare but mischievous actions of Wee People, but this is all in good fun and does not reflect the Fairy Kingdom in general. We've previously learned of some of the characters. Remember King Oberon and Queen Titania, who are royal fairies, and the mischievous sprite Puck, who causes a lot of trouble by putting spells on undeserving people with magical flower dust."

"I can tell ye for a fact that these mischievous sprites exist, as I, to me great annoyance, wear one atop me shoulder every day," pipes up Henry.

"Oh, Henry," responds Violet, "I know you're referrin' to yer friend Punt, who's one o' your dearest friends in the world despite his fickle nature."

"Aye," agrees Henry. "Punt's me faithful sidekick. If only he kept to his own affairs and daedna get his jollies from interfering in mine. The connivin' Wee One is bound and determined to have me ostracized to Hades."

"Henry, are ye going to Hades? Can I go wi' ye?" inquires Malkie.

"Ah, Malkie, ye daena know onything. Hades is Hell," exclaims Telford.

"Daena tell me things I already know, Telford," replies Malkie with irritation.

"Malkie, ye daena ken onything! Yer afraid o' yer own shadow," declares Telford teasingly. Malkie decides to ignore his brother for the time being with no rebuttal, but gives him a dirty look before turning his attention to Henry.

"Henry," he inquires, "is Punt the mirkie Wee One who got ye in mischief wi' Annie MacGivens? Did he cause the trouble that made Ol' MacGivens mad?"

"Malkie, cease meddling," answers Adam Sr., "or off to bed ye go."

"Malkie," rejoins Emma, "ye know nothing o' love acause you're so dimwitted."

"Hush, Emma," says her father gently. "We must begin this story as it is a long, complicated one. Get on with it, Violet. Begin, please!"

"Children," interjects Violet quickly, before anyone can say another word, "this is a play o' comedy and fantasy that takes place in a magical forest where fairies dwell. We'll cover the royal wedding o' the Duke of Athens and Amazonian Hippolyta on anither day. Listen carefully so ye get the names straight and comprehend the storyline. As mentioned, yer all acquainted by now with the King and Queen o' the Fairies and the knavish Puck, who is an all-around jokester and a scalawag." Violet clears her throat and proceeds with the tale while the children remain uncharacteristically quiet in great anticipation of the drama to come.

"King Oberon, King of the Fairies, is mad at his wife Queen Titania because she adopted a changeling boy from a king in India, whom she adores, as he is a beautiful child. King Oberon is jealous and full of wrath and wants to use the boy as a knight in his king's brigade. The king and queen are not speaking, although they, by chance, run into each other in the woods, for the queen has traveled to Athens for the upcoming wedding of the Duke of Athens (Theseus) and the Queen of the Amazons (Hippolyta) that King Oberon is attending as well.

"Before the nuptials, Egeus, the father of beautiful Hermia, relays to his friend, Duke Theseus his distress over his daughter's love for a man named Lysander, as he has already arranged for her betrothal to Demetrius. Hermia tells them she is in love with Lysander and will never agree to marry Demetrius. Enraged, Duke Theseus calls on an ancient Athenian decree that a daughter must marry the man her father desires her to marry or face death. Oberon gives her another choice: marry Demetrius, who her father has chosen, or become a chaste nun worshipping the goddess Diana. The distraught Hermia and her lover, Lysander, have no choice but to run away through the forest to another city when they find out they cannot marry legally in Athens. Demetrius finds out from a jealous Helena, who desires Demetrius's affections, that Lysander and Hermia plan to secretly marry, and follows them into the forest to prevent their getting away.

"Meanwhile, in the forest, there is a mischievous sprite called Robin Goodfellow (also known as Puck), working for King Oberon, who has been instructed to cast a spell on Queen Titania to make her love an animal in the forest, in order to humiliate her and cause her to give up her changeling boy. The mischievous Puck mistakenly casts a spell on Lysander by applying a flower juice to his eyelids so that he no longer desires the beautiful Hermia, and is now in love with Helena, who has been desperately, but unsuccessfully, fighting for Demetrius's love. King Oberon finds out Puck has cast a spell on Demetrius, so now both are in love with Helena, and neither have affection for the beautiful Hermia any longer. He sends Puck back to try again to cast a spell on Queen Titania, and this time he scatters magical dust that causes Titania to fall in love with a laborer called Bottom, who is rehearsing for the play to be performed for the nuptials. It turns him into a donkey-headed man. Queen Titania, sleeping in the forest, wakes up, and the first person she sees is Bottom with the donkey head. She immediately falls in love.

"Lysander and Demetrius, who are still under a spell, both in love with Helena, set up a duel to battle for her. Helena thinks both men are mocking her because neither loved her before – that is, she thinks they are playing a cruel joke on her by pretending to love her. King Oberon has Puck keep the two duelers apart until the spell can be uncast. Eventually the spell is uncast on Lysander, and he goes back to loving Hermia. The spell remains in effect on Demetrius and he continues to love Helena, which is fine with Helena. So now, all the lovers are together with their true loves.

"Children, we'll continue this story at a later date and learn o' the fanciful wedding and play that takes place," says Violet. In anither Story Hour we'll cover the bumbling characters workin' for King Oberon, selected to put on a play for the royal wedding. They, too, are in the magical forest practicing for the play."

III. Whaur o' Whaur Has Poor Mary Gone?

Since Mary's death, once the children are tucked in for the night,

Violet has the formidable task of mollifying their fears of dying in their sleep. She attempts to soothe their inconsolable sorrow by inspiring them to believe in a divine universal plan.

"I canna go to sleep," whispers Malkie in trepidation. "What if I'm next to be taken?" He points his finger skyward and grimaces, trying to dispel the imminent danger that he fears is coming to him, and him alone, as he sees himself as the least virtuous of his siblings, being that he is prone to trouble, almost as much as his brother, Henry.

"Ye'll be next for certain, Malkie, acause ye're the one who gets in the most tangles; that is, except for Henry," teases Emma. She, unlike Janet and Malkie, is the only child not visibly grief-stricken over Mary's death because of her extraordinary knowledge.

"It could be ye, Emma. You're the one who knows the Wee People, and they might desire to make ye one o' them," taunts Janet, who now sleeps in her own bed at night with the other children when not resting downstairs by the fire. "They steal children. Ye could become a changeling."

"Nae," replies Emma, "only bad fairies steal children, just like they're bad people. Most Wee Folks are honorable. Elor and Twixie tell me they've seen visions o' me in the future. I'm goin' to stay down on earth and be a verra important person when I'm grown," she states proudly.

"Mebbe ye'll become a gypsy fortune teller earnin' money telling tall tales," replies Malkie.

"Ye're an eejit, Malkie," replies Emma.

Says Janet sadly, "I daena mind if I'm chosen to go acause mebbe I'll meet Mary again. Mary and I were to be blood sisters. We belong thegither through thick and thin. We were goin' to mix our bloods in a river ceremony, but not 'til spring when the water was warmer. Now, her blood's frozen foriver and iver in the cauld ground." Janet begins to weep.

"Daena leave us, Janet," pleads Emma. "You're not ready to

depart the world. If ye depart ye canna come back. Ye'd be lost to us foriver and iver."

"Hush, children, let's no get ahead o' ourselves," says Violet. "Rest assured that since her departure from Bridge o' Allan dear Mary's doin' well. The Wee People tell me she's verra happy in her new role as an angel's apprentice. She's learning to be part o' the Order o' Angels, those angels who aid in the success and wellbeing o' mankind and other universal affairs. Someday she'll be a full-fledged angel."

"What's mankind?" inquires Malkie.

"'Tis all people residing on earth," replies Violet. "The angels are looking out for us at all times, casting a golden protective light o'er those who're kind and have good intentions. They help us in all aspects o' life, from protecting us from harm, to giving us clarity o' mind in makin' the right decisions, to matters o' love and friendship and good health, as well as business relations wi' others. People on earth who die and go to Heaven choose their time o' departure for a reason. 'Tis usually a choice the person makes afore he's born, as a person's lifespan is a choice. The time one lives on earth is a matter that depends on what one needs to accomplish here."

"I've a lot to accomplish here," boasts Malkie. "I'll be down here for a verra long time."

"Ye daena know that, Malkie. Ye daena seem that busy to me," baits Telford. Malkie ignores his brother, as he is accustomed to Telford teasing him.

"What's a lifespan?" Malkie inquires

"'Tis the number o' years ye live on earth, ma dear," replies Violet solemnly.

"Is Mary looking down on us and watching o'er us?" inquires Janet.

"Mebbe sometimes, though she's important duties to perform regardin' the spiritual wellbein' o' folks o'er the world. Her duties could be in Scotland, in anither country, in anither era, or mebbe anither plane in the universe. Mary possesses a verra sacred, awe-inspiring, and spiritually fulfilling existence whaur she resides."

"Oh," replies Janet, "if that's true, mebbe we should apply to be angels."

"Nae, ma dear lassie," replies Violet. "Ye've a verra important mission on Earth. More than likely, ye've been chosen to live a very long and satisfying life wi' a lovin' family o' yer own. Our fervent desire for all ye children is being happy and living long lives. We certainly daena desire ye to leave us too soon."

IV. Janet's Visit to the MacLaines' House

A few weeks after Mary freezes to death in the sheep pasture, Janet announces out of the blue at breakfast that she must visit the MacLaines to be assured that "they're na feeling sad and alone wi'oot thair Mary." Janet is still recovering from her near-death experience and is thin and frail, her face gaunt, her big blue eyes cloudy and protruding slightly, but her strength is coming back little by little. She has an improved appetite with the help of Violet and Cook, who go out of their way to make her favorite foods of vanilla custards, rice puddings, apple pies, fruit-nut breads, and oatcakes. Janet's strong, compassionate, fun-loving personality shows traces of revival, as evidenced in that she is joining the morning hikes with her siblings and Violet – only when the sun is shining, that is – and manifesting signs of a curious, playful child again, picking wildflowers and pebbles along the road, and mimicking the tunes of the birds serenading her from the trees. Janet fears cold of any kind, staying indoors on blustery days and steering far away from the cold water of the streams, where her brothers wade in search of frogs for their races. Occasionally, she will break into one of her endearing little girl giggles when something in nature catches her fancy, like the beautiful snowy white gannet flying overhead from the sea, the perfect diamond shape of a red and yellow leaf falling down on the path before her, or the tantalizing scent of a wildflower that has the fragrance of honeysuckle.

No degree of persuasion on the part of her parents will change her mind about seeing the MacLaines. Her face becomes pathetically sorrowful as she laments on the suffering of the MacLaines without their Mary, touching the hearts of those around her; alternately, her face becomes aglow with light and love when she talks of plans to visit the MacLaines once again.

"What'll the MacLaines dae wi'oot thair Mary?" she inquires, in a somber soliloquy to the room in general, as if she were on stage in a play, her cute little mouth enunciating perfectly through the gap in teeth, her shoulders slouched in conveyance of the weight of such a grave uncertainty.

"Please let me visit the MacLaines. They'll love to see me and will be so happy acause I'm Mary's best friend," she pleads, her face showing distress at the thought of the MacLaines without their Mary.

By putting themselves in the shoes of the MacLaines, the senior Bairds and Violet are able to empathize greatly with the loss of their only child, as they came so close to losing their dear Janet, and for a short time thought that indeed they had lost her. Mary was the light of the MacLaines' lives, and perhaps Janet is doing what is best for them by traveling a short distance down the lane to offer her condolences. And as Janet says, "Without their wee Mary, the MacLaines' world might be dark and gloomy foriver." Janet feels the excruciating weight of other people's pain, and cannot tolerate suffering, especially in those she is close to. Her compassion for the less fortunate will come to the forefront in her adult life and lead her to a rewarding career path helping the less fortunate. She will be instrumental in establishing social programs to aid those wretched souls caught up in the horrid conditions of the Edinburgh slums.

The elder Bairds are talked into the idea with a little coaxing from Violet, for she thinks it would be a beneficial to Janet's recovery, as well as the MacLaines' wellbeing, to share their loss together. "The walk in the fresh air would certainly do her a great amount of good," voices Violet encouragingly.

"Might it be painful for Janet to see the MacLaines in their grief?" Adam Sr. inquires. "It might set her back in her recovery to be subjected to that kind of pain again, which must be wracking their spirits. I can only imagine them submerged in a river of grief that will be hard to extricate themselves from for a very long time."

"No, Mr. Baird. Janet has a strong spirit," replies Violet. "I believe it'll aid her recovery to spend time wi' the MacLaines. She'll be benefited by the act o' helping others, as that's what Janet chose as her role in life long before she came into this world."

Jean clears her throat and looks mystified, skeptical that her child was preordained before birth for any particular role. "Though Janet's yet a child, she does have a lot o' compassion for others," she agrees. "I daena know if it'll always be part o' her nature, but 'tis certainly the case now. We can't hold her back from doing what she desires to do for the good of others."

Adam Jr. is not convinced, as he had been involved firsthand in the making of Mary's coffin, and attended the wake for Mary, both of which he had found excruciatingly painful. Janet tries to convince Adam that it is the right thing to do.

"Adam," she implores, "I must visit the MacLaines. I fear they'll not be well without Mary. I must offer myself to them in her place. Mebbe I should live wi' them for a time, be their daughter, help make them feel like they still have a lassie."

"Daena be silly, Janet. Nothing will replace Mary for them. Ye willna be able to take the place o' their daughter," responds Adam, trying not to sound too harsh, though the thought of Janet leaving them to live somewhere else does not bode well with him.

"Just for a time, I'll stay wi' them and we can talk o' Mary. I'll tell them what Emma tells us 'bout Mary bein' an angel workin' for the Almichty. I'll tell them all 'bout her new role in Heaven."

Adam gives in, as he knows the strength of his sister's will. No amount of convincing will change her mind. "Janet, ye canna live wi' the MacLaines, but I'm certain they'd appreciate a visit from ye, as they did say to me that they would desire to see ye at the wake. I'll take ye o'er to the MacLaines efter schule."

"Nae, Adam, I must go alone. I must do this by myself, so they feel when I'm wi' them that I'm part o' their Mary, and they feel for a time that I'm their daughter. Mary and I were to be bluid sisters," she says sorrowfully under her breath.

Adam does not want Janet to go alone; never does he want to see her walk down the lane to the MacLaines' house as on the day the two lassies left together, and it was feared they were both dead.

"Awricht, Janet, I'll walk wi' ye and tell Mr. and Mrs. MacLaine that I'll return for ye when they're ready. We'll find out if they're busy and how long they'll desire ye to visit. I'll return when the MacLaines tell me. That way I'll know you're safe. Just understand they might want to visit wi' ye for only a short time, as it might be too sad for them to see ye without their Mary. In that case, I'll stay and visit wi' ye."

V. Wee Lassies Discuss Death

Emma coaches Janet on what she is to tell the MacLaines about Mary's role in Heaven. "'Tis important for ye to tell them how special Mary is," says Emma. "I've talked to Mary and she tells me she's an angel aidin' ither children from gettin' into trouble and dyin'. She's sent to aid children in danger of dyin', but are no supposed to die acause they're needed on earth. Tell the MacLaines that Mary's savin' all the bairns."

"Emma," inquires Janet in frustration, "why daedna an angel save Mary, if there are angels out on earth saving children? Why daena angels save ither children from drownin' and sickness?"

"Mary waesna supposed to be saved acause she'd a verra important job to do in the universe," says Emma. "She chose to do this job acause 'tis special and gets her closer to becoming an angel. Some children choose to have short lives and live anither life, in anither time, in anither place. Mary tells me there are so many wonderful things about being an angel. 'Tis the most wonderful job in the universe."

VI. Comforting the MacLaines

Adam holds Janet's hand tightly as they walk down the lane to the MacLaines, more for his own need to find comfort in closeness from her unblemished wee spirit than for her protection. He's soothed by the preciousness of his sister. He prays her spirit is not shattered by what she finds at the MacLaines.

The frosty landscape of November is stark, with a few scraggly leaves clinging to life for as long as they can hold out, but the sun shines brightly and warms them in their soulful journey. When they reach the MacLaines' farm everything appears the same to Janet, not as empty and bleak as she had thought it would be without Mary. The yard is clean and tidy, and the barn with its creaky, rusted weather vane atop has been recently painted to a reddish brown, the color that Janet and Mary had suggested to Mr. MacLaine a few months ago. The MacLaines are overjoyed to see Janet, almost in tears, as if a family reunion after years of separation is finally taking place. Mr. and Mrs. MacLaine appear thin and haggard looking in Adam's estimation, but he sees a positive change in them since the wake. They have an accepting, resigned look in their eyes, having succeeded in wading through the labyrinth of the monumentally difficult challenge of facing the death of Mary and burying her. In Adam's estimation, there is a badge of courage that can be read in both of their countenances – they have succeeded, amazingly, in coming to terms with loss. Surprising to Adam, they are still standing and engaged in the process of living. He thinks that if Janet had died, the Baird family would not be functioning well at all, would have been torn asunder, his mother never recovering fully and spending the rest of her days in bed. Adam assesses that the MacLaines will always wear a badge of courage and strength. People will be drawn to them because of this.

Adam apologizes to the MacLaines for not sending word in advance of their coming, and asks them if they would like Janet to stay and visit for a few minutes, or if they'd desire for him to come back to pick up Janet at an allotted time.

"Ah, mebbe she can stay the nicht?" asks Mrs. MacLaine, her face lighting up in the remembrance of past sleepovers with the lassies. "Ye can wear one of Mary's nightgowns, Janet, as she possessed so many. I must give ye some o' her best clothes anyway, as I know she'd desire ye to have them."

"Thank you, Mrs. MacLaine. I'd love them." She turns to Adam and says, "Please let me stay wi' them through the nicht. We'll have a glorious time talkin' o' our wonderful Mary."

Adam agrees, as he sees the MacLaines really would relish this, but on the condition that Janet promises she won't leave the MacLaines' house until he comes to fetch her in the morning.

Janet and the MacLaines have a very beneficial visit. The MacLaines are grieving terribly, and the sight of the wee lassie, appearing so forlorn and pathetic, because she's also grieving for their daughter, helps them immeasurably in deflecting some of their own pain. They willingly step out of their own sorrow for a bit to tend to the broken heart of this wee child. The MacLaines fuss over Janet, who appears very frail, pale, and thin in their estimation. Mrs. MacLaine sets to work in the kitchen, a task she used to relish but has approached half-heartedly since Mary's death. There has been no one left to prepare special treats for, those sweets that Janet and Mary used to enjoy together after their egg-collecting duties, like chocolate puddings and oatmeal-raisin cookies. Janet helps Mrs. MacLaine with the baking and stovetop puddings, and the aroma of luscious foods lends to her a better appetite than she's had in a long time.

Janet tells the MacLaines that Emma has been in contact with Mary and that Mary is doing well. She tells them of Mary's important role as an angel. The MacLaines don't have second-sight but they are true believers in fairies and angels, as many Scots are, being that they have remnants of childhood memories of their fairy friends. They try hard to accept what Janet tells them, at first hesitatingly, as it sounds farfetched, but it does help them immensely to envision their wee daughter in a heavenly role, wherein she is aiding the universe in grand ways. They soon begin to take on the notion wholeheartedly that Mary is up in the heavens working for the Almichty, as their Mary was by far a superbly intelligent child whom they knew would go on to achieve great things.

When Adam comes to pick up Janet the next morning, Janet brings up the subject of egg collecting as they are leaving.

"Who's collecting eggs from the farmers now that Mary and I daena collect?"

"Ah," replies Mr. MacLaine, "I do the collecting myself now."

"But Mr. MacLaine, doesn't that keep ye away from farmin' duties?" inquires Janet.

"Well, I make the time, as 'tis a necessary source o' income for us. Mrs. MacLaine aids me, but she has a bad knee and canna walk verra far, so I go the distance."

"Adam," beseeches Janet, "I must do the collectin' to aid the MacLaines."

"Och, Janet, ye canna go out and collect eggs alone efter what happened. Besides, ye're still weak from the freezin' ye got," says Adam severely. His color rises and he wants to kick himself for mentioning "the freezin'" of Janet in front of the MacLaines.

"Daena worry," says Janet confidingly to the MacLaines. "We'll figure something out. Mary would want me to continue wi' the eggs," she says determinedly. Since her near-death experience she has been getting more of her way with her parents and siblings, and she's assured that she'll get her way on this matter.

Back at home, Janet talks to Telford and Malkie and works out a deal with them. They'll aid her in collecting eggs in the afternoon, and she'll aid them with their homework, as Janet is a very good student and Malkie struggles to keep up. Telford is a good student but relishes being out in the open air any chance he gets.

Adam has no reservations of Janet collecting eggs for the MacLaines with her older brothers, as long as they stay together. From then on, every other day, the three tromp down the lane to the MacLaines, gather their baskets from the barn, and set out for the assigned farms in the vicinity. On their first day out to collect the eggs, Adam watches them head down the road with a bit of sadness. He remembers the dainty ballerinas that once danced down the country road to their chore. Now he observes a vagabond troupe, incongruent in size, age, and mannerism, two awkward, gangling laddies and dainty wisp of a lassie, the laddies veering off the beaten track now and again as they spy things they want to explore further.

"'Tis really good for Janet to be out in the sun," says Violet. The family notices that Janet is getting stronger and gaining weight, and has more color in her face. The satisfaction from helping Mary's parents has caused Janet's characteristic giggles to spontaneously arise much more often.

As for the MacLaines, their lives have become happier because they see Janet and the laddies every other day. Mrs. MacLaine goes out of her way to provide a delicious snack for the three egg collectors. In a year, the MacLaines adopt a child in need. Mrs. MacGivens's second cousin and her husband are killed in a buggy accident. A baby girl comes to be an integral part of the MacLaines' lives.

Chapter Three

I. Annie and Henry — 25 November 1863

A month has passed since the storm and Annie and Henry have seen each other only twice. In a rare coming together, they discuss their future.

"Why are yer folks so strongly opposed to our union, Annie? They think I'm not good eneuch for ye?"

"Ah, Henry, they'll come round in time." Annie's mouth curves up into a half-smile, showing the tops of her small, pearly-white teeth. Her peachy complexion has taken on a glowing vibrancy in pregnancy, so that she appears to have just stepped out of a Renaissance painting of a beautiful Madonna. She pats Henry's hand gently with her small, delicately-boned hand. Henry feels the warmth penetrating through his skin and is immediately put at ease by the confidence she exudes.

"'Tis just Faither's way. He daesna take readily to change. Life must be totally in concert for him, smooth sailin' as a vessel on calm waters. He becomes rattled easily, breaks down to a sorry state when he's threatened, 'specially when it comes to his family." With a questioning tilt to her head, Annie peers questioningly at Henry to gauge if he's sympathetic to her father's plight. She tightens her hold of his hands, covering them both tightly with hers.

"Mum concedes to onything Faither does and says. 'Tis not that she daesna have a mind o' her own; 'tis that she's been conditioned by years o' agreein' wi' Faither to spare conflict and give her peace o' mind, and also to appease her own guilt for what she feels is her fault in somethin' that happened in their lives long ago.

"He's not a bad sort o' chap, Henry. Just plagued by a miserable past.

Ye'd comprehend if you were privy to his early years. He fears onything that might take his family from him, as he's experienced tragedies in his own life. Indeed, he lost his entire family, parents, three brothers, and a sister, at an early age in a fire. Was an orphan by age twelve."

"I might've liked him better as an orphan. Could have given him a barrel-full of pointers on how to make it in the world usin' one's charm," jokes Henry.

"Ah, Henry," chuckles Annie. "I'm his only living child." Annie sighs deeply and clears her throat before attempting a painful revelation of her family's hardships. "I daedna tell ye o' the plight o' me wee brither. He was scalded to death in the bathtub afore we moved to Bridge o' Allan. 'Tis when we lived in a verra poor quarter o' Edinburgh whaur conditions were deplorable; not nice as here. We'd bathe in a big kitchen tub behind a partition once a week. A tragic, sad event occurred when wee Brodie, me brither, climbed into the hot boiling water o' the tub whilst me Mum turned away from the tub for just a few seconds to draw cold water to add to the hot from the kitchen. She told Brodie to wait and not get in, but he was eager to play wi' his toy boat floatin' o'er the water. He was two years o' age, and I was six months auld. He opened the curtain and jumped into the tub afore Mum could prevent him, and was burned o'er most o' his body. He died at home a few days later from the burns, as the doctor said the unhealthy conditions at the hospital would add to his poor condition. My parents were devastated. To this day, Mum blames herself and Faither blames the world. Soon thereafter, we fled from the sadness o' that place by movin' to Bridge o' Allan, though one can niver escape past horrors that haunt."

"I'm sorry, Annie," responds Henry, his face revealing great sympathy, as if he had experienced the tragedy himself. "This explains a lot. I ayeweys wondered what was behind the behavior o' yer faither. I've true compassion for him, truly, but I daena know if it'll lend favor to me in his eyes, even though I daena feel any anger towards him and would gladly be his friend. I've been banned from crossing yer path iver again. He's conveyed to me faither, in no uncertain terms, that I'm anathema. No conversin' wi' ye or yer family iver. 'Tis what he's laid down as the law o' the land. Faither says he rudely wagged his finger in his face in anger."

"'Tis illogical for us not to see one anither as we're in school thegither," Annie replies, laughing lightly. "Faither's just venting his frustration."

"He's been acquainted wi' the Baird family for almost the entirety o' me life, so he must be privy to the fact I spring from a genteel family," says Henry. "I'm the epitome o' respectability," he jokes, "acause o' me verra gentle nature and forthrightness. I'm even respected by animals and fairies."

"Henry, Faither's cognizant o' yer fine upbringing. 'Tis the upheaval o' emotion from the situation o' me bein' unmarried and wi' bairn," says Annie. "He insists I marry a Catholic, for he believes that Catholics adhere to a more virtuous path than people o' ither religions, and transcend to Heaven acause they are devout and virtuous."

"There are verra naughty Catholic laddies I'd like to introduce to yer faither."

Annie clears her throat and the color rises in her cheeks, which alerts Henry she's about to broach a delicate subject.

"What, Annie? Speak openly to me. We'll be thegither. We're bound thegither for life acause o' the bairn."

"Henry," replies Annie quickly, "that willna be possible for a time. I'm to sojourn at me Aunt Ethie's in Glasgow prior to me condition becomin' apparent." Her color deepens to a dusky rosy shade, by which Henry is spellbound, captivated by her beauty and endeared by her awkwardness in dealing with this difficult topic.

"I'll deliver our bairn at Auntie's house wi' the aid o' her long-time physician-friend, Dr. Mackenzie. They've made arrangements for me to give the bairn at St. Anthony's Catholic Adoption Center, but that plan willna reach fruition. O'er me dead body! We must figure out a way to keep our bairn. Auntie will go along wi' me request as long as me parents are not present. Ye'll love Auntie Ethie. She's verra intelligent and progressive, and sympathetic to me situation, but ma parents insisted she start the adoption process. She says she daed but only to appease me folks."

"Aye, our wee bairn willna be taken from us."

"Aye," responds Annie soberly. "Rightfully so, we're the bairn's God-given parents."

"Annie, dae ye feel good 'bout goin' to Glasgow? Are ye scared to leave yer family to have the bairn away from home?"

"Ah, Henry. 'Tis a comfortin' solution to be far away from me folks and able to relax in Auntie's cozy home. She's a gentle, understanding soul, a kindred spirit, and will be a great asset to me."

"Annie, I promise we'll travel to America posthaste as soon as the bairn is mature eneuch to voyage on a steamer. According to Adam, a vessel leaves bi-monthly from Glasgow for the Americas, as fast as they're built for the American war effort. We'll marry in Glasgow secretly whilst yer residing wi' yer auntie. I'll be staying in Glasgow by then wi' Adam and Adam can aid me in finding contacts for work whilst I reside wi' him and Larry, being verra near ye and the bairn, which is beneficial. Adam will be departin' for America in the next couple o' months. The family willna object to us goin' to America once we're married, 'specially wi' family in America to greet us."

"Aye, Henry. It'll be a dream come true when we sail off to America wi' a bundle o' joy in our arms."

"I adore ye, Annie. Dae ye iver wonder why?"

"Why is that, pray tell?" inquires Annie, her eyes glimmering like stars.

"Ye comprehend life and you're so gentle wi' people, even yer hardened faither. To ye, folks are all perfectly wonderful, even those who're maddening beyond reason."

"Good Lord, Henry," replies Annie, "I'm no saint. Ye're bein' overly generous wi' yer compliments. 'Tis ye who sees light in people and ye revere everyone. I grew up in a harsher environment than ye. I've had to deal wi' Faither pained by onything the world has to offer, lashing out on a regular basis. I've come to tolerate negativity. But yer world, Henry, is but a dream! The Bairds lead fun and joyous lives, wonderfully happy thegither. Yer family lives in a beautiful environment wi' literature, music, and laughter, and fun outdoor games. The closeness ye have wi' one anither is admirable. Henry, ye've been privileged to have that kind o' world; acause o' that ye can joke and be content in life."

"Annie, ye've risen above yer upbringing. Ye're born into this world a perfect creature, a lovely angel that makes the world a better place just by yer mere presence. Ye've an exceptional quality o' true excellence 'bout ye. That's why I love ye."

"And ye, Henry, ye I love acause ye're so real, so comedic, so transparent in yer kindness. Everyone takes delight in yer presence. Henry, never change, even if I change. Ye're funny and witty, and people admire ye for that fine sparkle. They're drawn to ye acause ye make folks feel fine wi' themselves."

"Well, now that we've established that we're wonderful and amazing people," says Henry jokingly, "let's go have fun down by the river and relish in the delights o' the day. The water looks lovely, eh? The river's calm wi' a bonnie color o' blue like the color o' the sea at dusk. Annie, we'll be fine as long as we're thegither. We'll be verra happy when our bairn arrives."

II. Annie MacGivens — A Promising Future

Annie MacGivens walks down the street from her home on Keir

Street and turns right onto Henderson on her way to school. She exudes a brightness of spirit despite the encumbrances of her life, and thus has the ability to lighten the moods of people around her with her cheery, open smile and friendly greetings, offered heartily to one and all crossing her path.

To the town drunk she calls out, "Hallo, Mr. Ferguson, a great morn to receive the sun's blessing." He is slouched precariously on a bench in front of the Furry Beast Pub waiting to be let in.

She then gives a greeting to the middle-aged town gossip, Mrs. Gertrude Fenton, who has much to say that is unflattering about Annie behind her back, especially with recent rumors of her pregnancy.

"Hallo, Mrs. Fenton. Ye're looking verra fine indeed on this lovely day. 'Tis a fine blue tweed that ye wear! So pretty wi' yer eyes."

Mrs. Fenton looks extremely pleased and waves happily to Annie, but as soon as Annie is farther down the lane, the old biddy's thoughts are focused on informing her friends, soon to be seated beside her for their morning chat, of Annie's developing figure.

Annie is very popular in school despite her handmade clothes of inexpensive fabric (secondhand clothes done over), her much gossiped about tumultuous family situation, and the fact that she is not a Bridge of Allan native, though no one knows she's originally from the ghettos of Edinburgh. Her clothes look perfect on her lovely petite figure – her mother is an excellent tailor and Annie would look good in a burlap sack. She has the doll-like beauty of a child with a perfect rosebud of a mouth, intense blue eyes, and a small, cutely upturned nose. Her wise eyes, with their intelligent, friendly, curious gaze, have the maturity of someone beyond her years. Her mannerisms and speech are smooth and graceful. Annie, to sum it up, is in a class of her own – having the rare qualities of being charismatic, beautiful, personable, and intelligent.

Annie is never fazed by the inordinate number of crises that plague her life, in particular the burden of achieving peace in the environment of her father's volatile mood swings, a father whom she honors with patience and allegiance. She maintains an aura of equanimity and acceptance of her plight, reminiscent of a beautiful flower in a meadow of weeds, bending and swaying agilely in compliance with harsh heat and the downing winds of discord, coming upright as they abate, never to be torn or uprooted.

Annie's God-given innate sweetness has been a lifesaving buoy in her family's ever-constant environment of volatility and discord. To counteract her father's temper and her mother's sad, defeated presence, she offers an uplifting mood, a constant influence of love, understanding, and acceptance, like the presence of a calming sea that uplifts the senses. Her family conditions have been distressing, and she has adapted by living in a state of gratitude no matter what hand she is being dealt, rising above it all through her faith. Every day she prays for patience and happiness for her future. This is not to say she has not had to wrestle with sorrow and despair, but her kindly acceptance and good nature to what has been dealt to her in her life have overridden the burden, making it possible for her to be outwardly content, maintain healthy friendships in school, and excel academically. She is her own person outside her tumultuous home life, and carries none of the baggage brought on by her family. When Annie's father is in a foul mood, which is every evening after work, he takes to the couch for a nap before dinner. Annie brings down his slippers from upstairs and pulls off his work boots so he can put up his feet; she routinely fetches him cold ale before his nap, as well as a warm compress to cover his weary, bloodshot eyes, while he sinks into a deep slumber interspersed by grossly loud snores.

"How was yer day, Faither?" asks Annie brightly, as he drops his large, bulky frame down onto the lumpy sofa.

"Same as yesterday, blithering monotony and drudgery."

"Faither, ye must have found somethin' ye liked in yer day?"

"Canna say I daed."

"What o' the look o' beautiful dawn in the morning as ye walked to work, or the scent o' trees and flowers and the dusky, inky blue evening sky on yer way home?'

"Aye, lassie, there's much in the world to admire if I wasn't walking me way into a damn hellhole at work, and wasn't so damn tuckered out on the way home."

"Oh, Faither, ye're bein' impossible!" replies Annie, with an exaggerated gesture of defeat in her pouty look, followed by a musical chuckle. "I might as well try to lasso the moon than bring ye good cheer."

MacGivens's craggy face breaks into a smile as he reflects on this image, though he's heard this many times before, and always imagines his Annie flying towards a silver-faced moon with a golden rope in her hand to lasso the moon for him. Annie's the only person in the world who can steal a smile from Mr. MacGivens.

"Aye, me lassie, I'd dive to the bottom o' the sea to find ye the perfect pearl, if I could. Lass, ye're the one pleasurable thing in me day; only ye can soothe me more than a lager."

"What o' Mum? Daesna she bring ye smiles? So gentle and kind to ye."

"Aye, she'd fetch me a smile if she wasn't dunked in a deevil's brew o' sorrow."

"Ah, Faither, ye must try harder!" is all Annie suffices to exclaim each day, though she perseveres in displaying a wide, encouraging smile to assure him that everything will be fine in their world.

Alas, Annie's prayers have been answered. She's incredibly proud being pregnant with Henry's child, and anticipates with excitement the prospect of a life in America with their bairn. A sense of newfound freedom has come to her despite the scandal of being unmarried with child, as if her body and spirit have been prompted to bloom to their fullest, under a warm, gentle sun, nourished by the larger-than-life presence of Henry. She is soon to be free of the discord she's dealt with for so long in her home life, although she'll miss her parents and worry greatly about them. An innate sense of survival guides her to go forward to a new life free of guilt. Henry, a lad who is lighthearted and kind-hearted, is the answer to her prayers. The tumultuous winds of a storm she has braced against her entire life are lessening due to the bairn inside of her and the laddie who will be at her side. Henry will always lift her up and protect her. Annie can feel the new life growing like magic within her. She takes a big breath of air and sighs in relief.

III. Double Blow of the Grim Reaper — 3 February 1864

Since leaving school, Adam continues to work full-time as an apprentice wheelwright and coffin maker throughout the winter of 1863 and into spring of 1864. He will turn eighteen years old on 29 April 1864. In the fourth year of his apprenticeship at the shop, another tragedy involving a child reels the townspeople of Bridge of Allan, causing them, understandably, to fear for the safety of their children and question the longevity of their children's lives. Cammie MacLeod, an eleven-year-old country lad, came into town with his father on Friday's Market Day, the customary day of the week that hogs are auctioned off. He met up with his school chums, and, on a dare, performed a more-than-foolish balancing act atop the wood railing of the bridge overlooking the River Allan. The laddie initially exhibited an admirable feat of athleticism in the estimation of his buddies, with inspiring acrobatic agility, but sadly he lost his footing a few yards into his quest due to the swooping of a seagull too closely overhead. The creature's aviary dive caused Cammie to fall backwards off the bridge into the mighty currents of River Allan. The choppy waters and swift current took him under almost immediately. The poor child disappeared into the fathomless depths, resurfacing three miles downstream, where his lifeless form was caught on rocks at the river's eastern bank.

Adam is once again called on to make a child's coffin for one of his sibling's friends, a school chum of Malkie's, and to top off his discomfort, he is chosen by his boss to make another painful delivery of a small pine box to the MacLeod family. He prepares the wagon and horse, this time decking out old Jackie in a ceremonial blanket and a decorative feather. The old horse performs admirably as he clip-clops through town and out a country road to the Macleod farm. As with Mary's wake, the family gloms onto Adam with open arms as if he is the messiah, a special emissary from God, coming to their rescue, assigned to be in charge of their lost loved one's transport to Heaven. They beg for him to stay for refreshments, and talk in torrents about Cammie's many talents and their aspirations for him, as though he is temporarily out of town. Adam wonders if their minds are rummy with grief and lack of sleep, their inevitable grieving process having not yet begun; perhaps they are playacting as a coping mechanism, a way of keeping the raw staggering emotions of the final dissolution of their son at bay. Adam wonders how folks survive such grief, how people go on living with this happening to them.

He is reminded of a William Blake poem that he learned in school, which gives him a modicum of comfort:

O! He gives to us his joy
That our grief he may destroy;
Till our grief is fled gone
He doth sit by us and moan.

Malkie's sensitive soul takes a severe beating. So distraught he is by his friend's death that every bit of his usual spunk and adolescent mischievousness is drained out of him. He no longer teases his brothers and sisters with his bravado, and has ceased to be interested in frog racing or playing outdoor games. Coming to grips with the death of Mary, four months previously, was very hard for him, and another tragedy laid down so soon has made him terribly fearful of death. Malkie refuses to go to school for a week after Cammie drowns. Adam and Henry try console him by telling him he'll be able to visit them out West when they're settled, and that they'll send him the steamer passage money when he's old enough.

"Please daena go out West," he begs of his brothers. "Ye're goin' to die out there. We'll niver find out what happened to ye. We canna visit ye in the church graveyard iver acause we won't be able to get ye back to Scotland. Ye'll be buried on some plain or mountain."

"We'll be fine," answers Henry. "We're takin' lessons in scalping Indians and practicing shootin' our rifles to the mark between the eyes," he says in jest. Malkie looks horrified.

"Henry's teasin' ye," says Violet. "Yer brithers will be fine out West, as both are smart and strong. Indians will adore Henry. Ye must realize he has a special way wi' folks!"

Emma and Janet try to console Malkie, as it is disconcerting for them to see their feisty brother change into a weakling. "The auld Malkie has left us," says Emma sadly. She tries to bring her brother out of his grieving stupor.

"Malkie," says Emma, "I'm certain that Cammie's awricht whauriver he might have gone efter he died. He's probably up wi' Mary workin' wi' ither angels as a messenger."

"No," replies Malkie. "He's gone for good and will reside wi' all the ither children in the graveyard foriver. He daesna talk to me when I go there to visit him acause he's really just 'come part o' the dirt."

"No, Malkie. Ye're wrong. His spirit lives on. Ye have to believe that."

"I daena believe in onything," declares Malkie.

"Malkie," says Janet, "ye've got to believe in life efter people die. Acause we're all goin' to die, and ye've got to believe that we'll be awricht efter we die and can visit each ither."

"I know that Mary's awricht up in Heaven, and so that means that Cammie's awricht," says Emma.

"How do ye know for certain?" asks Malkie, awash in tears, but trying hard to accept their words. His awkward adolescent features twist in agony.

"Acause," replies Emma, "Mary's talked to me from up there." She points to the sky. "I have talked to Mary and she's awricht."

Malkie appears to be pacified, as the next day he goes to school, and by the end of the week he's back to his lively boisterous self, which everyone is overjoyed to see despite the irritating pranks, like having another frog crawl down Emma's back.

IV. More and More Wee Coffins

Adam's experiences at the coffin/wheelwright shop have made him all too aware of the brevity of life. Coffin building has surrounded him with death every day on the job, lending him a bleak outlook on the shortness of the life experience for many: sweet babies succumbing to whooping cough and pneumonia; young, vibrant mothers dying in childbirth; unfortunate freak accidents happening to strong, healthy farmers; many elderly stricken by winter influenza and pneumonia. He's seen too many sorrows in his lifetime, hardening his perspective on the fairness of life and God's reliability in providing everyone a decent life. He imagines souls floating up to the heavens from earth in a constant stream of defection, rising to the realm called Heaven. Being exposed to death on a daily basis at the wheelwright shop has not made him any more immune to death – quite the opposite. He's continually fearful for the welfare of his family.

He reflects that death could happen to someone close to him, thinking it nearly stole away Janet. *Anither reason to go to America, so I daena have to be round to see anither child's coffin. Next time it could be one o' me own family's.* He plans to make money for the family to keep them well fed and healthy, with plenty of ranch hands to lighten his father's load and bring in bountiful crops. Great sadness lurks o'er Bridge o' Allan – too many memories. *A dark cloud shadows the beauty o' this land*, he has concluded after dealing with so much death.

His brother, Henry, who has been in possession of the fey magic his entire life, can joke about life and death, even in the face of all this gruesomeness, which is mind-boggling to Adam. Adam wonders how Henry is able to make light of the Grim Reaper coming to town after everything that has happened.

"The Grim Reaper was in town the other day looking for passengers for the Hades train, but when he made his rounds o' the taverns in Town Square he took a look round and said, 'Na thank ye' and made an abrupt turnaround, hightailing out of town," quips Henry.

"Why's that?" inquires Malkie. "Aren't we like everyone else o'er the world?"

"The Grim Reaper sighed, stuck out his slimy tongue, and said, 'Blimey, Scotsmen are so bloody cheery wi' their whiskey breaths, they'd turn Hell into a festive saloon. Their dispositions are tainted so that they'd be inclined to party day and nicht in Hades. They're jus' too damn stubborn to accept the bleakness o' death – damn happy-go-lucky heid-bangers in plaid skirts; difficult to control acause o' their whiskey-blood.'"

"Aye," agrees Emma, "we've the Wee People on our side as well. They keep us safe and sound in Heaven and on earth."

"Henry Baird," chastises Violet, "no more conversation 'bout death in front o' the bairns. They daena understand the macabre, bein' they're so young."

"None o' us comprehends life and death, Violet. 'Tis the reason we're caught up in this life contract. God asked his people if they wanted to live down on a bonnie land called Earth, but he didn't tell them they'd have to pick up and leave at his discretion, wi' wee notice."

"Och," wails Malkie. "Ye mean we could be called up just that swiftly?" he inquires, with the snap of his fingers, his voice wavering.

"No," moans Violet in disgust. "Henry Baird, see what ye've done! Ye've seeded nightmares in the bairns' minds. Ye're a troublemaker, young laddie. If only Adam Sr. were to witness this, ye'd get yer hide tanned."

"Have him stand in line for that!" responds Henry with uncharacteristic soberness.

"Oh, Henry, naebody desires ye to suffer," she responds in her motherly way, to cheer him after her admonishments.

V. Adam and Henry's Pastoral Discussion

"Why do children have to grow up, Henry? Efter we're gone, the family will go on wi' daily life as usual; the land will go through its seasonal cycles as usual; but niver will it be the same for us. Like the end o' a book … eh, like the end o' a fairy tale. Verra sad indeed for parents to have their offspring scatter like dandelion seeds to wind. When we depart, the bonds that glue the family thegither will be severed, and not rejoined in the same way. Do ye not feel this part o' life windin' down, Henry? Difficult to depart, but it would be harder to stay. I feel like me verra existence would be diminished to mediocrity. To hold one's heid up high, a chap has to be able to slay a couple o' dragons. Wi' me limited perspective o' the world, I'm unfit to fight the evil o' the world and find me proper place in life."

"Like a village dunce?" jokes Henry.

"Ye know what I'm conveying to ye."

"Aye, Adam, but I'm goin' acause our destinies call to us. I'm departin' acause 'tis the nature o' life for creatures to fly from the nest as soon as they can spread their wings."

Adam and Henry have been herding sheep with their Australian shepherds, Reg and Alpin, all morning in the western pasture under a lovely cerulean sky and warm spring sun. The air is crisp and breezy, and new bursts of tall blue-green grasses and spreads of wildflowers from a very wet winter have set the hills ablaze with yellows, blues, oranges, and whites. The land is mesmerizing with the hum of wildlife. The lads rest on a vista that overlooks the River Allan and the tops of the town's stone buildings. They leave the dogs to herd the stray, stubborn sheep into formation as they enjoy the bucolic scenery. Adam sucks on a piece of dried stem while contemplating his impending voyage. Henry lies flat on his back mulling over the billowy cloud formations overhead, on the verge of drifting off to sleep. He's been spending countless sleepless nights planning his wedding day in Glasgow, as well as his itinerary to America with Annie and the bairn.

"I've seriously set me mind to departin' in the next month for Glasgow," Adam remarks to Henry out of the blue, stirring Henry from his catnap. Henry sits up, yawns loudly, and wipes his forehead with his handkerchief. Adam's plans having become a reality, taking place in only a month's time, gives him an urgent desire to set his own timetable for departure.

"If I daena go soon, I'll niver be away. There's ayeweys goin' to arise hindrances to me plans," says Adam.

"Aye," responds Henry, in a cheery, upbeat voice that doesn't fool

Adam. "I'll be staying in Scotland for a spell 'til Annie gives birth, but we've definite plans to depart for America soon efter that. Her bluidy faither's more strongly opposed to our union than iver. I'm forbidden to see her iver again; that's according to the dictates o' Ol' Man MacGivens. When I approached the house couple o' days ago, the auld scourge had it out wi' me, wi' vengeful words from his window, as if I was Scotland's most infamous outlaw, though he daedna come out to smack me as last time."

"How's Annie coping wi' all o' this?" inquires Adam.

"Despite poppycock from a deplorable faither, Annie's keeping the faith, in possession o' her sweet, sensible self. Her fine disposition's keeping her strong; her spirit's bein' buoyed by anticipation o' our beautiful bairn and upcomin' adventure to America. 'What's meant to be will be' is her motto. Niver has there been such a brave lassie as Annie. She possesses many close chums that ordinarily would support her, but circumstances prevent her from seein' them outside o' schule. I do know many are beginnin' to suspect something's awry. Niver have I heard an angry or derogatory word uttered from Annie's mouth towards her parents, who're treatin' her verra shabbily at a time when she requires tender lovin' care. Mr. MacGivens forbids her leavin' the house except for schule, wi' an ulterior motive o' keepin' us apart, but at least we can see one anither at the schule house. Next month, she'll be departin' for Glasgow to reside wi' her Aunt Ethie. The bairn is due in May. Till then, we plan to see each other on the sly afore and aft schule. I'm happiest when Annie's at me side."

"I'm sorry 'tis so difficult for ye and Annie, Henry, but life will work out for ye. A day will come when ye'll be thegither. I wish I could wait for ye 'til you're ready to depart."

"No, Adam, ye'd best depart whilst ye can. It'll be easier for us if ye lay down the tracks afore we arrive and lend us pointers as to whaur to live and work. Daena fret, brither, I'll remain and aid Faither in the runnin' o' the ranch for at least six months. I'll continue on for three months efter the bairn's born so he or she's mature eneuch to travel. A month afore the bairn's born, I'll move to Glasgow and Annie and I'll marry," he states emphatically, "but I'll come back to Drumdruils. I plan to leave Annie in Glasgow at Aunt Ethie's efter the birth and visit her on weekends. Now that we've the extra burden o' the western pasture, I'll tend to ranchin', as well as aid Mum and Violet wi' the children. The children will be in need o' extra doses o' attention acause they'll be missin' ye terribly. In a year's time, they'll have sprouted up eneuch to fend for themselves, and perhaps Telford will take o'er management. I'll meet up wi' ye whauriver ye may be in less than six months' time efter yer departure. Write often o' yer whereabouts, at least once a week, so that I can seek ye out. Annie and I will be ready to leave next autumn when the bairn's o' proper age for travel."

"I'm no goin' on any grand voyage yet, Henry, only to Glasgow to seek employment in carpentry. I'll be returning to visit once or twice per month 'til I find a means to travel West. It'll take a fair stretch o' time afore I've procured eneuch funds to travel to the frontier."

"I'm betting that once ye get to Glasgow and view the steamboats on the River Clyde headin' for America, ye'll get the itch to take yer leave. What's to tie ye down to Glasgow, efter all? Mebbe the bonnie lasses, but they'll most assuredly turn up their noses when they encounter a country bumpkin as the likes o' ye," jokes Henry.

Adam again senses that his brother is covering his true feelings, and tries to console him, for it's been Henry and Adam's avid dream that they'd be in America together.

"Henry, you're coming soon. I feel it in me bones. Thegither, we've the best chance o' makin' a fortune in the New World. So ye must keep yer plans alive."

"Aye, daena fret for me. I'll be following yer footprints," he replies assuredly.

"Henry, I ken we'll reunite soon in the Americas," assures Adam.

"There's no way ye'll not be coming as soon as ye can. Annie and the new bairn will thrive in the New World. We can all begin a bonnie life anew o' the frontier, wi' a fine future for a new family. To succeed, we've a better chance as a team, and we can send for the rest of the family, whoever desires to come. I'm certain the brithers and mebbe lassies will have the itch to join us in a few years."

"Aye," replies Henry. "We Bairds need to own our piece o' the world. What Mum and Faither have here on this fine ranch is perfect for them, but we belong to the fabric o' this life only when young. We've created naething to call our own. 'Tis like tryin' to lasso cattle – the ultimate achievement in life is ropin' yer dreams, that which yer soul calls out loudly for ye to do."

Rather than dwell on the stark reality of leaving his home, for the distance, on close scrutiny, seems as far as the moon, Adam's mind goes over again, for the umpteenth time, his itinerary, as he rests in the grass. *First, I'll travel to Glasgow to find carpentry work; next, find a ship for New York; then inquire whaur I can meet up wi' the track builders o' the Union Pacific.*

VI. Adam Prepares for Departure to Glasgow

24 May 1864 — Age 18

Adam's method of handling his emotional departure is to put on a brave, confident face and take charge of his plans step by step. The first step is to get to Glasgow and work until he has earned enough money to purchase passage on a steamer to New York. The transition of living away from home for the first time will be eased by frequent visits to Drumdruils, every other weekend. His final goodbye before boarding a ship for America will be most difficult, but as long as he remains confident in his decision, he's hoping to find the strength for the ultimate breaking away. He finds it cathartic to imagine a lucky charm coming to his aid in America – though he in no way has retained his imaginary childhood beliefs. Emma and Violet say fairies are not present in physical form in the West, though something charmed by them, like a magic rock or feather, can protect him if he runs into trouble. Emma has given him a magic rock from the dun-shi.

Perhaps, he reflects, *magic will be America, in the midst of the wilderness; magic might be in the sky and the trees and plants and rocks. I'll make it exist in me imagination! Just imagining its existence will soothe me and remind me o' me homeland, as a child's lullaby soothes, or as a magic star looks o'er me.*

He remembers the Wee Ones from when he was very small, but can't remember exactly at what age they were present and when they disappeared. He recalls his childhood friend, a Wee One named Jack, whom he hasn't thought of since he was seven, but whom he would talk to when he was out in the woods by himself. When he was six, the little man helped him swim the width of the river after he had fallen in, but the recollection is blurred, and now he thinks it might have been his imagination. He does remember falling in the river and somehow miraculously making it to the side, swimming with a swift current much stronger than he was.

On Adam's last night at home before leaving for Glasgow to work along the docks, the children settle in around him, competing for physical proximity. They gaze at him longingly, as if to memorize a lasting picture of him.

Janet leans into him. "Daena leave, Adam," she pleads. "We're meant to be thegither acause we're family. We should stick thegither like glue, so if we're in trouble and need aid ye can rescue us. We might be drowning and ye willna be here."

"Janet, dear, when grown up ye'll understand that I must take a leap forward to unknown places that might seem scary now, but it'll be necessary to become a man by forging ahead. Henry and Telford will save ye if ye're in trouble."

"Adam," says Emma, "the Wee People will save ye. They think 'tis a wonderful adventure for ye. Ye must be verra careful. They say there's no Wee Ones in America in body, but they can track yer activities and come to yer rescue if there's a problem, like being lost."

"But who'll play wi' us?" inquires Janet. "We need ye to be here to aid us when we're playing." Janet pouts for a short time, then recovers admirably for such a young lass, accepting the fact that her big brother, a rock solid foundation in her life, is leaving. She springs up to her feet, gracefully flinging her arms to the sky, her face glowing with inspiration.

"Adam, when ye look up and see a really blue sky, will ye think of me, please? Send me a message in the blue sky wi' yer mind."

Adam replies, "Aye, 'tis easy eneuch, Janet. There will be many, many blue skies so I'll think o' ye often, lassie."

"When will ye reflect on me, Adam?" inquires little Emma, as she snuggles against his side.

"When I see a cave, or a burrow, or a hillock, I'll see ye and yer Wee Ones. Mebbe yer friends will come out in the spirit o' the sky and trees to tell me how ye're doin'. I'll send greetings to ye through them. They'll mebbe report back to ye how I'm gettin' on."

"No, Adam," corrects Janet. "Violet says the Wee Ones daena abide in the New World, so ye canna view their dwellings for there are none there. They live only in the Old World whaur they've lived for centuries. I canna see them, though. I'm too auld for that."

"She's richt," says Emma. "Elor says they daena have Wee People living in the Americas. They abide on this side o' the ocean. The Wee Ones say they'll ayeweys remain in yer heart and in yer mind, and ye can call on them when ye need their help. Folks that ken Wee People here in Scotland can call on them from the New World, if they're really needed. Wee Ones can aid ye even from here. I daena understand how, but mebbe they'll send angels to aid ye," says Emma soberly.

Explains Violet, "They daena exist in physical form in the New World; that is, thair dun-shis are not in the hills of America, but the Wee Ones are multidimensional. They travel invisibly wi' their minds everywhere to aid ye. They can sense if ye're in trouble and help ye out. Once ye've been friends wi' Wee Ones as a child, they're yer friends for eternity. They'll send an angel if a physical presence is needed."

"Aye," agrees Adam. "They'll be in me heart and soul, and I'll remember their special magic to help me wi' tough times." Adam wants to believe this for his own sake, as he's feeling insecure about leaving, and wants to reassure his brothers and sisters that he'll be okay, as well as himself.

"Emma," says Adam softly with emotion, "when I look up to the stars o' nicht, I'll think o' ye looking up as well, and I'll send a message to the stars to keep ye safe.

"Janet, when I look to the Heavens, I'll think o' ye dancin' wi' the splendor o' the dancin' stars, and be assured that you're looking up to the heavens as well.

"Malkie, when I see frogs and toads, which I'm sure there'll be plenty o' in America, I'll think o' ye and how ye are fond o' racin' them. Telford, I'll see many trains o' the New World and remember yer love o' them."

"And what o' Henry and Baby Susan? What'll remind ye o' them?"

"Ah," replies Adam, "'tis easy. Henry will be wi' me soon; 'til then, when I see a white woman or an Indian squaw, I'll reflect on his jokes about women. And Baby Susan will be in me heart whaniver I view a wee bairn."

On the day of his departure, Adam bids farewell to the family, his throat wadding into a tight ball. He swallows repeatedly, his eyes cast down, reticent to speak or look up at them for fear of shedding a tear, even though this is not his final farewell. He'll be back on the weekends, which gives him the courage to make it to Glasgow. Knowing that he can return on a whim if homesick, or if he changes his mind about leaving for America altogether, makes the breaking away more bearable. And he'll be only a half-day's buggy ride from home.

"I'm coming down wi' a wee crochle, I fear! Me throat's dry as straw from the outside cauld!"

Henry comments teasingly, "Adam, if ye desire to attract bonnie lasses in Glasgow, and no hyenas, yer voice has to be a couple o' octaves lower!"

"Remember, I'll not be far off. I'll return soon and describe to ye the bustling city life in Glasgow."

Adam hugs every member of his large family and walks forlornly down to the village square, where he catches a ride with a neighboring rancher, Langdon Innes, whose flat wagon is pulled by two of his prized Clydesdales loaded with produce for the market in Glasgow. He plans to catch a ride back to Bridge of Allan weekly on Mr. Innes's trips to and from Glasgow for Market Day.

VII. Wee People in the New Land? Emma Questions Elor

May 1864

On their customary morning walk, Violet intentionally leads the children into the woodland by a small rickety bridge crossing a narrow stream, at which point they come across their Wee Friends, Elor and Twixie, who are out collecting wild blackberries that they intend to put up for the winter. Nineteenth century Scotland is not privy yet to refrigeration, but the Wee People use advanced technologies and have a freezer box in their dun-shi scullery. A beautiful spring day sets the scene, with light showers coming down sporadically during the first part of walk. The sun is winning its battle over the cloud cover, and fluffy cotton balls sail off to the north to disperse, rendering the skies clear and dry above the hiking group, which is proceeding erratically down the path. Emma, who is anxious and fearful about Adam's impending trip, wishes to talk to her Wee Ones about him. He's left for Glasgow, and will be off to America soon.

"Elor, Adam's goin' to need yer aid in America. It'll be verra, verra dangerous wi' Injuns and wild animals. Please send the Wee People to watch o'er him."

"Ah, Emma, Adam will be juist fine," says Twixie sympathetically, as she stands next to Emma in the woodland. Twixie strokes Emma's hair and tries to allay her fears.

"Emma, ma dear, ye ken the Wee People daena live in America," replies Elor. "We've lived here on this continent for eons" – he points his forefinger to the damp soil – "in the heart o' the European world, and have niver ventured to America."

"I beg o' ye, Elor, send someone to watch o'er Adam."

"Now, daena fret yer bonnie wee head. If we sense Adam's in trouble, we'll be there for him, no in physical form, but we'll be watching o'er him in ither ways – mebbe sending an angel apprentice or two when he's in trouble. I hear Henry's goin' o'er soon to America wi' his Annie and bairn. Yer brither, Henry, is the one we must look efter in America! He's the laddie we've been on the brink o' disaster with from the time he was two years auld. Och, that wild rascal daena get any better wi' age!" declares Elor in jest. He strokes his beard and takes up his pipe while reflecting on Henry's zestful personality. The Wee People have always loved Henry because of his jig-spiritedness, similar to Elor's son, Punt.

"I'm just jesting," says Elor. "Henry's just bein' Henry," he says, with a touch of fondness to his voice. "He's goin' to be a tad overly spirited always, as his nature dictates this." Elor's demeanor changes, his posture becoming more upright as he waves his pipe in the air with gusto. "Mebbe Punt should go wi' Henry? It would do Punt good to grow up a bit out in West and take on the hardships o' a rugged life. He could be our first representative in America. Would be a fine education for him!" declares Elor.

Says Violet, "I'm na positive Henry would desire Punt to traipse efter him all round, as he can be a nuisance and stir up trouble. But a fine idea for someone to look efter Henry!"

"I'll ponder o'er this, but I guarantee ye that Punt would love to go in physical earthly form, as he adores Henry and will miss him greatly," replies Elor.

BOOK FOUR

Chapter One

I. Spring 1864 — Adam's Arrival in Glasgow

Adam arrives in Glasgow, a bustling port city on the River Clyde, in the late spring of 1864. The great city has grown significantly with the advent of its shipbuilding and train industries that have boomed since the start of the American Civil War. The last time Adam was in Glasgow was as a child, when the family made one of its rare visits to town to view the Hunterian Museum exhibition adjacent to the University of Glasgow campus. At that time, they went to a Wild West show. Glasgow has flourished since his last visit, with many modern buildings, cultural event sites, and beautiful homes built by the wealthiest citizens. In the early 1800s, there was a great inequity in the distribution of wealth. Elite entrepreneurs were making expansive fortunes in the booming industries and built grand mansions in the West End. This was in marked contrast to the narrow, windy roads and closeness of the poor East End tenements, where typhus and cholera epidemics were rampant. In 1832, a cholera outbreak in Scotland killed 10,000 people. Between the 1830s and the late 1850s, death rates in the cities rose to peaks not seen since the seventeenth century. Glasgow has upped its public health efforts in the last two decades, and many of the East End tenements have been removed, but there is still a large, very squalid class of Glaswegians. Adam sees evidence of the very poor selling sparse goods along the docks and main thoroughfares. Tearing at his heart, he sees ragged-clothed children with haunted faces of misery selling small bundles of posies they have picked in the fields. He sees his brothers and sisters reflected in their pathetic, ghostly faces.

Viable energy pulsates throughout the city, as if it was a living entity bursting with new appendages, the result of the great ship building industry that has risen up along the River Clyde. The main street is alive with the clip-clop of carriage horses pulling gentry and and horse-drawn flat wagons hauling goods loaded off the ships. Little shops and new businesses lined up along the quay offer all kinds of sundries for the sprouting industrious city. A menagerie of street vendors – costermongers, fishmongers, and vendors selling household goods such as pots and pans – market their wares from flat wagons. Throngs of people are shopping up and down the dusty, cobbled streets. Rickety little bungalows for dockworkers have been erected along the shores of the great River Clyde, a tributary to the Atlantic. This pulsating, electric vitality lifts Adam's spirits. His anxiety of being separated from his family is quelled somewhat, but not entirely.

Before his arrival in Glasgow, Adam went about securing a job and a place to live, which has eased some of the difficulty of a transition to his new life. He had contacted his old school chum, Laurence Ross, from Bridge of Allan, for possible work, as his father runs a contracting business in Glasgow that Larry is now working for. Larry's father had been happy to set Adam up as a housepainter in the newly constructed neighborhoods springing up at an amazing pace, whereby whole sections of land are being transformed into housing within weeks. Larry had written back inviting Adam to room with him in his small workman's cottage across from the quay.

To have made contact with someone from his home village lends Adam a sense of familiarity and confidence, an assurance that he will be secure and comfortable in his new environs away from his family. In Glasgow he starts his new life, proud of his success in moving towards his dream. A month into his painting job, which he performs conscientiously to the best of his ability, working overtime many days, one of the local carpenters suggests that he try procuring work as a pattern maker, estimating that Adam would be well suited for this kind of work, which offers a much higher salary. A position serendipitously opens up when a worker leaves for America unexpectedly, which Adam secures without too much effort, for he has a good reputation as being an honest, hard-working individual, as well as Larry's father giving him a stellar recommendation.

Being in Glasgow on the docks of the River Clyde, Adam is at the heart of the city's major industry where there is great demand for ships for the war effort going on in America. Most of the boats being built are for the Confederate Army. Adam's new job as a pattern maker is on a steamer named the *Will-o-the-Wisp*, a paddleboat designed, engineered, and being built by Messrs. Simon & Company, made for the purpose of outrunning the Union blockade.

The new job suits Adam's abilities and interests well, and he is delighted in finding work on the docks close to the very ships he hopes will transport him across the Atlantic. He is one step closer to achieving the goal that he's visualized since his schoolboy days in Bridge of Allan.

Adam finds his work as a pattern maker very interesting and far more challenging than painting buildings. Pattern making for ships embraces the main types of engineering construction for the molding of patterns in loam and greensand, and the castings of hand and machine gearing and parts – pulleys, pipes, columns, sheathes, screws, pumps, and cocks. The *Will-o-the-Wisp* will be traveling to America once completed.

During this time away from his family, Adam becomes more extroverted, uncharacteristically enthused to engage in conversations with strangers and work comrades, taking the liberty to initiate friendly chats with local vendors and business owners along the quay. Characteristic of shy people, he has, in the past, been reticent to approach those he doesn't know, for he has found interactions with strangers difficult and awkward for him, thereby making it futile to convey aspects of his warm, intelligent personality; conversely, for Adam, it's difficult to intuit what's going on in the minds of others, unlike his brother Henry, who reads people like a book. Adam's people skills are deficient to the point that he lacks the innate ability to discern what part of himself he should share with others. True to form for shy individuals in social interactions, he is taken aback and his energy drained by the complexity of other individuals, especially those who are overbearing, loquacious, or extremely extroverted.

Adam's emergence from a shy, withdrawn person is brought about by the fact that his way of life is now so different. He feels himself with an entirely re-invented personality. He no longer lives in the shadow of his charismatic and extroverted brother. Henry has always been in top form when interacting with strangers, for he has a natural ability to intuit what makes an individual tick, the core essence emanating from a person's soul. Henry derives great energy and knowledge of life from new people he encounters, and they respond to him with utmost reverence. Everyone wants to be Henry's special friend, to be in the domain of his charismatic and energetic persona. When in the company of Henry, people often feel good about themselves, as they sense they are being understood and appreciated. The emergence of Adam from his shell and his newfound ability to hold his own part of a conversation is very encouraging, for he'll need this ability out on the frontier for his survival. Personalities will be more diverse due to ethnic and cultural differences, and it will be far more complex to unravel the nuances of peoples' intentions than those in his little township in Scotland.

In Glasgow, he experiences an immense relief that his woman troubles are behind him. At the same time, looking back to the fact that he was an object of desire by women has given his ego a boost. Endowed with a great boost of confidence in that he has a job and lives away from home, he no longer lives within the defined boundaries of being the responsible eldest son in his large Drumdruils family, whereby he has always maintained a quasi-parental role for his siblings, as well as sharing a responsibility with his father for the welfare of the ranch and its employees.

Adam is quite content in Glasgow, working in the shipyards, as he is not so far from his family – it has been reassuring knowing that they are only 36 miles away and he can reach them within a half-day's ride. He's able to ride home to visit almost every other weekend, but as the days draw closer to boarding a ship to America – he has halfway decided to board the *Will-o-the-Wisp* that he is working on, once it's completed, as he has had a part in its creation – his anxiety is manifested by sleepless nights. When sleep finally does come to him, it is not deep or relaxing but fitful; he awakens often with a fast heartbeat. His appetite is suffering as well. The ultimate step he will be taking, once he's on the ship and out at sea, has a rather scary finality for him. It's the loss of everyone and everything he knows and loves, as daunting as embarking on a trip to a distant planet. He decides not to think and just act – going through the motions step by step is the best way to leave. When the *Will-o-the-Wisp* is finished and ready to steam off to America, he plans to mindlessly board her, to go forward with his plans, no matter how parts of his mind warn him not to go, for there will be no going back.

II. Annie and Henry Wed in Glasgow — 4 June 1864 — Awaiting the Birth

Henry learns from Annie, via a letter that Adam delivers to him from Glasgow, that she is to deliver in the next few weeks. He immediately makes arrangements to move to Glasgow. On June 1, at the end of the weekend, Henry, who has been actively managing the ranch in Adam's absence, rides back to Glasgow with Adam after the weekend on Mr. Innes's flatbed. Henry plans to stay with Adam and Lawrence until the birth.

With strained relations with Annie's parents, there is virtually no one left in Annie's extended family but her great-aunt Ethie. A favorite of Annie's, Ethie lives in Glasgow in a quaint bungalow, and has been a widow since her early forties. Annie is grateful for a safe haven for herself and her unborn child, where she will be pampered and kept mentally and physically healthy, an escape from the negativity of her parents' constrained environment. Ethie is a free-spirited woman in her early seventies, with a long career as a midwife and nurse. Having been privy to a plethora of difficult life situations from a diverse sampling of society, Aunt Ethie has, accordingly, developed pragmatic, liberal views on how to conduct one's life with utmost freedom and happiness. Her motto is "Do not listen to the good opinion of others but follow the direction of your own heart and soul," for solutions to dilemmas are most certainly going to materialize in one form or another with intuition, patience, and good intent. She has no qualms with Annie's pregnancy, especially in light of the fact that the unborn bairn is a child conceived out of love, and goes out of her way to accommodate the two young lovers. When Henry comes to town, she enthusiastically carries out the necessary planning for a small wedding to be held at her bungalow, to be officiated by her friend, the Reverend Duncan Farley, pastor of her local community church.

On June 4, three days after Henry's arrival in town, the Reverend Farley marries the handsome young couple in Aunt Ethie's parlor. It is a simple ceremony imbued with a sacred, somber air, with Adam acting as best man and Aunt Ethie as the matron of honor. Annie is stunningly beautiful in a loose, empire-waist, cream-colored organza and lace dress, with a simple strand of pearls. Her golden hair is tied back with a weave of honeysuckle from the garden. She glows with a spiritual light, as if the heavens have cast a golden aura down on her, encompassing her with a halo. In Henry's eyes, she looks like an angel about to take flight. After the vows, they have a simple supper in the dining room with the reverend and Adam toasting the new couple. There is a photographer and a few dear friends of Ethie's to share in the celebration. The scrumptious supper consists of roast pork, applesauce, and green beans, and for dessert a white wedding cake topped with pink miniature roses from a famed Glasgow bakery, McFarland's. After the wedding, Henry stays on to live with Adam and Larry in their small rented cottage down by the docks, helping Adam prepare for his imminent departure and visiting Annie daily.

III. Adam's Departure for America — The S.S. Will-o-the-Wisp — 6 June 1864

The *Will-o-the-Wisp* is scheduled to depart the Glasgow port two days after the wedding, on June 6. Adam will be taking the ultimate step, embarking onto a steamer whose every nook and cranny he has come to know and love, with a destination far away from his beloved homeland. Fortunately, his anxiety has been significantly quelled by the distractions of the wedding. Henry kept Adam constantly by his side when not at work, integrally involving him in the preparations for a small, intimate affair, which invariably required a lot of planning and orchestration of food, drinks, and flowers. Adam has savored every last moment he could spend time with his brother. Henry has promised Adam that he, Annie, and the bairn will be on a ship in the next three months, most likely at the end of the summer before seasonal storms set in, which also makes Adam's leaving less foreboding; yet he is unsure of Henry's organizational skills in the complexities of getting himself and his family afloat at the right place and time, with the necessary accoutrements for life out West.

Adam is saddened that he won't be present for the birth of his first niece or nephew, which is to be any day now, but his opportunity to be on the ship has helped build can't be thrown away, as the steamer lends him a sense of familiarity and security. He has spent many days in the finely crafted boat's creation, and is bolstered with a sense of great pride that he was involved in its creation. In his spare time, when not working or helping Henry with wedding preparations, Adam built a beautiful cradle of hardwood for the bairn and a tiny wooden chest of drawers as wedding presents. These gifts he presented to Annie and Henry on their wedding day, and they were greatly appreciated. Annie said they would keep them in the family for generations to come.

Henry plans to stay on at Larry Ross's house after Adam's departure, as Adam has paid for the entire month of June, and Larry enjoys Henry's company very much. Henry, in true form, has been a breath of fresh air in an otherwise laborious work environment. On the morning of his departure, Henry and Adam walk onto the ship carrying all of Adam's possessions for the journey in a lug box: his satchel from Grandfaither, his little trunk full of his prized books and clothes, pictures of his family, and, most importantly, his compass and carpentry tools.

Henry hugs his brother on deck and quickly removes himself to the dock. He waves heartily from the shore as he watches as the *Will-o-the-Wisp* in all its powerful glory steam away, disappearing over the horizon like a little toy being gulped up by the vast sea. As he waves farewell, the thought comes to Henry, magnifying his sense of forlornness, that he has never been separated from his brother for any length of time. How grand it would have been if he, Annie, and the bairn could have been on the mighty *Will-o-the-*

Wisp. Henry goes directly to see Annie once the boat has departed to discuss, in full, the particulars of their own voyage to America in the coming months. This makes Adam's leaving a little easier to bear. He is invigorated by visions of himself and his new family reuniting in an exciting, beautiful environment.

For two weeks after the wedding and Adam's departure, Henry continues to visit Aunt Ethie's house daily, spending the entire afternoon with Annie out in the garden, in the shade of the grand old beech tree, amongst the melodic hum of insects and bees, the twitter and flutter of birds fervently engaged in bathing and feeding, and the aromatic flowers of the divine sweet honeysuckle and jasmine. The newlyweds enjoy this time of complete togetherness and continue discussing their voyage to America that will take place, to their best estimation, in early September before winter sets in. Their bairn is at the heart of their planning, as the birth is soon to be a reality, and they know it is no small venture to take a child so young on a long voyage. They chart out the type of blankets they will need for the trip, all the paraphernalia to keep the bairn safe and warm, and medicines to take along in case the bairn falls ill. Annie is a much better planner than Henry and covers their every possible need. Aunt Ethie is very accommodating to Henry and Annie, each day serving them dinner along with sweet lemonade under the beech tree. She totes out tea and shortcakes in late afternoon. Oftentimes, on the long, warm June evenings that stay light 'til after ten, she sits and chats with them about the glories of the atypical warm weather, her prized, award-winning plants, and the many births she has participated in, like the time a woman had a home delivery without medical aid, and then came to the clinic a day later, not feeling quite right, and delivered two more babies that she hadn't counted on. Being ebullient and fun-loving, Ethie is masterful in dishing out choice pieces of gossip going around town. She is a match for Henry in her storytelling abilities. Henry tries to pay back her kindness to himself and Annie with small repairs to her house, fixing loose roof tiles and worn-out window frames, masonry work on her chimney, and grouting her bathroom and kitchen tiles.

Ethie has arranged for her good friend and personal physician, Dr. Earl Mackenzie, to deliver the baby, and Ethie, a skilled midwife, will be his trusted attendant during the delivery. Henry and Annie feel very grateful for the excellent professional help they'll receive at home, as the Glasgow hospitals are not the healthiest places to deliver, laden with bacteria and oftentimes filth.

On June 20, Henry arrives at the cottage for his afternoon visit to be greeted by Ethie, who comes charging out the door onto the front porch like a bull let out of the pen, waving her hands wildly in excitement.

Says Henry, "Ethie, ye've yer lassie spirit o' yore back."

"Aye, that's how I feel," she replies, as she conveys that Annie is in the beginning stages of labor, in a joyous, emotionally charged vigor that sets him to lamenting the fact that she was not Annie's God-given mother.

"Dr. Mackenzie's been sent for and should be arriving shortly."

Henry is taken into Annie's room to wait with her for Dr. McKenzie's arrival. She lies tucked in like a doll under freshly starched sheets, a fragrant magenta rose in a crystal vase by her bedside; a fresh flower in perfect bloom is how Henry sees Annie. *She could niver look more bonnie than this*, he reflects as he approaches the bed and kisses her cheek. He holds her hand gallantly during bouts of pain, mentally trying to transfer some of the pain to himself. In between contractions, the couple makes solemn vows of their love for one another, and for their soon-to-be-born child, an impromptu re-enactment of their wedding vows, which helps Annie keep her mind off the sporadic, unrelenting sharp surges of pain.

Once Dr. Mackenzie arrives, Henry is escorted out of the room and not allowed to visit Annie again. Henry covers up his displeasure in having to leave by jokingly declaring that he is an outcast of the "privileged delivery game" because there is fear that he might cause Mackenzie and Ethie to fumble and "drop the ball." Ethie assures him that everything will be fine, that Annie's labor is progressing smoothly. She promises Henry that she'll keep Annie comfortable and give him regular updates when she's free to leave Annie for a few minutes. Henry is comforted in knowing that Ethie is a very experienced midwife. He waits patiently outside in the lovely sunny garden all afternoon, communing with the birds, clouds, and trees for company. There is a very petite sparrow that seems to have taken a fancy to him, chirping away all afternoon by his side. "Tell me more of yer woes, me wee friend. Why daena ye get yer sorrows off yer chest?" coos Henry.

Finally, towards nightfall, Ethie comes out and tells him that Annie is doing fine. "Doc Mackenzie says she's bravely holding her own and has admirable physical endurance for such a wee lass."

Ethie then tells him matter-of-factly, so as not to alarm him, that the bairn repositioned itself to a breech position in the last few hours, which is a concern to Dr. Mackenzie, but it is being repositioned with each contraction by manual manipulations of the doc. Ethie tells Henry it will be a long, drawn-out birth because of the breech factor, and invites him to stay at the house overnight. She makes him up a bed on the couch in the little office off the dining room, well away from the back of the house where the bedrooms are located. Due to the locality, he is unable to hear much of what is going on in the bedroom, but stays awake throughout the night gauging Annie's progress from Aunt Ethie, who comes to him every hour or so to report that labor is progressing nicely. It is not until early morning, around four o'clock, that he hears from Ethie that the baby's head is crowning and delivery is imminent. He waits patiently, lying awake atop his office daybed. Another hour passes, and then another, with no news. Finally, around six o'clock, he hears the startling wailing of a bairn, sounding to him like a wild animal caught in a trap. Henry jumps up off the bed and rushes down the hall to Annie's shut bedroom door. He can no longer hear the wailing bairn, only sharp creaks in the floorboards from active to and fro movements in the room. He waits impatiently outside. An interminable few minutes pass, and neither Dr. Mackenzie nor Aunt Ethie emerges. Finally, Dr. Mackenzie startles Henry by thrusting himself abruptly out the door. Clad in his bloodied white apron, white linen cap, and gauze facemask, he appears to Henry to be a warrior returning from battle, all hyped up on adrenaline. His demeanor transfigures within seconds, like a stilling wind deflating a sail. The good doctor becomes a presence that Henry does not wish to or expect to encounter – an extremely tired, overworked, aged man. His jowls are drooped and his expression sad, revealing that his well-fought battle was lost.

"I regret wi' all me heart to inform ye, laddie" – he comes out with this in a raspy voice, almost on the verge of tears – "yer wife has passed away from a great loss o' blood. A large placental tear occurred and bleeding couldn't be abated; hemorrhagin' o' this sort is sadly verra common in childbirth."

Dr. Mackenzie comes close to tears, with a look of total despair and defeat on his countenance. "Ye've a fine female bairn born this hour, laddie. She's goin' to depend on ye immensely," he states quite emphatically.

After what seems an interminable amount of time, Henry is allowed into the room to find Annie lying peacefully in bed as if in a deep sleep, her eyes closed, her visage white and stony as marble. Aunt Ethie, devastated by the loss of her niece to the point of speechlessness, unwraps the blanket to show him the sweet face of his bairn. She pats Henry on his back and quickly leaves the room with the tightly swaddled newborn in her arms. On seeing Annie, the image of Snow White comes to mind; Henry wishes he were a prince coming in to wake her up. He walks up to the bed, takes her cool, lifeless hand to his breast, and tearfully kisses her goodbye on her cheek. A subliminal prodding pulls him away from the room –

Annie, he senses, is outside the room with her bairn. He walks out mindlessly in a state of complete denial, convincing himself that he has dreamt of Annie's death while dozing on the office daybed, and he hasn't just seen Annie lying in her bed. He finds Aunt Ethie leaning over the kitchen table with the bairn cradled against her chest, teaching her to suckle a cloth soaked in boiled goat's milk. Henry is soothed by the smell of fresh coffee percolating, and warmth from the wood-burning stove. His mind is dulled from exhaustion, and it takes a garnering of many diverse, runaway thoughts for him to reconcile the circumstantial duality of his situation – a death for a life. Annie is gone and a bairn has taken her place. Ethie places his new daughter in his arms to console him. Henry, momentarily lost in the moment, is consumed by the presence of this tiny new life, rosy, delicate, and perfect, making adorable cooing sounds with her mouth. He begins to sense the spirit of Annie next to him, and looks over to see if she is actually present, uncertain of anything in his state of mind from shock and lack of sleep. He knows that Annie would not miss out on seeing his holding their newborn for the first time.

The rest of the day is dreamlike to Henry, as if he were living in the shoes of someone else. Annie's body is taken away in the late afternoon by a D.S. Dodd Mortuary carriage while Henry stays in the kitchen, holding his bairn. Ethie goes out in search of a wet nurse so the bairn can be fed. A burial service is held two days later in the Glasgow Ramshorn Cemetery where Aunt Ethie's family is buried. She writes a long letter to be sent by a messenger on horseback to her parents of Annie's death, the time and place of the funeral, and of the birth of their granddaughter, Mary Alice Baird. She doesn't expect that they will come to Glasgow for the burial. Ethie tells them in her correspondence that Henry will bring the bairn back to Bridge of Allan in a month when it is safe for the bairn to travel, and he will visit them at that time to discuss arrangements for the bairn's future. She receives a sharp reply one day later via the messenger, penned by Mr. MacGivens, his large, childlike scribble stating emphatically that they don't ever care to see Henry or the bairn.

"Our Annie's the only one we cared about and Henry Baird killed her wi' his lust. The spawn o' sic a deplorable lecher isna welcome to our home."

The day after Annie's death, Henry looks out to the glorious early summer day, profuse in vibrant colors and sensuous floral scents, and wishes it would all go away – such an uplifting demonstration of beauty isn't appropriate to mark Annie's death. He'd prefer a grey, cloudy day to match the somber occasion. The world, he concludes in dismay, is very unsympathetic to his loss – summer, an uncompassionate friend, flaunts its bountifulness at the expense of his loss of all of life's beauty. As the days progress, Henry's grieving process manifests itself in the form of emotional numbness. He is not the Henry of old with twinkling to his eyes and humor and wit abounding, once with a boundless source of delightful quips flowing unabated from his mouth. Aunt Ethie takes very good care of Henry; her mission is to keep him balanced to ensure a full recovery, making sure he eats well and sleeps soundly. She encourages him to take long walks outside in the sunshine. Henry resides in Glasgow for a month after the funeral at Aunt Ethie's, appearing to be as fit and as well as the thriving bairn, and then takes his wee lass home to Drumdruils to meet the family.

IV. Adam's Arrival in America — July 1864

Just off the steamer, Adam stands on dry land for the first time in over a month. Embarrassing sea legs cripple him for the first couple of yards, and he wobbles awkwardly along the wood planking, willing himself not to topple over and make a fool of himself. He breathes in unfamiliar scents, feels a subtle, unfamiliar nuance to the sun and wind – blinding bright sun and a crisp, sweet-smelling breeze – and views a different kind of sky, not the pastel grays and blues as Scotland's, but less opaque and more vivid. An exciting, alien world presents itself to him. From the New York Harbor, he gazes in sheer delight at the towering buildings, astounded by their high climb into the sky with so much grace and elegance, as if they intend to keep on growing all the way to the highest clouds. He is giddy with excitement, for he has finally reached the shores of his imagined dreamland, the first step of his journey into the vast unknown wilderness. Adam is thinking that each day will bring a delightful gift of new beauty and awe, and that this will go on and on for his lifetime, like an extended good-feeling dream. A friendly chap with an Eastern European accent and light blond hair approaches him.

"Where do you hail from?" inquires the young man with sparkling, smiling eyes. "You're a Scot, I suspect?"

"Aye," replies Adam hesitantly, shy and hesitant at first from being sought out by a stranger so soon off the boat. "Most folks surmise I'm either Irish or a Scotsman acause o' me reddish hair, I suppose," he answers out of politeness.

"Ah, we do have redheads from where I hail from as well. Just by your speech I ascertained you're a Scotsman. I heard you bidding the captain farewell as you disembarked. There's something so distinctive about that accent, though the brogue is sometimes hard to understand. I met another Scotsman back in Europe whose talk sounded like gibberish. The dialect was called Gaelic, I learned later. At least I can understand you. My name is Adrian." He extends his hand warmly and they shake.

Adam takes this as a compliment, as he was dismayed when some of the deckhands had a hard time understanding his accent.

"Adam Baird's my name. Gaelic is o' the Highlands, and I'm from the Midlands o' the country," replies Adam. "Whaur ye from?"

"Austria," replies the young man. "The Hapsburg Empire of Queen Elisabeth and Emperor Francis Joseph. I'm homesick already for my beautiful homeland of Bad Ischl."

"Why did ye leave?" inquires Adam, proud that he is engaging in conversation so easily and posing questions to another without hesitation.

"My father and mother are a duke and duchess, and the royal class holds to strict social requirements that members must conform to, which boils down to marrying someone of the same class – inevitably someone picked out for one in childhood."

Adam bonds immediately with this exuberant lad, very happy to have someone to talk to in his new, somewhat overwhelming environment. He learns that he and Adrian are the same age, and that Adrian is from a very wealthy family of royal descent, a second cousin, once removed, to the Emperor of Austria. Adrian is seeking adventure and running away from his arranged marriage to a girl he does not fancy.

"She's an ugly duckling, as thick in the waist as a tree trunk, with silly, inane thoughts running circles in her head, usually pertaining to her social events or the wellbeing of her pernicious Pomeranian lap dog, who bares its teeth whenever I approach; that is, the dog, I mean to say, not Constance. Constance has nothing better to offer a man than an extremely large dowry."

"Aye, I'd hate an arranged marriage. Ye have to be compatible wi' yer wife."

"Ah, yes indeed! Well, Adam, do you have room and board yet? If not, I can take you to the roominghouse where I have lodgings and introduce you to my charming landlady, Mrs. Larkin. Not a grand hotel by any means, but very clean, and Mrs. Larkin makes a fine breakfast akin to a banquet to keep one going most the day, and for a modest fee!"

"That would be just what I desire. A clean bed to rest me weary, sea-ravaged body on and a hearty meal," answers Adam with enthusiasm, pleased with himself and feeling secure and prideful in that he has found a friend and a place to lodge so soon off the boat. Adam learns more about Adrian the next morning over a large breakfast of eggs, bacon, scalloped potatoes, sausage, hotcakes, porridge, fresh fruits, and hot coffee. Adam is accustomed to drinking tea, but relishes the hot, strong coffee, the way it washes the heavy meal down so well and fortifies him with added energy and alertness. *'Tis why Americans have so much gusto*, he thinks.

Adam learns that Adrian studied geological engineering at the University of Vienna in Austria, and upon graduation wrote to mining officials in the Sutro mines in Nevada, which his professor had referred him to, to inquire of their need for skilled mining engineers. He was immediately sent an offer letter for a job in the Caledonia Mines in Virginia City, Nevada Territory, without an interview, with a detailed map and itinerary as the best and most expeditious way to reach the mines. The mining supervisor, John MacInnes, had written back to say Adrian was greatly needed, as skilled workers were at a minimum, and that Adrian would have a good-paying job as soon as he reached Nevada. Because of his mechanical skills, Adrian hopes to find jobs along the route to Nevada to earn money. If not, he can use the money his parents gave him to build a house in the West. Adam decides to go with him in the hope of getting a good carpentry job along the railway lines, or perhaps work in the mines alongside Adrian.

Adrian and Adam first travel to Omaha, and, on arrival, hear that there is a great demand for laborers in North Platte, 290 miles from Omaha. The lads go to work as section hands in Omaha, but find the jobs unsatisfactory as they pay very poorly. They decide to go to Julesberg, Nebraska, to procure government jobs that that they have heard pay fair wages.

V. Adrian and Adam in Julesburg on the Nebraska/Colorado Divide

Adam and Adrian got work as oxen drivers hauling freight between Julesberg, Nebraska and a military outpost. Several years later it would be reorganized into a major military fort named Ft. Fetterman after Captain William J. Fetterman who was killed in an Indian battle near Fort Phil Kearny. Their first sighting of Indians in Julesberg gives them a shock and thrill they will never forget for their entire lives. The Pawnees, working for the federal government, are given free passage on the trains going through the towns. Three flatbed cars full of tribe members come rolling in, in a shockingly colorful display; each man is holding up a sapling ornamented with a human scalp. The Indians exhibit a sense of prideful achievement in their demeanor, and apparently have brought their warheads along for show.

"Christ Almighty, Adam, what do you make of that? You'd think they'd be arrested for flaunting human remains like Aborigines. What a bizarre sight!"

"'Tis their culture, Adrian," explains Adam, less disturbed by the sight than Adrian, who had never lived the rugged life of a farmer and been exposed to the rawness and bestiality of animals. "They're keeping record o' their successes in war like we wear medals for bravery in battle." Adam had read about this practice in his extensive studies of the West back in Scotland, but had no idea he'd come face to face with a display of this so soon. He is pleased with himself for having prior knowledge of this aspect of frontier life.

"Well, certainly a gruesome showing of their winnings; but, as you say, it's part of their culture and belief system," replies Adrian.

One of the carpenters looks on in disgust. "The government should shoot them savages on the spot for such revoltin' behavior, yet here they're gettin' paid better than us," he fumes. "I'm out of here! Not working for this damn government affair. Headin' back to Omaha, where it's civilized."

Adrian and Adam wave good-naturedly to him as he packs up his tools and bustles off belligerently. After the worker has departed, Adrian turns to Adam and says, "You're right. It's a part of their rituals. We've got to respect their practices. After all, we're on their land."

"Aye," replies Adam. "That carpenter feigned disgust just acause he daesna desire the job. An excuse to quit hard labor."

"I viewed him slacking off a number of times on the job – not a trained carpenter either," adds Adrian.

"Aye, he wouldn't have worked out," replies Adam, feeling blessed that he ran into Adrian when he did, the best companion for his trip across this daunting land, someone with common sense, intelligence, and compassion for indigenous people.

VI. Baird Family Anxiously Await Word from Adam

Adam set foot on American soil for the first time on 9 July 1864. By the third week in July, the Baird family has received no news of his safe passage, over a month after his departure, knowing only that he steamed off on the *S.S. Will-o-the-Wisp* on the sixth of June. Henry had described to them Adam's departure on June 10 in a letter from Glasgow, and an account of his lovely wedding to Annie on the fourth of June.

The family becomes more and more desperate to hear of Adam's safe arrival. On June 21, Henry relays to them the sad news of Annie's death in a short, solemn letter, and requests to bring the new bairn home to Drumdruils when the child has matured "a wee bit more." He asks them to inquire around for a wet nurse who can provide milk for the baby. Added to their worry over Adam's safety is the news of Annie's tragic death, and their worry over Henry and the bairn's wellbeing.

The family had become accustomed to Adam's regular correspondence from Glasgow, letters arriving within two days on the mail buggy that travels to and fro twice per day from Glasgow. Adam's last letter alerted them that he would be boarding the *S.S. Will-o-the-Wisp* at the Clyde River Port in Glasgow on the fourth of June. It is the long interlude of nothingness, of not hearing anything, that disturbs their equanimity and makes them rather fearful for Adam's safety due to imaginings of the worse kind.

One month after Annie's death, the third week of July, Henry arrives home from Glasgow with his wee bairn, appearing bedraggled and deflated with grief, but becoming more animated with pride in showing off his darling daughter. Despite his misery, Henry describes to his family, in vivid detail, the thrill of Adam's sendoff, the impressive image of the *Will-o-the-Wisp* steaming mightily across the foamy, wave-crested Atlantic, and of waving excitedly to Adam as Adam waved back, until the ship dipped into the horizon like a red speck of sun going down. Still they have heard nothing of Adam. His exact whereabouts are wide open to speculation, which has disposed the family to imaginative scenarios as to his fate – whether or not he made it to America on the treacherous seas is questionable to those with little knowledge of seafaring. The Baird family has read of fabled disasters of ships sinking in storms and passengers dying of disease en route, even murdered by travelers in the steerage compartment, and so they must rely on hope and faith that Adam is safe.

Malkie has wild visions of his brother living with the Indians by now, riding a beautiful white pony across open plains in search of buffalo, his red hair tied back with a leather strap, his feet shod in colorful beaded moccasins. Janet surmises that he's laden down with so much gold that he can't travel very fast due to the load, so he has purchased a team of mules. Henry, despite his mourning for Annie, jokes that Adam has been kidnapped by a band of bawdy "ladies of the night" who have put him to work as a slave in their establishment. Jean has visions of her poor son falling overboard on the high seas in a great storm, as they had endured such horrendous storms in Bridge of Allan the previous winter, and has mental pictures of her dear laddie succumbing to every other imaginable disaster that could beset a human being on a ship and in a savage land. It takes a cup of Violet's calming brandy and elderflower elixir to raise Jean up to a more positive frame of mind. The Wee Ones have conveyed to Emma and Violet that Adam is safe, has reached the American continent in good form, and have given them the exact time and date that he arrived at New York Harbor. The Wee Ones have explained that letters from Adam will take months to reach them, so they must be patient, but they can indeed rest assured that he is out of harm's way from the savage sea. The family is not reassured by what Emma and Violet convey to them. They have only a modicum of faith in the communications of Wee People, especially when coming secondhand from Emma and Violet, second-sighters not as reliably accurate as correspondence, as far as they are concerned. To ease his wife's fears, Adam Sr. makes a day trip to Glasgow to the Port Authority to check on the status of the *S.S. Will-o-the-Wisp*. He learns that the ship reached New York Harbor at Pier 18 on July 9, and that it is on its way back to Scotland. Weeks later, an article in the *New York Evening Express*, which the family found in the Glasgow City-County Library, confirmed the ship's arrival. Finally, in October, a clump of Adam's letters arrives at the post office in Bridge of Allan – he had mailed one a week, starting from the first day of his arrival in America.

Postmaster Dean Macleod, a Mason brother of Adam Sr.'s in the Glasgow Chapter, sends his messenger, Birdie Dowd, up the hill to alert the anxious Bairds. All along the route, Birdie tells everyone he meets of the news of Adam, and as a result of Birdie's circuitous route up into the hills to Drumdruils, the entire town is informed of Adam's fate hours before the Baird family. Malkie runs out to the mailbox to intercept the postmaster's messenger as he spies Mr. Dowd stashing a large bundle of letters into the box. Scratchy, guttural whoops of joy resonate in the morning air as Malkie runs back to the house. On receipt of Adam's letters, the family gathers around to hear Adam Sr. read the descriptions of his voyage across the Atlantic on the *Will-o-the-Wisp*. Thereafter, the thrilled family clan gathers in the sitting room each evening as customary, but in lieu of their usual Robert Burns, Shakespeare or Brothers Grimm, they read aloud, over and over, Adam's letters describing his exciting life out West. Adam is descriptive in details of his adventures on the vast, rugged plains, up in the high, daunting mountains, and of the fast-paced, monstrous railroad being constructed that will stretch across the entire continent, with the eventual coming together of the eastern and western lines. He makes a point to write eloquently of his experiences as a way of entertaining his family, and for him to remain always in their thoughts.

VII. First Letter from Adam — October 1864

Dear family,

I've reached America! What a grand country with so many novel sights and sounds. Met up right off the steamer with an Austrian gold miner/mining engineer. We traveled to Omaha together and got no work, but found there was great demand for labor on the Union Pacific Railroad, which is working north of Platte, 290 miles from Omaha, Nebraska. Got a job as a section hand, but unsatisfactory work and low pay. Heard there was demand for carpenters in government jobs. We got work as oxen drivers in a town called Julesberg, with a wagon train hauling freight between Julesburg and a military outpost.

In the wagon train there are about sixty wagons. Each driver has six yoke of oxen, which pull two wagons loaded with freight. The freight is used for building a new government post. Each morning the train starts before sun up and drives about twelve miles, which is a day's journey with oxen. In the evening about sunset, two wagon bosses will go ahead to select a camping site where there is water to be had. When they reach a suitable point, the wagon boss detours from the road. The first wagon drives the oxen to the right to start forming a half circle and the second drives to the left, forming the other side of the circle, meeting the first wagon at the head of the circle. The following wagons will alternate, one driving to the right and the next to the left, until the circle is completed, and this acts as a temporary corral in which the oxen are confined. After un-harnessing the oxen, they are turned loose from the corral with herders to watch over during the night. In the morning they are herded into the corral, and the wagon bosses on horseback ride around the outside of the corral, calling loudly "Cattle in the corral. Cattle in the corral." This is the signal for the drivers to get up and hitch their oxen. This means that the driver will have to enter the corral where there are over three hundred oxen and pick out first his wheelers (the oxen which come next to the wagon), put the yokes on them, attach them to the wagon, and so on, until his train of six oxen is complete. Each man has to know his own oxen intimately to achieve this.

Your loving son and brother,

Adam

Chapter Two

I. Henry Returns to Drumdruils After Annie's Death

When Henry arrives back at Bridge of Allan with his precious bundle of joy, it appears to his family that he is handling his grief over the loss of Annie admirably. That he bears internal sadness, which he certainly does, is not evident to the Bairds. Henry appears to be the same dynamic personality, witty and upbeat in his remarks, and exhibits great pleasure over the attention that he and his new bairn receive. The family concludes that he has come to terms with Annie's death by focusing on the present exigencies of his wee daughter.

The family is overjoyed with Wee Mary, "a perfect wee, rosy angel," as Violet describes her. They focus on the bairn rather than the death of the bairn's mother, and the household has a jubilant air as they look forward to the prospect of a merry future with this beautiful child. The convivial atmosphere at Drumdruils aids Henry in keeping his grief hidden before his family. At times, it seems to him that they have forgotten about Annie altogether, which is understandable to him, as Annie had never been part of their lives. Only Violet is aware that Henry's spirit is shattered at its deepest layers. She attempts to talk to him about Annie and the great love he had for her, so he can let out his emotions and deal with them, not bottle everything up inside and pretend everything is normal.

"Henry, ye're verra lucky to have experienced a closeness to anither human bein' as ye did wi' Annie. She'll be wi' ye in spirit for the rest o' yer life, and ye'll take wi' ye all her wonderful golden essence, the beautiful fabric o' her being, wi' ye whauriver ye go in life. What Annie bestowed to ye by her lovin' presence has expanded yer own spirit so that ye'll have a verra positive effect o' ithers, 'specially on yer daughter."

"Aye, Violet. I'll try to keep Annie wi' me in me heart." He brings his hands to his chest in a steeple of prayer. "She was a lovely jewel, and her golden essence was beyond measure, but I fear I'll forget her. I'm forgettin' what she looked like even now, and she's only been departed from this earth a short while."

"Na, Henry, ye'll niver forget her. She'll come back to ye in many ways, in many shapes and forms, throughout the entirety o' yer life. And at the end o' yer life, ye'll come to grips wi' a greater understandin' o' life and death."

"I pray that ye're correct, Violet. I do hope so," replies Henry soberly. "I've Wee Mary to raise into a fine woman; hopefully, she'll be as fine as her mother."

Contrary to his family's observations of Henry's wellbeing, townspeople and friends that he encounters notice the twinkle has gone from his eyes and his smile is not quite as bright. A wizened yet shrewd and empathetic old-timer at the Furry Beast remarks, "The fine lofty spirit o' the laddie has faded." Henry continues to amuse people with his witty comments and observations, and is attentive to everyone's problems and needs whenever he's in town, whether he comes in for farming errands or for drinks at the Furry Beast, but time will be necessary for him to fully recover his bounce and give so much of his energy to others. The grieving process is just that – a process – even for Henry, who has always seemed to others to have a unique mastery over life.

Though people are not aware of this, Henry's thoughts are constantly centered on Annie, especially when he is away from his bairn and family, even while he ministers to others, giving him less focus and energy to tend to the needs of friends and townsfolk. He has in the past been like a gardener nurturing his plants, his brilliant charm, compassion, and intuitiveness lifting everyone up to thrive in the fertile environment he has created for them. Townspeople, especially those in the tavern, notice Henry is still reaching out to engage others just the same as before, though they are dismayed that the intense spark and jovialness are lacking and his charms are not quite as effective as before. They pray that he will be renewed in totality to his charming self somewhere down the road.

With the help of Violet, who prompts Henry with suggestions that the clan chief, Elor, has given her as to the likely whereabouts of a spirit that has ascended from earth to the heavens, Henry daydreams of Annie soaring beyond the stars, somewhere so magical that mere humans can't fathom the wondrousness of it all. He is given comfort by the thought that she is in a beautiful, ethereal environment of kindness and tranquility where her good works can be appreciated. Violet tells Henry that Annie will be looking in on him and the bairn now and again, particularly watching over their beautiful daughter Mary, to guide and protect her from harm and help nurture her sweet spirit. Henry often looks up to the sky, to a place where there is an opening up between the layered clouds. *Annie must be up there somewhaur*, he thinks. He has an intense desire to jump into the space between the clouds and catch hold of her, to be assured that she definitely exists somewhere on another plane. He wonders how a tragedy like this can befall a laddie like himself, who loves life so much, who appreciates the gloriousness of life more than most. He hates to see his appreciation for life diminished because of his own personal tragedy, his wit and humor at a loss because tragic events in his life have taken a toll on his spirit. These thoughts are a positive part of Henry's grieving process in that he worries about his own well-being, a sign that his strong spirit for life will be returning slowly but surely.

Suggestive of his healing spirit is Henry's coming to terms with

Annie's demise. Henry concludes that Annie was too good for this world – she belonged somewhere better than a world of imperfection. There was no other reason for the Almichty to snatch her away so young and healthy. Henry has never thought about the imperfectness of the world or its imperfect people before, though his role has always been to minister the weak and fragmented citizens of Bridge of Allan, whom he has always empathized with and found endearing in their multilayered, problematic personalities. Henry also ponders on the death of wee Mary MacLaine, who died amongst the sheep. He has concluded that Mary MacLaine and Annie MacGivens were both special emissaries of the Almichty from beyond a place of worldly comprehension, both semi-angels who didn't plan to abide on the human plane for long, coming down to grace their presence on the earthly realm, to offer a bit o' honey to sweeten a bitter world, a warm, fragrant breeze to assuage the raggedness that humans create for themselves due to their imperfections.

When will Henry's jig-spiritedness return? Violet has asked this question of Elor, and Elor has assured Violet that Henry's innate nature can't be altered, and he'll come back just as buds sprout anew in perfect harmony on trees and plants after a long winter frost. Elor has given Violet a vision of Henry's future. *Our Henry,* he says, *will marry another wonderful woman down the road that he'll meet in the San Joaquin Valley of California after a number of years in America. That union with this outstanding woman will occur after Henry has matured to middle age.*

Violet is gratified by this news, and mollified by the fact that Henry will be in America someday with Adam and find another love, but for a good many years will be living a meaningful life in Scotland close to her and the rest of the Baird family where she can watch over him. She will treasure more years with her dear Henry close by as much as she treasures the morning sun.

II. Henry Discusses Death with Telford and Malkie

While groping for a lifeline in the bottomless pit of sorrow over losing Annie, Henry attempts to reach out and console his younger brothers, Malkie and Telford, who have become unsure of their safety in life, and in Malkie's case, fearful of stepping outside or going to sleep at night without imagining the bogeyman lurking in the closet or under his bed. Henry's approach is upbeat. He tries to manifest some of his old charm and humor, which he finds is a way out of his own bleak hole of despair. In this way, Henry works at renewing his own faith by helping his younger brothers, which has taken a harsh beating despite his talks with Violet, his own personal knowledge of Wee People as semi-angels, and the existence of pure angels that are emissaries of God. Death is the loss of the physical part of a person, and no matter what faith abounds, it is a great loss because the person who has died has transitioned to another invisible plane and can no longer be physically touched.

Malkie, the most sensitive of the Baird children, is not sleeping well at night and cries out in his sleep with nightmares. He has never gotten over the death of Mary MacLaine, and Annie's death has only fueled the fire of his fear of his own life being struck down at any moment in time.

"Henry, why do young, happy people die?" inquires Malkie, vigorously shaking his blond shaggy head back and forth, as if to dispel the evils surrounding him. "Why did the Almichty take your Annie away? It means that it could happen to me, or anyone o' us. God could swoop down a' take me from this world wi' a swoosh o' his hand. I'm the kind o' laddie that's bound to be taken acause o' me way o' findin' mischief all the time."

"Malkie, me laddie, I assure ye that Annie is in good hands and ye're not goin' onywhaur acause God needs ye down here. What would God do wi' a laddie like ye, who's fearful o' his own shadow? God certainly will want ye to stay on earth and work out yer shadow-fear, just as people must learn to be unafraid o' ghosts, goblins, and boogies that are all part o' imagination. Once ye learn how to shake hands wi' yer shadow, and have no fear, yer free to go from here!"

"I daena want to be free to go onywhaur. I desire to stay down here," proclaims Malkie, pointing at the ground.

"Well," says Henry, "if ye stand on yer head at night against a wall whaur there's an image o' ye on the wall, and reach out and shake yer shadow's hand, God'll view ye as being a brave laddie, and mebbe decide ye're richt for this world."

"Och, Henry, ye're jestin' wi me!"

"Aye, laddie, that I am, but let me inform ye o' this fact. God wants ye to stay acause he knows ye're the nicest o' the Baird siblings."

"How do ye know that? I'm verra nice indeed, but am I really the nicest o' all of us? How do ye know?" asks Malkie, looking pleased and coming around to believing Henry.

"Aye, laddie, God really wants ye to stay wi' the Bairds and has heard from many of the young lassies at church, as I've heard, that ye're verra, verra nice."

"What?" inquires Malkie incredulously. "Lassies at church daena like me. Lassies niver notice me. They niver iver speak to me."

"Well, ye have to pay attention to what's goin' on round ye, Malkie. I've heard from four different lassies that they find ye 'specially nice. They've come up to me and have inquired 'Are ye Malkie's brither?' When I reply aye, they say 'If only he'd notice me.'"

"Aye," says Malkie, in total consternation. "I'll pay more attention to what's goin' on at church. Usually I've me heid in me prayer book, so no one will notice I'm no singin'."

Telford inquires very soberly in his analytical way of thinking,

"What 'bout Annie? Henry, are ye awricht wi' yer emotions? Has this no affected yer ability to live happily? How're ye goin' to live without yer Annie? Ye must be verra lonely. How ye goin' to get past such a big loss and not be sad foriver?"

"Annie'll likely be an angel workin' on God's behalf. She has a pure, golden spirit and belongs to some heavenly order that's worthy o' her. 'Tis our purpose on earth to live exemplary lives and be honest and virtuous always for ithers to follow. Annie set a fine example for me to live by."

Henry clears his throat to hide a surge of emotion, which comes up without warning at inopportune times. "I'm na lonely, Telford," declares Henry emphatically. "I've me wee bairn and all o' ye Bairds in me family to carry me through this difficult time. I'll have to do me best, and be on me best behavior from now on, acause I've a daughter to bring up. No more jolly pranks for me. Wee Mary has no mother and she'll have to rely on me and all o' the Bairds for her love. Albeit, I expect to be waited on hand and foot by me brithers due to me misfortune," he teases.

"Well," says Telford kindly, "if ye need someone to talk to and help ye be happy again, I'm offering me services."

"Thank ye, Telford. That is very considerate o' ye. I might take ye up on that when I need to go on a long hike to get away from me troubles. I'll go wi' ye to yer healing woods, sit by a pond, and throw stones in for good luck, or catch some minnows in the stream to soothe me soul."

"Henry, I still daena ken why people have to die," says Malkie sullenly, not being at all uplifted by Henry's attempts to assure them that all is well with Annie. "Annie daedna do no wrong. Why did God take her away from ye and from her wee bairn who needs her for milk?"

"Me dear laddie," replies Henry, "if only I had the answer I would have gone to the ends o' the earth to avoid Annie's passing from me sphere o' life. God works in mysterious ways. We must go on wi' our lives and wait and see what transpires. Mebbe there's a pot o' gold at the end o' the rainbow, at the end o' our lives. Mebbe all those we've lost will be reunited wi' us someday at the end of our time on earth."

Whilst Henry is manifesting his humorous side with his brothers, he becomes so preoccupied that his grief is abated temporarily. When alone with his thoughts, it all comes pouring down in torrents, drowning him in sorrow, and he must work hard at keeping afloat. Violet is there for him, to help him remember the vastness of the universe and the wondrous places Annie might be dwelling in. Henry also finds solace in his wee bairn's presence. He adores her beyond measure. Each day, he rocks Wee Mary in his arms and sings to her, and is always present to put her to bed at night. Henry loves to look into Wee Mary's bright blue eyes that are so much like Annie's. He finds that they reflect beauty and the wondrous magic that exists in life. The existence of such a beautiful wee creature reassures him that life has purpose and meaning. And, of course, the existence of his Wee People friends like Punt, who has remained on his shoulder when out working on the land, is proof that there are other domains of God's universe where Annie is dwelling. "The Almichty must be all around," he reflects, "acause the Wee People are flitting o'er the earth, exhibitin' their charm and brilliant minds, and undeniably part o' God's workings. Whaur else would they be comin' from?" wonders Henry.

III. Sorrowful Letter from Henry to Adam

At a camp near what will be named Ft. Fetterman, where Adam was first able to mail letters home, he receives the letter from Henry with the shocking news of Annie's death. By the time he's gotten word,

Annie's been dead and buried for many months. Adam is overcome with shock, and worries greatly about what his brother must be going through. Annie was the shining light in his world, guiding him to a bright future.

1 August 1864
Dear Adam,
Annie had a sweet wee lass who is doing well. I've terribly sad news about Annie. She died in childbirth two weeks after you sailed, her death caused by the shock to her system from loss of blood. Miraculously, the baby, Mary Alice Baird, is alive and kicking. My heart lies shattered into a thousand pieces. Don't know if I'll ever recover from a loss of this magnitude, but just seeing the wee bairn so strong and energetic keeps me mind from doom. A lot of women die in childbirth, but poor Annie was not deserving of this because of her kind, wonderful spirit. I was with her for the birth of Wee Mary at Aunt Ethie's, but her parents were nowhere in the picture. They disowned Annie and her child before her death when they found out I was seeing her in Glasgow. Now the MacGivenses will have nothing to do with Wee Mary. I suppose they're too auld to care for a bairn anyway. Mr. MacGivens is well into his fifties, and in poor health from lung disease.

Happily, the bairn has come to live at Drumdruils in the care of our diligent and loving family. She's a wonderful bairn with a very sweet temperament, and makes everyone very happy. We've not had a baby living in the home since Wee Susan. The children, especially Emma and Janet, are delighted that they have another Mary to make up for the loss of their beloved Mary MacLaine. Faither and Mum are delighted with this wee lassie, and we have decided that she'll be brought up as a sibling to the others, though it's my responsibility to support her. Wee Mary will be aware that I'm her true father.

'Tis the reason for not corresponding sooner. I'm planning on departing to America next month. I cannot expect the folks to feed and clothe another child without financial assistance. No work to be found in Scotland because the recession has worsened. Times are hard on the farm wi' poor profits. I'll send more news as my plans become more definite. Take care o' yourself. I'm eager to shake your hand and give you a bear hug on the American frontier.

Your loving brother, Henry

When the tragic news arrives, Adam hikes out from camp to sit forlornly atop a high granite outcrop twenty yards away from the corral, with a bird's eye view of the oxen that graze languidly on the meager tufts of grass. He throws a couple of stones down to them, but they do not stir, too preoccupied in their feeding. In his present sullen mindset, he envies the oxen – lucky and naïve creatures not having to bear complex depths of emotion like humans. They are dumbly and blindly living in the present moment, oblivious to the past and future.

His brother's loss is akin to a heart-wrenching personal loss. He envisions Henry floundering in a maelstrom of pain, his spirit diminished. Guilt arises in Adam like an unwelcome guest – he is not at home to comfort Henry and the family, though he would gladly be a stand-in for Henry's suffering, if he could.

When Adam received the news from the outpost courier, images of a dying Annie, a grieving Henry, and a motherless child have been plaguing his thoughts as he goes about his daily activities. He has told no one of the death of Annie except his best friend Adrian. Adam cannot escape the tragedy even while sleeping, for he wakes with a start periodically throughout the night, barraged with the cold, incomprehensible reality of death. Nonetheless, there is a magical glory going on above as he lies awake. The nighttime sky speaks in flickers and twinkles, with a periodic show of comets and falling stars, and he wonders if life and death are but random occurrences of nature, like falling stars and meteors. Adam's faith in a higher power has, once again, been blown off its pedestal, cracking into pieces of uncertainty. He questions the existence of a loving God having a masterful plan for each individual on earth when so many die senselessly, especially the children he's helped bury. He concludes that nothing in life is guaranteed, just as wee Mary MacLaine froze to death in the sheep pasture by his sister's side and Annie died in childbirth.

Three months have passed by since Annie's death and I daedna know me brither was suffering terribly. I should've sensed his pain, which must've altered the entire well-being o' the family. Annie died a mere two weeks efter I departed!

The thought appalls him, as Annie was so beautifully alive and in the full bloom of pregnancy when he last saw her at her wedding. *She was a wonderful lassie and perfect for Henry*, he thinks.

Adam's total alienation from his family, mentally and physically, shrouds him with an acute feeling of aloneness. He questions whether he should've come to America. Adam is overcome with worry for Henry, and considers his options: he can turn around and head back home, or keep going west on his journey to the silver mines of Nevada. He has seen the frontier in all its glory, Indians galore and beauty abounding, but the work has been very tough and the wages dismal. There's not enough to send home to the family, just enough to eat and buy the basic necessities for travel to Virginia City. Has it been a selfish, self-indulgent trip with little consideration for his family's welfare? Nevertheless, Nevada lurks on the horizon as a chance for making a proper wage, maybe even a fortune, and the prospect of this possibility cannot blithely be set aside. Adam decides to venture on in his journey across the beautiful, vast frontier.

IV. Adam's Letter of Condolence

Dear Henry,

I was so terribly saddened when I heard the news o' Annie. I cannot imagine what you're going through. You're the strongest person I know, so I hope all your wit and intelligence, your extraordinary insight into the meaning of life, and your knowledge of the exquisite harmony going on in the universe will help you through this sad time. Poor Annie – she was like a brilliant gem, so lovely, gentle, and giving, and you must miss her greatly. Your bairn must surely be beautiful like Annie, and I'm certain she gives you a lot of joy, but this in no way negates the loss of your exceptional Annie. The best remedy for you, I believe, is to come to the West, away from all the pain associated with the places that you and she frequented. Please join me in America, if you can get away. Life has so many twists and turns, but I assure you that you'll find peace and harmony and will be safe in this vast beautiful land where anything and everything is possible.

Your loving brother, Adam

V. The Regal U.S. Pawnee Soldiers — 3 September 1864

In the following weeks, Adam is able to mail more correspondence home, as his party of oxen drivers moves in closer to the military fort. Scouts carry mail from their outlying camping grounds. When the family receives Adam's letters, over a month has passed since they were mailed.

Around this time, near the newly built, Adam sees Pawnees dressed up in U.S. uniforms acting as scouts in the employ of the U.S. government. He describes this remarkable vision in his letters, though neglects to tell his family the sordid details of the human heads on poles.

Dear Family,
There are Pawnee Indians working for the government. Working as an oxen driver, I came across three flat cars full of Indians dressed up in U.S. military uniforms. They were Pawnee scouts in the employ of the U.S. government to guard railroad builders from warring tribes. The government had arranged with Pawnee scouts to protect the overland building of the railroad and protect graders and track builders. The Pawnees had a battle with the Sioux, who were vehemently opposed to whites on their land. The Massacre of Plum Creek between Sioux (the most powerful of the Indian tribes) and the Pawnee practically ended all opposition to the building of the railroad. Many Sioux were killed. It is quite tragic, as they are a beautiful, industrious people. Both tribes have their merits and I wouldn't want to choose between them.

I will not end this letter on a sober note. I am enjoying the West immensely in all its glory. I have decent work, good food, and the companionship of my good friend Adrian. I think o' ye all in the "Land of Drums," and oftentimes at night I wake up and think I'm at home in Scotland. It is a disappointment when it registers otherwise.

Your loving son and brother,
Adam

"Listen up, children!" Adam Sr. exclaims excitedly, uncharacteristic of his typically stern, composed demeanor. "Adam's met up with Indians already! Says they're regal and handsome, nothing resembling the stereotype ye get from the Wild West shows in Edinburgh and Glasgow."

Later that evening, Malkie, Telford, Janet, and Emma are on the sun porch discussing Adam's letters and reliving his experiences in their imaginary play. Malkie imagines aloud with his eyes gazing out the window, "The Indians are riding across the plains. I'm riding at the head and we spy a giant buffalo to slaughter for supper;

the creature appears so mammoth, like a small hill."

Emma replies, "Malkie, ye numbskull, Indians daena have supper in America, nor do they have tea time, breakfast, or dinner."

Malkie says, "Well, they've some sort o' meal when they eat thegither and enjoy their kill. They enjoy eatin' much more than we Scots, for they have worked verra hard for their game, and are proud o' their brave feats."

"Aye," rejoins Telford. "I read that buffalo are very sacred creatures to the Indians, and when they partake in their flesh, they take in some o' the spirit o' the buffalo, which endows them sacred energy, and makes them much stronger than ordinary people."

"Aye," adds Malkie, "they eat raw hearts that are drippin' wi' blood!"

"Mebbe eatin' buffalo is like goin' to church for them," replies Janet.

Says Emma, "Aye, their homes are verra beautiful and they make beautiful baskets and jewelry that are magical acause their squaws' hands have created these wi' the energy from the spirit o' the buffalo."

"I'm eating the raw heart o' the buffalo as I'm the brave who made the first kill," says Malkie, pantomiming his mouth full o' red meat. He makes an *Mmmm* sound while chewing.

"Och, Malkie," says Emma in disgust, "ye're na an Indian and ye daena ken how to eat buffalo."

Says Janet, "The women stay home and make their beautiful things like woven rugs and woven baskets to carry water, and even baskets for their bairn. I would love to do that kind o' task. Think how pretty our house would be wi' beautiful baskets decorating the shelves."

"Mebbe Adam could send us some baskets," says Telford.

Replies Malkie, "Is that all ye can think 'bout, is weavin' ugly baskets? Daena ye know the total beauty o' the Indian way of life, wi' so much freedom, livin' off the land, roaming across the plains, followin' the great buffalo spirit?"

"Malkie," says Telford, "I'd give me two front teeth for one o' their precious rugs or baskets."

VI. Adam's Heroic Rescue of Fellow Teamster

15 September 1864
Dear Family,
While driving oxen a scary incident happened. I went antelope hunting with a group of fellows when in camp. We had to get back to camp by crossing the creek. This meant taking off our clothes and swimming across, with clothes tied on a rope that men on the other side helped to pull across. Martino, another teamster, tied his clothes on the rope and jumped in, not realizing the water would be over his head. He immediately started struggling, for he couldn't swim. By the time I reached him he had come to the surface three times and then sunk down for good. I had to go down under and find him on the murky bottom and haul him to shore. He was unconscious and not breathing when I brought him in, so he was put over a barrel and rolled back and forth until the water poured out of his lungs. After that he revived nicely and was the same unlikeable personality as before, though would not go close to water again.

Your loving son and brother,
Adam

Adam doesn't mention to his parents that Martino Bellini is a young man of questionable character who had made fun of him many times because of his accent. On one occasion, he had asked

Adam if he had a lisp, and why his words were "garbled" all the time. On another occasion, he'd heard Martino mocking him to the other fellows, chanting a singsong of "That Scot has a sock up his snout." A lot of laughter had ensued, and in fear of more ridicule, Adam had shied away from talking to anyone but Adrian for the next couple of days. Adam had cringed whenever Martino pretended to not understand him, which was often. Martino spoke in choppy short sentences with a definite accent as well, as he was Italian, which makes him a candidate to be made fun of, though no one had the nerve to do so. The fellows sense Martino is not as good-natured as Adam.

Adam also neglects to tell his family that his own life had been in great jeopardy from hypothermia from being in the cold water for so long while rescuing Martino. When he came out of the water, he had to be revived by the fire. He also fails to tell them that Martino had been declared dead when he was first brought out, and it had been a last crazy attempt to revive him by rolling him over a barrel – no one thought this would work – that had brought him miraculously back to life.

Martino was not the same for a couple of weeks after his resuscitation, and it became clear he had some long-term effects from oxygen deprivation, as he had trouble with orientation. He eventually recovered, but would never go near the water again, even to wash. He never criticized Adam's Scottish accent again, but had not thanked Adam for saving his life. Adam got the impression that Martino would have greatly preferred had someone else saved him. Everyone in the camp cast Adam as a hero after that day.

20 September 1864

Dear Family,

We finally reached a military outpost, and found there was no work, so we had to turn around and go back to Julesberg. Got work with a railway company while in Julesberg. I am working on a road that will eventually reach Ogden, Utah, a distance of 800 miles. My friend, Adrian, had a job lined up in Virginia City, and left with a wagon train of Mormon settlers once we reached the post. Hated to see my first and only friend in America go and leave me on my own again. I decided to keep working on the railway to earn much-needed money so I will be able to set up house once I'm in Nevada, as well as send a wee bit home after starting work. Adrian will secure me a job in the mines as a carpenter, as he has many contacts. He promises a very good job waiting for me when I arrive, though this might be many more months. If you don't hear from me, please don't be alarmed. I will be out in a vast stretch of wilderness where track is being laid with no direct mail lines. I will keep writing, though, and once I reach a major outpost will send my correspondence in a batch.

Affectionately,

Adam

P.S. The West is as beautiful as Scotland but unlike Scotland. The terrain is diverse, with many very high mountains decked with forests, and vast plains as far as the eye can see. The total effect is vast swaths o' land as unlimited as the stars in the sky. The magnificent mountains, many that could be ranked as Wonders of the World, are spiritually inspiring to any tired soul that has traveled from afar. 'Tis because of the vastness o' the land that one becomes overjoyed wi' a feeling of God's eternity, for this land gives credence to the belief that there's a divine plan behind the snow-topped mountains, bright blue skies, roaring rivers and streams, verdant forests, and colorful woodlands, a needed revival to my faith in the Almichty that I take solace in.

Sadly, right before he wrote to his family, Adam bid farewell to Adrian, for Adrian was starting out for Virginia City to his engineering job in the mines. Adam's long-time companion joined a party of mostly young men from the eastern shore of Massachusetts who were also heading to Nevada for the mines. The young men would be traveling with a party of Mormons until they reached Utah.

Adam was despondent and lonely after Adrian left, for his jovial friend has been a constant companion and security net in the New World. Outgoing and charismatic, Adrian acted as his brother Henry had in Scotland, attracting groups of friendly and informative people to them. Adam reflects that he'll have to learn to be more outgoing after he strikes out on his own in order to get information or find human companionship. He gave Adrian a long bear hug and wished him a safe journey. He promised to hightail to Nevada as soon as the track-laying job was completed.

Chapter Three

I. Aftermath o' Annie's Death — Autumn of 1864

Henry's grieving process takes a turn for the worse as the autumnal environment loses its pleasurable warmth and golden colors, becoming enveloped in a dismal gray and chilling cloud cover, a harbinger of a cold winter to come. Annie has been gone since summertime, and Henry's been working valiantly on maintaining a positive outlook on life. *People leave the earth physically*, he tells himself, *but they continue to exist spiritually elsewhere*. He plays this mantra over and over in his mind to defeat his sorrow. Annie had greater things to do in this grand universe.

Henry visits the Furry Beast Pub almost every day after work. With the aid of his sidekick Punt, he has come up with an arsenal of outlandish jokes to please an eager entourage. This gives him a temporary reprieve from the pain of his loss, but the devastation is like an open wound that refuses to heal completely, resurging when memories of what was and thoughts of what could have been come into play. As time goes by he feels the distance between himself and Annie lengthening. In the early days after Annie's death, Henry could sense her beautiful spirit close by, no longer physically there, but a lingering, soothing presence at the periphery of his awareness. He had been consoled by the fact that her presence, albeit ethereal, would be everlasting. Lately, though, he's become aware that he's forgetting what Annie looked like, as her image is dimming, and he's lost a sense of her presence hovering ever so subtly at the back of his mind. Aunt Ethie sent pictures of the wedding day, taken by a renowned Glasgow photographer, a good friend of hers, who attended the post-nuptial supper at the bungalow. Henry couldn't bear to give the beautiful pictures more than a cursory glance, as it was too painful to see what he had lost.

For Henry, life has become a fallow, rocky field whose soil is not tillable, a vast expanse of grey, chilling nothingness, devoid of light or dimension, with dreams not worth the trouble of sowing because Annie is not by his side. The sky, without Annie, does not appear wondrous and magical to him. Sunlight is inconsequential, nighttime stars are but dull, yellowish rocks, and the pale moon is a flat and pathetically lifeless rock. His days are bearable only because of his daughter's existence. Wee Mary reminds him so much of Annie. Henry tries valiantly to focus on the miracle of his daughter being alive. *Efter all, me wee bairn might've as easily hiv died alongside Annie.*

Poor Wee Mary! Mary will niver ken Annie, the woman who loved and nurtured her in the womb, reflects Henry. *She'll hiv me, o' course, but I'm a shell o' the man I wis withoot Annie, and I'll be goin' afar to America. Sadly, wee Mary might forget me.*

In America, Henry hopes to distill his pain. The whole of Scotland represents to him a ground of lost dreams. Plans of traveling to America are a lifeline that he intuitively grasps onto, as the thought of a far-off destination away from everything sad grants him a modicum of relief from his despair. He can well justify his travel, as it is a proper means of gaining support for his daughter. He and Annie had, many times, discussed their desire to send their child to college, and it is his steadfast desire to fulfill all the wishes that Annie had for her daughter. Henry's secure in the fact that Mother and Violet will take very good care of Wee Mary while he's away. *Until I return, God willing, she'll be happy wi' the family; she'll thrive in the Baird home wi' the siblings*, rationalizes Henry.

Henry mourns greatly over the next several months. His travel plans to America and his newborn daughter are the only reasons for him to get out of bed in the morning. His family, friends, and acquaintances watch their beloved comedic star, who stands for all that is fun and joyful in life, go through the motions of being fun and witty, but appearing so beaten down and dispirited that they wonder if he'll ever climb out of his hole.

Henry has reached out to the MacGivenses to visit their grandchild at Drumdruils, just as Ethie had beseeched them to come to Glasgow shortly after the bairn's birth. They haven't acknowledged receipt of his invitation to Drumdruils. The MacGivenses, who are devastated over the loss of their beloved Annie, continue to reject the bairn, not recognizing her as any relation of theirs. Henry is so proud of his beautiful and sweet daughter that he can't fathom their attitude and thinks they'll come around eventually. This has not been the case. Mr. MacGivens has been heard around the pubs in town spouting out in a drunken stupor that the bairn's blood is tainted with Satan's. Henry has taken full responsibility for supporting Wee Mary, and he's definitely decided that the only way to support his child well is in America.

Me child'll be fine at Drumdruils whether I stay or gae. She'll be happy wi' the ither children to play wi', and wi' Violet and the folks round she'll thrive, just as I've thrived growing up here, he reflects.

Punt sticks to Henry like glue during this difficult period of mourning, always perched on his shoulder whenever Henry leaves the house, recounting lame jokes in his ear nonstop. The merry sprite pulls pranks on the townspeople to which Henry feigns a half-hearted laughter, though his spirit is not livened.

About two months after Annie's death, he is in town on an errand to buy salve for a sheep wound inflicted by wire fencing. Punt tags along, and before Henry can stop him, the wee jokester has popped the buttons off the bodices of two middle-aged, bosomy biddies, who are in the throes of juicy gossip as they sit on a bench in the town square. Punt's maneuver necessitates the ladies to shield their chests with their forearms and run for cover behind a thick hedge. On another fun-filled day for Punt, a drunken man's shoe soles were dabbed with sugary tree sap while he was drinking in the pub, so that when the poor man tried to walk, his feet had difficulty getting off the ground. Henry had tried to laugh at Punt's antics, but could only manage a half-smile.

A "Most Wanted" poster for the derelict who assaulted the women is put up in the Bridge of Allan post office. The two distressed biddies put out a version of Punt far off from his true diminutive size. Their description of the assailant is a chunky man of about 5'5", a large square jowl and unshaven bristled chin, broad shoulders, and long, agile fingers, enabling the perpetrator to rip open bodices with lightning speed. The assailant ran into a nearby pub and was never seen exiting. It's been surmised that he was a phantom, as stories of lifetime regulars who have died in the pub and now reside there are legendary. Punt is overjoyed with his post office depiction. Suffice it to say, the sprite began to dress in Western attire, trying to resemble the rugged outlaw on his "Most Wanted" poster.

II. Plains, Trains, and Indians — Ogden, Utah — September 1864

When Adam caught sight of the Pawnees for the first time he gasped at the surreal image before him, a mindboggling spectacle for an impressionable young man. As he told his children in later years, it was comparable to viewing a motion picture for the first time, or sighting a fast moving, newly invented roadster roaring down a country lane at an impressive speed. The Plains Indians were so different than his preconceived notion – entirely outside the box of anything he could have imagined. They were not fierce aborigines with short, squat, brown bodies, a notch below human beings, as he had been told. Standing in all their glory before him were magnificent specimens, fine-featured and bronze, with beautifully proportioned bodies and fluid movements. What surprised him most of all was their belongingness to the environs – he sensed them to be as much a part of the land as the beautiful rivers, lakes, trees, and valleys. To Adam, it seemed as though this glorious country had been created for their existence, so they could blossom and prosper. He was spellbound and rendered speechless by their awesome sight. When he listened to one brave conversing with the cavalry officer in perfect English, Adam apprised him to be an intelligent human being who demonstrated qualities of integrity, forethought, and civility. He would have liked to converse with them, to show his admiration, but he was too timid, and so stood gazing at them "like a lump on a log," as he told his children many years later. Adam observed the Indians closely as a cavalry officer handed one of them an official document and shook his hand. The Pawnees trotted off on their horses as gracefully as birds taking flight to the sky, and it wouldn't have surprised him in the least if they could fly like birds.

Dear Family,
The Indians have lithe, muscular bodies and carry themselves with an air of being totally at ease in their physical bodies. They have absolute authority over their physical environment, as evidenced in the way they are very friendly and winked at me like I was a young spellbound child, which is what I felt like. Perhaps they could sense that I found them regal and was awestruck by them. They remind me of Henry in some ways, in his carefree, fearless attitude about life, as Henry is comfortable in his own skin as well. Henry would get along with these Indians admirably.

Love with all my heart,

Adam

P.S. Henry, daena let this gae to yer heid, whit I just wrote!

While he was viewing the Indians, Adam had looked around at his fellow European comrades to gauge the differences between the white and Indian races. The Europeans, he had assessed, are visitors traveling over the land to other places to find profit in the gold and silver mines, benefiting from the plentiful fish and game of the land, chopping down trees for train tracks and housing, and killing off the buffalo that the Indians depend on for food. The visitors, he had reflected, regard Indians to be bizarre savages, a lowly order of man. The Indians see white men as heathen interlopers who have no respect for land or life, and kill all the buffalo as well as their brethren without forethought. Adam empathized with the Indian viewpoint. Perhaps white men are an irreverent, ghostly predator species from a faraway part of the earth that have no sense of the sacred. He feels an affinity to the Indian way of life, and often imagines himself mounting a horse and galloping across the plains with them, abandoning the white race altogether. Some day, some how, he pledges to do his part in making up for white man's transgressions.

III. Henry's Travel Plans Delayed — October 1864

Henry's intention to join Adam in America in October 1864, six months after Adam's departure, as he and Annie had planned, doesn't pan out. Adam Sr., in his early seventies, becomes increasingly plagued by arthritis and back pain, and spends many days inside working at his desk on the farm ledgers, relying more on more on Henry to manage the seasonal berry picking crew (June through late September), which gives him little leeway for embarking on a steamer before winter sets in. Henry, being the eldest son living on the ranch, feels it is his duty to pitch in to keep the ranch afloat, at least until the economic tide has taken an upswing and his father is better. The recession in Scotland is worsening, feed for the animals is more expensive, and the jams and jellies, considered a luxury item for many, are not as profitable in a poor economy. Henry also feels a responsibility to his daughter to ensure she is happy and thriving. Wee Mary is at home, well cared for by Violet and his mother in the daytime. He spends much time in the evening entertaining her and the other children.

After the berry harvest, Henry supervises the annual sheep shearing in early October, which must be completed before the severe cold of winter sets in, as well as the mending of fences and pruning of berry plants for the next season. His parents also insist that Henry finish his last year of school now that he has a child to support and will need a career. He spends his mornings and early afternoons at the schoolhouse, and another six hours ranching.

Miss Carroway quizzes him almost daily regarding Adam's whereabouts, but Henry has to disappoint her time and time again, as they haven't heard from Adam in a very long time – finally, Mr. Dodson brought the batch of letters, in December 1864, those that Adam had mailed from a military outpost in Wyoming. At that time, he had carried a letter to Miss Carroway from Adam, parts of which she read to the rest of the class; the more intimate parts she kept to herself. The lovely letter found a home in Miss Carroway's hope chest, to be cherished for the rest of her short life. Henry decides to leave for America in late spring of 1865, when he has graduated from school and Mary is out of infancy.

Letter from Adam:

Dear Miss Carroway (Edna),

I hope this letter finds you in merry spirits and well in constitution. I will forever think fondly o' the quaint schoolhouse in Bridge o' Allan presided over with such love and devotion by you, a faithful servant to knowledge, and will remember your wonderful teaching methods and your unabated dedication and belief in all your pupils. We students were indeed fortunate.

The intimate times I spent with you will be cherished as a gift that comes in handy when out alone in the wilderness for so many months, sometimes with no one to talk to but birds and bees, and sundry living creatures, large and small, that go "boo" in the night. Our friendship was warm, sensual, and lovely, yet regrettably our relationship was destined to be short. I will never forget the generosity in love that you gave to me, a young, curious, inexperienced laddie.

The West is everything that it is made out to be. The country is more beautiful than can be imagined, the vastness and purity of nature awe-inspiring. I think you would find it to your liking, but it is a rugged and untamed land, not made for someone with fragile sensitivities to transit easily. Some day it will be tamed with train travel, but I fear the awesome grandeur will be lost as time progresses, with more and more tracks laid down and more settlers moving in. For now, think of me in a beautiful place, almost like Heaven.

With great respect and admiration,

Adam Baird

P.S. I am attaching souvenir images that you can share with your class, which I have procured at some of the major stops along the way, mostly forts and large outposts, where I have been able to mail letters. The images give one an idea of the natural beauty of the open landscape, but in no way come close to its true grandeur.

IV. Bridge o' Allan — Christmas 1864

For Christmas, the children receive a large, beautifully constructed train set that had been made by Adam in the Bridge of Allan wheelwright's shop before he left for Glasgow. Mr. MacDuffy, Adam's old boss, personally delivers the gift to the Drumdruils farm. The children are overjoyed and spend endless hours building train stations and connecting wood tracks through the cities that Adam has written about along the 800-mile route of the great Union Pacific Railway across the continent. It is a special, magical Christmas that they'll treasure in their hearts. The train set will remain at Drumdruils for future generations.

The children have new kittens in the house that play alongside the children, batting at the cars as they come round the bend. Kipper the dog, who desires to be in on the fun, puts up his head and howls at the sound of the train's whistle as it roars down the track. The children play cowboys and Indians with their train set, and set up Indian statues on the flatbed cars, which they have constructed from papier mâché. Adam had described to them that Pawnees ride standing up on the flatbeds.

V. Wee Mary Alice Baird Gravely Ill — February 1865

Two months after Christmas, Wee Mary Alice Baird, eight months of age, comes down with pneumonia and gives the family a terrible scare. Emma and Janet are filled with dread and stand vigil at Mary's bedside when not in school, fearful that Mary will be taken from them despite assurances from the Wee People that she'll recover in full.

"D'ye think God will take anither Mary?" inquires Emma. "The Wee Ones say she'll recover, but what if they're wrong?"

"Mebbe the Almichty favors Marys in his Heaven," replies Janet.

"Ah, I daena desire our Wee Mary to leave us. We canna live

without our sweet precious bairn. The Wee Ones say she'll na be ailin' for long, but I daena ken if that means she'll abide here wi' us, or be somewhaur afar in the universe whaur she's na ailin'. Aye, mebbe God takes Marys to Heaven acause they've the name o' the Mother o' Jesus. Mebbe there's a special place for Marys in Heaven," says Emma.

"Emma," replies Janet with great trepidation, "ye better check wi' the Wee Ones again. Find out if all the Marys go to Heaven as children, and if our Wee Mary dies, will she become an angel like Mary MacLaine?"

The lasses continue to stand vigil over Mary throughout the week. Mary is having extreme difficulty breathing from pneumonia. Violet brings home some medicine from Twixie, Punt's sister, in the form of an herbal poultice to wrap around her neck. She also brews a special tea for Wee Mary with herbs that Twixie has recommended. Twixie brings over a special moldy cheese that they spread on toast for Mary, and instructs them to give her a piece twice per day. In a week's time, the bairn is on the road to recovery. Her health is frail for several weeks thereafter, and she has lost a lot of weight. Henry is afraid to leave her for fear that she will have a recurrence due to her weak constitution and postpones leaving for America until the following year.

Henry spends his free time playing with his Wee Mary and the other children, taking charge over the Baird outdoor games that he and Adam had refereed together. Wee Mary is a beautiful, bright child and looks a lot like Annie, though with the strong-willed, lively temperament of the Bairds. Henry derives great solace in having a living link to his late wife.

Story Time becomes an immensely pleasurable sojourn for him, as he can sink into an imaginary life that the children are naturally in tune with. He and Violet read to the children in lieu of Adam Sr., who habitually lies on the couch to ease his severe back pain. He greatly enjoys being in the room to participate, voicing his strong opinions, and keeping the children in line – in particular, the adolescent laddies, Malkie and Telford, who have a tendency to wrestle and vocalize at inappropriate moments.

Henry says to Emma, "Select yer tale for tonicht, lassie." Emma picks Shakespeare's *A Midsummer Night's Dream* again, as it deals with Wee People royalty, the King and Queen of the Fairies, Oberon and Titania. The children never cease to be charmed by the wee changeling that the queen has stolen, or traded for, whom she adores and won't give up.

VI. A Midsummer Night's Dream

Violet summarizes the play that has thus far been read at the previous Story Time – the children know by heart the main parts, as they have heard it three to four times. She then summarizes the second half of the play about the wedding, as well as the play that the motley group of actors act in.

"I'll cover the rest of the play quickly so we may move forward with another story this evening before dinner, as Emma has already chosen anither fairy tale from *Grimms' Fairy Tales* and is eager to hear it again, as she is writing a report on it for school.

"As we left off in *A Midsummer Night's Dream*, the two young couples are sleeping in the woods, as well as Queen Titania, all having been given a strong brew by the mischievous sprite named Puck," summarizes Violet. "Now, we begin the story of what happens next in the woods."

The four lovers (Lysander, Hermia, Demetrius, and Helena) are awakened by Theseus, Hippolyta (his future bride), and Hermia's father. They've ventured into the magical woods to watch Theseus's actors rehearse their play. Most of the brew has worn off, so Lysander again loves Hermia, but Demetrius continues to love

Helen, for the love juice remains in his eyes. Hermia's father persists in his demand that his daughter, Hermia, marry Demetrius, but since that young man no longer wants her, and all four are happy with their partners, he ceases to oppose Lysander marrying his daughter. Theseus gives them permission to marry on the day set for his own wedding to Hippolyta.

Queen Titania also awakens. As the others, she thinks that she has been dreaming. Puck removes the ass's head from Bottom, and the bewildered weaver makes his way back to Athens, reaching the Greek city just in time to act in the play, and saving the day, since he is to act out the part of Pyramus, the hero. The Master of the Revels tries to dissuade Theseus from choosing the laborer's play for the wedding night. Theseus, however, is intrigued by a play that has a reputation as being brief, merry, tragic, and tedious. So Bottom and his troupe present an entertaining, albeit awful, *Pyramus and Thisbe*, much to the merriment of all the guests, who think it's a comedy. After the play, the two bridal couples retire to their suites, and Oberon and Titania sing a fairy song over them, promising that they and all of their children will be blessed.

"And Shakespeare concludes his play on a verra happy note," says Violet. "Everyone ends up marrying the person they're intended to marry. The couples will be happy foriver. Even the King Oberon and Queen Titania, royalty o' the magical fairy kingdom, come back thegither, for they do love one anither despite their constant bickering o'er the changeling."

VII. Henry with Wee Mary at Drumdruils Farm — 1864 – 1866

Life for Henry becomes routine in the running of Drumdruils.

He sinks himself into managing the ranch, a catharsis in combating his grief over the loss of his precious Annie. It is a pleasure to spend his time outdoors in the fresh air of the golden pastures surrounded by woods where tranquil sheep and cows graze, and, seasonally, amongst the sweet-smelling strawberry, currant, and gooseberry fields. For the next couple of years, Henry puts off joining Adam in America because he is very much needed on the ranch. By the end of 1866, Malkie and Telford have matured into strong, competent adolescents of fourteen and fifteen years of age, respectively, and have voiced their desire to take over the major duties of running the farm in lieu of continuing their educations. Henry continues to waver in his once strong desire to go to America, and is considering staying at Drumdruils for good. Wee Mary is a major factor in his indecision of staying or heading out West. He is more on the staying side of the fence. Mary will turn three years old in June 1867, and has blossomed into a lovely and robust child with second-sight. Henry is immeasurably proud of his daughter, but worries that her second-sight might cause her complications in life, as the gift has brought difficulties to his own, though he concludes the benefits of being second-sighted far outweigh the strife. Being a second-sighter as an adult comes with a genius-like ability to witness firsthand the complex synchronicity of the earth and universe, and thereby the wondrous interplay of different planes of reality. A second-sighter has a unique perspective on universal life in all its forms, most invisible to those on earth, including seeing the engaging Wee Ones.

The downside of having second-sight past childhood is that it brands an adult so different on many planes from his friends and peers. In Henry's case, it has endowed him with a lot of spunk, but there were many times as an adolescent that he was involved in wayward behavior through the orchestrations of Punt. Other people sense that a second-sighter is different, even sometimes odd, but in Henry's case the gift has worked to his advantage because he is so endearingly funny and personable. Wee Mary, Henry is certain, will possess second-sight as an adult, and Violet agrees, as Mary already has an uncanny ability to foresee events that other children with second-sight aren't in tune with.

Punt has latched onto the child because she is part of Henry's world, and the two tours de force, the Wee Sprite and the Wee Lassie, have become bosom buddies, freeing Henry up from Punt's constant diligence over him. As Violet puts it, Punt and Wee Mary, being the same size and temperament, are perfect playmates, as they both possess the same insatiable energy and curiosity. Punt tries to be the leader in their playful interactions, and Mary, strong-willed and spoiled by the older Baird children, resists the directives of the self-named leader, and oftentimes gets her own way with the softhearted sprite.

The Baird family hasn't heard from Adam since his last batch of letters in December 1864, written several months prior in October. The time they last heard from him, he was in the Platte River Valley, continuing his work as a carpenter on the tracks. In that letter, Adam had informed them that his friend, Adrian, had left for Virginia City, Nevada.

I'll probably not make it to Nevada for a long while, not 'til the tracks are laid all the way to Ogden, Utah, Adam had written.

Finally, three months later in March 1865, the family receives their latest news of Adam's journey in a letter mailed from Cheyenne, Wyoming.

January 1865
Dear Family,
I'm still working with the railway company. The road reached Cheyenne and my crew was sent to build a bridge across Dale Creek. This was near the summit of the Black Hills, a spur of the Rocky Mountains, and it is the highest point on the overland road, about 9,000 feet. I will not be able to mail this letter until I reach civilization in Ogden, Utah, which will be months. Don't worry if you don't hear

from me for a while.

Love,

Adam

VIII. Laying Down Track and Building Trestles, Platte River Valley — 1865 – 1867

The excitement and novelty of America doesn't combat Adam's homesickness for his family, but as his journey progresses, he relishes in the extraordinary sights, scents, and sounds of the new land, a sensual utopia that lifts his spirit and lends to him a surety that his decision to come to America was undeniably a good choice. He makes an effort to convey the beauty of his experiences to those he left behind in Bridge of Allan, through his descriptions, in order that they may uplifted by the excitement of his travels, and with the hope of inspiring his younger brothers to join him. Adam has a smidgeon of guilt that he is enjoying himself whilst his family is being stretched financially, though he rationalizes that he is one less mouth to feed, and he will be sending money home as soon as he starts work in Nevada.

The country is extraordinarily awe-inspiring as they pass through newly discovered territories of the West. He looks up to majestic mountains and stunning waterfalls and is humbled in appreciation. Adam thinks the magnitude of its glory can only be the work of a higher power. As he encounters the unparalleled beauty of each new territory, some never before trod by white men, his spirit is sent soaring, shivers running up and down his spine. The West lends to Adam precisely what he'd been searching for – a sense of the limitless possibilities in life, as the unfathomable immenseness and magical dimension of the land bestows in him a confidence in his own potential.

Adam tells himself he will never again settle for an ordinary life back in Scotland. He concludes that if he'd stayed in his homeland, he would not have experienced this newfound growth of mind, body, and soul, would have lived his life in a closed off, one-dimensional state of mind, though he would not have realized the humdrumness of his life. He would have been content, but not inspired to soar and grow his spirit as he has in the New World. He remembers the parable he heard in a pub recounted by an old timer. It regarded a man who came to a fork in the road and was given a choice as to which way to go. One path led to a comfortable, serene, and uneventful life; the other was a path that was a steep uphill climb with a peak that might never be reached, but if great obstacles were conquered and the mountaintop reached, a feeling of intense satisfaction in accomplishment would be granted to this individual and his spirit would be immeasurably loftier.

Most people daena choose the uphill battle, thinks Adam. He is proud in that he sees himself moving on the difficult uphill grade of the American frontier in order that his spirit will forever soar and feel free.

Adam has immense pride in his opportunity to experience the West, and he tries to convey to his family in his letters a sense of the historical value of his having the rare opportunity that only a minority will have of experiencing the new land in its pristine state and meeting its indigenous people, for he senses that the land and its people will not remain untarnished. He envies the Indians for having had possession of this land from the beginning of time, as the elders, the guardians of their history, have orally conveyed. Adam desires to own a piece of this land someday and this desire renders him slightly guilty, in that he wants to hold onto a piece of this awesome beauty for himself that is not rightfully his, and yet he does not want this for too many others. He can rationalize this by promising himself to be one of a few who will responsibly fight to protect its pristine beauty and the rights of its native inhabitants. Adam cringes at the destructiveness of the emigrants who have inflicted great damage to the Indian way of life in a habitat that rightfully belongs to them. *The problem can only get worse the more folks that tread through this land without worshiping or even respecting it*, he surmises.

When Adam sees something extraordinary or bizarre, he jots down notes in the little pocket diary, which he carries at all times in his breast pocket for future use in letters to his family. Indeed, conversing with "Plains savages" for the first time inspired him to transcribe his conversations word for word. There is little opportunity to send letters home when out in the wilderness laying track – he is crippled by tiredness at the end of each day and there is no mail service, and thus, he jots down a chronology of the day's events in the evening when he is not too tired to write. On rest days, when he has time to compose letters, he stashes them away in his grandfather's leather travel satchel until they can be mailed.

Adam has gotten word that they will reach Ogden, Utah, in a couple of weeks where correspondence can be sent eastward, and there will be a lapse in the work schedule. Until then, he continues writing and holding onto his letters, hoping his family doesn't feel that he's forgotten them, or think that he's in trouble.

IX. Adam's Work on the Railway — 800 Miles of Track

1865 – 1867

Adam takes in a panorama of new country each day as he travels along the tracks of the Union Pacific Railway, working with the engineering company unit that has taken him on as a carpenter. The railway route has left him astounded by the diverse varieties of landscape – flora and fauna that flaunt extravagant eye-pleasing displays of beauty with each new stretch, bend, dip, and climb along the newly installed line, dramatically changing mile by mile as they proceed on their journey westward as the tracks are laid down. He assesses the Almichty has gone to extremes in his creation of an unparalleled masterpiece. Unlike Scotland, a bonnie, bonnie land indeed, he thinks, but with a predictable color theme to its lochs, moors, and jagged peaks, the landscape of the American frontier is bold and dramatic, vividly polychromatic, unsurpassed in its flaunting of the total color spectrum. Every body of water possesses individuality and instills vitality to those in its presence; each mountain is a breathtaking, stunning vision, a testament to the existence of the Almichty weaving magical glory through the terrain. *Who else could hiv created sic a fine work?*

As Adam comes upon each pristine river or lake, he is overcome with emotion. The idea that this beautiful river or lake has been present for eons before mankind's presence, existing for the benefit of the creatures living along their shores, or the birds flying overhead, lends him appreciation to the sacredness of other life forms. Each species flourishes in a sacred haven bestowed by the Creator's masterful hand in a grand cyclic interplay of predator and prey for the continuance of all life on earth, and the survival of the earth itself.

Every evening as camp is being set up and supper is being eaten around a campfire, the sun displays a most splendid sunset, and he is touched with melancholy that another beautiful day is ending, will never exist in this particular display of vivid beauty for him again. The thought that he will never again pass through a stretch of beautiful country is heart-wrenching, and he often makes a pledge that he will come back over this same route on his way home, if he ever goes home. In the morning, he is back on his mule riding to the worksite under a glorious sunrise, experiencing new beauty as he has never experienced before. His spirit is once again lifted, and he looks forward with excitement to what he will see and experience on that day.

X. Winter 1866 — Railroad to Cheyenne, Wyoming

In later years, he admits to his children and wife how homesick he was. Every time he had seen something wondrous in a newly discovered territory, he had wished his family were there to share it with him. Since Adrian's departure for Nevada, fellow railway workers have provided his only companionship. He appreciates being in a country of primarily English-speaking people, although many have a hard time understanding him unless he speaks very slowly and clearly in the Queen's English. At first he was incensed that people did not understand a speaker from the homeland of the English language. Later, when he met Europeans and South Americans struggling to learn English, so eager to be understood, he empathized with their struggles and counted himself lucky. Adam comes to respect the Europeans and foreigners from Asia and South America for their adventuresome and courageous natures, coming up against the threat of danger at every bend in the road while unable to understand what is going on, knowing that their very survival in finding work and food depends on learning English to navigate successfully across a hostile frontier. He observes their valiant efforts to learn the language, and how very quickly, out of necessity, they pick up the necessary English words to communicate.

There are many fine people he meets along the way that make

Adam's journey interesting and keep his homesickness at bay. He learns to love and appreciate a diverse group of people from all over the world, and is thankful for the existence of these gentle souls who cross his path and enlighten him with their different cultures and philosophies of life and religion.

At other times, some of the hardcore ruffians – crude, immoral, bigoted, and drunken – dismay him to no end. Many such despicable men are Indian haters, who use bigotry to elevate their egos and status, as they consider themselves the rightful possessors of the land due to their European ancestry. Indians that don't work for the government are considered fair game to be shot mercilessly on the spot, as if they were game.

To Adam, a surprising number of his white brethren taint the environment with their lack of ethics and vulgarity and give a bad name to the white race. *A beautiful pristine land,* he thinks, *should be regarded as sacred, not contaminated by loathsome elements of the human race.* The railway company does its own share of damage to the purity of the land, cutting down trees, infecting the rivers with creosote and tar, building ramshackle huts and tents along the track route that are left to wither in the elements, and leaving the garbage of the work crews strewn across the land.

XI. Spring 1867 — Bridge Building

Note from Adam's journal:

The bridge over Dale Creek, a little west of Cheyenne, Wyoming, was finished this spring, and now working on the crossing of the Laramie plains, in Wyoming. The West also has vast grassy plains that extend as far as the eye can see, with mammoth buffalo roaming the plains. The plains lend a feeling of total freedom and lack of encumbrance, as not seen in the old country where the land ends at the sea, and doesn't go for hundreds and hundreds of miles without end. Now I know why people risk their lives to live out here.

XII. Summer 1867 — Medicine Bow Creek

Adam's been working on erecting a water tank at Medicine Bow Creek in Wyoming. The old one was built too close to the creek, which gradually undermined it, and one day while the engineer of a train was getting water, the whole thing toppled back into the creek. It came near to ending the life of one of the workmen.

Notes from Adam's journal:
It was generally believed that the building of the Overland Railroad would meet with strong opposition from the Indians, but this expectation was not realized. The government arranged with the Pawnee tribe of Indians to act as scouts and protect the graders and track builders. They had not been organized very long when they had a battle with the Sioux, who were at that time the most powerful of the Indian tribes. The result of the fight was a big list of killed and wounded Sioux warriors, and it practically ended the opposition to the building of the road.

Shortly thereafter, Adam went to work in the bridge yard in Julesberg. The workers in the yard were astonished to see a train come into the station one day, consisting of three flat cars on which was a large Pawnee outfit, a complete moving camp in itself. Nearly every one of the Indians had a sapling, which was ornamented at the top by an Indian scalp. One carpenter who had worked only a day or two picked up his tools, remarking that he cared not to see that kind of atrocity ever again, and left for Omaha.

Adam writes to his family about what he has seen though leaves out the part about human heads on poles. The family doesn't see the letter for months:

Dear Family,
I was awestruck! Thought I was viewing creatures from another planet. They're so exotic yet so human and handsome. They tell jokes and laugh amongst themselves like regular folk, and there's such intelligence and spirit in thair eyes, and a confidence like they have inside knowledge o' life. Their attire with beadwork and jewelry is lovely, and makes for a fine picture to relish in my mind.

On the day Adam sees the 'Injuns' riding the rails with heads on spikes, dressed in their beautiful leather and bead attire, he is beside himself with the excitement of the spectacle.

"My Lord," he exclaims out loud, embarrassed at first by his outcry, though no one was in hearing range. His thoughts went along the lines of, "If only Henry could see the Injuns all dressed up in such finery with heads on poles! Henry would be making jokes about all the heads on the spikes, something to the effect that the white race should also mount some of their more deserving citizens along with the deer, antelope and bears!" The sight does not appall Adam, as he's seen it all before.

XIII. Track Graders Jailed — Big Bear Creek — December 1868 – Summer 1869

Dear family,
These are exciting times, maybe because there are so many people

from diverse backgrounds that are doing things their own way and don't always do right by other people. There was some violence between graders and trackers. Small communities have arisen wherever the graders come in and lay down track. Business needs have been met as these small towns have grown. In Big Bear, a small community south of Salt Lake City, the town built a jail for those graders who did not mind their manners. The town organized forces in expectation o' trouble, and the graders made preparation for attacking at once. A volley of fire killed five men in fast succession. The fort near Bear River took over controlling the violence for a while thereafter.

Correspondence to come when we reach Ogden. Have little time to write now, but you will hear everything going on as soon as I get my letters mailed. Hope everyone is doing well. I do miss Scotland a lot, and sometimes dream at night of being home in my special country of birth.

Love,

Adam

BOOK FIVE

HENRY GOES WEST

Chapter One

I. Adam Senior's Request of Henry — June 1869

The Baird family is wholly naïve as to what travel in America entails, but have been relatively confident, with a good dose of worry, of their son's competence in his quest to reach the silver mines of Virginia City, Nevada. Of late, however, they are greatly troubled that they have not heard from Adam in over a year; to be exact, one year and five months have gone by. The last news of Adam's whereabouts was in Ogden, Utah, in January 1868. Adam did forewarn them that it would be difficult to mail letters from remote areas along the track-building route, but the family has no conception of the vastness of the American frontier, the thousands of miles of virgin land that is being covered by the new railroad. To their fertile, imaginative minds, the West is full of danger and hostility, which Adam might have come up against, and that could be the reason for not hearing from him. In prior correspondence from Adam, he had managed to reach a city or town to mail letters home every three to four months. To the eyes of people living on the small, waterlocked island of Great Britain, the length of time of even one month in not seeing a town or city is incomprehensible, as even the gargantuan Atlantic Ocean is crossed in a little over a month from Glasgow, and the great oceans must be far vaster than the American frontier.

Has he run into foul play, or become sick, or run out of food and money? Or the worst of all scenarios, is he being held captive by Indians?

These questions run constantly through the minds of the family. An entire year without hearing anything is of great concern to even the levelheaded patriarch of the Baird family. Adam Sr. makes a decision uncharacteristic of his conservative nature, which he brings up as the family dines one cool summer evening.

"Henry, would ye consider traveling out to the West to seek out your brother? That is, if you're willing to leave your daughter and the ranch for a time? Your mother will not rest easy 'til she's assured Adam's safe."

Henry can't believe what he's hearing. Uncharacteristically, he is caught off-guard by his father's out-of-the-blue entreaty. It takes more than a few seconds to garner a response.

"Umm, Faither, I'll certainly ponder this wi' all the seriousness it requires." Jokingly, he inquires, "Daes this mean me skills as a great outdoorsman and tracker have finally come to light?"

Adam Sr. replies sternly, "Henry, don't joke on something as serious as your brother's wellbeing. I don't ask this o' ye lightly, as I know you have responsibility for Wee Mary's welfare, and are an integral part o' the running of the ranch, but you are the next eldest and the only one in a position to go."

Henry mulls over the pros and cons for the next couple of weeks of whether to leave his life in Scotland. Alas, the pros for going to America outweigh the cons. First, the window of opportunity to leave for America is closing in on Henry – he figures that if he waits any longer, he'll never get away from Bridge of Allan to see the land that Adam praises so much. The surprising go-ahead from his father, due to his concern for Adam's safety, rekindles Henry's dream of adventure and obliterates the obstacle of seeking parental approval.

It has been over five years since Adam's departure and Henry is at a ripe age for adventure, a mature twenty-three years of age. He struggles with the idea of leaving his daughter and family for such a long duration – the reality does not elude him that he might be away far more than a year. His concern for Wee Mary's welfare tops everything. She is now five years of age and a full-fledged member of the Baird family. The family has not shied away from making it known to her that Henry is her father, and her relationship with Henry, whom she calls Papa, is a very close one. Mary considers herself one of the Baird siblings as well.

Henry plans to tell her about her about Annie when she is older. Mary has not been lacking in maternal love, with Violet and Jean helping to raise her, and she has been the recipient of unabated doting from her siblings. Henry has given Mary a great deal of attention in the evenings, and has taken a prominent role in her book learning and creative development. Mary has shown a proclivity for second-sight, which has lent Violet and Henry the task of overseeing her gift discreetly. Her abilities enable her to view other planes of reality, past and future periods of time, and to appreciate the earth as a living, breathing entity whose creatures are all integral parts of a grand cosmic scheme. Mary needs to receive educational instruction from semi-angels, Wee Ones, on protecting Mother Earth, and on many other matters of universal interplay. She must also learn from Wee Ones, as Henry did, to take advantage of her abilities without seeming different to others; that is, with her unique perspective of the universe and life on earth, to use her talents to aid the people of her community without giving the impression that she possesses supernatural qualities. Above all else, she must not appear to be a demonic creature or a witch to the many superstitious pagan believers around her. Henry has concluded that having Emma and Violet aid in the development of his daughter's creative powers is highly beneficial, being that they are second-sighted and understand what the powers entail for a female.

Before Adam Sr. brought up the possibility of Henry traveling to the West to find Adam, Henry had put to rest his dream of leaving Bridge of Allan, surrendering to the priorities brought on by Annie's tragic death and his family's needs – his role in life, unconditionally accepted by him, was rearing his child and aiding in the success of the ranch. Once the possibility of travel to America is put on the table, the thrill of experiencing an exciting Western adventure is, once again, reinvigorated.

Adam Sr. says in earnest to Henry, trying not to sound pessimistic, "I've my doubts that ye can find Adam easily, as there is a vast amount of territory to cover."

"It willna be difficult if I travel directly to Virginia City, as 'tis the city Adam intended as his final destination," Henry assures his father.

"I've my doubts that Adam ever reached Virginia City," replies his father gravely. "Surely we'd have heard from him by now. Something must've happened. I've checked at the Bridge of Allan post office, and they assure me that mail service is readily available from the Comstock Lode by train and steamer – that it takes a little over two months to get a letter from Virginia City to Bridge of Allan."

"I'm certain if he's not arrived yet, he'll be there by the time I make the trip," replies Henry.

Henry refrains from telling his family that he's certain he'll have success in tracking down Adam. With the help of the Wee People, in particular Punt and Elor, Adam's whereabouts have already been pinpointed with an advanced technology – global positioning satellite (GPS). Elor informed Henry that his coordinates show that Adam reached Nevada, near Elko, in late September 1869. In all likelihood, unless Adam takes a detour or decides to stay put, he'll be reaching Virginia City in the next few weeks, by late October, as Elko and Virginia City are a little over 200 miles apart. He figures a wagon can cover fifteen to twenty miles per day (only 10 days' travel between the two towns, but there could be rest stops and detours along the way that would make the going slower).

Henry is excited by the prospect of seeing his brother whom he hasn't seen in five years, and may very well never see again if he doesn't take the plunge. Henry decides to leave his options open as to how long he'll stay in the West. An exciting travel adventure is opening up to him, and he can come back to Drumdruils in a year's time – that is, if he doesn't find lucrative work worth staying for.

Weighing in on this decision to travel is his duty to help the family financially, particularly because they are supporting Wee Mary. It is an added enticement that he will be able to earn money for Mary's future education, as well as to help his family with their financial hardship. Foremost on his agenda is to reach Adam in Virginia City and assure his parents that Adam is alive and kicking. After that, he will research whether it is feasible to earn a good income out West. With this course of action in mind, keeping his options open as to what would be most beneficial for the family, and particularly for Mary, he'll be free to decide the best time to head home to Scotland without any time constraints. In getting in touch with his true feelings on the matter, Henry has concluded that he will miss his daughter and family in Scotland terribly, to the point of desiring to return as soon as he's had a good visit with his beloved brother.

There is another pro in favor of Henry's leaving at this time. For the past five years, ever since Annie's death and Mary's birth, he has been managing the Drumdruils ranch as a necessity because of his father's debilitating back pain, which has progressively worsened, and presently prevents him from any farm work. In the last couple of years, though, his two younger brothers have matured and are now capable of taking on a lot more responsibility. Telford and Malkie are now seventeen and sixteen years of age, respectively. As a team, they are capable of managing the entire ranch themselves, with the help of their two ranch hands. Even more heartening, both his younger brothers have shown a great aptitude for ranching, with no desire to further their educations in college. Henry had promised Adam he'd come, and with Wee Mary permanently entrenched in the Baird home with the only family she's ever known, the time seems right. The Baird children are her siblings, and Adam Sr. and Jean her beloved grandparents. Henry's sense of duty to earn money to support his child prevails, and a feeling of guilt in leaving her has been lifted. America holds promise for Henry to earn a better living than anywhere in Scotland, and he'll be able to reinvent himself as an intrepid explorer of a new land and not a grieving husband whose spirit is continually being weighed down by the pain of Annie's death and thoughts of what could have been had she lived.

II. Baird Children Discuss Adam's Fate

The children become very concerned about Adam when they hear of the behind-the-scenes plans for Henry to travel to America to find him.

"'Tis been too long since he's written. He might be dead, scalped by Indians," says Malkie remorsefully. Malkie looks like he's going to cry.

"He could be merely captured by Indians," says Janet, more optimistically. "He might be teachin' them to read and how to talk the Queen's tongue. Adam really loves Indians and they woudna kill him acause he's a friend. Mebbe they're teaching Adam how to hunt big buffalo."

"That's richt," says Emma. "Adam's na deid. I'd feel it in me bones if somethin' iver happened to Adam. Besides, Elor would have told us if he was deid. Mebbe he's on his way home and wants to surprise us!"

"It is a big, big land! He could get lost but mebbe the Indians will help him find his way back to us," says Janet.

Pipes in five-year-old Mary Alice, "Papa's goin' to find Adam," she says with assurance. "I ken he will. Punt tells me that he's safe and they'll find him. I believe Punt acause he's ayeweys richt."

"Aye," agrees Emma confidently, "Adam's na deid. Daena fear."

III. Henry Embarks on Voyage to America, September 1869

In late September 1869, Henry boards a ship for New York from Glasgow. Elor had informed him that Adam will arrive in Virginia City in mid-October, and advised him to go directly to Nevada to meet up with him.

It was very difficult for Henry as the final days before his trip approached – leaving Wee Mary and the rest of his family tore at his heart. Punt, Elor, and Twixie assured him that he'd be able to stay in touch with Wee Mary through the Wee People. As it turned out, Punt could not bear for his best friend to leave him behind and decided to go with Henry. As he told Elor, "Someone has to keep Henry out of trouble."

"Mary has second-sight and will learn to communicate with us," Elor tells Henry. "If she isn't able to at first, Violet can help her. We have a direct line of communication with Punt, who is going with you, in case you haven't heard, and he can probably communicate with Mary right off, as they've been reading one another's minds since Mary was a bairn. As Wee Mary gets older, she will be able to access you with her mind directly through remote viewing."

In Glasgow, on his way to board the steamer, Henry stops by to inform Aunt Ethie that he is leaving for America, and hands her a letter of invitation from his parents to visit Wee Mary in Bridge o' Allan anytime she desires. Since he took the newborn back to Bridge o' Allan, Henry has taken his lassie to visit Aunt Ethie each year on the anniversary of Annie's death and Wee Mary's birth. On his final visit, Aunt Ethie has news that both of Annie's parents passed away during the winter, Mr. MacGivens due to lung disease and Carrie MacGivens succumbing to breast cancer.

The Civil War has ended, and not as many steamers are being built, but Henry goes to the Glasgow Port Authority and gets a listing of ships crossing the Atlantic. Henry boards an Anchor Line steamer, the *SS Caledonia*, on 25 September 1869, with Aunt Ethie and Dr. Mackenzie seeing him off with jubilant fanfare.

Chapter Two

I. Henry Reaches America

The *SS Caledonia* makes it across the Atlantic in very good time – just over a month due to favorable weather. Henry disembarks the ship at New York Harbor in October 1869 and sets out on the Union Pacific line across the country to Omaha, Nebraska. From Omaha, he is one of the earliest travelers to enjoy transcontinental train service toward Sacramento on the Central Pacific Line, which was launched five months earlier, with the ceremonial driving of the Golden Spike on 10 May 1869. Adam had a hand in the building of the railway, although Henry doesn't realize this at the time. From Sacramento, Henry takes an eastern-bound train to Steamboat Springs, Nevada. In Steamboat Springs, he catches a stagecoach that stops in Reno, and then clambers up the steep foothills into the Sierra forests to Virginia City. Henry arrives in the quaint city in November 1869, just over two months after Adam's arrival. Adam had been working on the railway for five years, making his way across the grand continent to reach his final destination of Virginia City.

While Henry is still at sea and almost to New York Harbor, Adam's belated letters arrive in Bridge of Allan. He informs his family that he is on his way to Virginia City, and should reach the silver mining Nevadan city by September 1869. Henry will hopefully get word of Adam's arrival in Virginia City from the family when the ship reaches New York Harbor in October.

II. Letters from Virginia City to the Family — September 1869

Dear family,

I reached Virginia City in September! Took a stagecoach from Steamboat Springs, Nevada, to Virginia City. Adrian was there to greet me, and it was a great reunion of old, dear friends, with much elation, for it has been three years since I've seen him. He has arranged a job for me in the Caledonia mines as a carpenter, as he has quite a lot of clout, as his father-in-law is the manager, and he is head engineer of the entire mining operation. He married a wonderful lass, and they seem very happy in this beautiful wee city. The climate here is very refreshing, as we are up at over 1,874 meters in the foothills of the Sierra Nevada range. It snows here in the winter (twice since my arrival), but it is not terribly cold. The snow is gone within a day of its falling, melted by the intense mountain sun that provides a wonderful warmth, even as we close in on winter.

Love,
Adam

III. Adam Learns of Henry's Departure for Nevada

The reunion with his friend Adrian in Nevada is a gratifying occasion for Adam, who has been virtually isolated from close companionship for several years. Adrian and his wife, Elise, greet him with much fanfare as the stagecoach from Steamboat Springs pulls into Virginia City's main thoroughfare. A banjo plays "America, My Home." Festive banners and signs along the street read "WELCOME HOME, ADAM." Adrian's fellow Masons wave, clap, and jump up and down. Adam has never been the center of so much attention, and tries to overcome his shyness with smiles and waves as he greets the enthusiastic town.

Adrian has recently married Elise, the beautiful blonde daughter of the supervisor of the Caledonia mines, John MacInnes. They have built a large house on C Street in Virginia City with the money Adrian's parents gave him on his departure from Austria. Adrian is making an excellent salary as the chief mining engineer for the Caledonia mines, as well as being engineer for a lucrative mine in Gold Hill, a few miles up the mountainside.

After a heartwarming welcoming and a luncheon in his honor at Virginia City's famous Silver Spoon Café, Adrian and Elise take Adam over to their elegant two-story Victorian home, where they have a comfortable room waiting for him: a feather bed with a down comforter of deep red velvet, matching chairs of red and blue silk damask, an elaborate wood-carved headboard, a mahogany armoire, and two marble-topped dressers of fine quality mahogany. Adam has never experienced such luxury. The newlyweds assure Adam he is more than welcome to live with them as long as he wishes. Adam thanks them graciously, but has already made up his mind not to impose on them for long. He plans to engage in a concerted effort to find his own lodgings after a few weeks on the job.

On Adam's first day in Nevada, he walks down the planked board sidewalks, admiring the colorful storefronts, and heads to the Virginia City post office to register his new address. He is surprised and overjoyed to find his family's letters awaiting him. The fact that they knew to send them to Virginia City is a pleasant surprise, but, then again, nothing is impossible with his family, he reflects, not with the multi-talented, second-sighted Violet and Henry in the mix. He reads his family's letters as long-lost treasures, and is overjoyed to learn that Henry is on his way to Nevada and will be reaching Virginia City in late autumn. When Adam learns Henry will be in Virginia City by mid-November, he goes out the following week and finds a small, inexpensive one-bedroom cottage in town on B Street that will be available the following month. He also has plans to save a good part of his salary over the next several months for a small plot of land that he and Henry can build a cabin on.

Adam, with much excitement and joy, writes:

Dear family,
I eagerly await Henry! To put it more truthfully, I am so excited I can barely contain myself. I have rented a two-room cottage in town with outhouse at back, with plenty of room for both of us. I have plans to purchase a plot of land in the hills above town (on the way up to the mines) as soon as possible. Henry will be able to help me in my quest to build a nice wooden structure during the winter and early spring months, and in better time than by myself.

With love to all,
Adam

After Adam moves to his rented cottage, Adrian and Elise invite Adam over for Sunday dinners on a regular basis. This provides Adam with a much-needed sense of home life. They offer him the pick of their dog's first litter two weeks after he moves to his cottage. Elise volunteers to keep the puppy during the day, and so every evening after work Adam walks over to Adrian and Elise's house to pick up his puppy. His golden retriever, Amber, is his constant companion, and he cuddles with her like a baby at the end of a long day. Occasionally after work, he and Adrian go for drinks in one of the many saloons along Virginia City's B and C streets, where he soaks in the rowdy and colorful razzle-dazzle of the booming mining city.

Adam soon grows tired of the drinking and gambling scene of the saloons, though, wishing for more intellectual and philosophical gatherings in Virginia City. Adrian helps him gain invitation to the Masons, and Adam goes through his initiation rites soon thereafter. Adam enjoys the camaraderie of the Masons very much, and participates in their civic-minded duties for the betterment of the community.

IV. Perilous Work in the Caledonia Mines

It is his first day of work on 15 September 1869. With his carpentry skills in high demand, and with the help of Adrian, Adam had registered and procured his job in town at the Nevada Mines office on B Street the day before. Adrian kept his promise, and the office had his name on file, with two stellar references, one from his old boss at the wheelwright shop in Bridge of Allan that he had given Adrian on his departure from Fort Fetterman, and the other from Adrian. An excellent paying job had been waiting for him.

Adam tours the mines on his first day with the foreman, John MacInnes, Elise's father, and co-supervisor Hank Rogers, as well as Adrian, who is there for support (and to translate for Adam if his shy nature and thick brogue become an impediment). There is no problem at all, as John MacInnes is a Scotsman from Glasgow and understands Adam perfectly, and Hank is a kind, decent Italian, with curly dark hair, a strong burly build, and an engaging sense of humor.

The crew transport Adam down the mineshaft in a wood-caged lift to the deepest bowels of the mine. Adam begins to appreciate the excitement and complexities, as well as the perils, of mining.

The elevator car travels hundreds of feet down through depths of darkness on thin cables; overloaded boxcars haul up ore on a maze of tracks that trundle around the upper regions of the mine, giving off high-pitched grating sounds that, to Adam, sound like warnings of peril. Men and donkeys haul the loaded carts down the hill from the mine to a waiting train, where it will be transported for shipment. Workers go to and fro, up and down along the tracks in carts to the back regions of the mine, performing their designated jobs, lanterns and pickaxes in their hands, laughing, cussing, and joking. There is constant danger of being trapped in a cave-in, but everyone seems to be oblivious to this but Adam. The new employee is thrilled by all the sights and sounds, but is constantly wary of cave-ins or falling rocks, shutting his eyes on his descent down into the mine. Soon enough, Adam becomes as immune to danger as everyone else, for performance is hindered by the threat of death hanging over a miner. This job will provide a very good salary for the first time in his life, and he's doing something he is skilled at and loves to do, no matter what the risk.

V. Lake Tahoe — Emerald Gem of the Sierras

On a long holiday weekend, a few weeks before Henry's arrival, Adam travels a short distance to Lake Tahoe and camps at Emerald Bay. The lake is a green-blue jewel with its crystal clear waters of seemingly endless depth. Adam is enraptured by the splendor of this great body of water with the majestic, snow-capped Sierra Mountains in the backdrop.

Adam wishes there was someone to enjoy this wondrous scenery with him. Henry will be with him shortly, but he is thinking more along the lines of female companionship for this romantic setting. How wonderful it would be to have a lovely gentlewoman on his arm to stroll the paths around this lovely lake, to peer down into its depths to try to see the bottom, a silhouette of a man and a woman side by side viewing their reflections in the blue, glassy-mirrored water. He finds Lake Tahoe a miraculous lake that is healing to his mind and soul, bringing him closer to the divine and to his inner desires of what he wants out of life.

Adam decides, then and there, with inspiration enveloping his spirit from this incredibly beautiful environment, that he would be much happier if he had a wife to share special moments in life. The problem is that Adam has not come across many available, reputable women in the West, though there is an abundance of married women who have traveled with their husbands to these parts. Most of the single women are saloon and brothel workers servicing the miners as the best way out of poverty, or Chinese laundry workers and cooks that do not mix socially with whites.

Although Adam is very engaged with his work in the mines all day, he often finds himself lonesome in the evening. He can't wait for Henry to arrive, as he is without any close friends except for Adrian, who is busy with his new wife. They are expecting their first child in four months. He writes to his family often, at least once a week, and thinks fondly of his sisters, Janet and Emma and Baby Susan, who is no longer a baby but in school now, and his brothers, Malkie and Telford. He wishes he could meet Wee Mary. How they would love beautiful Nevada! The laddies must have changed greatly in the five years he's been gone. He thinks of Malkie and Telford, no longer children, busily running the ranch. He has a nostalgic remembrance of when he was ranching at Drumdruils as a teenager. From recent letters, he has learned that Janet and Emma have both decided to go to the University of Edinburgh once they have graduated from school in Bridge of Allan, as Miss Carroway has instilled in them prospects of bright futures with a university education. That is what he had hoped for, and he has plans to help pay for their educations. He would love to see them, as he pictures them as beautiful young lassies at ages fifteen and fourteen. The chance of seeing any of his family out West besides Henry is probably not going to happen, which saddens him greatly.

In reflecting on his lovely sisters, Adam's mind segues to Ruthie Malcolm, the sweet lassie he left behind, saddened every time he thinks of her death, as it hasn't sunk in entirely that she passed away tragically. The individuals away from him who have died are as much alive in his mind as those truly alive, for he hasn't seen anybody from back home for years. *'Tis aw relative*, he thinks. *There're many people I'll niver see iver again from Bridge o' Allan.*

He can't bear thinking of never seeing his family again. They are, and always will be, very much alive in his mind, and he plans on seeing each and every one of them again when he visits home someday.

Ruthie's sad death sheds light on the shortened paths some individuals in life are destined for, perhaps many, and the burden of pain for those left behind, just as Henry bears the burden of pain from Annie's death.

Adam has fond memories of his and Ruthie's very comfortable rapport. During the course of their relationship, it was expected, almost guaranteed, that life would open up like a rose to a satisfying fullness, to meet their every whim and dream, which made them giddy with pleasurable anticipation for their futures. *We were young and naïve*, thinks Adam. He and Ruthie had been stepping out together for almost three years before he left for Glasgow to work. He recalls the great fun they had had socializing together with their Bridge o' Allan and Helensburgh group of friends. He had halfway planned to contact Ruthie after he had established himself in Nevada, depending on his circumstances, to coax her into coming out West. He feels terribly guilty that he didn't visit her before boarding the *S.S. Will-o-the-Wisp*, or even writing to her informing her of his departure, though his date of passage on the ship had come up quickly, and he hadn't had time to even go back to Drumdruils for a final visit.

Mebbe that one act o' neglect had been the catalyst for her death. What if the hope that I might have given her for our life thegither might have kept her alive, kept her from succumbing to a grave illness?

Adam's last correspondence with Ruthie had been during the months he was working in Glasgow. In America, when he had received the terrible news of Ruthie's death, he found it necessary to read the letter three times, for the written word did not register in his mind. The reality of her death was incomprehensible at first.

Poor Ruthie had died while he was on the ship, a few weeks before his reaching America; and, in retrospect, by no coincidence, she had been on his mind constantly as he lay in his berth below deck, sickened by the fierceness of the sea that rocked the boat violently. The wee steamer was tossed around like a weightless cork. *This must've been at the same time she was on her deathbed, sick and in pain*, he reflects. *We were both suffering.*

Adam had survived and she had not, but it could just as likely have been the other way around. Adam reflects on the sad fact that life is not guaranteed; it can be taken away shockingly fast, leaving those left behind bowled over with doubt as to what life is all about, what is in store for them.

That someone as vibrant as Ruthie could die so young is regarded by Adam as a waste of fine human potential, a severing of the golden threads of life of a beautiful, deserving person.

Aye, he reflects, *a cord is severed to bring people into this world, and a cord severed to take them out at any time.*

Adam's mind is transferred back to the harsh mindset of his coffin-building days when death was an everyday occurrence. He thinks of Henry's Annie, whom he learned had died when he reached New York City. Two beautiful lasses passing away while he was at sea. *No life is guaranteed*, he reflects. Adam resolves to make the most of his gift of life.

Adam recalls Ruthie's younger tomboy sister, Catherine Malcolm. He can't imagine Catherine succumbing to an infection like her sister, as Catherine was so spirited with health and vitality. He and Catherine were great pals and engaged in many outdoor activities together with a group of other young teenagers from the church, consisting of her school friends and his younger brothers and their friends. Adam was one of the youth group's leaders. It seemed that Catherine and he had a natural rapport – it was a brother/younger sister relationship, with a lot of teasing and jokes thrown about. Catherine was always trying to outdo him with her athletic prowess. They found humor in many of the same things, and alone, he was very much at ease with her, without the least bit of shyness, being that she was an adventurous, high-spirited lassie much like his sisters, and was Ruthie's rambunctious kid sister.

Adam recalls her personality as being agreeable, and her looks lovely like her sister's. She was taller and less fragile than Ruthie, her complexion more colorful because of her time spent outdoors, and her build more athletic than Ruthie's. Catherine was free-spirited, strong-willed, and full of energy and *joie de vivre*, a lassie of fourteen when he last saw her. Adam wonders what Catherine looks like now, almost twenty years of age. Some lassies get prettier as they develop into young women; others, unfortunately, become coarser and heavier. He is certain that Catherine must have grown into a beauty like her sister, as she was a very pretty wee lassie when he last saw her.

Adam decides to learn of Catherine Malcolm's whereabouts by writing his mum, requesting that she correspond with Catherine's mother, although this is an embarrassing prospect for him. This correspondence might send the wrong message by conveying to his family that he is desperately lonely and unhappy, not liking life in Virginia City at all, and to combat his depression, scrambling for any available lassie to be his wife. His brothers will be thinking "Henry is coming – why a wife now? Henry is much more fun than a mere lassie." Adam can only imagine them making coarse love jokes about him and Catherine.

Despite all the fuss, he considers it a long shot that Catherine will be available. Chances are she has her own family by now, though he's very curious about the Malcolm family's wellbeing, as they having endured so much grief with the death of Ruthie, and a couple of years earlier the loss of Mr. Malcolm. On Adam's second letter from Virginia City, he makes a request to his mother to get in touch with the Malcolm family.

VI. Adam's Request of His Mother — November 1869

Dear Mother,

Would ye be so kind as to be an intermediary for me? I would like you to correspond with Mrs. Abigail Malcolm, to make an inquiry about Catherine's circumstances, whether she still resides in the Helensburgh area and remains single. If so, might she be willing to correspond with me? To ease Mrs. Malcolm's mind as to the suitability of her daughter corresponding with me, you might ensure her o' my secure employment at the Caledonia Mine in Virginia City, which is about a two-hour wagon ride from beautiful Lake Tahoe. The lake is a gem, the most beautiful lake I've ever seen. I would love to share the beauty of the Sierra Nevada country with a wife, but don't tell Mrs. Malcolm I have any romantic notions, or am seeking a wife. Convey that I'm only curious about what happened to Catherine and her mother after the tragic death of Ruthie.

Again, apologize for my letter of condolence not getting through. Are they well and adjusting? Would Catherine like a pen pal?

Your loving son,

Adam

BOOK SIX

CATHERINE LEAVES SCOTLAND

Chapter One

I. Catherine's Voyage to America — 28 February 1870

3 March 1870

I am continually, terribly sick when below deck, as are all the passengers because of the high rolling waves that never cease, causing my stomach to churn in agony. My only relief is to keep looking out the porthole in my room. The sea is as green as I feel, like green pea soup, and the ship is like a bottle on the waves being tossed about. I would be better off up on deck in the open air than below in my cramped compartment, wherein there is but one little porthole, but the weather is poor and the passengers are not allowed up on deck for the water spills across the wood in thick planes of wetness, and is very slippery. The deckhands on the ship wear special canvas weatherproof cloaks coated with linseed oil, and heavy oiled boots up to their knees that they wear in storms, and they still get soaked to the core, poor lads! There are only three other passengers on board including me – a very nice widow, Mrs. Oakwood, going to live with her daughter in Illinois, and a young man, Gregory Smith, a little older than myself, who is going to California to meet up with his brothers; the brother is running a store in the Mother Lode, catering to miners, selling mostly pants and flannels. There is also the ship doctor, Dr. Knoll, and the navigator, Mr. MacLean, both very gentlemanly. They are always up on deck tending to their jobs. As soon as the weather is good, I will definitely spend my time on deck, as I am quite claustrophobic.

7 March 1870

A horrible event occurred today. I'm still shaking. We heard that a young man, part of the crew, jumped overboard out of despondency. I cannot help but wonder why he was born in the first place if he was to die by his own hand so early on. What benefit is it to live through childhood and young adulthood and then cease forevermore? Father would have said what happened was for a reason, that life has many inexplicable twists and turns that are the Lord's business and not ours to dwell on. The poor lad might have been just terribly seasick, deranged in the head to the point of wanting to end his suffering. The crew sleep way in the bowels of the ship with no portholes whatsoever. I would die without a porthole.

Perhaps the laddie lived to his fullest potential in the short time he was on earth, his life and mind accelerated, his experiences adding up to as many years as a man of eighty. Surely, this kind of thinking is merely to console myself. Just the same, perhaps he does have other better universal places to journey to in the grand scheme of things. It is still so very sad, too sad for words, and everyone is upset that this has happened on our ship, for we feel a sense of camaraderie with all the men who are braving the harsh circumstances together on this perilous voyage to get us safely across this vast formidable sea. We're hoping he was the only member of the crew with plans to end it all on a whim. Maybe this is a common thing among seamen? I can't get this tragedy out o' my mind!

II. Starry Skies, Moonlit Nights, A Very Handsome Captain

From the diary of Catherine:

10 March 1870

I was able to go on deck today, as the weather was fine and I met the handsome Captain Nathaniel Noble. He invited Mrs. Oakwood and myself to dine with him this evening. We've been on the ship for a week and the weather has turned calm, almost balmy. We are allowed on deck to view the ocean that seems to be alive in the way it dances, sprays, and changes colors all at once. It is mindboggling in its depth and vastness. The captain is very gentlemanly, and so gallant and gracious, inquiring delicately, and with much concern, about how I am bearing up. He assures me that the voyage will be "smooth-going" most of the time, and that I won't always be seasick. He is an educated gentleman from Edinburgh whose father was a sea captain as well. Captain Noble studied navigation and astronomy at the University of Edinburgh, and tells me he is more at home on the wide-open sea than on the land, that there is breathing room out here, and when he is on land too long he becomes stir crazy.

14 March 1870

Captain Noble seems to like me very much. I am aware of this because of the way his eyes light up when he sees me – he rushes over to kiss my hand and to converse with me whenever I'm on deck. The touch of his hand is like a baby's bottom. I wonder what his face feels like. This attention is only because I am young and pretty. Mum always warned me not to let this kind of attention to go to my head, that men will bow down to me and act charming, but that doesn't necessarily mean they are going to be dear, loyal friends for an eternity.

Mum was very smart about these things, as she was very beautiful when young. She says she learned early on all about what is important in life and how to respond to the advances of men. Mum told me in some ways it is a curse to be attractive because men don't see the inner beauty, only what's on the outside – they don't take the time to delve into the substance of a woman before professing their undying love.

This is so true! Would the captain like me for who I am if I were homely? It makes me wonder if true love is a sham. Mother warned me to guard against men's advances, and that is why she was so thankful that Adam Baird's mother had contacted her. Mum trusted the integrity of the Baird family, and always found Adam to be a responsible, gentle soul when he stepped out with Ruthie. I think she was afraid that I might be left on my own some day – this has come to pass – and that I would be prey to unscrupulous men who might take advantage of me. She feared that I would marry unwisely because of my passionate nature. Mum said that there are many fickle gentlemen who have no intent to settling down to a home life.

The captain is very virile, and sometimes I am overwhelmed by his mature age of forty years, and his intense masculinity. I am shy and feel slightly uneasy in getting too close to a man like the captain. What does he see in me? Sometimes, by that look in his eyes, it appears he's about to swoop me up and carry me off to his cabin. This would be very scary and improper, but then again, I might be tempted, as I feel like the sea is another planet and I'm in a dream world where anything is possible. I hope Mum was wrong about my inability to control my passionate nature.

16 March 1870

Captain's teaching me to navigate by the stars and this is a thrilling endeavor. He tells me that all one has to do is follow the stars to chart our course, and he points out all the constellations to me. I spend a lot of time on deck in this pleasant balmy weather, and I feel more alive and free than I have ever been in my life. I'm in wonderful health from the sun and sea breezes, and feel a glowing vibrancy as never before. I see why Captain Noble thinks the sea is the best place on earth to be. It renders so much vitality, and the winds and water lift one's spirits with unlimited energy.

25 March 1870

I call him Captain now – no surname necessary! Aye, indeed,

Captain is very charming, and the most handsome man I've ever known! To diffuse my vanity, I must admit he is interested in me because I'm the only eligible young woman on the ship. Mrs. Oakwood is well over fifty, a widow and quite dowdy. Mrs. Oakwood says that Captain Noble is far too old for me and I shouldn't be out on deck with him alone, but she is a wilted ol' frump. This is very unkind of me to write, but what does she know of friendship with the opposite sex? I'll make it up to Mrs. Oakwood for my unkind thoughts by inviting her to stroll on the deck with me before dinner.

Captain is very appealing because he has that know-all look in his twinkling eyes that comely men have, a look that proclaims he has mastery over life, that he finds living amusing because it is so easy for him. He appreciates the opposite sex very much, maybe because he goes for long stretches on the sea without seeing women. He is the kind of man that women are attracted to because of the authority he conveys, his great confidence, his erect, commanding posture, his vast fund of knowledge of everything under the sun, and the stars! Literally. What a great intellect! Did I mention his fine features, sculpted like a god? Those too! He is a beautiful looking man. When he sweeps his vivid blue eyes over each feature of my face and body like he's drinking me in, I become helplessly self-conscious and giddy, and have the urge to giggle. What would Mother say? That I should be wary of all this charm, that this has nothing to do with love.

Catherine has had admiring looks from men many times before, and being a pragmatic lassie, she is wary of the captain's power over her, but she consciously allows herself to be drawn in by his masculine charms. This is the nature of being young and full of life, she rationalizes to herself, to let one's better judgment breathe – at least loosen its restraints a wee bit – in order to fully seize the magical moments of being young and alive. *After all, I won't be young forever!*

She tells herself that she has the ability to control the situation if it gets out of hand. That is, she'll definitely not allow herself to completely succumb to the captain's charms, but she'll just enjoy them for what they are: a special time in her young life. She allows herself to daydream about his fine looks and muscular physique, about how it would feel to kiss him.

Catherine finds the captain more and more intriguing as they spend time together, which is over elegant, candlelit dinners at the captain's table, on deck in the late mornings, and after supper while stargazing at twilight. In the late morning, after her slight seasickness has subsided, she finds the courage to venture up on deck to soak up the golden warmth of the sun, to watch the playful breezes stirring up the water, the waves dancing rhythmically as if to a song. During these hours, she observes, with a great fascination, the goings-on of the crew in performance of their duties.

The captain goes about his inspection of the ship with great thoroughness and authority. When he spots Catherine out on deck, he rushes over to bid her a good morning, inquiring as to how she has slept, and if there is anything at all she needs to make her voyage more comfortable. She finds the intelligent glint in his eyes most appealing, indicating to her that this gentleman has total mastery over his ship as well as the world at large. This observation makes her feel safe and secure in her daunting solo journey over thousands of miles of fathomless sea. The captain, she finds, approaches life with a carefree amusement, as if there is nothing that he can't handle. This inculcates in Catherine a desire to be as strong and as self-assured as the captain.

Catherine writes in her diary that night:
The captain is a truly magical individual in his command o'er life – he has a worldly power o'er the universe. He rules his sailors with an almost supernatural talent, and they have a high regard for him; in the same way, he takes command over the ship and guides it

towards its destination, as if the ship is moving grandly over the sea because of his power over it. He is truly masterful in everything he does, be it navigation, decision making, or ensuring his passengers and crew are at home on the open seas. I have become truly smitten by his charms, and yet have to chastise myself for being so taken in by this gentleman. I have always had a practical and skeptical nature when it comes to men and their attraction to me. Is it the vastness and magic of this great beautiful sea that grants me the privilege of being open to an illogical romance?

When the captain makes flattering comments about Catherine's flushed cheeks or attire, tingles run up and down her spine. *Surely, he doesn't look at all women like he does at me, or through me,* she thinks. She reads the discerning positive appraisal of her looks in his intelligent eyes as they sweep over each of her features, in the same manner in which he assesses the direction of the winds or approaching clouds. She is acutely aware that this gentleman has the art of seduction mastered. Catherine admires the cunning arch of his brow as he inquires about her personal life. She relays to him that she is traveling to Virginia City in Nevada to marry a laddie from Bridge of Allan, Scotland.

"What's the character of this lad, Adam, whom ye plan to marry? Ye must love him greatly to travel so far to be wi' him."

Catherine is taken aback by the question, as she admits to herself that she doesn't truly know Adam's character after so many years, or love him at all, at least not yet; she hardly remembers what he looks like. She blushes and hesitates before replying. "Well, I haven't seen Adam since I was a wee lass of fourteen years old, but he was a fine laddie then, when I knew him." She doesn't reveal to the captain that he was her sister's romantic interest.

The captain raises his thick, dark brow skeptically, as would a doctor in assessing the wellbeing of his patient, an indication she interprets to imply that perhaps he thinks her very fickle to cross the ocean and a vast swath of land to marry a man she's not sure of. Catherine is sorry she's been so forthcoming with the captain in revealing that she's not well acquainted with Adam. It raises skepticism in her own thoughts as to the rationale behind her trip.

"Ah, 'tis an arranged marriage by your parents?"

"Not at all. Adam inquired about my whereabouts through his mother, who corresponded with my mum. Adam and I were very good friends, as we spent a lot of time outdoors together in my youth. He was one of the leaders of my church youth group. I really looked up to him as an older brother."

The captain reflects for a moment and then tosses his response gallantly to the receptive sea, which he gazes pensively on. "Well, if it weren't for Adam, I wouldn't have had the honor o' meeting ye, and so I'm forever in Adam's debt, no matter the uncertainty of his character and the reasoning behind your voyage."

III. Dancing on the Deck by the Light of the Moon

Catherine and the captain dance to a lovely Celtic melody called "*The Braes of Balquhidder*" on deck, played admirably by the fiddler, Sam Boxer, who is down in the dining hall entertaining the crew after supper. As they dance, the frothy waves, driven by the gravitational force of the moon, lap against the ship in rhythm with their moves. The stars up above are spotlights, illuminating the gorgeous scene below: a handsome gentleman and a lovely lady in each other's arms, twirling on the deck at the bow of the ship. Catherine's gown shimmers in the light, the same iridescent blue-green color as the sea. The night is warm, as scattered clouds had rolled in to trap the warmth from the afternoon's rays, providing an almost tropical balminess to the air.

The captain has a loving, seductive look in his eyes, the look that women respond to with goose bumps, a look of absolute, profound awe of Catherine's total being. She finds this look to be a candid revelation of the captain's thoughts, and Catherine is rendered breathless, slightly embarrassed to be the object of a man's tender emotions. She senses a strong magnetic current emanating from his being as they dance, as if the power of the universe has settled in him and is being transmitted to her. To Catherine this experience is equivalent to possessing a million stars in the sky – she will never have mastery over the intense brilliance of the stars, nor over the captain's exalted being, for he is the personification of a god to her, nor will she be part of this life forever, as the long voyage will alas end, but despite this, she enjoys owning all this grandeur for a short interval, in this magical sliver of time, on this magical ship. She is aware that she owns this man's affection, and that she radiates powerful vibrations from the sea, the stars, and her own feminine energy, on a voyaging steamer out in the middle of nowhere at a special time in her young, impressionable life. The experience is owned by her and no one but her, and Catherine is able to step outside of her reservations to relish in this ownership.

She reflects that the captain knows her very well in such a short time, is in tune with her inner being and passions; he sees down to the depths of her soul. She concludes they are kindred spirits, carved from the same universal mold, as stars inhabiting the same part of the skies were once one entity and reflect off one another. She considers the fact that Adam Baird doesn't know her soul like this man, doesn't know who she really is like the captain does. Adam has displayed little understanding of what love means to life. He desired marriage with Ruthie because he said he loved her, and then let go of that love like it was something expendable so he could travel. He broke Ruthie's heart and then she died! Where was the passion in that love? Certainly, there was passion for travel and adventure, but not enough passion for the finest woman ever. Now at the end of his quest for travel and adventure, he is looking for a steady partner in life. Catherine has often thought of herself as a convenient replacement, like a secondhand piece of clothing. *How do I know he will ever truly love me?*

Every day at sea has brought on more doubts about Adam as a marriage partner. Catherine wonders if she is confusing qualities she has always taken pride in about herself, levelheadedness and pragmatism, with sheer foolishness in traveling thousands of miles to marry a man she hardly knows. Catherine recalls Adam as a kind, thoughtful, steady, and reliant person, at least during his school years, but she wonders if he will make a good husband, if he will be a fitting complement to her own unique, spiritually vibrant being, or a total mismatch because of his quiet, shy, and steady, down-to-earth nature that she remembers him to possess.

The captain has her heart for now, and she has a secret inner desire to be his wife. She relishes the idea of a perfect union with the handsome gentleman. The fervor of her youthful heart responds to the magic moments with him, the tender and spine-tingling emotions he provokes. It is exciting for her to dream of an enchanting, charmed life that could open up for her with a man like the captain. The possibilities of such a life seem quite feasible as she receives powerful positive inspiration from the energy of the sea, and from the captain.

The captain continues to look lovingly at her, moved by Catherine's enchanting presence as they sway to the music and the motion of the waves. He bends over and kisses her fully on the lips in a tender and protracted manner, the likes of which she has never experienced before. Aye, she has had gentleman callers kiss her on the cheek, or briefly on the mouth in a polite goodbye, but the captain's passionate kiss is so full of sexual energy that she becomes entrenched in a sea of desire. She can feel his soft beard on her cheeks, and picks up the scent of his musky cologne and the damp wool of his navy-blue jacket, scents that reminds her of the misty moors of her homeland. More than all those sensations, she feels so much at home and secure in his all-encompassing embrace. *So this is what it is like to be with a true love*, she thinks. Catherine finally pulls away, ashamed that she has let her desire for the captain overtake her, and highly embarrassed by her actions, wonders if someone else on deck might be observing an intense romantic encounter.

"My dear Catherine," says the captain, "I can't bear for you to leave my life entirely and traipse across to country to the savage western land of Nevada. I must ask you now if you will consider being my wife, and drop this fanciful idea of marriage to a childhood friend."

Catherine is flustered and blushes to an attractive hue of a salmon-colored rose, the same color of the sunset they stand under each evening as the sun dips into the receptacle of the horizon. She is stunned by the captain's earnestness, and does not answer for several moments, for what he is saying does not seem quite real. Indeed, she can find no words to respond, so tongue-tied she is. The fact that she knew his proposal was forthcoming doesn't negate the shock of hearing it. Her reaction is quite different from what she had thought it would be – she finds herself on the verge of saying "Aye."

Blown away by pure emotion, she finally gains enough presence of mind to stammer in a Scots dialect that she rarely uses, "Oh, Captain, if only I could, but I canna break me engagement to Adam. 'Tis a union wi' Adam me mum desired o' me. Though Mum's passed on, it would break her heart if she lived and kent I wis abandonin' poor Adam, who's patiently awaitin' me. I must honor her wishes as a way o' honorin' her love, the one who gave me life."

"I understand completely," replies the captain gallantly, not appearing dejected or saddened by her response. "Granted, though, I've time on my side, wi' a great expanse o' ocean to change yer mind. I sincerely honor your decision for the present. May the Almichty be my witness when I declare that I'll try my utmost to dissuade you from going to Nevada. I stand before you an earnest and doting man, a living and breathing presence professing his everlasting love for you. I must express to you, in no uncertain terms, that your ideas o' Adam's character are not real, only a figment o' a long ago memory o' a teenaged laddie in Scotland.

"I won't kiss you again in that passionate manner for the time being – not until you've given my proposal more thought and you've come to a sound decision. I ken you have to make up your mind about my proposal alone, without my influence. I don't want to be too persuasive in my love for you while you are torn and deciding your fate. I fear if I act too aggressively, you might decide to marry me but later regret your decision."

When the captain responds so very generously to her rejection, eloquently convincing her of his undying love, granting her the leeway she's requested yet declaring he's not abandoning his quest for reciprocation of his love, Catherine is genuinely moved. *What a passionate, alluring response he has given me, and it reveals that the captain is truly a gentleman.* The sincerity of his response alone makes her question her decision to marry Adam. In her heart, she doesn't want the captain to give up on her and rescind his proposal, for she depends on him for her wellbeing. Without his love and attentiveness, there is sheer aloneness to deal with in her world, with many scary unknowns in her future. She has come to believe there is nobody in her world as important to her as the captain.

In the days following the proposal, Catherine berates her fate in life, the lack of favorable timing, for how unfair the circumstances are to present the wonderful captain in her life at a time she is traveling to marry another man! *'Tis like waving unbearable, impossible conflicts in front of me*, she thinks, *for no matter what I decide someone will be hurt.*

She's upset with herself in not having accepted the captain's proposal on the spot. *What was I thinking? I should've said aye!* Not only is she affianced to a man that that she hardly knows, she has shunned the kind captain's proposal, an excellent fit for her, a kindred spirit who is intelligent, handsome, and manly. Why does the universe offer her a man so perfect and not let that love transpire? Indeed, what an imperfect world it is!

Catherine desires something to happen so she'll have a reason to call off her marriage to Adam and not hurt his feelings. She wants to run into the captain's arms, lay her head on his chest, listen to the steady beat of his heart, and take in his masculine scents of whiskey, sea salt, sweat, tobacco, and misty wool, scents that remind her of her father, an elixir that comforts her aloneness.

Catherine views the captain as the perfect man and is of the opinion that a perfect union with him would inevitably transpire. Adam is never going to measure up to the captain, and Catherine very much desires a charmed life. Mother would have wanted her to be truly happy, she is certain.

She writes in her journal that night:

Perhaps I should not let this opportunity in life pass me by, to be with a man I'm extremely suited for, a gentleman I'm in love with. It isn't likely that I'll be attracted to and love Adam at this phenomenal, majestic level. Mum didn't understand the ways that men and women come together, a powerful uniting of like spirits, maybe because she was married for so many years and forgot that kind of true love exists, not just comfortable friendship-type love as with Father, but passionate love wherein spirits soar to the highest levels of existence. I can honestly say that I could easily be very happy and proud to be married to the captain, and my spirit would fly higher than birds can fly, up to touch the stars.

Chapter Two

I. Catherine's Near-Death Experience —A Ship in Distress

That night Catherine goes to bed and has vivid, lucid dreams of the titillating thrill of dancing in the captain's arms, but wakes up at two o'clock to hear the continual grinding noise of the ship's engines, sounding to her like an animal in perpetual agony, as if a battle for its life is taking place in the bowels of the vessel. And then the engines shut down completely and the ship comes to an abrupt, eerie halt, as if the steamer has lost her will to fight any longer. *She has died,* thinks Catherine.

Catherine sleeps little for the rest of the night, but does not leave her berth, as passengers have been instructed by the steward to stay below. Dr. Knoll, the ship's doctor, who was up on deck during the entire night aiding the crew, breaks the news to them in the early morning that the ship is completely surrounded by ice, but so as not to alarm the ladies does not convey the whole picture or the gravity of the situation. At first light, Catherine insists on going up on deck to see for herself that the *S.S. Alabama* has run into a massive iceberg, which has caused a gaping hole in her bow. There is excitement, dread, and a sense of calamity in the air. Even the birds in the sky are squawking preternaturally, as if they sense an oncoming doom.

Seeing the spectacle firsthand, she assesses that the ship might not make it out of its precarious situation. The beautiful vessel, in her once robust, stately glory, is taking on water at an alarming rate and will be enveloped by the monstrous sea if the damage cannot be repaired. Catherine has initial thoughts of going down with the ship to a final desolate burial ground on the murky ocean floor. *This could be the last day of my life*, she reflects calmly, panic quelled by the tired, dream-like state of her mind. An inner voice tells Catherine that it does not help to think about dying in an icy sea. She commends herself for being so brave, at the same time wondering how she can be so fearless. *'Tis in God's hands as to whether I live or die*, she decides, although she holds out hope that she will live. There is a subtle inkling in the back of her mind that relays to her that she will not die at sea, which lends to her a vestige of courage, but she wavers back and forth in trusting the accuracy of her senses in such a calamitous situation.

Catherine reflects that it has been a wonderful life, yet a short one if she dies, just as her sister had a short life. She has second-sight, lending her courage, telling her there are other great things out in the universe that she will experience if she dies. Because she is young and naïve, she does not lament over what she will be missing out on in her present lifetime, as she has only a vague conception of the future coming joys that life has to offer. Catherine is only disappointed that she might not be marrying the captain or Adam.

Catherine gives credence to the thought that maybe it was not so awful that the poor laddie on ship jumped overboard in his emotional distress, as they might all be doomed to die anyway; all may have very well been pre-ordained. She wonders if perhaps this disaster was planned in order for her to join her parents and sister in another more perfect world, for she might not have fit into the captain's nomadic life, no matter how great their love, nor have been happy in the savage wilds of America with a pensive, introverted man like Adam. She pictures Adam in a rosier light now that she is facing death; the disappointment that she might not ever see him again makes her sad.

Poor Adam's going to be disappointed when he learns his future wife drowned at sea, she laments. *He'll most likely be distraught for a time, for our friendship has grown close from the many letters that we've written each other. But how can he truly mourn someone he doesn't really know?*

On further reflection, she is of the opinion that Adam will be able to survive any loss merely by the awesome happenings taking place each day in his life. *America in all its glory is Adam's true love,* she decides, *and 'tis maybe fortunate that we never came to be reacquainted.*

Adam, she thinks, *will receive solace from the love of his new country, which he has described in his letters as being more beautiful than words can describe and worth traveling for months to reach.* Catherine assesses that she might never have loved the so-called magnificent land as much as Adam to stay there, but is sorry she'll never experience it. Adam has written so much about the glorious country that she has a picture of the beauty in her mind's eye, like her vision of Lake Tahoe, which, according to Adam, is an extremely beautiful emerald-blue lake that is like a natural jewel.

Maybe I'll die in the arms of the gallant Captain Noble, and that will be a great love to relish before I die, she reflects stoically, *for the captain would have been a good match for me. He is a Scotsman from a fine family and extremely intelligent and well educated – maybe a little too old for me, having turned forty, but that's probably not an issue in the grand scheme of things, wherein men are desirable at any age if they are good breadwinners and can produce a family. And now there won't be any problem with age or children if we die together at sea. If we miraculously live through this disaster, it could be an omen that we were meant to be together no matter what the circumstances of his age or career.* She reflects on the irony of her continuing to make plans for her life when she is facing so much danger. *'Tis because I don't believe I'm really going to die!*

Catherine stays on deck all morning viewing the monolithic iceberg towering over the ship. The crystalline blue statuesque ice sculpture rising out of the ocean stuns her, as it appears to be growing upward into the sky. *So scary and cold, yet so lovely*, she thinks. The monstrous ice rises out of the water like a Gothic cathedral, shimmering blue and silver tones in the early morning light, so stunning and blinding to her eyes, yet so terrifyingly close to the ship. *If it topples*, she thinks, *tons of ice will come down onto the ship*.

There is an all-out, well-orchestrated activity on the part of the crew to save the *S.S. Alabama* as well as everyone on board from disaster. The crew is trained to function as a unit in an emergency, as they have braved many storms together, but running into an iceberg is an unparalleled disaster that they have never experienced before. The fires are stoked to give the engine its utmost power; deckhands climb the ropes to the sky and peer down from above to view the site of impact. Finally, after many unsuccessful attempts, a crescendo of harsh clanking comes from the ship's engine as it jerks, quakes, and hisses like an alley cat before coming back to life. Once fired up, the steamer attempts to back away from the monster clutching it, the scraping sound of ice and the spine-chilling pitch of the steam engine dueling. The ship is hopelessly stuck fast to the towering monstrosity. The ship's engine sounds like a screeching animal that is using all its life's stamina to pry itself loose. Catherine envisions a big ice monster devouring a wee sea creature. She's never seen the captain so intense and focused in his actions, and so vocal in his authority. His command of the situation is extraordinary – there is an edge to his voice as he calls out orders to his men; its tone is revealing to her, conveying that he does not have total control over the situation.

After much ado, they have success in breaking loose. The pried-away vessel is backed a short distance away from the monster's clutches. Crewmen are lowered down by rope to inspect the bow. Twenty minutes later, the men holler to be pulled up, and report that there is a gaping hole over five feet wide and three feet deep in a section of the bow. The boat is taking on water, but it is determined that water is seeping into only one enclosed part of the bow, and other sectioned-off compartments are free of damage and remain watertight. The navigator has calculated they are only fifty-five miles off the coast of Newfoundland, and they must try to make it to land before the ship takes on enough water to sink; that is, if they can keep the engines fired up. The ship lurches forward and starts a slow, jerky course towards a lifesaving land.

II. Life in St. John's, Newfoundland — A Sparkling Winter Wonderland

The brave captain and his men have valiantly labored all day and continue into the night to get the engines to work again after freeing the damaged ship from the ice. Catherine notes in her diary, "She continues to take on water! We are going off course to find the nearest land, which Nathaniel says is Newfoundland, off the eastern coast of Canada. It has a port city named St. John's, which is the capital of Newfoundland, named after John the Baptist, says the good doctor. If the ship makes it to port before too much water is taken on, the ship can be repaired. I've been told all this through hearsay, not by the captain, as he has been too busy to talk to me. We steam very slowly and very jerkily the entire day and into night towards land (I nap on and off, and wake up often to make sure we're still moving and not sinking under)."

At dawn, the ship passes through a narrow passage that leads to the docks of St. John's. The skies are a beautiful rose-gold color striped with lavender. *Never have I seen a more glorious sunrise, which is auspicious to our now certain survival,* Catherine thinks. *The captain, in my eyes, is a hero for saving us from disaster, and perhaps I should give him an agreement for marriage, although I know he could break my heart, as he loves his sea as much as Adam loves his land. Yet he is so magnetic and intelligent that it is hard to resist his advances.* After they docked in St. John's Harbor, he came up to confide in her and told her that all is well, that they'd be in this town for several months for extensive repairs to be made, as the ship has been ravaged. The captain promises he will be stopping by to see her in the evenings whenever he's able, after his work on the ship is completed. He has arranged for his three cabin passengers, as well as Dr. Knoll and the navigator, to stay in homes of the townspeople. Catherine will be staying at the house of a young married couple.

The ship's crew remains on board each day, working on repairs under the captain's supervision, and spend their evenings in town at Lottie's Place and the Yellowbelly Brewery and Public House on George Street, all relatively new buildings since the Great Fire in 1846, which burned a great chunk along Duckworth, King, and George streets and Queen's Lane. The men retire in the late hours of the night, or wee early hours of the morn, to Molly Mallory's Boarding House.

Catherine arrives in St. John's to be welcomed enthusiastically by the townspeople, all very hospitable and kind. It is not hard to find families willing to take in the ship's passengers. She is fortunate to be the guest of an extremely nice and outgoing young couple. Catherine takes an immediate liking to Suzanna and Albert Ross, who are in their early twenties, only a few years older than she, and full of fun and laughter. They, and the future children that they plan to have – Suzanna has already picked out names for four – intend to migrate to Virginia City in five years' time, which gives Catherine hope that she'll have supportive friends in her new life, if she decides to marry Adam.

Suzanna is twenty-three years of age, two years older than Catherine, and has been married two years to the town's furrier. Catherine was graciously invited to stay with them in their small, charming yellow cottage, surrounded by a white picket fence, on the edge of town, which Albert inherited from his aunt. She feels immediately at home, and loves walking around the quaint neighborhood with the couple, meeting many of the neighbors, who are intrigued by Catherine.

Suzanna is a small, redheaded spitfire of a lassie, and very proficient when it comes to domestic chores: cleaning, laundry, shopping, and particularly cooking, with a lot of laughter added to the pot. She masters her chores with great gusto as she dances around the kitchen, clanking pots and pans, dust and debris flying as she sweeps, water flying as she mops, all the while chatting and joking a mile a minute.

Suzanna and Catherine shop in town each day for groceries, but because of the freezing climate it's not hard to keep food fresh in Newfoundland. Suzanna stores her meat and other perishables she wants to freeze outside in an ice hole; meat, if not used up, will stay frozen until spring. They have stored up a lot of deer and antelope meat from hunters that have bartered with Albert, at his furrier shop, for a good fur hat. There is really no need to freeze fish, for they can buy freshly caught beauties every day in the harbor market.

Catherine finds Suzanna hilarious in her imitations of townspeople, whom she been introduced to on their long walks – people that Suzanna has known her entire life – and Catherine is educated to all their mannerisms and eccentricities back at the cottage. Suzanna is not cruel in her depictions, but right on the mark, at the same time displaying a fondness for her subjects.

She and Albert are teaching Catherine to ice skate, and they think she is quite a natural at it. Catherine knows she will never be as skilled as those who have grown up in Newfoundland who are put on the ice as toddlers – most children learn to skate as soon as they can walk. By early childhood, wee skaters can spin and do jumps, with no apprehension of not landing in an upright position.

Besides skating on most evenings, Suzanna and Catherine take walks to town during the day, and often venture to the far outskirts of the village, to where vast woodlands begin, which gradually rise into the foothills of great forested mountains. They trek across a mile or two of flat, snowy plain that sparkles and glistens in prismatic crystalline splendor, a truly magical winter wonderland that Catherine delights in. Sometimes she forgets that she is not out on her beloved moors of Scotland in winter. Besides outdoor adventures and skating, there are some more refined ladies' functions: the lassies have attended three tea parties, one a luncheon given in honor of Mrs. Oakwood and Catherine (Mrs. Oakwood is being housed by a kindly widow in town in her fifties).

Albert works in the center of town on George Street, but comes home for his mid-day meal, which Suzanne and Catherine prepare together while having fun. Albert entertains them with gossip of the village, as many confide in him while they are having furs attached or reattached to their coats, mittens, and mufflers.

Catherine writes in her diary after being in St. John's for a week: Albert thinks we are silly lasses, for we laugh to our hearts' content, sometimes making ourselves teary-eyed and red in the face. We find everything funny as we cook. Albert says we sound like a raucous pack of hyenas. We do get enjoyment in coming up with new recipes each day, which Albert greatly appreciates. I have increased my cooking skills immensely, which will be necessary if I become someone's wife, particularly Adam's. Will I or won't I marry Adam, or love him if I do marry him? That is the question. Should I travel thousands of miles to Virginia City? Perhaps I would be happier staying here with Suzanna and Albert, and having the brave captain come to visit me often when he's not at sea. This town feels like home. I am safe and secure here, and have friends. What more could I ask for? What would Mum think? I'm sure she would have a strong opinion, probably veering towards Adam and Nevada.

III. Skating to Strauss on a Frosty Winter Night

The townspeople skate to the spirited music of an organist who is playing his pipe organ atop the rink, gliding the instrument smoothly around the ice as if it, too, were on skates. Catherine imagines the organ has a mind of its own, and a set of lungs that projects musical notes to far corners of the rink, going wherever it desires to serenade. She admires the skilled expertise of the ice skaters; they appear to her like dancers who belong to a professional dance troupe, not your run-of-the-mill citizens of St. John's, some quite elderly. One old man spins expertly in figure-eight configurations; another younger man does a back flip expertly on the ice and lands upright with perfect grace. Catherine takes delight in watching folks having so much fun in this country of ice and snow, of short dreary days, but magnificent twilight hours when the sky stays peacock blue all night long.

After the evening meal is when everyone comes out and the best skating is done. Catherine always imagined that those living in places as cold as Scotland stayed indoors in the wintertime, huddled around a fire after the sun went down, as people in Helensburgh do. Scotland is cold and clammy in the winter, but Newfoundland is even colder, and just as humid as Helensburgh, being that it lies close to a large body of water. Catherine reflects that expending energy outdoors on the ice for a couple of hours each evening may keep the cold at bay and all the people healthy.

Here, everyone, even folks in their eighties, brave the cold for the evening's festivities, the women dressed elegantly in colorful, long wool coats and fur muffs, collars, and tuques. Catherine also admires the lads and men in patterned wool sweaters and tight, colorful breeches that show off their muscular legs.

The captain had promised Catherine he would visit her in St. John's whenever he could get away from his ship's duties early enough to spend the evening with her. He apologizes profusely for not coming to visit her every evening, as he would like, explaining that there are times he gets in late at night from the ship for only a break to sleep. When he does visit, about three times a week, he bears lovely gifts, and always gives her the tender, protracted embrace of a lover having been separated for too long.

Catherine is sorely disappointed on evenings that he doesn't come knocking at the cottage door with a bouquet of flowers wrapped in colorful lacy paper, expensive French perfumes, or bottles of wine or cognac that she shares with Suzanna and Albert, along with the lavish meals she and Suzanna concoct. The captain has accompanied Catherine out at night to the skating rink several times, which has made the experience of learning to skate all the more thrilling. Enfolding her lightly in his arms for romantic Strauss waltzes, her favorite being "Southern Rose Waltz," lends to her the blissful feeling of flying. With the captain's arms around her, she is completely fearless on the ice, wherein she forgets she is on a very slick surface and not dancing on the smooth deck of the ship.

At twenty-one years of age, Catherine, despite her second-sight and pragmatism, is hopelessly drawn to the charms of the captain, so handsome and engaging to the extent that she finds it virtually impossible to see anything but a perfect human being.

Catherine's diary:
4 May 1870
I try not to be taken in by the captain's charms, but his charms are like a magnet, the same force that draws me to the stars and the moon. How can I not be attracted to brilliant celestial objects and a larger-than-life man of the sea? I know so many women are, as I hear them talk admirably of the captain in town, and even Suzanna

is quite flirtatious with him when he visits. The fact that so many women are attracted to this gentleman makes me not want to be attracted to him, but I can't help myself. I think even women who are married would like attention from him, so they can feel as I do around him, like a revered goddess, so wonderfully alive. Back in Helensburgh, I did have a revelation while daydreaming that I'd have three loves in my life, one a great love, and I think I've found my great love in the captain. He tells me I am a very beautiful young woman, and I don't know how to respond to this but to blush and show my gratitude by giving him a hug. I have received this remark from gentleman suitors before, but when others have relayed this I have felt quite deflated, with the impression that I was something to be bought and possessed. They did not see me for who I truly am, someone of substance with deep thoughts, opinions, and feelings, someone with a practical intelligence. But when the captain admires my looks, I come alive, knowing he sees far more in me than what's on the exterior. We have covered so many intellectual topics, like the state of affairs in Scotland and the British monarchy. He values my opinions and he has a knack for reading my thoughts. He is very interested in my life back in Scotland, and loves to hear about Mum and Father and Ruthie. He was tangibly moved, almost to tears, when I told him about Ruthie and how she died.

I'm hoping I will love Adam as much as the captain when I get to know him; that is, if I decide to go on to Virginia City. I don't love him now and have reservations about traveling a great distance across a strange territory, with Indians and wild animals galore, for a man I hardly know. As for the captain, I, of course, love him like I do the stars, the moon, and the night sky, but it is not practical love; it is romantic, magical love that will probably not last, just as the full moon wanes and disappears, and the stars dim and die.

To think in practical terms, the captain lives on his ship 300 days out of the year. He continually urges me to marry him instead of Adam, to live in St. John's in his house on the edge of the bay. If I marry the captain, I picture myself living in a large abode with many gables, with the sound of waves and seagulls waking me in the morn, standing patiently at a widow's watch, waiting for his ship to come in. That would be fine by me, yet I've been led to believe the captain has women friends in every port. His time away might bring out some jealousy on my part. Even in Newfoundland he has other women friends who know him quite well! Some act as if they are on intimate terms with him. Would he end those friendships if I married him?

Suzanna would like very much for me to remain here as we are such close friends now, but she warns me of the captain's chameleon-like nature, that his affections can change like the direction of winds. She has told me she knows the captain has a special woman in the village, and then becomes close-mouthed about it. Sometimes I think she is envious of my relationship with the captain by the way she acts around him. Maybe she exaggerates a wee bit about his dalliances? Of course, Captain knows a lot of women in St. John's. He is the type of man that women buzz around like busy bees, but I know he adores me above all. I can feel it in my heart and in the depths of my soul. I feel magic between us!

Looking into his eyes I see the light of a million stars sparkling with truths about the mysteries of the world – I'm confident that I can trust this fine gentleman who has so much mastery over the universe. He looks at me with much awe, and I become aware of the effect of my persona on him, which imbues me with a feeling of power that I, too, have mastery over the universe. I know it is vanity to garner power from a man that way, but I let it happen anyway. After all, I will not be young forever. I should enjoy my young life as long as I can. I almost died at sea!

The captain comes often to visit Catherine in St. John's after his long days on board the *S.S. Alabama*, putting his revered ship back into seaworthy shape. He is so charismatic that even Suzanna, a discerning student of peoples' characters, and a married woman to boot, doesn't find anything amusing about him to imitate.

Catherine is very honored that the captain sees something special in her and takes time out of his busy schedule to visit her, though her insecurity about her place in his heart has been stoked by things Suzanna has said. "The captain, most likely, has a lass in every port! He's never been for want of female companions. He loves his drink and card playing in the evening very much."

Catherine's diary:
I think the captain finds something special in me because I'm educated and not fickle like a lot of ladies, and am interested in him as a person. Perhaps he sees me as his counterpart, a kindred soul, and likes my high-spiritedness, as he, too, is high-spirited, even more so than myself. I think he also realizes that I am intuitive and can see beyond his innate charms to the man he truly is, a complex individual with much depth to his character, but with kindness and gentility woven into these layers. I truly admire this man! Where does this leave me but in a terrible fix? I'm in love with a man I shouldn't marry, and engaged to a man I don't really know, and probably won't like. The captain is still trying to change my mind about marrying Adam, and I'm giving him hope by not mentioning Adam in his presence. Maybe this is the wrong way to go. The captain has my undying affection forever, and I truly wish, deep down inside, that I could marry him, but I have my reservations.

As for Adam Baird, I shall lists the pros and cons of a marriage to him. I reflect on the cons often.

The laddie didn't even want me at first – he desired my sister. We did have some good times together, but I'm secondhand goods. Adam is someone I do not know! Probably he's not worldly at all in nature like the captain.

Will Adam make a good husband? I know he'll be true to me as he was always reliable, steadfast, and devoted to the Baird family.

These are the qualities of a good man to marry, but there has to be love and attraction as well. I'm just not in love with Adam from his letters.

The captain has my heart for now and will always own a part of my youthful self.

She is up in the air as to what she'll do – go to Virginia City or stay in beautiful Newfoundland. For now, she is happy to bide her time in the lovely city of St. John's.

In later years, Catherine came to realize that the only reason she got away from the captain and didn't abandon her plans to continue on to Nevada was because of her long stay in Newfoundland. When she became an integral part of St. John's society, acquainted with many of the townsfolk, and privy to their gossip, she learned that the captain had quite a reputation in town. At first she didn't believe all the talk – that the captain had one woman in particular that he visited frequently in town, an older woman in her thirties! Catherine couldn't understand how the captain could spend time with this other woman when he loved her. Thinking on this later in life, she was certain beyond any doubt that captain was a kindred spirit of hers. This was apparent by their physical attraction and the synchrony of their thoughts and emotions.

It was as if our spirits had melded and we were two halves of a perfect whole, and no other two human beings could be so complementary. The captain was someone who belonged to me for a short period time, but he was not meant to be with me for a lifetime, she thinks.

The memory of Captain Noble was an extraordinary gift in giving her a snapshot of herself as a young woman, a wonderful memory, splendid to warm her spirit on cold winter evenings, a blanket of cozy memories to wrap around herself. Even the scent of the captain remains in her memory, particularly when she smells the sea, wet wool, and aromatic tobacco. This gift has kept her believing in miracles and a magical universe in her old age. Looking back through the years, Catherine is glad that she met the captain. *There was something truly magical that occurred to stir my youthful spirit and lend to me fond memories of my youthful passions.*

Two and a half months in St. John's went by quickly, and in seventy-five days the ship was repaired and ready to complete its journey to New York. Catherine had to make a decision as whether to stay and marry the captain or to continue her westward course to marry Adam. It was a difficult decision to make, but an incident occurred that made the decision easier.

IV. Who in Heaven's Name is Elizabeth O'Grady?

Catherine found out that the captain's special friend was named Elizabeth O'Grady, and that he provided financially for her. Subsequently, she learned from Suzanna, who decided to tell her everything for her own good, that Elizabeth O'Grady had a son by the captain.

"I wasn't going to tell you and hurt your feelings, and probably wreck our friendship, because I thought you'd be leaving and wouldn't need to learn the rotten truth," said Suzanna. "The captain has a child with Liz O'Grady, and when he's not over visiting you, or playing cards, he's probably with Liz and his son." Catherine's heart sinks when she hears this.

Catherine confronts the captain with this information, but his response confuses her.

"Ye've a son and a woman whom you keep, and visit often? You didn't tell me this. Why is she not your wife?"

"Liz O'Grady has a son by me acause she planned to become

pregnant so I'd marry her. Frankly, I did not want to marry her. She's not the right kind o' woman for me."

"What kind o' woman is she?"

"Ah, she's a woman who's had some tough breaks in life and has a survivor's mentality – she knows what she needs and goes after it. Liz is a content lassie now, having obtained what she desires. I'll give her credit for bein' a good mother to our son, only a young woman I don't click with emotionally or intellectually – not educated and spirited as you. She was workin' in a brothel when I met her. I only do what is required o' me by providin' for both child and mother, giving them a lifestyle that is comfortable, and for the sake of my son, ample support to keep her from having to sell her body anymore."

"How do I know this won't happen to me? Ye'll marry me, give me children to care for, and house me in town so I'm available to ye when ye come back from sea? Ye might tire of me soon enough, not have time to visit often acause ye've anither family ye must tend to and limited time on your hands."

"Catherine, you're verra special to me above everything else in this world. You're someone that I don't want to get away from me. Ye give me such joy, inspire me to believe that 'tis possible to be verra happy in life wi' the right person. Together we're an unconquerable team. I'd never abandon ye, and I'd always make time for ye."

Catherine writes in her diary that night:

The captain is charming, so very charming. So very charismatic and handsome that every lass he encounters swoons and bows down to him. He makes women feel that they are special. And he wants to marry me? Why? He probably has a girl in every port, not just St. John's – he's never lonely, is well established in town with friends, and he loves his drink and card playing. And now I find out he has a family to support. Will the captain be a good husband? Maybe he finds a quality in me that he needs to feel complete. Who knows what this quality is, for I don't always see myself as others do? It might be because I appear even-headed, and that's what he lacks in life, a stable foundation. He also sees my spirited side, but I think he realizes that I will settle down to domesticity in married life and be content to raise children; whereas, he has a wild side with adventure and travel to many foreign ports, which will always be part of his life. I know what I must do. I must get away from the captain before it is too late.

I said my goodbyes to Suzanna and Albert, and all the wonderful townspeople I have met here, whom I will always consider my friends. They'll be so far away but so close to my heart forever. I am completely hopeless at goodbyes, and must've sounded like a crying loon. What memories I've made here! Mother and Father would be proud of me. I sense they've been watching over me. I will say my sad goodbyes to the captain once we reach New York Harbor. I sense Mum, on the other side, is guiding me, helping me through this fateful decision in life.

BOOK SEVEN

HENRY ARRIVES IN NEVADA

Chapter One

I. November 1869 — Henry Joins Adam in Virginia City — And Punt, Too!

In 1869, six years after Adam's departure, Annie's death, and Mary's birth, Henry Baird, twenty-three years of age, sets off for America. Adam is in the process of buying land to build a house on, and has been seriously seeking a wife, corresponding with Catherine Malcolm of Helensburgh in the hope of enticing her to join him in America. Adam has tentatively procured Henry a carpentry job in the Caledonia Mines with the help of Adrian. His brother might have another type of job in mind that he'd prefer to find on his own, so it has not been made into a definite position.

II. Adam's Near-Death Experience in the Caledonia Mines, Virginia City — Saved by the Valiant Punt — June 1870

Henry has been in Virginia City for four months, and the brothers excitedly await Catherine Malcolm's arrival, which is estimated to be next week according to the train schedule. Adam was wired that her ship docked safely in New York Harbor and that she boarded a westbound train the next week.

In the months before Catherine's arrival, the brothers have had many adventures and misadventures together. There've been times that Adam wondered if he'd live to see his wedding day. The West is dangerous in many unexpected ways. Henry is thankful that Punt accompanied him, as the Wee One does come in handy in helping them out in jams and in saving their lives.

On his second day in Virginia City, Henry started a job in the Caledonia mines that Adrian helped procure for him. The miners soon get to know Henry, and value this charismatic, personable addition to the crew. Henry's presence inspires the men to adopt more camaraderie with one another. They look forward to coming to work each morning, as Henry has a God-given knack for entertaining, commiserating with those in need, and making the overall work experience of the miners a more positive experience.

Each day, the two Baird brothers hike up into the hills to the Caledonia mines from their rental lodging on C Street, along a steep, mile-long, gritty dirt path, winding up into the lower Sierra foothills of the Nevada range, in terrain dotted with chaparral, sagebrush, and fledgling pine. Along the way, they pass by, with pride, the redwood-log bungalow they've been constructing on weekends, which is near completion thanks to the help of the town. Seventy-five men and women attended a community house-raising party last week, hosted by their Caledonia Mining Association, with co-workers, townsfolk, and friends all in attendance. Thankfully, the house will be ready, with all its trimmings and amenities, in time for Catherine's arrival. The brothers are pleased with the solidly built redwood construction that is eye-catching, and are assured that Catherine will appreciate beginning her married life in this idyllic woodland setting. The interior of the home is lovely with its light pine-board floors, lofty ceilings, large airy rooms, and tall windows set to catch the morning light. The main room and kitchen have handmade tables, chairs, and cabinets of oak and cedar cut from nearby trees, as well as a beautiful dark walnut desk. The two bedrooms have mahogany dressers, armoires, and bedsteads purchased from Sacramento, California.

III. Exhausting Work in the Caledonia Mines

Adam's job in the Caledonia mines, with Henry to assist him now, entails checking on the wooden structures traversing deep into the mine and repairing any weaknesses tantamount to keeping the mine from caving in. The shaft of the mine goes down through subterranean layers into three compartments.

It's a physically demanding and dangerous occupation for the miners and carpenters, especially transporting the workers up and down the shaft. Hoisting the cage that carries the crew into the mineshaft is precarious on any day. On Henry's second week on the job, he and Adam arrive at work around seven in the morning to find the entire crew gathered around the mining framework, looking up at the elevator cage that habitually runs up and down the shaft of the mine, carrying the workers. Up overhead, there is a steam engine on a large building framework that houses the shaft called a gallows frame, with a large pulley atop the wood contraption. When working properly, the elevator cage is attached to the cable pulley that is run by a motor. A strong wire cable passes from the engine over the pulley on to the gallows frame and down the shaft to the mine. Presently, they find that the cage is caught in the cables. Not an unusual occurrence – this happens at least twice a week, as the cables can get entwined at the start, or anywhere along the way down. Accidents can happen when the cable gets caught up in the pulley mechanism so the cage can't progress.

The miners are in fine moods on this beautiful warm morning, the tone jovial, as workers are being given extra time above ground with pay, which is quite a precious respite considering the quality of air in the shaft. Adam sees the cage is dangling precariously above the shaft like a marionette, displaying an awkward side-sway dance, bouncing around the twisted cable as it tries unsuccessfully to descend by the power-driven pulley. A few planks have been set across the shaft and a ladder set atop in preparation for someone to climb up, reach overhead, and free the twisted cable from the pulley mechanism, allowing the cage to descend into the shaft. The cage is quite high up and requires a tall man to be able to reach that far.

No one is doing anything to alleviate the situation, and so Adam volunteers to climb up on the ladder set atop the planks to reach up and free the cage from the cables it is entangled in. He is up on the ladder only for a few seconds when one of the planks on which the ladder is balanced starts to break in half. Adam hears the sickening sound of breaking wood, and in a split second realizes he is going to be hurled down the shaft. With lightning speed, and just in the knick of time, Billy Lowe, the supervisor/engineer in charge of the engine, stabilizes the ladder for Adam by quickly, and with great force, shoving an unbroken plank next to the broken one, laying it parallel, so Adam can step onto it quickly. Billy is able to hold the ladder on the good plank before the broken plank splits entirely in two and falls down the shaft. After the cracking noise, Adam visualizes his body free-falling for hundreds of yards down the shaft to his death. He becomes shaken and very pale, and begins to sweat profusely. The men make him sit down to gather his wits.

Unbeknownst to the workers, Henry's spritely friend Punt has been coming to work each day with Henry, standing on his shoulder, acting as though he were at a sporting event. Punt immediately comes to Adam's aid in a way that no one but Henry is aware of. Punt is able to move an alternate plank over the cracked one with lightning speed to make it look like Billy's response time is commendably ultra-quick in steadying the ladder. If not for Punt with the help of Billy Lowe moving in to steady the ladder on the solid plank, Adam would certainly have been hurled to his death down the shaft. Accidents are not uncommon around mining shafts, wherein cables maim men when they become entangled in them, or cables break off completely and send workers hurtling down the shaft to their deaths.

Adam described the incident of the shaft breakage in a letter home to his family to impart the frequency of mining accidents, but failed to relay the severity of this incident and how close to death he'd actually come.

Adam reflects on what would have happened if he'd fallen down the shaft and had been killed. *The world would have ended for him. Probably would've made me into a larger-than-life hero. Mebbe 'tis na so bad to die and be worshipped – that is, if there's somewhaur better to go to efter death.*

Henry often wonders what would have happened if Punt hadn't been there to save his brother on that day. *I'll niver be irritated by the presence o' that Wee Man, niver again, no matter what he daes. Niver will I tell him to skedaddle*, thinks Henry.

IV. Repaired S.S. Alabama En Route to New York from St. John's

The rest of the voyage goes smoothly for Catherine. The seas are calm, and there is no seasickness among the passengers. The repaired *S.S. Alabama* steams into New York Harbor on a beautiful spring morning. Catherine is thrilled with the sighting of the Statue of Liberty in the harbor. The captain persists fervently in his courtship of her. His charms are very compelling, and Catherine finds herself being drawn more and more to him despite her reservations. She has already made her decision to continue on to

Virginia City, however, and is adamant that she'll not change her mind. Enjoying the captain on the last leg of the voyage is a way to say goodbye, as she knows she will probably never see him again.

Catherine writes in her diary:
10 May 1870
I have said my farewells to all the passengers and crew, and to my dear Captain Noble. I address him as Nathaniel now. He is resigned to the inevitable, that I'm to be married to Adam Baird as soon as I reach Nevada, but has informed me that he thinks we will be reunited some day in the future, hopefully sooner than later. He holds out hope that the relationship will not work out for me and Adam, and that once I reach Nevada I'll decide I can't go through with the marriage – he has said something to the effect that if Adam turns out to have been full of "blarney" (his words) that I should write him and he'll send me money to travel back to St. John's. He reminds me that I really don't know Adam well enough to marry right away. Nathaniel says that we should keep in touch even if I do marry Adam, for the future may bring circumstances whereby I become a widow – this is very pessimistic talk, and alarms me, as Adam does have a very dangerous mining job. I know the captain is just venting his hurt feelings about me leaving.

Captain Noble escorted me to the Transcontinental Railway, the Union Pacific, going west across the country to Ogden. I am to transfer to the Central Pacific in Ogden that will take me to Sacramento. From Sacramento I will head up to Steamboat Springs by stagecoach, and them on to Reno, Nevada. Adam will meet me in Reno. The entire trip will be approximately thirty-four days.

Later in life, Catherine, as a middle-aged mother of six children (Belle, Will, Jean, Margaret, Ethel, and Mary) will attribute the captain's power over her to the magic of the sea, the thrill and freedom of being out on a vast expanse of formidable ocean for days on end to cross the Atlantic, entirely at the mercy of nature and the expert navigational skills of Captain Noble, whom she found unbelievably handsome. It was the colorful rhythmic waves as they frolicked in the wind, the magic of moonlit decks, and being held close by the captain while dancing under the stars on balmy nights. In St. John's, it was the extravagant dinners out on the town while being seen in the company of this handsome man, the envy of the all ladies, the presents from the captain, as well as skating with him on the charming ice rink. All of these things exude enchanting memories. Above all, it was the vulnerable situation of being alone in the world, and to have someone to look after her wellbeing, to lend her a sense of security. Now in her later years, Catherine looks back and is amazed by the courage that she possessed in her youth. The fact that the captain was handsome, charismatic, and charming sealed the great attraction, and her loving admiration for this genteel man would last for the rest of her life. His power over her was limited by what she willingly surrendered to him; it was her own spirited nature that permitted her to seek out and experience the romantic enticements of the captain, and eventually the pragmatism of her intellect to have the wherewithal to pull back when it was necessary to leave. She is not sorry for either of these actions. She savors the wonderful memories to look back on. Catherine will never forget the captain. Nathanial Noble will always be in her dreams.

V. Drumdruils Ranch 1870 — Baird Children Fret Over the Fate of Their Brothers

Emma, fourteen, Janet, sixteen, Malkie, seventeen, and Telford, nineteen, as well as Susan, eight, and Wee Mary Alice, six, continue to spend a lot of their free time discussing their brothers in America.

Before bedtime, they gather and talk over the situation of Adam and Henry being so far away where they have no access to them. The old playroom is their sanctuary, a place where they can discuss their innermost feelings with one another, away from the ears of adults.

The Baird siblings fear they will never see their older brothers again, being that they are "as far away as the moon," and they have not seen Adam in six years.

"Why are we na goin' to visit Adam and Henry? If we daena go we'll niver see them again. 'Tis like they're deid. They could be deid!" croaks Malkie, looking crushed and close to tears. "We'll niver see them our whole lives, as long as we live." Malkie grabs Scruffy Bear and throws him across the room.

"Na," says Janet emphatically. "They're na goin' to be deid to us. We'll hear from them often. They'll write."

"What's the difference?" says Malkie. "We daena iver see thair faces. Like they might change and we woudna ken them. 'Tis kind o' like they're deid."

Emma says, "They're na deid. We can sense them, communicate wi' them wi' our thoughts. They're out there somewhaur."

Pipes in Mary, "I see Faither acause I hiv second-sight and he's na deid. I dae sense him, and I ken he'll look efter me."

Replies Emma, "I'll tell ye what they say and what they're doin', and how they look."

"Aye," says Janet, "we daena have second-sight. Ye must tell us when ye can sense that they're in danger, so we can pray for them."

"Just the same," says Telford, "I'm goin' out West to make me fortune as soon as I can get away from ranching duties. I've written Henry and Adam, and I'll meet them in Virginia City."

The Bairds receive regular letters from both Henry and Adam, and are thrilled to no end to read about their lives, but it takes a month or more to get these letters, which means they're not kept up to date. Adam, being a prolific letter writer, continues with his weekly newsletter to the family of the goings-on in Virginia City, his last letter informing them of Henry's arrival, of Catherine Malcolm being en route to marry him (by the time they get news of Catherine coming, she and Adam are already married), the house he and Henry have built, the friends and townspeople who helped them build their new home, and their work in the mines.

"Why daena we hear from Adam and Henry more often?" inquires Telford on one of their daily walks out in the woods with Violet.

"'Tis like they're deid," says Malkie, a theme he's latched onto and continually brings up when feeling down and missing his brothers.

"Na," responds Janet. "I'm telling ye, Malkie, they're not deid."

"We willna iver view their faces again," says Malkie. "They might've changed and be different now. Mebbe dressin' and speakin' like Indians."

Says Wee Mary Alice, "Faither's not changed at all. I can sense him."

Rejoins Emma, "Mary's right. We can sense our brithers and communicate wi' them from afar wi' our minds acause we've the second-sight."

Telford reiterates for the umpteenth time, "I'm goin' to America to see for myself that they're alright just the same."

VI. Baird Brothers, a United Front

Before Catherine's arrival, the two Baird brothers enjoy being together once again, just like the old days in Drumdruils. Together they forge a comfortable life in Virginia City. Adam, with Henry by his side, and with a little imagination, can pretend that their homeland of Scotland is nearby, not thousands of miles away. It is only when Henry arrives that Adam realizes how homesick for his family he's been. The two brothers' relationship picks up where it left off six years before, a warm, trusting, and noncompetitive bond, with brotherly affection and humor, and added to the mix a panoramic Western backdrop where adventure and danger lurk around each corner.

Adam feels more secure on the job, pleased to have Henry at his side, as they've worked together in synchrony since they were young children, not having to second-guess one another's actions in making life-and-death decisions. Case in point: the time Adam warned Henry away as he started to walk into a small cave-like stretch of the mine. Henry's curiosity got the better of him, for the section gave the appearance of an enticing cave of treasures that he would have loved to explore as a lad. Punt was not there on that day to warn Henry, as the Wee One had decided he loathed the dusty, gritty atmosphere of the mine, and his small lungs were not physiologically adapted to breathe congested air. Adam's warning came as a fear reaction – a bracing of his body and an atavistic grunt that Henry picked up on, as he knew his brother so well. In a flash of recognition, Adam sensed the precarious nature of that particular section as he glanced overhead and saw beams showing new cracking. Henry knew to trust Adam's instincts. Sure enough, within seconds of Henry backing away, the beams broke and heavy silt and clay came rushing down to fill the entire chamber.

There are many other adventures and challenges in their new life that have nothing to do with mining. Virginia City is a town that lives up to the wild stories of the West. The two brothers got into a bar brawl one evening while peacefully drinking their whiskies. Two drunken brutes started punching them off their stools, and everyone in the bar was drawn into the melee. The brothers fought admirably alongside the others until the sheriff was able to take control and arrest the two instigators. Adam is very appreciative of Henry's presence, as an onslaught of more difficulties arise.

VII. Punt — Rootin' Tootin' Cowpoke o' the West

Punt truly relishes his stay out West, and takes his experience to another level by adopting the rustic lifestyle and attire of a bona fide cowpoke. He decks himself out in Western cowboy boots and a gold and green Stetson hat, a green and moss-colored plaid lumberjack shirt, a green denim jacket with a fleece collar, and dark green leather chaps. Henry finds his get-up ridiculously comical.

"Punt, ye he look like a leprechaun whose been kidnapped by outlaws."

True to form, Punt is also up to his customary antics of stirring up a little trouble in town to keep himself amused, though Henry isn't amused at all. Punt has played pranks on several old biddies in town, as well as inebriated patrons wobbling unsteadily out of the saloons who are easy targets for a "wee bit o' teasing." Punt's favorite prank is to fly up behind a drunk in his bee-sized form and draw in chalk the word "Roostered" (Punt's favorite slang word for a drunk) on the inebriated man's back. When the man gets home, his wife will be alerted to his drinking, if she doesn't know already.

VIII. Man, Monkey, and Building Blown to Smithereens on B Street

One of the most tragic events in Henry and Adam's time in Virginia City was the loss of their beloved supervisor to an explosion in town. To Adam, it is ironic that the mines, with all their inherent dangers, did no harm to poor Billy; simply sleeping innocently in his own bed in the center of town is what killed his good friend. Adam, again, has to wonder about the fairness of life – is there a universal plan behind such inequities? Why do some good people die young and other less deserving men have long lives? It was Billy, only thirty-five years of age, who had played an integral role in saving Adam's life as he had stood precariously over the mining shaft on the verge of falling in. If only he had been there for Billy to return the favor. Adam is bowled over with guilt and grief for not being able to save him.

According to *The Territorial Enterprise*, an explosive fire started at the residence of a Mr. Van B, who had owned a gunpowder agency dealing in the distribution of gunpowder which had gone out of business. Mr. Van B, having lost his agency, was trying to concoct the right formulation of explosives so he could build up another lucrative business. In preparation for his new business, he was storing nitroglycerin in his room and performing tests to produce a better product that would sell. In the middle of the night, his pet monkey allegedly got into the nitro and caused a severe explosion that wiped out entire blocks on B and C streets. Many buildings in blocks of C Street and B Street were completely obliterated.

Adam's superintendent, Billy Lowe, lived in one of the three-story buildings and was trapped inside. Adam and his other mining comrades rushed over to try to find Billy when they heard the explosion, which was loud enough to awaken everyone in town. The firemen wouldn't let them inside the building to find their poor friend, as the floors had all collapsed into the cellar. Poor Billy's body was never recovered, but Mr. Van B's body was found stark naked in the street. His monkey was spotted climbing up a tree, and then disappeared for good.

This massive explosion was a few years after another big fire in Virginia City had wiped out a large section of blocks at the heart of the city, and had left several thousand people homeless. This fire had crossed B and C streets at Taylor, as well as crossing again below D Street, where it destroyed the Catholic church, the Methodist church, and many fine residences. In the western part of the town, the stately homes of John Mackey, J.P. Martin, Charles Forman, Charles Rawson, and other prominent citizens were lost. Many other more modest homes were destroyed, as well as a great number of the city's businesses. On the west side of C Street a clean sweep was made, from and including Marte's large new brick building all the way out to Carson Street. Virginia City was able to rebuild itself quickly and often, and it took only a few years for people to put behind them each of the many tragedies that had occurred.

Dear family,
Glad to hear ye are all faring well and that happy times abound for every one at Drumdruils. It was good to hear about the children and that they are doing well in school. Things are fair here in Virginia City. As usual a lot goes on. Don't know how to explain the unusual frequent unfortunate occurrences of the West. We had some bad news with the foreman of the mine who died in an explosion, a very well-liked man and a good friend of mine. A man by the name of Van B had an agency for a powder company and was keeping dynamite in his room. He blew up the whole building with the help of his pet monkey. My friend unfortunately resided in the building. Henry is doing well, and will write you in a separate letter. Suffice it to say, I so enjoy his company out here.

Your loving son and brother,
Adam

IX. The Temperance Society and Scotch Pete

Adam and Henry are elected by the management of the Caledonia Mine to take another miner, a fellow Scotsman, Pete Macintyre, to the Temperance Society, for a bid to become a member of a group of men who are sworn to sobriety. The man is called "Scotch Pete" because of his great liking of Scotch whiskey. They are not close friends of Pete's, but because they are fellow Scotsmen, the management deemed it appropriate that they aid in Pete's recovery. Adam is incensed that one lone alcoholic Scotsman could give the whole country of Scotland a bad name. Henry appeases him by saying there are alcoholics in all countries, but they're elected to help Pete because they can talk the vernacular and can better convey to Pete the consequences of his actions. The matter is grim, for Pete is on the verge of losing his job because of his drinking problem. His co-workers have reported him for imbibing on the job, a very foolish action in a very dangerous occupation, risking the lives of not only himself but the other miners as well. Pete has been given one last chance to clean up his act, and that is only because he is a tremendously strong, burly fellow who can load more ore carts each day than any other worker.

Adam and Henry, with Punt on his shoulder, escort Scotch Pete down B Street to a Temperance Society meeting. Along the route, there are various saloons that Scotch Pete is enticed by, almost taking a detour into one. Punt doesn't help matters at all, for he loves, with a passion, the lively, rowdy saloon life, and telepathically puts thoughts in Pete's head to tantalize him to step inside for one last evening of barhopping.

"I've got to have one last drink for posterity afore I'm doomed to sobriety, then I'll quit cold turkey," he promises the brothers. Adam and Henry can't dissuade such a strong man with an addiction away from his physiological need. But one drink is not enough. At every saloon they pass, Pete insists on going in, time and again exhibiting his unquenchable thirst for the hard stuff. The brothers sigh in resignation, caving in on their endeavor to save Pete's job. Punt is in seventh heaven. He adores saloons – the game playing, the clink of the roulette tables and the shuffling of cards on the felt tables, the clanking of pool balls, and the scantily clad barwomen performing outlandish, uninhibited moves to the lively piano and banjo music. Punt tells Henry he'll help him win at cards. Henry declines. Often, when they are in a bar, Punt gets up to his usual pranks by tickling a lady and having the man sitting next to her take the blame. In one bar, he is the cause of a fight that breaks out when a young man's girlfriend is tickled and an innocent gentleman of good standing, a bank clerk, sitting on the other side of the lass at the bar, is blamed. The boyfriend starts pummeling the innocent fellow with his fist, and they are both thrown out into the street.

When Henry, Adam, and Pete finally arrive at the Temperance Society, located in a building adjoining Piper's Opera House, Scotch Pete is full of liquor, but surprisingly is able to sign the forms and is given membership. Having membership is to no avail, as Pete's drinking starts up again several weeks later. He is fired from his job and takes a new job in the Red Bucket Saloon on Main Street.

X. Scotch Pete Beats His Addiction wi' a Wee Bit o' Help

At the next meeting of the Temperance Society, Adam and Henry attempt, once again, to get Pete sober. Punt, who is sorry he has caused so much trouble for Pete, tells Henry he can make Pete stop drinking, and now that they've had their fill of fun in the saloons, he'll make a concerted effort to enable Pete to get back his job in the mines. As they walk down B Street to the Temperance Society meeting, Pete, out of habit, is drawn to the bright lights and music emanating from the saloons along their route. He promises he'll stop in for only one drink. There is no way of preventing the large

Scot, willfully and physically strong, from swinging open the double doors and walking into the Lucky Lady Saloon.

"Pete," whispers Punt in his ear, "you're a fine specimen of a human. Daena spoil it wi' the liquor. If ye desire to spend time in saloons, take only one or two drinks, and then sassafras for the rest o' the evening. Will hiv the same effect as the alcohol, keep ye lively and talkative, but ye willna be drunk." Punt has inside information on Pete that is important in getting through to him. Specifically, Pete is an extremely shy person and loves to be around people; consequently, when he's drinking in saloons, he's able to talk up a storm without being self-conscious.

Of course, Pete doesn't see Punt as he whispers in his ear, but the message registers loud and clear. Pete looks around in perturbation, as if someone has said something disgusting to him. He can't find the source of the voice he's hearing in his head, and decides to ignore it. He draws another long drink of amber whiskey, chugging a full glass down.

Henry, privy to this lecture coming from his wee sprite friend, is surprised at Punt's maturity in trying to help Pete. Throughout his boyhood years, Henry has witnessed only the playful jokester side of Punt. He hadn't realized there was another more mature component to this wee creature. Being part human, Punt's human side on earth is definitely maturing. As he gets older, he is still drawn to having fun in the earthly dimension, as that is a normal, elemental side of being a sprite; in other dimensional realms, he's been living up to his father's wishes, a very astute and wise near-angel, who's trying to get his wings to become a full-fledged angel. His role on earth is to aid mankind in its development, and as he matures he's come to find this purposefulness much more satisfying than being a jokester, and certainly more rewarding.

Punt sees that he's not getting the desired results from Pete, so he tries another tactic and whispers softly in Pete's ear again. "Pete, do ye ken how long your life is goin' to be if ye daena cease the drink?

I fear only a couple o' more years for ye to be alive, me good fellow. Lookin' into yer future, I see a verra sorrowful man in bed, nearin' death's door. Yer face's yellow, ye've black teeth, and ye're rottin' away at the core; yer innards are riddled like a puckered pickle."

Pete looks around again to locate who's talking to him. He rubs his ears as if a pesky bug was buzzing around inside. In an attempt to make the intrusion go away, he holds his ears momentarily and tries to block out the sound of Punt's voice. He draws a long drink, presuming that he's half-asleep and dreaming, and slaps his cheek lightly to wake himself up.

The bartender refills his glass on Pete's demand, but Punt puts a spell on Pete's whiskey to make it taste like turpentine. At first, Pete doesn't notice as he takes a long, drawn-out chug, emptying his glass. Soon, though, the toxic taste hits his palate and a look of abhorrent disgust comes over his visage. He attempts to spit the residual taste out of his mouth back into the glass.

"Hey, barkeep, I've got a bad lot o' whiskey here," he yells angrily to the bartender as he throws his glass over the bar onto the floor. "Give me anither shot. Use the good stuff this time round. None o' yer crappy slops, or I'll throw it back in yer face."

Punt tries another ploy. "Pete, I see ye in a successful business in the future selling pants for the miners. Money to buy yer own home. And I spy a verra bonnie lassie at yer side. Ah, so cute, a couple o' sweet bairns lying in a crib. I do spy twins! This'll niver come to pass, na happen iver, if ye're drinkin'."

The bartender gives Pete another shot of whiskey from a fresh bottle. He makes a point of opening it in front of the aggrieved customer. Pete takes a small sip and spits it out. He looks around in a daze, bug-eyed, as if he'd just been hit over the head with a sledgehammer. He then states somberly, "I'm goin' baurmie wi' the drink; 'tis na tastin' richt to me no more. Me taste for it has gone awry. I crave it, but daena like it. Let's get out of here."

Adam is bowled over in amazement. He's not been privy to

what's transpired, and can't fathom what's caused the about-face in Pete's behavior. He concludes that Pete must have been given shots from bottles of whiskey from a spoiled case, extremely distasteful to the point of making alcohol repulsive to Pete. *It must've been like drinking a spoiled batch of milk, getting sick, and never wanting to drink milk again*, he muses. Adam and Henry had been drinking ale, and he figures they're lucky to have not tried the hard stuff. With no resistance, the brothers guide their despondent workmate down to the Temperance Society meeting.

BOOK EIGHT

CATHERINE

Chapter One

I. Catherine Malcolm's Arrival in Virginia City

Catherine reaches Reno, located in Washoe Valley of Nevada, in the summer of 1870, tired, excited, and relieved that her overland journey is near completion. The kind and personable porter tells her Virginia City is only a two-hour buggy ride away. She waits for nearly half an hour on a bench at the train depot for Adam, her body stiff from lack of movement, and her mind weary after sitting and sleeping in a cramped compartment on the train for so many days. As she's eager to explore her first Western town ever, the porter directs her to a teashop in the shopping district a block away on the main street of town. She leaves word with Mr. Jacks, the porter, that an unusually tall laddie with red hair will come looking for her, and to please direct him to the teashop.

The climate is very warm, the skies the bluest of blues, clear and cloudless, the desert-mountain air dry and invigorating, as Catherine makes her way down the street to a quaint little café that is welcoming to her with its pretty curtains appliquéd with daisies and a chalkboard menu written in curlicue italics out front. Catherine loves the high-altitude air, and takes in a deep breath to alleviate her travel fatigue. Fifteen minutes later, as she is being served strong black tea and buttermilk biscuits with quince jam at a small table by the front window, Catherine's heart almost leaps out of her chest as she spots Adam riding down the street in a buggy drawn by a large bay horse. Out of the corner of his eye, he catches sight of her standing up and waving exuberantly in the open window. Catherine has no recall of willing herself to a stand, so spontaneously has she acted. He waves back. She sits down in embarrassment and waits for him to dismount. Adam tethers the horse to a hitching post across the street as Catherine tries to steady her pounding heart and shaking hands with deep breaths and long sips of tea. He crosses effortlessly over the wide rutted road with long, easy strides in a matter of seconds, and makes his way to the café's entrance, having to stoop down to clear the doorway, bells jingling loudly atop his head as he enters. Catherine takes in a very tall, strikingly handsome gentleman dressed in a finely tailored riding outfit, a laddie that any woman would love to have on her arm. She is surprised at her own reaction to seeing Adam, of how proud she is in knowing that this fine man is coming for her, for her alone, for the purpose of marriage, a feeling that she hadn't experienced with the captain when they were together, even after the captain's proposal. She wonders why there is a difference in her response to Adam. Does she not know the inner workings of her own heart, mind, and emotions? The other female patrons and staff in the café are gazing up at him in awe, as if a prince has just landed in the room from out of a fairy tale.

At Catherine's first sighting of Adam, an immediate resurgence of feelings that she'd long ago squashed come tumbling forth. She had revered him, had sought his attention zestfully and giddily as an adolescent, her newfound sexuality intrigued by him. She only now confesses this to herself. Catherine revisits the jealous sting of when Adam began stepping out with Ruthie. From that time on, until his departure to the West, the disappointment of his being with her sister had overridden all the positive feelings she'd had for him; that is, until meeting Adam in person again today.

Adam's essence comes back to her – the intelligent, reserved, extremely kind laddie who acted as one of the youth counselors, an attentive instructor who ensured an educational and enriching experience in nature for the kids. He became a special friend of hers only because she had latched onto him eagerly and unabashedly.

They had developed a mutual bond; and, as she recalls, he had been very mindful of her safety when she was at that stage of brazen fearlessness. Memories flood in of their times spent together: the church outings in nature, the dances wherein the counselors and older kids taught the younger lads and lasses the intricate steps of Scottish folk dances and ballroom dancing (she was Adam's partner); the ice cream parties and supper socials; the kirkyard jumbles they had worked on side by side to raise money for the youth group; all their inside jokes and the harmless pranks they played on each other. Catherine remembers the ease she had felt around Adam as a teen, talking a mile a minute, with interspersions of spontaneous laughter, during which they waded in muddy ponds, sweated on rocky climbs, swam in sun-kissed lochs, raced across moors and hills, and collected specimens for their notebooks. They came back each day exhausted and fully quenched by nature's bounty.

She had adored Adam when she was twelve and thirteen years of age; by the time she was fourteen, she had a full-blown crush on him. He was a representation of the mysteriously compelling opposite sex. As a lassie, the way to get Adam's devotion, she had thought, was by demonstrating her athletic prowess. She remembers showing off for him, demonstrating her fearlessness, how strong and fast she could run, swim, and hike. She wanted to grow up fast so she could continue to capture more and more of his attention, to revel in his admiration of her feats. All that attention stopped before she turned fifteen. Adam spent less time as a youth leader, and eventually none at all. It was incomprehensible to Catherine why a laddie like Adam would be taken in by a lassie like her sister, beautiful yet so docile and domestic in her homebound activities – no desire for outdoor adventure at all. There was not a firm muscle on Ruthie's body, no color in her cheeks. Ruthie's skin was as white as her mother's pearls. It just didn't make sense to her.

Adam bends down to kiss her lightly on the cheek and settles in a chair across from her, giving her an appraising look.

"My goodness, Catherine! Ye've grown into a verra bonnie young woman. I'd no idea! Your pictures do ye no justice."

As they commence talking, she is at first flustered and blushes at the novelty and awkwardness of their first encounter, and then becomes cognizant of her inner thoughts and impressions – a nostalgic sense of reconnection to her life in Scotland, a common golden thread of shared history together that brings on a comforting sense of relief that she is no longer alone in the world. Seeing Adam, of her beloved homeland, sitting across from her at a café table draws her back to Bridge of Allan and Helensburgh, as if she's never left. She momentarily forgets that her parents and sister are buried, that her beloved moors and lochs are not right outside the door. She relaxes and smiles widely, and begins to enjoy herself in Adam's presence.

In the first few minutes of their conversation, a surprising and stark realization comes to her out of the blue. Adam is by far a better marriage choice than the captain. Later, upon further reflection, after a few months of her marriage to Adam, Catherine admits that she was enchanted beyond reason by the captain's doting on her. She also admits that there was no roadmap for the future in their relationship – it was a dream romance created by the magical sea. The great expanse of ocean lent the impression that the relationship was sound and would go on interminably, but the mesmerizing façade was soon to come to an end when they hit the monolithic iceberg that subsequently led to her placement in St. John's, away from the beautiful deception.

During the voyage, Catherine tried to impress the captain with her depth of character and intelligence, setting forth on many historical and literary topics of the world for discussion, and trying to find witty answers to his question about her, or expansive remarks to his observations. She wanted to be his intellectual equal, not just a tantalizing jewel to admire. Was she fully appreciated by the captain? Did he come to appreciate her in totality, inside and out, or just on the outside, as her mother had warned her? She contemplates the difference. Her mother had lectured her a lot about love, especially in the final year of her life. Catherine had thought it was unnecessary advice given her age and experience as a teacher.

"There is love that starts with a foundation of camaraderie and grows into true love, and there's romantic, magical love that comes on quickly and electrifyingly warm and glowing, and goes by the wayside just as quickly as it comes on," Mrs. Malcolm had lectured her. "Ye want to have the former lastin' kind o' love, me dear. Don't settle for a fanciful romance that'll end abruptly and leave ye broken into pieces. There'll be a lot o' men vying for your attention. Make certain your heart and soul, as well as yer sound judgment, are in the mix, and not just fantastical whims."

"Aye, Mum, I'm certainly aware o' the fickleness o' romance, as some o' my friends have been stung. That certainly won't happen to me! Ye must ken I'm fully in control o' my actions at all times, that I'm as level-headed as they come."

"Aye, Catherine, ye've always been quite level-headed, but that willna prevent some gentleman from knockin' ye off center. All it takes is the magnetism o' one handsome man."

"Ah, Mum, I doubt there'll be any o' that sort out West. From all the newspaper pictures I've viewed, the men are scrubby and dirty, on the whole an uncouth-lookin' lot."

All feelings of doubt about Adam, whom she hasn't seen for years, and her regret in having to leave the handsome Captain Noble, fly out the window as soon as she sees him. Throughout the entire train ride across the American continent, she was remorseful, increasingly so, as the distance steadily increased and drew her farther and farther away from the captain, the gentleman who conjured up images and sensations of moonlight dances in protective arms, starry, balmy nights, and a vast sea of dancing, glimmering waves. The fond memories will last her a lifetime.

Catherine is warmed by the fact that Adam is so visibly excited to see her, which assures her that he truly relishes their past friendship in Scotland, a bond they shared apart from Ruthie. Adam suggests that they take a meal in town before heading up to Virginia City, about a two-hour ride, he explains, across the desert and up into the mountainous woodland terrain of the lower Sierras. Catherine finishes her tea as Adam sips on a glass of lemonade served reverently to him by the waitress, after which time they walk a short distance down the street to the Red Brick Steak House. They are served an excellent venison stew with a red wine sauce, a butter lettuce salad with poppyseed dressing, and Irish soda bread. For dessert there is scrumptious caramel pudding, Catherine's favorite. Her appetite is surprisingly good despite her jitters around Adam, as the high altitude of Reno works its magic. It is lovely little city encircled by snow-capped mountains even in the summer.

When they reach Virginia City in the late afternoon, a large party of enthusiastic townsfolk is lined up along the sidewalks to greet them, just as Adrian's friends and townsfolk had greeted Adam a couple of years earlier. Red, white, and blue welcome banners wave gaily in a warm, gentle Sierra breeze for the Fourth of July, and signs posted in the storefront windows along the sidewalk promenade announce Catherine's arrival on July Fourth. In parentheses it reads that Catherine is betrothed to Adam Baird. Catherine's face is perspiring and highly flushed to a rose color, so overwhelmed is she by the fanfare over her arrival. The colorful signs stating she is to be Adam's wife on the Fourth of July are particularly adrenaline-inducing, because she has forgotten that he had mentioned in his letter that the ceremony would occur the evening she arrived. She had brushed this off as his being overly eager. Until Adam had informed her on their trip up from Reno of their ceremony that evening, she'd been thinking they'd marry in perhaps a month's time after they were fully reacquainted. Now she's settled on the idea and is quite eager, thinking it will be best to marry Adam on this day, as her life with him started the moment he arrived at the café. Catherine is touched and gratified that so many people are aware of her arrival, and that they desire to make her acquaintance. This speaks volumes to her of the respect the community has for Adam.

Catherine steps down from the coach into Adam's arms, and once her feet are planted firmly on the ground, she looks up to gaze into the twinkling greenish-blue eyes of none other than Adam's younger brother, Henry Baird, who winks at her and smiles broadly, showing off his beautiful white teeth and charming dimples. He appears overjoyed to see her, even more so than Adam's enthusiasm had been on first seeing her. Henry, Catherine finds, is far less reserved and more animated. He comes up and embraces her tightly, lifting her off her feet and twirling her in a complete circle, as if she were a lightweight rag doll, which makes her fully conscious of her weight. After the long, drawn-out hug, she peers closely at his face and gasps aloud in amazement at Henry's transformation from a skinny teenager to a superb-looking man – he's the kind of man that women can't keep their eyes off of. She finds herself one of those women as she gazes up at Henry in awe. She hopes that Adam doesn't notice her reaction to his younger brother, but Henry is just so captivating in his overall charm and animal magnetism, unrivaled by other men. Adam seems to be accustomed to the effect Henry has on women, and takes everything in stride, standing back with a proud look on his face.

As Catherine recalls, Henry was the Baird brother with quite a reputation, the one known for his wit and also the one with a propensity for trouble. She recalls that he had fathered a child out of wedlock and then married, but had tragically lost his wife in childbirth. Henry has certainly changed, she thinks, with a maturity that is evident by the ease with which he carries himself, so remarkably self-possessed, as if he owns the world. She had no idea that he was out West with his brother. Later she learns that Henry has not been in Nevada that long. Up until six months ago, he had been living in Scotland, only a short distance from her. That their paths never crossed in Scotland isn't surprising, as Henry was preoccupied with managing the Drumdruils ranch and Catherine very busy teaching in Helensburgh, and subsequently dealing with her mother's sickness and eventual death. Catherine finds it ironic that they now meet thousands of miles away from where they both lived last year, only forty miles apart.

Catherine thinks back to the last time she saw Henry. He was a laddie of sixteen attending one of the church youth functions. She is, again, taken aback by his remarkable handsomeness. Adam is very good looking with his muscular physique, beautiful red hair, and fine chiseled features, but Henry is uncommonly handsome in a way that can't be measured by physical assets alone. He exudes a remarkable degree of magnetism and spirit, someone with uncanny energy that uplifts others by his mere presence.

Catherine is truly glad to see him, as he represents another person from home to help combat her homesickness for her beloved Scotland. The thought crosses her mind, and is guiltily erased within seconds, that Henry might be a better match for her than Adam, though she can't define why. She detects something in Henry that prompts her to believe that there is a likeness in spirit between them at a core level, as she in tune with an energy exuding from him that is more than charisma. Henry smiles at her flirtatiously, and she can read in his eyes his endless store of humor. He reminds her somewhat of the captain in his beguiling effect, and she must remind herself that terribly handsome men can lead her astray, erase her better judgment of what is good for her, as did the captain.

Catherine then notices a Wee One atop Henry's shoulder, the size of a tiny hummingbird, clapping and jumping up and down in excitement, waving a little red, white, and blue flag. She comprehends immediately that she and Henry do indeed share kindred spirits, and that likeness is second-sight. She tries to conceal her laughter as she observes the comical Wee Fellow with his amusing gestures and facial expressions, but is unsuccessful and chuckles aloud. Henry, right away, becomes aware that she can see Punt.

"What do ye find amusin' 'bout Henry, me dear? I ken he's full o' blarney, but na many react to him in that manner."

Catherine tries to cover up her initial surprise in seeing Henry's Wee Friend, as well as her awe over Henry's vibrant presence and looks. If one can call a man beautiful, Henry certainly fits the bill.

"Oh, I'm juist verra surprised to find Henry in America. I daedna ken he was in this town wi' ye." Catherine reverts to her colloquial Scots around the brothers, who have quite heavy accents.

"So glad to see ye, Catherine. Ye're a lovely sight, as though ye brought a touch o' our beloved Scotland wi' ye. Indeed, those beautiful green eyes are the color o' lochs."

"Thank ye, Henry. I'd no idea ye were here in America. 'Tis good to see people from home, 'specially anither Baird brother."

"Henry's been in Virginia City for about six months, and I'd no idea he was comin', so I daedna write to ye o' this. He was sent by Faither to investigate whither I had been captured by Injuns! Communication's verra slow and unreliable in the wilds, and the family was terribly worried."

Catherine decides that even with Henry's looks and charisma, she's better off with Adam than having to share a man with a demanding Wee One. From her dealings with them, she knows they can be quite possessive. As a child, her Wee One friend was jealous when she played with her schoolmates, even those schoolmates with second-sight.

After Catherine, Henry, and Adam go back to the new house, she and Henry are left alone for a few minutes while Adam goes outside to retrieve firewood for the evening. She immediately asks Henry about Punt.

"I'd no idea Wee Folks lived in America. I saw a very lively Wee One on your shoulder this afternoon at the coach stop."

"I daedna realize that ye're blessed, or shall I say cursed, wi' the second-sight," replies Henry with surprise. "I suppose a lot o' adult Scots have second-sight and daena confess to it. I suspect Punt might be the only sprite in America."

"Well, I daena use my second-sight often. Only now and again do I see Wee Ones flying o'er the moors whaur I walk. I've no ongoing relationship wi' them now, as I did as a child when I was verra close to one. They've helped me since me mother's death by keepin' the family graves tidy and planted wi' wildflowers, and commiseratin' wi' me telepathically about my loss." Catherine, when around Scots who speak the dialect, tends to fall naturally into the colloquialism, but as a teacher and at home with her parents, she was raised to speak the Queen's English.

"My best Wee Friend, Randa, disappeared when I was ten years old. She must've died. I was crestfallen when she disappeared from me life. 'Twas years afore I got o'er her."

"Wee People daena die. She might have left for anither dimension, mebbe for noble purposes o' a higher order."

"Aye, but I was so young, and she daedna tell me she was leavin' me," replies Catherine sadly. "She was just gone permanently, which to a child is death. She was me closest confidant, and I miss her to this day."

"I'm sorry," says Henry, looking at Catherine with empathy. Trying to make her feel better, he says jokingly, "By now yer Wee Friend's probably an angel lookin' o'er ye. I'm sure she watches o'er ye whaniver ye're in trouble. Mebbe she helped ye cross the treacherous seas."

Catherine considers this seriously. *Maybe an angel did help me survive my near-death experience.* She likes the idea that it might have been a protector angel named Randa.

"And your Wee One? How long has he been wi' ye?"

"Foriver and iver! Too long," replies Henry jokingly. "Fortunately," he laughs, "Punt's me one and only Wee Friend in America. His faither's chief o' the Bridge o' Allan clan, and he's most likely stayin' only for a wee bit o' time, as I've been told. He's out here temporarily whilst in training for grander ventures, to put it mildly. Punt, who is very intellectually gifted in matters of science and technology, is Elor's successor. Elor's tryin' to groom his son's character to be more o' a leader, which is quite a chore, to put it lightly! Suffice it to say, Punt has attributes o' a full-blown earthly sprite in every sense o' the word, a perpetual jokester and troublemaker. He's been round me since afore I can remember, gettin' me into all sorts o' jams, though part o' that is na his fault but me own inclination to get into scrapes. He's enjoyin' verra much the West, is excited by the novelty o' it all, but I ken he'll eventually go back to Scotland, as soon as I'm settled in. He's missin' his own kind, and as a result has lost some o' his spunk. Exactly what his father, Elor, had hoped for! Ideally, Punt will go back to our homeland a more mature fellow and contribute to the advancement o' civilization. Elor's told us there's a lot o' innovations in science and technology on the way for our world, 'specially comin' from England and Scotland."

II. Early Evening Vows at the Presbyterian Church on C Street

Adam comes back inside with an armful of logs and kindling, and he and Henry take Catherine on a tour of the new house that they are so proud to have built themselves. The house has the delightful new-wood scents of cedar, pine, and oak, from the floor, built-in cabinets, and new furniture. Catherine notices that the house has a lot of wonderful storage space in each room, especially the kitchen. Adam shows her to an empty spare bedroom where he has placed her trunk, and tells her the wedding will take place in the evening at six o'clock. Catherine's heart starts to beat wildly, and she sits down abruptly on the lavender-rose quilt-covered bed. She is very tired from the journey, and appreciative that Adam thoughtfully allotted time for her to be alone, rest, unpack her clothes, and dress. There are several hours left in the afternoon before the grand event. Her wedding dress is wrinkled, she sees, as she lifts it out of the cedar chest. She hangs it by an open window so it can catch the breeze. After unpacking her beautiful gown, she lies down and falls asleep for an hour, waking up feeling rested and restored, and very excited about her wedding.

5 July 1870
Dear family,
Catherine and I were married yesterday in the beautiful Presbyterian church in Virginia City. I was so happy to have Henry as my best man. People said Catherine was the most beautiful bride they'd ever seen. She wore a lovely silk and pearl-buttoned gown, brought with her from Scotland that was her mother's. It was a wonderful ceremony, truly a family occasion. I feel very blessed to have had a lovely bride and me brither at me side in this place far away from home. Wish ye had all been here, but thought of everyone during the ceremony.

The town is beautiful with three large churches, an opera house, and many stores. The layout of the town is hilly, and the streets sweep upwards to the piney foothills. I am awestruck by the beautiful landscape. At an elevation of over 6,000 feet, the air is fresh and the dry desert climate makes for superb sunshine. The snow is soft and lacy, though surprisingly the winter air is mild with brilliant sunlight, nothing like the raw, humid coldness of Scotland in the winter. Up in the mountains above the town and the mines, there are streams full of fish and all kinds of wildlife like deer and elk. The town is affluent and bustling from the Silver Boom. There is a lot of energy that one can feel from nature, from the affluence of the town, and happy settlers.

With love,

Adam

Catherine writes in her diary that night of the wedding as she sits in bed waiting for Adam:

4 July 1870

I'm a married woman now! And I'm verra happy to be here in my own wee home with a husband, my dear friend from my childhood. I've become very attached to Adam, as my heart goes pitter-patter whenever he's around, which must mean that he's something special to me. I've so many blissful memories of the wonderful wedding celebration. The church was full, and we had an outdoor potluck that many of the townspeople attended after the ceremony. The evening was very warm and pleasant, and the stars and full moon were out to light up the night sky. There were red, yellow, and blue Chinese paper lanterns hung in the tree boughs to give our banquet a colorful, glowing, ethereal look. We had many toasts tonight, excellent red and white wines with the meal, and delightful French champagne with a French vanilla wedding cake. Scrumptious! I am truly a blessed lassie to have safely reached my destination to fulfill my fate in life. I feel so safe and loved.

III. Indians on the Warpath — Catherine's First Night in Nevada

Catherine and Adam's first night together is hardly the romantic event that the bride had envisioned. There is no time for what she had planned: a toast of brandy with Adam to relax with by a roaring fire, a moonlit walk around the garden to cool off from the warmth of the day, a cool jasmine-scented oil bath before slipping into her fancy cream lace lingerie, and then off to bed with her handsome husband to experience an intimate comingling, which she has only read about or heard about from her married friends. She does not quite understand the mechanics or highlights of an intimate relationship, and to Catherine, cuddling and kissing would be a sufficient display of love. She hopes that they will do only that on their first night together until she has overcome her shyness.

Catherine and Adam are just starting to relax by the fire with brandy cocktails in hand about an hour after the wedding supper event has wound down, close to midnight. A great commotion erupts, which is heard loud and clear coming from the Paiute Indian settlement, located up on the hill by a stream overlooking them, not more than 400 yards above their house. There is a lot of yelling and harsh cries. The encampment is located next to the site of where a Catholic church is being constructed. Catherine had observed this enclave of squalid huts when she'd first arrived, and had questioned Adam about the reason for its existence in town. Adam had explained that the Paiutes camping up on the hill are part a larger clan that live on the shores of their sacred Pyramid Lake.

"They're living in huts close to white people acause they need to work for food, and are offered menial tasks at the mines and other labor jobs in town for a wee bit o' wage. The squaws barter their handiwork o' baskets and jewelry in town in exchange for food. They can eke out just enough to get by on, but just barely. Several o' the Paiute men actually aided us greatly in the building o' this house."

Wailing chants and loud drumbeats reverberate like booming thunder, an overbearing presence drowning out the milder, ordinary sounds of rustling leaves in the breeze, owl hoots, wolves' howls, and the low-lying nocturnal avian and insect vocalizations of the night. Catherine's heart pulsates to the rhythmic beat, and her thoughts become clouded by fear that the Paiutes will cause harm to them, as their house is situated so close to the Paiute settlement. She tries not to appear alarmed. Adam picks up his rifle hanging in the hallway, and without another word charges outside, leaving Catherine to bear the storm alone. Catherine concludes that Adam is going off to battle Indians, which she'd read much about in Western literature while in Scotland. She wonders if he'll return in one piece. The thought comes to mind that she might become a widow on the same day she's become a bride. She can only sit patiently by the fire and pray that her journey to the West was not in vain. After an hour, Adam walks in with an air of nonchalance, as if he's been on a casual errand, and tells Catherine he went up to talk to one of the elders in the clan, whom he knows well and is friendly with. He tells her that the Paiutes are having a ritualistic ceremony to beseech the Great One for justice over a wrongdoing done to them. The wailing is their lamentations over the death of one of their braves. Apparently, he entered a store to purchase liquor and was killed by the white shopkeeper without provocation, other than the owner didn't like Indians. Ordinarily, the shopkeeper would have gotten away with this, but there were witnesses to the shooting who were sympathetic to the Indians.

"This outcome," Adam explains, "was lucky and a rarity." Adam tells Catherine that a white man has already been apprehended for the slaying. The sheriff has assured Adam that the man will stand trial when the circuit judge comes around next week. Until then, the murderer will stay behind bars. Adam says he told the elders that he will do everything in his power to ensure that the killer be brought to justice when the judge reviews the case. He explains to Catherine that many times these cases are dropped if it is a dispute between Indians and white people, and Indians are not allowed to sue.

Adam and Catherine sit up in bed throughout night as if at a concert, the drumbeating and wailing continuing on until first light. As the light of dawn begins to color the sky with pinks and oranges, the noise lets up gradually, as if it is being soaked up note by note, absorbed by the dissipating darkness. Catherine is quite relieved that on their first night they could sit and become reacquainted as the friends they were back in Bridge of Allan. They talk amicably through the night of their many adventures in nature together back in Scotland. Adam tells her, "Ye were a verra fine, energetic young lassie and a good outdoor companion acause o' yer athleticism."

Adam educates Catherine on the Indian race that he has come to admire, and describes to her the sacredness of this ancient race of people who live in accordance with the spirit of the earth. "They are somewhat similar to the Wee Ones in their philosophies," Adam explains. Housekeeper Violet had educated the Baird children, from early on, in the ways of the Wee People, how they revere the earth and its sacred life as whole entity, and strive to protect all components of the whole from harm, as each one complements the other. Catherine can relate to this, as she has second-sight and has had firsthand experience in the reverence given by the Wee Ones to the earth and all sacred creatures of the earth.

IV. Catherine Befriends the Paiute Indians

From the diary of Adam:
Catherine became well acquainted with the Paiutes and their customs, especially with a Paiute squaw named Mary, who did the family washing and cleaning. Catherine was very fond of Mary. I encouraged her to have Mary over to help with all other household affairs, as Catherine is with child, and so Mary started coming over

for the entire day to help out. At dinner time there'd be three or four bucks coming to share the food with Mary, but they started eating most of Mary's dinner. Catherine started making large meals for everyone, but didn't inform me until months later, not until after a tragic event had occurred. I suppose she thought I'd not approve.

V. Paiute Mary Begins Working for Baird Household

Catherine greets Mary enthusiastically on the first day she comes to help out in the house. Mary is very shy and doesn't speak a word to her, but manages an eclipsed smile with her head lowered in a display of reverence. Catherine, so excited in having someone come to her home, has dressed in her best everyday muslin, and had made cookies and a cake for her guest the day before. As soon as Catherine meets Mary she is immediately drawn to this very pretty, exotic-looking young woman. She's eager to become friends, as she has met few women since arriving in Virginia City besides Adrian's wife, who is very pregnant and bed-bound. Thus far, the only other women she's made the acquaintances of are store workers on her daily shopping expeditions in town. These women, Catherine has observed, have been obsequious and standoffish, and not very friendly to her. Catherine complained to Adam that no one is at ease with her. "They treat me like I'm an oddity, a fish out o' water," she had complained.

"'Tis acause they're in awe o' yer beauty and dress, Catherine. There's verra few refined Scottish women out West. Ye just have to show off your warm personality and they'll take to ye soon enough."

Catherine assumes Paiute Mary doesn't understand English, and tries to communicate with her new helper in rudimentary sign language. Mary is given a tour of the small house, which doesn't take long. She is shown all cupboards and closets where household mops, brooms and cleaning supplies are kept, and Catherine points to everything they will be using, pronouncing the words slowly and clearly: "Broom, mop, dust rag, dish soap, bath soap, laundry soap, pail." Mary smiles and repeats each word after Catherine, with the same Scottish inflection as Catherine.

Catherine is five months pregnant, and Adam has encouraged her to have Mary do all the basic household chores: cooking, laundry, sweeping and mopping of the wood floors, and the dusting of furniture. Catherine has no intention of having Mary do all the work, as she enjoys the physicality of cleaning. She is planning, with eagerness, to work alongside Mary as a teammate. The fact is, Catherine isn't sure if she's been cleaning properly as she has had very little experience – she's hoping Mary can give her some pointers and plans to follow Mary's lead as to how to mop and dust properly; that is, if she's able to communicate with Mary.

Adam hasn't complained about her housekeeping skills, but Catherine has found him too tired to notice anything by the end of the day when he comes home tired and hungry. She is unaccustomed to doing domestic chores, as her family was well enough off to hire help in Helensburgh. They had dear Mrs. MacCready every day from the time she was old enough to remember until the time of her mother's death. Mrs. MacCready died soon after her mother, and Catherine learned she was twenty years older than Mrs. Malcolm, which made her sixty-four at the time of her death.

After showing Mary where the cleaning supplies are kept, Catherine takes Mary outside onto the porch to show her where the tub and other accoutrements for washing clothes are located. Mary nods her head enthusiastically when shown all the laundry equipment and makes a wringing sign with her hands. Catherine jumps up and down and claps her hands enthusiastically. It feels good to jump, being that she has not been able to exercise much. Back in Scotland, she was accustomed to taking five-mile walks every day. Adam has warned her not to go out alone except on the major thoroughfare to the downtown where she isn't isolated, which is less than a mile away. And since she's been pregnant, he frowns on her doing any walking at all, even to town. Mary looks at her strangely, as if she's never seen a white woman jump up and down. Soon thereafter, Mary follows Catherine's lead and starts jumping. They both laugh hysterically. It reminds Catherine of her time in St. John's with Suzanna.

After completion of the house tour, in which Mary has not said anything besides parroting words in her newfound Scots accent, Catherine tells her they will start the next day. Catherine opens the door, hands her a basket laden with cookies and scones, and ushers her out, walking her part of the way up the hill to the Paiute encampment. Mary gives her a very perplexed look – a white woman walking her home to the encampment is like a white person stopping to offer her a ride in a buggy. Catherine hopes Mary understands that she is to return the next day.

"I will see you tomorrow," she enunciates slowly. Mary nods her head in agreement and smiles. Catherine wonders if Mary will show up the next day.

Catherine plans on doing all the cooking, as she developed a passion for it during her stay in St. John's, wherein she and Suzanna spent many enjoyable hours testing recipes and putting together a cookbook with their favorites for the St. John's Women's Club. Adam has told her she should have Mary cook the noontime and evening meals, but Catherine will not have it. It is her plan to have Mary as her cook mate, as she and Suzanna had had so much fun together in the kitchen together. Catherine loves surprising Adam with some of the delicacies she had learned to prepare in St. John's; and, at first, was very pleased that he relished everything she cooked for him. Being that he is ravenous after working in the mines all day at a physically demanding job, Adam cleans his plate in about two minutes. Catherine wishes that he would savor the food that she has spent many hours preparing.

When Mary comes to work on her second day, it is very early and Catherine is sitting in bed reading the paper, wearing one of the beautiful French lace nightdresses from her trousseau. Adam has already left for the mine. Mary comes up to Catherine and touches her arm gently. Catherine can't for the life of her figure out what Mary needs from her. Catherine stares at her quizzically. She sees Mary's jaw drop open and that she is waving her hand over her mouth to catch her breath. *Is something wrong with my arm?* It takes Catherine a minute to realize that Mary is completely bowled over by the lovely lace of her gown. Catherine laughs out loud at Mary's reaction, and then quickly stifles her amusement, sensitive to the fact that she might be hurting Mary's feelings by laughing at her first exposure to such finery, but Mary starts laughing alongside her. In a deep, husky chuckle, Mary continues to run her hand along the lace of her arm. Finally she says, "It's so very, very pretty." Catherine then realizes that Mary can speak some English, at least some words, and is just shy, and probably understands what she is telling her.

As the day progresses, and Mary and Catherine work side by side, Mary starts to relax. Catherine has an unaffected air about her that draws people to her, which was particularly useful when she was teaching in Helensburgh. All her students loved her because Catherine was as spontaneous and exuberant as the children. Mary comes to life like a beautiful flower opening up, and begins to show off her vivacious personality and her surprising mastery of the English language. Catherine finds her very charming and endearing, in that she is very curious about how the white race lives and of her married life with Adam. She loves all the furniture and dishes, and goes around the house browsing, as if she were in a store shopping.

Mary treats Catherine as if she were a goddess from a far-off planet. She comes up to her and touches her hair to feel its texture.

"Like beaver's hair and fox color!" she exclaims.

Catherine reciprocates and strokes Mary's lovely strands. "Verra soft," exclaims Catherine.

Everything Catherine says Mary finds humorous because of Catherine's Scottish accent, and Mary, in wanting to be just like Catherine, tries to copy her Scots' enunciation. "Verra, verra soft," repeats Mary. Catherine is so amused that Mary has the colloquial Scots intonation down pat.

Mary touches the skin on Catherine's arm. "Verra silky," she exclaims. "'Tis soft as water." Catherine can't help but to burst out laughing, but is touched by the sentiment of Mary being so impressed by her.

Catherine is eager to work alongside Mary, and being that she is a physically strong young woman, plans to stay active throughout her pregnancy, which is unheard of to Mary, as Paiute women take it easy during their pregnancies. When Catherine gets down on her hands and knees to work alongside Mary in wiping down the floor with a rag, Mary cries out in alarm.

"Baby coming, baby coming," she cries, thinking that Catherine has gone into premature labor.

Catherine jumps up off the floor very agilely, assuring Mary that she is perfectly fine. Mary has never seen a white woman move about like this before.

"I was merely aiding ye in cleaning the floors, Mary! I'm fine, Mary! No bairn yet. Not for quite some time. Many moons to go." Catherine holds up four fingers to show her the remaining months of her pregnancy, and then makes four circles with her arms to exemplify the moon, and rocks an imaginary baby in her arms.

Mary is in awe of this vivacious and athletic woman and calls Catherine by a Paiute name that can be translated to "Green-Eyed Colt Woman."

Mary is also full of vim and vigor and proud of her Paiute heritage, but sobers when relating the reality of her life. She tells

Catherine of the hardships of her life on Pyramid Lake, and that she is living in Virginia City in the encampment above the Baird house to help support her mother, father, and siblings, although she is married and lives with her husband when he's not on tribal land. Her husband goes back and forth between the lake and the Virginia City encampment every couple of days, bringing items to trade in the stores.

Mary is close in age to Catherine, but Catherine is very tall for a woman of her era, and Mary is short, big-boned, and powerfully muscular. In fact, Mary appears as powerful in her legs and arms as some of the Paiute braves Catherine has observed. As Catherine comes to be around her more, she begins to appreciate and admire the finer points of her beauty: glossy, raven-colored hair, braided with beads and shells woven in; perfect, large white teeth; a lovely mahogany-bronze colored skin; and fine, well-proportioned features. Her kind eyes are like beautiful sparkling amber jewels that are windows to her soul. Mary's tanned skin is indicative of having spent many days out in the hot desert sun, but Mary is still young and her skin has remained soft and void of wrinkles. Mary, overall, is a very handsome, healthy-looking young woman, which later on will prove to be her undoing.

Catherine learns from Mary, through roundabout questioning, that she is unhappily married. Her husband is abusive, beating her often for no apparent reason other than being insanely angry for her not living up to his high standards and accusing her of flirting with other braves. She had not wanted to marry this older man, but her parents had given her away to him in return for a half-acre swath of land. Her husband is considered wealthy by Paiute standards because he owns five acres of land and two horses, as well as a boat pulled up along the shore of Pyramid Lake, which he rents out to others for fishing.

"He say me Ugly Wooman," says Mary in her choppy enunciation. "He's good man when he's full of food and has no drink," she says brightly, as if this were a momentous occurrence. "If liquor there, the monster hits me like I wood to be hammered, makes me more ugly, a Ugly Wooman with black eye. He don't care and laugh at me when I with raccoon eyes."

"Oh, no, don't let him hit ye, Mary! When he tries, please run away from him. Run away and come down here. I'll protect ye."

"I belong to him. If I run away to here, he runs after me. Hit me maybe harder, and maybe hit ye. I stay away from work when he's wild animal. Nothing I can do 'bout it. I try no crying."

Catherine tears up at the cruelty and extreme hardship present in this young woman's life. *I hiv to do something about this problem*, she thinks.

"Ah, Mary, 'tis a verra bad predicament for ye. I must protect ye. Mebbe inform the sheriff what's goin' on."

"Sheriff no help Paiutes," Mary replies adamantly.

"I'll send Adam up to talk to your chief."

When Catherine approaches Adam about the problem of Mary's husband being brutal and that he must intervene, Adam replies adamantly, "Absolutely not. I willna be able to help Mary, as the Paiutes would resent me for interfering. We have to remain in good standin' wi' them for our own personal safety. We canna lose their respect."

As the weeks progress, Mary and Catherine become even more companionable, laughing together throughout the day at silly things, like finding Adam's night clothes strewn across the floor each morning, or the sight of the great mess they've made in the kitchen after having cooked up a storm, especially when the counters look like a war zone, piled high with pots and pans and splattered with food. On pie-making days, they have a flour mess all over the table, the floor, and themselves, like a fine dusting of snow. Mary and Catherine are both messy cooks, but Mary makes Catherine sit down for tea while she expertly cleans up any kitchen mess in a short time. The two friends enjoy sharing recipes and cooking methods. Catherine teaches Mary many of the recipes she learned in St. John's, and those in her mother's cookbook, which she brought out from her cedar chest. Mary shows her the recipes taught to her by her mother – a flatbread made from acorns cooked over an open fire with a griddle, and also recipes with pine nuts, using them for cake and porridge recipes. Catherine teaches Mary rudimentary Scottish cooking, from roasting a lamb to the preparation of mint jelly made with mint leaves, pectin, and sugar, and how to make the classic shortcake from only butter, flour, and sugar. Mary loves the shortcake, and at the end of each the day Catherine sends her home with a meat dish and a large tin of sweets for her husband – anything to keep Mary in good graces with him. This seems to appease the man, as Catherine has noticed that Mary's body and face are not marked with bruises anymore; and so, she concludes, Mary hasn't been beaten in awhile.

Henry comes over a couple of times a week in the late in the afternoon, or on a few occasions during his dinner hour, as he is not working in the mines any longer but has a job in town at the mining office. Mary reveres Henry, and her face lights up whenever she sees him. She claps her hands excitedly when she hears him climbing the steps to the porch. Henry has a knack for making anyone laugh, and especially Mary, who is in hysterics by Henry's antics, particularly when he performs his birdcalls for her, livens the room with a Scottish jig, or, as on one occasion, waltzes her around the kitchen while humming a Scottish ballad. Mary is overcome with laughter by just looking at Henry's comical demeanor.

Mary says to Catherine after Henry leaves, "Henry big chief man. Henry chief of white nation. Paiutes listen to Chief Henry. Beautiful Chief Man."

Mary is of great help to Catherine as her pregnancy progresses. Washing clothes is particularly taxing for Catherine, for it entails filling up a big tin vat with boiling water, soaping the clothes vigorously on a corrugated tin washboard in a flat wood box lined with metal, and then rinsing them in the large metal vat of boiling water. The final step is wringing out clothes by passing them through a large mangle contraption, and then hanging the wet, very heavy denim work clothes, as well as sheets and towels, out to dry. Catherine finds wringing the clothes with a mangle particularly taxing to her lower back, which has been sensitive since her first months of pregnancy.

Mary, with her exceptionally strong arms, can wring out clothes much more effectively than Catherine, especially the denim mining overalls of Adam's and the heavy muslin sheets that are tenfold their weight when wet. These burdensome items have to carried down the stairs off the porch to be wrung in the iron wringer and then hung out on the line, which Catherine has a hard time doing without getting thoroughly soaked, and the next day suffering from aching muscles and a bad back. Adam has told her to stop helping with the wash.

Mary finds all her chores very easy, as she is as strong as an ox and much accustomed to more onerous tasks. Paiute women are in charge of collecting and carrying, for very long distances, heavy loads of firewood and water for cooking, digging for roots out in the hot desert from sunset to sundown, and gathering up berries and acorns and grinding them on a stone mortar into a coarse flour. Since her marriage, Mary has been taking care of her husband's horses: finding them food and water and keeping them brushed to a gloss to meet his high standards.

Every noontime, Catherine feeds Mary a hearty lunch of warm meat pies, fruit, and cakes, but Mary adamantly declines to eat at Catherine's kitchen table with her. She insists on taking her lunch out on the porch, having been indoctrinated by white society of her lowly social class. Her tribe adheres to the belief that friendships with whites lead to trouble. Catherine is hurt by what she takes as a rebuff and wishes Mary would invite her to sit outside, as it is nicer outdoors on warm days, and not so pleasant to eat alone. She refrains from going out and plopping down next to her out of respect for Mary's feelings. *She sees me as someone grander than she is*, thinks Catherine, *someone to be honored as royalty. All I desire is a friend like my Suzanna in Newfoundland. Why can't Mary be a friend to enjoy dinner wi'?*

As Mary sits outside at the front porch redwood table with her lunch each noontime, it takes only a week or two before she begins to attract a number of the young bucks living in the temporary settlement above the Baird home. Either they smell the tantalizing aroma of delicious food or they are drawn to the beautiful squaw who has a newfound respect amongst her people because of her position in the Baird household. Mary always shares a portion of her lunch with the bucks. She knows they are desperately hungry, particularly those who haven't found work in a couple of days. Catherine has appalling firsthand knowledge now that the entire Paiute tribe is starving. Mary has explained that crooked Indian agents are shortchanging their federal ration allotments, and the pay for the work the Paiutes provide in town for white men is a pittance. Catherine begins to make enough food to feed all the bucks at dinner, and provides plates and glasses for all. Oftentimes, a group as large as five or six will congregate on the porch steps at noon to eat with Mary. Catherine notices they don't use silverware or glasses, and so she always provides plenty of cornbread for them to sop up their stew with, and extra bowls to drink beverage out of.

Adam has no clue of Catherine's noontime hospitality. She wisely keeps her noontime activities to herself, requesting that Henry not mention these luncheons to Adam, as Henry comes over at dinnertime often and sees what's going on, joining in a lively conversation with the braves and eating the delicious food in the kitchen with Catherine, which has been so expertly prepared by Catherine and Mary.

As much as Adam is an advocate and admirer of the American Indian race, Catherine, in the short time of their marriage, has become acutely aware of his high standards of propriety in regards to the activities of a proper lady. Adam is disapproving of her taking walks alone on the beautiful woodsy trails in their environs. And with all his respect and adoration of Indians, Adam would find it very improper for her to have a friendship with a Paiute, even a female friend like sweet Mary, who has so much to teach her about the Paiute culture. Catherine hides her annoyance and discontent for what she views as a major flaw in her husband's character. As she sees it, Adam is showing signs of hypocrisy by not living up to what he professes to believe. Admiring the American Indian culture from a distance is one thing, but turning around and viewing Paiutes as not worthy of friendship with the white race is quite disingenuous. The revelation that Adam does not believe in the cultures mixing socially brings out other faults Catherine has found in her husband – one being the irritating fact that Adam views women as powerless creatures who can't fend for themselves.

Growing up, Catherine was fiercely independent and strong willed. She was granted leeway to do what she wanted in the way of outdoors activities, often overriding her mother's views of what was proper for a young lady – indoor activities were recommended. Particularly worrisome to Mrs. Malcolm was her daughter spending many hours out on the moors by herself and swimming in the lochs alone. Mrs. Malcolm was somewhat tolerant of Catherine's tomboyish tendencies, and some leniency was granted, but only after Catherine endured a thorough lecturing on how to stay safe. "Ye must avoid the woods acause wild animals might be lurkin' there; keep your skin and hair covered from the sun; stay in shallow water to swim; ayeweys take snacks and water wi' ye," she had lectured. Abigail Malcolm saw something of herself in her daughter when she was young, and was reticent to stifle her daughter's youthful zest. Abigail remembered enjoying her freedom on the ranch that she grew up on. She had been a lively and energetic spirit when young as well.

"What wild animals, Mum?" Catherine would inquire. "I've niver had the acquaintance o' anything wilder than a wee boar or red deer, and other gentle creatures."

When Catherine was ten years of age, Mr. Malcolm brought home a Scottish deerhound to be Catherine's constant companion on her treks, which appeased Mrs. Malcolm's tendency for worry.

Catherine developed a strong sense of her own power in making her way in the world as she traversed her outside environment, as well as an inner sense of self-reliance would bring her more fulfillment in life than relying solely on a husband to dictate her activities and thinking. In her teaching career, she fed into this belief, teaching her students, male and female alike, to be strong, independent thinkers, and to rely on their own good judgments and sense of self to ensure that they thrived in the world.

Catherine complains to Henry. "Adam and I are not o' the same frame o' mind in our views o' the role o' women in the world. Regrettably, Adam has a somewhat cavalier attitude towards the female gender. To Adam, women are a weak, fragile gender, subordinate to men in many ways, physically and emotionally. He views the role o' males to be guardians o' women's fragile natures," she confides to Henry. "I don't understand this, as he grew up wi' yer sisters, who you've described to me as being quite independent, and some wi' second-sight.

"He'll never discuss intellectual topics wi' me, particularly politics, and he keeps me from the goings-on in Virginia City that he finds too lurid for the sensitivity o' a woman, like murders and brawls. He really would have been better off wi' Ruthie. She would've fit in well wi' that kind o' thinkin', but I've never been like my sister. I always had other ideas about women, maybe because of me second-sight."

"Aye, that daes resemble Adam's philosophy," agrees Henry. "He means well. Adam reveres ye, and he desires to keep ye away from all that is evil. He desires for ye to feel that you're safe and bein' protected in this rugged, sometimes brutal, frontier city, so that ye'll no want to go back to Scotland. He kens ye have the ability to support yourself and might decide to go home if ye get fed up wi' the uncivilized life here."

"I've never been afraid o' the world. How could he think that when I traveled 'cross the ocean on a ship by myself? There was a suicide, and I experienced an iceberg and a shipwreck and nearly drowning; and then a train, loaded with men of questionable character gawking at me and tryin' to converse wi' me all the way across this Godforsaken country."

"He knew ye were under the protection of the captain, and wouldn't be harmed by the crew. Well, that much was partially true; safety in the hands o' the captain's anither story!" chuckles Henry. "Also, on a train ride, the crew is hired to serve and protect. There're guards in every car, in case ye weren't aware."

Catherine looks up curiously, a little perplexed, and Henry laughs. She'd never told Henry about her romance with Captain Noble. She considers that Henry has a way of figuring out everything by his superb intuition. Possibly, he had read between the lines of her enthusiasm and exalted description of the sea journey, wherein she had described the great mastery the captain had over his ship in saving them from doom.

"How did ye know about my romance wi' the captain?"

"How could any man not be spellbound by your beauty? Out on the open sea wi' ye for that long! I hope this captain behaved himself!"

"The captain was a fine gentlemen, at all times, and made me feel special, one thing that Adam is incapable o' doin'; although I grant him leeway knowin' that workin' in the mines is verra hard and he's too tired in the evenin' to praise my cookin' or housework, or to look at me adoringly after I've taken great pains to dress and arrange my hair especially nice for him for dinner. Captain Noble asked me to marry him, but he accepted my decision to marry Adam, as I felt bound to Adam in that I'd already accepted his proposal and was on my way to America on passage paid for by him. Frankly, it was my mother's fervent desire for me to marry into the marvelously handsome and intelligent clan of Baird men!" exclaims Catherine jokingly.

Henry laughs, but doesn't look surprised by Catherine's revelation, and replies, "Adam sees women as sacred creatures to be revered and protected. He puts them on a pedestal and feels that 'tis a manly thing to do to keep them safe from the dangers o' the world."

"Aye, 'tis certainly true," replies Catherine. "He doesn't respect the power o' women. He views the opposite sex as delicate creatures unable to fend for themselves, to handle gruesome news o' the world, to be able to think their way out o' difficult situations, or to even talk intelligently about world events."

"Adam sees the role o' men is to care o' and protect women. He appreciates that women are his equals intellectually and emotionally, but he is wise to the nature o' his own sex, and is aware that there are men set on exploitin' the gentle natures o' women, if they have a chance," explains Henry.

"Henry, that means Adam sees women as being too feebleminded to know the motives of lecherous and dangerous types, and not able to protect themselves against this sordid quality in men."

"Nay, Catherine, Adam is aware of the power o' women, as all men are aware. The female's awesome power provokes some men wi' poor self-esteem and a sense of their own limitations. 'Tis why unsavory men desire to exploit women; 'tis acause they themselves daena feel manly and are jealous o' female fortitude. There're men that'll try to conquer and obliterate the power in women, and if they canna they'll try to kill them."

Mary tells Catherine that the braves think she is the most beautiful white woman they've ever seen, and also that she is very generous and a good cook. Mary says they love to come to dinner just to see Catherine. "Even no food, they come to see you," Mary tells her.

At first Catherine feels a little uncomfortable when the bucks stare at her almost longingly, their eyes drifting down and across her body, as if she were a novelty item in a shop to purchase, but she takes it in stride. After all, she's as different looking to them as they are to her. She finds many of the braves very handsome with their beautiful brown eyes and golden skin, and finds herself gazing at them as well. In time, everyone relaxes around one another as they become accustomed to their differences and become aware of how much alike they are. She tells Mary that the bucks are admiring her beauty as well, and that Mary should enjoy the attention as long as her husband doesn't find out.

Over the course of many days and many dinners, Mary befriends one of the bucks, a fine-looking fellow with almond-shaped eyes and a tall, languid body. Catherine finds him very nice and respectful of women, as he makes a point to thank her for her food every day. A little playful flirtation begins between Mary and this young man, but nothing untoward. Lo and behold, word gets out to other tribe members of the special friendship between Golden Eyes and Mary. Mary's husband, a gruff and belligerent man, whose persona could be representative a misogynist brute of any race, gets wind of the friendship between Mary and Golden Eyes, and believes that Mary is being unfaithful. He sets out to punish his wife in a most egregious way.

During the night in late January, a little over three months after Mary started working for the Bairds, with a full harvest moon of a fluorescent pinkish-orange hue lighting the skies to a daytime quality, Catherine is awakened to wailing, plaintive cries from the Paiute settlement. She hears drums reverberating in heart-jerking throbs, which keep her awake for the rest of the night. Adam doesn't stir from his slumber, as he's a very deep sleeper, being physically and mentally exhausted from his workday. As on her wedding night, and many other nights since, Catherine experiences the Paiute ceremonial tribal sound from the encampment up above. She speculates that a tribal ceremony of worship is taking place, but she has a disturbing gut feeling, which she tries to push away, that something sinister is occurring. The incessant beating of drums and lamenting vocalizations last until dawn.

Mary doesn't come to work the next day, and Catherine is beset with more and more worry. She walks bravely over to the settlement to inquire as to Mary's whereabouts. She has a sense of foreboding at the back of her mind that something calamitous has happened. As she approaches the settlement, one of the bucks she feeds dinner to steps out onto the road and holds her back from going any farther. He bends over and whispers in her ear, informing her that Mary was stoned to death that night. She also learns that the young buck, Golden Eyes, was also put to death, but in a different manner. He was tied behind the two horses and dragged to death. Catherine feels faint and almost collapses on the road. She is led back to her home with the help of the buck.

From Adam's diary:
Sadly, our sweet Paiute lassie, Mary, was stoned to death last night, and it took a while to find out that she had gone against her tribe's moral code. Catherine was devastated. I only wish I could have done something to help Mary. I will feel forever guilty. I told Catherine we could not have done anything to stop the stoning, as we didn't know it was occurring. I think it would have been disastrous for me to interfere, even if we had known.

Catherine at the time of Mary's stoning is eight months pregnant, and so distraught from the news of her death that she has premature labor pains and takes to her bed. She mourns for days over her wee Paiute friend.

"Why did I ever leave Scotland for this savage country? The

people o' Virginia City have no empathy for the protection o' women besides their own. Raising my children in this uncivilized land is at a great risk," she laments to Adam and Henry.

Adam doesn't help matters much by telling her that she must accept the customs of another culture, as Paiute laws have been in place for as long as the Paiute race has existed in America, for many thousands of years.

Catherine is bedbound for the rest of her pregnancy. Less than a month after Mary's stoning, on February 1, 1872, she gives birth to a baby girl whom they name Belle, after her father's mother. She secretly hopes that Mary is looking down from Heaven to see her wee bundle o' joy. She's certain that Mary would have loved her baby very much, and they would have had so much fun playing with her together. The birth of Belle keeps Catherine busy and content in her maternal role, as her heart overflows with the pride and joy and wonderment of her accomplishment in giving birth to what she views as the greatest gift ever from the Almighty.

Henry visits Catherine every day after Belle's birth, and by his charming and affable presence, and ability to comfort her, her grieving over Mary is lessened. She comes to have a more positive perspective of her life in Virginia City and its citizens. For a time she had channeled her grieving into anger at white citizens for their treatment of Paiutes. Her rationale, skewered with emotion, was that white people in their abuse and disrespect of Paiutes had led the aggrieved clan to resort to these same barbaric abuses against their own kind.

Mary becomes, in time, not a heartache for Catherine to endure but a fountain of fond memories of their times spent together, comparable to her great times with Suzanna in Newfoundland, though she can't write to Mary as she writes to Suzanna every week. Catherine often sends her thoughts to Mary in the form of meditation every morning, telling her what she plans for the day, what she will cook, and milestones that Belle has achieved. She will always cherish the cookbook of Paiute recipes that Mary taught her to make.

Henry is always enjoyable, entertaining Catherine with his silly jokes and anecdotes about the townsfolk, and, oftentimes, has Punt on his shoulder, which causes her great mirth, as Punt is a natural entertainer, putting on his comical faces that are right-on depictions of people in the town. Punt has been told not to speak when they're visiting Catherine, but oftentimes, he can't contain himself and dances a wee jig and sings for Baby Belle. Punt can't get enough of Belle, whom he adores. As Henry sits at her bedside, he holds wee Belle in his lap with Punt's little dimpled hand holding onto Belle's tiny infant hand. Catherine sometimes wishes that Henry were her husband, and Belle their child. *He would make such a handsome father*, thinks Catherine; *he's as handsome and charming as the captain.* She often looks into Henry's eyes as they converse, and he looks back with kind, twinkling eyes, and with a smile that brings dimples to his cheeks, which Catherine finds adorable. She is awed by the current of electricity that passes back and forth between them, a truly comforting feeling to be so connected so closely to another spirit in the world. *Henry is my kindred spirit – I am certain of that*, she thinks.

VI. A Lackluster Life with Adam

What a reticent man he is, thinks Catherine, sighing in resignation as she looks across the room to her husband in his armchair, wrapped up in his cozy little world of books and ongoing, in-depth ruminations of abstract thoughts on the nature of life itself. She envisions words floating to and fro through the air like musical notes, as if he were having tête-à-têtes with his revered philosophers. *He gives more time to them – those dead intellectuals with their exalted ideas – than to me.* She is glaringly aware that she and her husband hardly converse at all anymore, other than small talk over dinner, which entails news about Baby Belle's development and milestones, household concerns, or when he commends her on her cooking. She finds the silences between them unnerving. *What's that man thinking so intensely of?* Catherine wishes that while he sits in his horsehair-stuffed armchair surrounded by his family of books that he would have an occasional stirring, something on the order of a spark of light to his brain wherein he suddenly beholds the sight of her presence and finds it beautiful, or a zap to his sensitivities that he is in the presence of a woman with whom he can have an amazingly intelligent conversation. As they dine in the candlelight, whereby Catherine tries to set a quaint, romantic table, Adam is so hungry that he rarely has time for one or two words, which usually consist of compliments like "Excellent" or "Verra guid!" Certainly, he never compliments her on how nice she looks, though she goes out of her way to fix herself up for supper. Perhaps childbirth has taken a toll on her looks. Yet in town she is often aware of people staring at her admiringly, both male and female. She can tell that they are admiring of her looks by the way the womenfolk have clouded looks of dismay that she exists in such a refined state, and the men gawk a little longer than is proper. She would like to be friendly with the townspeople rather than being put on a pedestal. Does Adam ever think of her in romantic terms, envision her in his bed making love at times they are not in bed? It is evident that he doesn't like talking after lovemaking and desires only to sleep afterward, though she admits he is physically very fatigued from his work.

Am I such a nitwit as not to be able to discuss the broader issues of the world? He doesn't respect the breadth of my intellect, that I am capable of understanding esoteric complex thoughts, she reflects.

Catherine has tried being assertive and confident in bringing up the topic of Mary's demise, as it had been written up in the paper in a number of issues, only because she and Henry had walked down to the *Gazette* office and relayed to them the story of Mary.

"Ye ken, Adam, Mary shouldn't have had to die. There were ways to intervene, such as gettin' the community at large involved in the horrid practice o' stoning." Adam had looked completely baffled by her comment, as if she'd said something outlandish, and let the conversation drop after a one-sentence reply of "'Tis an interesting viewpoint, but the issue is far more complex than ye'll iver ken." Catherine is still upset about Mary and makes it known on a daily basis that there were steps they should have taken on Mary's behalf, so it had not happened, and they should ensure that it will never happen again to another squaw. Adam has patiently repeated his stance over and over again: "We daedna ken this was going to happen, so how could we have intervened?"

"We should've looked more closely into matters when they found out the horrid man was beating Mary," Catherine had responded angrily. "We should've taken our fears o' her treatment to the tribal chief, and if that didn't work, we should've taken the matter to the sheriff for the law to protect Mary."

"We canna interfere in anither set o' laws o' anither culture," Adam replies succinctly, and motions to let the conversation end by putting his hand out, as if he were halting a horse, hunkering down to the book in his lap with a look of frustration. Catherine rolls her eyes and squares her shoulders in defiance of his way of sloughing off the matter so blithely, but says nothing further.

Paiute culture shouldn't have been a deterrent to white law protecting Mary from being beaten, and 'tis so blatantly obvious, she thinks in defiance. *Adam's too preoccupied in his book to really care how I feel. I'm still very upset about this and will be for a long while.*

Catherine's annoyance with Adam is further amplified when she finds out he's hidden from her news of the trampling to death of a young Paiute brave by white men in the woods above Gold Hill, not far from their house. The white men had a trite justification for murder by stating that the young brave refused to move out of their way fast enough as they galloped their horses down the road on an urgent matter. The death was rationalized by the sheriff's viewpoint, after talking to the white men, that the brave showed total disrespect for "white authority."

As was later revealed in the newspapers, the brave had severe hearing loss and had his back to the horsemen as they approached from behind. He didn't hear their gruff shouts to move out of their way. This event occurred only a few weeks after Mary's stoning.

Adam considers that goings-on in town, the ones that he considers "delicate issues," would be damaging to Catherine's sensitivities, like the ignoble actions of drunken gamblers in a brawl downtown last week over card cheating, wherein ten unruly men were jailed for the night. Henry entertains Catherine with everything that is going on in the town with gusto and flair, and, if called for, a wee bit of humor added for effect. That is how she learns of killings, lynchings, and other crimes going on in town.

"The men were so drunk and stepping up onto tables and jumpin' down onto their opponents. The chairs and tables in the bar were splintered to wee bits. One fellow poured ale o'er awbody as he stood atop the piano. I viewed anither fellow swingin' from the chandelier. Needless to say, I heard that by the time the men were herded off to jail, they were all soppin' wet wi' ale. The jailhouse smelled like a brewery all night long."

"Henry," inquires Catherine with astonishment, "what in the world were ye doin' in the bar that night?"

"I wasn't in the bar. I happened to walk by and looked in the window at the maelstrom. I was takin' Miss Goodman home efter a supper engagement." Catherine tries hard to hide her envy as she pictures Miss Goodman, dressed in her finery, enjoying a night out on the town with handsome Henry in a nice restaurant. She and Adam never eat out.

Along with Henry's renditions of current events, Catherine is able to keep up on newsy gossip from shopkeepers in town as she goes about her about her daily errands.

Will she and Adam ever bond completely as marriage partners who are equal halves of a whole, Catherine wonders, as she had always imagined married couples to be two like-minded people with great rapport? *How will it be to live a lifetime with this even-keeled, mild-mannered Scotsman, to pass the entirety o' my life in mediocrity, not passionately exalting in the joys that are out there?*

He's not a thing like the captain, she thinks, although she's ashamed of herself for making comparisons between Adam and the captain, as she knows it isn't fair to Adam to be compared to a totally different personality, living a totally different lifestyle.

He doesn't revere me like the captain. I felt very special dancing in his arms on the deck. Adam and I never dance! He certainly isn't as sensitive to my feelings as the gallant captain, nor as charismatic, she thinks.

She sometimes wonders if her life would have been happier living in the captain's house, gazing out the bay window at the sea, waiting for his ship to come in. She has a romantic picture in her mind of the captain coming home and ravishing her with affection after many months at sea.

Catherine misses the tingly feeling of excitement coursing down her spine that she had when around the handsome seaman. Adam is not outwardly demonstrative of his emotions, and sometimes she picks up on his moods, wherein she can sense he's depressed about something that has happened at work, but remains closed off and will not discuss what is bothering him with her. He is often worn out in the evening, and she gives him his space, providing him a good meal and quiet time to relax in his armchair after supper while she tends to the baby's needs and cleaning up after the meal.

Does he really want a lover and a companion, or just a woman to keep his house? She has come to view their marriage as a business contract between two people that can aid one another in their quest for a comfortable life. *But where is spiritual connection?* she wonders.

Nevertheless, Catherine decides she does love Adam for being the kind, reticent man that he is. Because he is the man she chose to marry, she decides to work on their relationship with an open mind and compassionate heart. Perhaps they will grow a closer bond in future years. Adam, Catherine observes, does everything by the book, partitions all his thoughts, acts in accord to what life demands of him at any given moment, perhaps to keep a level head, to keep his fears at bay. She senses that Adam is a wee bit rigid because of his experiences in his travels across the country, that he has seen too much violence and met too many unsavory people. *God only knows what he experienced out on the plains of America coming to Virginia City. Perhaps he's trying to protect me from harm*, she thinks. Yet again, she thinks of Henry having lost far more in his life with the death of his wife Annie, but he's still retained his spunk and the twinkle in his eyes. Adam is the person she married, however, and Catherine tries to give him every consideration. After all, he is the one providing this wonderful life, her beautiful child, and this wonderful environment for them to live in – providing her food, protection, and family. *What more could a woman ask for?*

Catherine refrains from mentioning her seagoing romance with the captain to Adam, but she wonders if he might sense she's had a romantic affair with another man. Her love life with Adam is one that Catherine enjoys some of the time, but at other times Adam performs the act as a chore, as if it were a nightly ritual like brushing his teeth, and then he falls asleep immediately after. It's certainly not the romantic endeavor she envisions – not the satisfaction she would have derived from making love to the enchanting Captain Noble. Sometimes she imagines the captain in her bed instead of Adam. The captain has become a source of pleasurable fantasy, like a character in a romance novel, but better than that because he is real, although like a fading star in the nighttime sky. The captain is unobtainable to her now and she'll probably never see him again, she thinks sadly.

The captain has written to her twice since she's been in Virginia City. She has not shared the letters with Adam, and has placed them in a secret compartment in her dowry chest where she keeps the tablecloth and jewels that she brought from Scotland, a beautiful gold necklace with a green peridot stone, and a solid gold bracelet with a large amethyst stone, and her diamond and pearl earrings.

My dear Catherine,
I hope you are adjusting to your new life in the rugged State of Nevada. I have so many fond memories of our special times together at sea and in Newfoundland, and could kick myself for letting you ever leave my side. I will always cherish the times in the moonlight when your presence lit up my spirit. If you ever change your mind and decide to leave Virginia City, I can be reached in Newfoundland at Mrs. Lawton's Boarding House on Bay Street, where my ship comes to shore about every month. I have never had such a beautiful young passenger on my ship since your voyage, and never will, as who could be as lovely as you? I think we had a bond so special it must have been of a universal order. My proposal for marriage will always be open, and I hopefully await your return someday, if that is in the cards.

Affectionately yours forever,
Captain Noble (Nathan)

Catherine's heart is uplifted after reading her love letter from the captain. That night she had very pleasant dreams wherein she is dancing on the deck with the captain under a full moon and brilliant stars.

VII. Adam's Amorous Thoughts o' Catherine

Unbeknownst to Catherine, Adam reflects often on his relationship with his wife, at times when he appears to be intensely involved in his intellectual pursuits of the evening. Interspersed between philosophical readings of great scholars of yore – some of them he finds dull and convoluted – exists an awareness of the presence of a strikingly beautiful woman sitting in the wicker rocking chair across the room from him. It astounds Adam that he has taken Catherine as his wife, even after many months of marriage, wherein living with her has become routine. He is rendered awestruck whenever he gazes over at this exquisite Madonna-like woman, with her auburn hair picking up red-gold hues from the firelight, her peachy porcelain skin and classic features glowing in the light, and her tall, elegant figure, not soft or round, but with a firmness that speaks of strength. Adam remembers the athleticism of Catherine from her youth in Scotland. In their lovemaking, which he enjoys to no end, he is aware that her body is well toned and muscular under all the enchanting feminine curves, a surprising velvety firmness to her limbs, shoulders, breasts, and torso. He is confident that Catherine with her strength and verve would be able to put up a ferocious defense against any would-be attacker, though this doesn't guarantee her survival in the event of an attack when walking in the woods or to town alone, which she does quite often, despite his warnings. Adam fears that Catherine doesn't understand the risks involved in meeting an aggressive male perpetrator, white or Indian. He remembers how she spent her youth roaming the open moorlands by herself, but this was quite safe given that she was not likely to run into people in the desolate open country of Scotland.

Catherine is never aware of her husband glancing at her lovingly, as she's habitually looking down while mending, knitting, or reading, totally absorbed in her own thoughts. As he gazes at her now, Adam is thinking that his wife is very smart, very kind, very beautiful, everything he desires in a woman. *She's all things fine,* he reflects. He has often wanted to reach out to tell her all this and more, tell her of his romantic thoughts of her while away at work, tell her he cherishes her presence in his life, and is so very grateful that she became his wife. If only he could bring himself to express what is in his heart in a spontaneous way that doesn't come off as sounding trite. He fears that if he attempts expressing his feelings of love and admiration, his words would spill out in an insincere sounding and bumbling manner. *I haven't changed any since me younger days. I shy away from sentimental talk acause I daena have a knack wi' words as Henry. Niver did, niver will.*

He reflects on the miracle of Catherine becoming his wife; it was a marvelous, divine occurrence that he was able to impress her enough through his letters for her to travel thousands of miles over land and sea to reach him in Virginia City. He surmises that this was because he was able to express himself – the essence of who he really is – much more eloquently in writing than in speech. If he was more like Henry he could say something clever or funny right now and cut away at the frigid barrier that he senses between them as they sit in the drawing room, engaged in their own thoughts. Perhaps they could have an intimate conversation, and Catherine could tell him her innermost thoughts – how she feels about her life in Virginia City, and what steps he might take to make her life happier.

Adam would like to open up to his wife about his difficulty in sharing politics, literature, and the oftentimes crude, violent, and unjust happenings of Virginia City, and the world at large, due to his sheer exhaustion at the end of each workday. He's also very much aware that Catherine would like to have a social life, and wishes he had more energy to take her out on the town to a restaurant or a play at Piper's Opera House.

Adam finds Catherine too impulsive in her desire to intervene in the turbulent goings-on of the Paiutes. She'd act rashly, he fears, on injustices that she hears of, and put herself in harm's way. He has warned her to not venture up the hill anywhere near the Paiute encampment. If she had her druthers she would be up there discussing with the Paiute elders matters of unjust tribal laws and punishments like stoning. He's relieved that she's no longer serving dinner to a motley crew of braves since Mary's stoning. Catherine, he thinks, wears her heart on her sleeve, and he desires her to curtail her involvement in the Indian upheavals. She cannot save all the downtrodden Paiutes in Nevada.

Adam observes the budding friendship between Catherine and Henry, but is not jealous in the least, for he wants the two of them to be friends. Together, the atmosphere his brother and wife create is lighthearted and fun, their house filled with gaiety and laughter. *Who wouldna love me brother, Henry?* Catherine and Henry are so much alike in so many ways, and he understands why their relationship is so easy and relaxed. Adam doesn't worry that their friendship will become romantic, for he knows Henry too well, and understands Catherine more than he lets on to her. Henry will be grieving for Annie for the rest of his life, and is still at a stage wherein he carries the memory of their love with him like a badge of honor, to be cherished in his heart forever.

Adam is also very aware of the pragmatic side of Catherine's nature. He'd read a letter from Captain Noble that she had inadvertently dropped on the floor of their bedroom, just underneath the bed. In search of a slipper, before Catherine was in the bedroom, he had gone down on his hands and knees to the floor and had picked up the envelope and read the contents quickly, then put it back where he found it, leaving a bit of its edge exposed so she would find it. It was the final letter Catherine had received from the captain. Adam had been in bed for the night – presumably fast asleep by the time – and had observed Catherine bending over to retrieve the letter from floor as she climbed into bed. She had gasped softly, feigning a cough afterwards, and had stashed it away immediately in her lovely opal box of private correspondence, with the rest of the "love letters" from the captain. Fortunately, because it was under the bed on her side, she had presumed that Adam had not seen it there.

My dear Catherine,
I hope you are enduring your rugged life in the West. I pray it isn't too dusty and muddy, and the Westerners aren't too crude. Having you in my arms while dancing on deck and skating on ice was like holding the Goddess of Enchantments. I treasure our kiss that humbled me to the knowledge o' the exalted bond that can exist between a man and a woman. What else can I convey to ye but that my life has been profoundly touched by your exquisite presence? My perspective as to what a woman o' quality is has changed forever.

Again, if ye should ever change your mind and decide to leave Virginia City, I can still be reached, as always, in Newfoundland, at Mrs. Lawton's Boarding House on Bay Street. I receive my mail there rather than have it pile up at my empty house. I know we had a deep bond that was very special. It must have been in the stars that we'd be together on the open sea. My proposal for marriage will always be open, and I expectantly await your return someday, if that is in the cards.

Affectionately yours forever,
Captain Noble (Nathan)

The captain had been very much in love with Catherine, Adam was stunned to learn from the letter, and he's aggrieved that his wife had been weighing in on staying with Captain Noble in St. John's and not coming to Virginia City. On further assessment, Adam was surprised Catherine hadn't stayed in Newfoundland with the captain, as she knew the seaman far better than she knew him. She couldn't have had any notion what a marriage to a mining carpenter that she hardly knew would be like. Catherine last saw him as an immature lad of seventeen. Adam's first reaction is to be highly incensed that this auld chuff, the captain, is still throwing himself at his wife after her marriage. She made her decision! Had Catherine been in love with Captain Noble and come to Virginia City out of a sense of duty, a promise that had been made to her mother, or an acceptance to a marriage proposal she didn't feel she could back out of because she had agreed to marry him and paid for her trip? Adam had sensed that there had been a significant romance in his wife's past, but had assumed it had been back in Scotland. Is the captain aware that she was in love with him and was undecided about coming to Virginia City? Is he now trying to get her back?

When he first saw Catherine in Reno, after so many years apart, he could read in her gestures, her eyes, in her stance, her modest self-assuredness, in the totality of her demeanor that she was a woman who had previously experienced a great romance. Not that Adam was very experienced in detecting a woman's past in her bearing, but he had known Catherine as an adolescent, and he could see the change, not only in overall maturity but also in a glint of knowing that comes about after having given one's heart to another. Adam is assured Catherine didn't give herself physically to the captain, for she was a virgin when she married him, but he senses she'd experienced great passion and perhaps had given her heart to this gentleman during their time at sea and in St. John's. The fact that Catherine had decided against the captain and had come to him in Virginia City is very gratifying to Adam, for it affirms that which he had assessed about his wife's character, her intuitiveness of his nature from his letters and her mature pragmatic approach to life. Adam is thankful that Catherine was able to discern between love based on substance and love based on the enticements of an open-sea romance and courtship in a crystalline winter wonderland, for Catherine had described to him in glowing words her enchanting life in St. John's, and had even mentioned the crew from the *S.S. Alabama* living in St. John's and working on the ship during those months.

As to Catherine's relationship with Henry, Adam is pretty much assured that his brother would never betray him – he knows Henry well – and he's pretty much assured Catherine would never betray him, particularly since they have Baby Belle in their lives.

Catherine, he admits, loves Henry in a very special way, as everyone loves Henry for his contagious humor, wit, charm, handsomeness, and perhaps even more so than any of his other women admirers, for she and Henry are definitely kindred spirits in being able to share the Wee Folks, even if they don't truly exist but are merely shared fantasies from childhood. Adam is uncertain of the existence of Wee Ones, but likes to pretend that they are present when he needs a lucky talisman. He's certain that Catherine loves him now that they have lived together as man and wife and have a child together. He can tell by the way she cares for all his needs, in their lovemaking, and the way her eyes light up when he comes home to her in the evening safe and sound. If only the love Catherine has for her partner in marriage was expressed more openly outside the domain of their marital bed. If only it was easier for Adam to convey his feelings of upmost love and admiration for Catherine. Adam is once again amazed at the twists and turns of his love life, that he, shy Adam Baird, is presently, and has been in the past, embroiled in many manifestations of women's love and doesn't quite understand the feminine mystique.

VIII. Catherine in Love with Henry?

Catherine's main delights of her life in Virginia City – she does count her blessings – are her wonderfully crafted home that has the scent of fine wood, and warmth from its glowing walls and plank hardwood floors; the beauty of the high-desert mountain terrain with its wooded forests and snowy Sierra peaks; Baby Belle, her adorable daughter, who's blossoming into quite a personality in her own right; her marriage to the kind-hearted, intellectual Adam; and, above all, the presence of Henry, who has made her day-to-day existence entertaining and exciting.

Catherine, Adam, and Henry have had many enjoyable times together taking in the sights of the beautiful, newly formed western states of Nevada and California. Henry's company has been a delight to both of them, lighting their way with humor and high-spirited enthusiasm as they have explored lovely parts of the beautiful West. One weekend, in the spring of 1871, after Adam and Catherine had been married close to ten months, they traveled by train from Reno on the scenic California Zephyr line, which was built in the 1860s. The train chugged slowly along the twisting, snowy mountain pass, climbing to its highest elevation of over 7,000 feet, lending passengers a spectacular bird's-eye view of the high-altitude terrain, sparsely studded with stunted, bent-over trees. From the summit, the Zephyr steamed down the mountain pass, winding through lush forestland to the port city of Sacramento, a bustling community along the waterfront of the Sacramento River. The picturesque city of eye-catching European-style architecture was booming with an ever-growing population of immigrants. New construction had sprung up during the Gold Rush affluence of the 1850s, and was continuing its growth to the downtown area and to the city's periphery where grand homes were being built. Catherine observed that many of the hotels, restaurants, and stores exhibited wrought iron railings on balconies, and high-arched doorways and windows of classic European design, which lent a charming Spanish and Parisian flavor.

The threesome splurged by checking into a plush suite at the high-end California Hotel located on the Sacramento riverfront, comprising two large bedrooms and a plush parlor, which made Catherine feel like visiting royalty. The next day, the travel enthusiasts rode out by buggy through the verdant grassy hills of the Sacramento Valley, viewing an entirely different terrain than the Sierras – beautiful orange, purple, and yellow wildflowers, patches of gnarly oak trees whose limbs fanned out to great widths, and smaller species of shrubby oak interspersed with fruit trees and sycamore, plus many unfamiliar varieties of trees and plants not indigenous to Scotland. Their destination was John Sutter's Mill, to view firsthand the site where gold was first discovered.

Catherine was aware during that glorious weekend that she was experiencing a lofty aliveness to her spirit, a renewed excitement, eagerness, and energy because of Henry's presence. *If only life could be like this all of the time*, she had reflected. She observed that Adam was a livelier, more engaging person around Henry. The two brothers, she noted, shared a special camaraderie. It became apparent to Catherine on the Sacramento trip, as well as the other trips they'd taken with Henry, that Adam is more outgoing and talkative around his brother, in marked contrast to his quiet, introspective nature at home with her, wherein all he desires after work is to enjoy a substantial dinner and to sit down with a good book and a small tumbler of whiskey. Catherine only wishes her husband would display that vital spark o' spirit with her in their home life that he shares with Henry. The two brothers have so much to talk about. She would love to have that special kind of relationship wherein intellectual topics go back and forth nonstop with ease and enthusiasm.

Many times, Catherine has tried to engage Adam in intelligent conversation but has been rebuffed. To one of her advances to discuss the book he was absorbed in, he had responded politely, "I canna explain the convoluted theories conveyed by this great thinker unless one starts at the beginning o' the book and spends hours goin' o'er his ideas point by point."

Adding to her frustration, Catherine has not had much success engaging in any kind of enjoyable intellectual conversation on current affairs of the world, or that of their active and often volatile city. Again, Adam has responded to her initiation of conversation about the turbulent affairs of Virginia City, from civic matters to shootings to Indian unrest, by replying, "Catherine, I just daena hiv time nor energy to keep up wi' onything goin' on in town. Mostly petty things bein' reported o' no significance. 'Tis all in the newspapers, if ye're wantin' to learn the gossip; albeit, I daena want ye gettin' all riled up on Indian matters."

On a particularly memorable holiday trip in September, seven months after the birth of Belle, Adam, Catherine, Belle, and Henry, with Punt in tow, spend four days camping along the shores of Lake Tahoe at Emerald Bay. To Adam, this is sacred ground – the place where he had several years before dreamed of finding someone special to share his life with, and soon thereafter had come up with the idea of contacting his mother to look into Catherine Malcolm's whereabouts. Adam is gratified that his dream has come true, that Catherine had the insight to see a potential for love to blossom between them. The amazing courage she possessed to travel so far is not lost on him, to risk the long, hazardous voyage across sea and land to America, and all alone, and based entirely on intuition of his good character based on a childhood bond she'd shared with him, as well as the sporadic correspondence they had exchanged.

Catherine has revealed to him in so many ways since their marriage that she is truly a rare individual of fine quality, who is giving and cares passionately for others, willing to fight for the rights of downtrodden Paiutes at her own personal risk, which has made him fearful of her safety. Since Mary's stoning, Catherine has continued to feed hungry Paiutes at dinner despite his desire for her to cease, and has sent many baskets of food up to the encampment. Each week on her way to town she buys baskets, trinkets, and jewelry from the Paiutes selling along the road.

Adam romanticizes his wife's character, putting her on equal footing with Florence Nightingale, who gave so much of herself in the Crimean War effort between Britain and Russia. The war left a lasting impression on Adam's childhood, and thus Florence Nightingale left an everlasting imprint of the greatness of this woman in his mind. His idol Leon Tolstoy was a Russian soldier in the

Crimean War and wrote of it in his *Sevastopol Sketches*. It is even more impressionable to Adam that such a great writer as Tolstoy could have lost his life to the British Empire, which has brought to light for him the fact that there are fine people on both sides of a battle. He goes over one of the patriotic rhymes he learned as a young student in school regarding a victory Great Britain and her allies achieved in the Siege of Seavastopol:

I remember, I remember the tenth of November,
Sevastopol, powder and shot,
When General Liprandi charged John, Pat, and Sandy,
And a jolly good licking he got.

Adam senses the tensions in his marriage, which distresses him greatly, and thus he makes a mental note to be more in tune with Catherine's sensitivities and needs, no matter how tired and disgruntled he is at the end of a long workday. One of the problems in their relationship, he has come to realize, is the amount of time he spends away from her. He's perpetually tied up at work, coming home many evenings long after sundown, as his duties have been expanded with the opening of a new shaft, wherein the newly built tunnel walls must be reinforced with wood structures to prevent them from caving in. Adam's fine and careful craftsmanship is truly appreciated by the miners, who must spend their entire shifts down in the shafts and risk being asphyxiated in a cave-in if the walls haven't been secured properly.

Catherine worries about Adam inside the mines at night and tells him so as a way to demonstrate her love.

"Adam, the shafts are extremely dangerous. I worry the entire evening and into the night when ye don't come home 'til well past bedtime. I fear that ye've fallen down into the mine, as ye almost did a few years ago. Henry told me the board broke when ye tried to repair the lift, and the only thing that saved you was Punt."

"Punt! 'Tis nonsense an imaginary sprite saved me from anything. You're bein' silly, Catherine. 'Tis always night inside the cave, whativer the hour, and a lantern's sufficient to see, as I've excellent night vision."

Personally, he is touched by the fact that she's worried, but he doesn't let on to this, as he becomes tongue-tied in trying to express his gratitude that she worries over his safety. Inspired by the beautiful Lake Tahoe environment, the thought comes to him again that he must muster up courage and express his feelings openly to Catherine, tell her how much he reveres her and appreciates her concern for his safety, no matter how much o' a bumbling eediot he comes across as.

On their Lake Tahoe trip, Catherine is thrilled and exhilarated by the cerulean, gem-like lake, unlike any body of water she's ever encountered, deeper than any loch in Scotland, barring the Loch Ness in Inverness that she'd visited many times with her family. She, Henry, and Adam absorb into their beings the spellbinding spiritual gifts offered by the magical body of clear water, awe-inspiring in its majestic display of nature's perfection. They walk reverently along the sandy beach, and Henry and Adam venture out to wade in the very chilly water as playful waves ebb and flow and soothe their bare feet. Catherine and Belle watch from the shoreline. With Henry along, there is an added sense of wonderment and exhilaration with glorious displays of wildlife, as Henry magically orchestrates the avian world with his talented bird calling. The birds respond to his magnetic energy and rare affiliation to all forms of life in nature. There exists a language of boastfulness and competition amongst the avian wildlife, like and unlike species, all wanting to get noticed by Henry. As a result, there is continual lively back and forth of chatter, chirps, whistles, and bellows, as well as beautiful displays of aerodynamics for their enjoyment. Henry runs along the shores flapping his arms like wings, vocalizing his outlandish calls, while birds hover over him as if they were chicks following their long-lost mother. Belle, at only seven months, laughs and claps, finding Henry's antics with his bird friends hilarious, especially when he loses his footing and falls into the water.

IX. Henry and Catherine — Close Confidants

Back home in Virginia City, after the Tahoe trip, Henry starts a new job in the mining office in town as a financial accountant for the Caledonia Mining Corporation. While working in the mines with Adam when first arriving in Virginia City, he had come to the realization that he was not the skilled carpenter that Adam was, and he abhorred underground work away from the sight of the sun or sky for ten hours at a time. He had applied for a job in town, and with a good word from Adrian, senior engineer of the mines, he was soon promoted to a senior position in the accounting office. Henry had managed the financial books for Drumdruils Ranch in Scotland for over five years, and had acquired valuable accounting experience. Good accountants are hard to come by out West, as a majority of the mining workers are either uneducated or not well versed in English, and so Henry has risen quickly in his profession to senior financial accountant for the Caledonia mines.

The bond between Henry and Catherine has been strengthened after Paiute Mary's death. Henry has been a constant source of comfort and understanding as she's mourned. The terrible emotional upheaval brought about by Mary's death left Catherine numb and questioning her decision to come to live out West. At one point, she had voiced to Henry, "Mebbe Belle and I would be better off back in Scotland. I could support her alone in my teachin' profession."

"Catherine, me lassie, ye must be more jolly aboot yer life. Ye've so much to live for – Adam loves ye greatly, and ye hiv Belle to adore and groom into a fine young lady; and o' course ye've got me, who adores ye. Also, ye must help me stay out o' tribble," he says teasingly.

With his new position, Henry is off work at an early hour, which gives him time to spend with Catherine and Baby Belle, whom he adores, as she reminds him so much of his beloved daughter in Scotland, Mary Alice. Almost every day since Belle has become old enough to be aware of the world around her, Henry and Catherine have taken her on long hikes in the pine-studded foothills. Belle is a happy-go-lucky baby who delights in the outdoors with little coos and screeches at each novel sight she comes across. On warm and sunny days, they enjoy hiking up and down the woodland paths above the house, wherein sometimes they pass by the Paiute encampment without any danger (though Catherine feels some remorse when passing by), or they walk into town to fetch items Catherine needs from the local stores.

Of course, on their long walks, the dynamic Punt always tags along, whether invited or not. Catherine is delighted to see the Wee Sprite, as he reminds her of home on the moors in Scotland, where her Wee Friends flitted about gaily and entertained her with their comical antics, and showed her the best places to find beautiful rocks and colorful stones to add to her collection, and, above all, they escorted her to the best places to find wildflowers to take home to her mother in a way of appeasement for being out alone on one of her foolhardy quests for hours on end, as Mrs. Malcolm would call it.

Catherine and Henry, being second-sighted, commune with the many aspects of nature available to those with inherent insights into the underlying synchrony of the environment. They enjoy watching the integral relationship that creatures display with one another, and observe with amusement the reaction of these critters' first encounters with a Wee Person. All creatures seem to accept Punt as one of their own species, and so he is able to go up to any one of them and have a lively interaction. Catherine and Henry find it fascinating the way he communes with foxes, deer, raccoons, and even bobcats that become quite docile in his presence. Catherine becomes quite anxious whenever they spot a bobcat on the trail, but Punt tells her, "Fear na, me lady, I'll protect ye wi' me life." He proceeds to jump on the back of one of these wildcats as if it were a horse and rides around with ease.

"Ye'll not be harmed by mountain lions or bobcats or any wild cat, as long as ye are wi' me."

"If Punt waesna present, the cats would most likely be in hiding," Henry tells Catherine.

Punt speaks in chatters, mimicries, and the other vocalizations of birds, and so does Henry. On their daily walks, Henry performs his perfect birdcalls. His quail cry is quite delightful to Catherine. Punt is totally enamored by Belle, who chatters away in her own obscure language with Punt. He seems to understand everything she says, and interprets for her mother and Henry. Punt spends most of his time entertaining Baby Belle with his acrobatics and jig dances, and even conjures up a fiddle to play for her.

"What's that ye say, Belle?" Punt inquires. "Ye tell me ye desire for me to play 'Twinkle, Twinkle, Little Star.'" Belle treats Punt as if he were a talking doll, and often reaches out to play with his long, flaxen hair.

Punt, being the silliest of creatures, has Catherine and Henry on the edge of hysterics whenever they're out with him. He tells them corny jokes along the way and gets them riled up to the point of their laughing out loud. During these special times, Catherine has a change of attitude about her life, forgets she is in mourning for Mary, and is proud to be living in such a beautiful place.

Today, Punt is wearing his fancy Western ensemble in green, as he loves to play the part of a rootin' tootin' cowboy.

Says Punt to Henry, "Daed ye ken that I'm a true Western cowboy in anither dimension? Yep, I roped me a steer just the ither day. Was out on me ranch and desired a wee bit o' tender beef. The steer let me lasso him in, but then said to me, 'Punt, what're ye doin'? I'll teach ye how to tame a bucking bull if ye let go o' me – not that I canna get away by myself.'

"'Ye mean I can become a professional bull rider?' I inquired. 'That would be a fine profession for me, as I haven't found me calling in life yet.' And the bucking bull agreed to teach me to stay on his back like the best o' them."

Catherine and Henry can just picture the wee fairy riding a bull that would outsize him by a thousandfold, comparable to a fly on a bull.

"So I got on his back, and he says to me that he'll go easy on me at first, but within four seconds' time he threw me wi' great micht o'er his heid, and that was that. Luckily, I can fly. I got back on and he said for me to try stayin' on once more. He then threw me off in two seconds' time. The bull apologized to me for not letting me ride longer, but he said I'm not big enough to even attempt to tamper w' his fierceness.

"'Next time, ride a calf!' he said. So I took his advice. Rode me a wee calf round all day long, and the wee calf and I became the best o' friends."

"Ye look ridiculous in that apparel," says Henry, kiddingly.

"Tell me 'bout ridiculous next time I see ye bein' laid out on the ground by the likes o' auld MacGivens. Remember that?" Punt tells Catherine how he saved Henry from a vicious attack by his then-future father-in-law.

Catherine finds herself often laughing out loud at Punt's outlandish play, uncharacteristic of her usual reserved demeanor that has been particularly somber. The wee sprite continually stirs up hilarity in the wake of his lame jokes and silly dances. As such, by the time of the six-month anniversary of Mary's death, Catherine's depression and sorrow have lifted considerably. She feels magically alive on her outings with Henry and Belle, more content in this natural, outdoor environment than anywhere else. As such, she had agreed to camp at Lake Tahoe with Adam, Henry, and Belle.

Catherine and Henry are alike, as two peas in a pod, both receptive to out-of-the-ordinary realms of consciousness due their second-sightedness. On their daily walks, they are more cognizant of what's going on at a subliminal level in nature, thus recognizing the oneness in the rhythm of the universe, in tune with integral, intertwining components of life going on all about them, and in their own aliveness in response to nature and to one another. They can pick up readily on the state of each other's emotions as they relish the natural environment. When they are together in nature, there is an intense feeling of wellbeing, as if there's an alignment of cosmic energy enveloping them with light, peace, and inspiration.

A physical attraction is not what brings the two together, although Catherine, despite her conscious thoughts not to fantasize about Henry, often finds herself drawn to him physically when he is in her presence, as she can't overlook his beauty and charisma. Periodically, her anger at Adam for not preventing Mary's stoning by the Paiutes arises, and she uses these unresolved emotions as an excuse to turn to Henry as her best friend and confidant over her husband. When confronted with angry thoughts of Adam, she veers closer to overstepping the boundary separating her from Henry, which only accentuates their burgeoning attraction. Most of the time, she is able to control her emotions and keep up positive thoughts of her husband.

Catherine loves Henry deeply because of their easy bond, but in a different way than she loves Adam, for she has searched her heart and has discovered that she does indeed love her husband despite his inability to share his intimate thoughts with her as she and Henry are able to share with one another. Catherine decides that she must work harder to strengthen the bond with Adam. This is the best path to a happy marriage, she has concluded. "Try harder to bring Adam out of his shell" has become her motto. She has become very pragmatic and careful in matters of her heart regarding Henry, especially since her dealings with the captain.

Aye, everyone reveres Henry, she reflects. *My love for Henry is not based on practicality. To revere Henry, who is a godly representation of the male gender, is sheer fantasy and evokes fantastical flights o' the mind. Henry's the same caliber as the captain, so awesome, charismatic, and magical, but love for him is based on a fanciful bond, wherein a prince and a princess live happily ever after, as one reads of in fairy tales.*

Catherine views Adam, with all his reticence and inability to display emotion or share his deepest thoughts, as a down-to-earth and steadfast individual of the finest substance, like a fine seaworthy ship that never falters in its ability to provide for safety and overall wellbeing. Catherine has come to find Adam's shyness and inability to express emotion rather endearing. He touches her heart in the same way as some of her past pupils had touched her. A few of her students had possessed traits of great shyness, pronunciation problems, or hearing defects that prevented them from conveying to others their true selves, and she had developed a true empathy for them that had touched her very core. She had gone out of her way to bring those pupils out of their shells and aid them in developing their individuality. Catherine decides she must develop a stronger relationship with Adam, as he will always be the pillar of her life and Belle's.

Catherine will continue for her entire life to have splendid dreams about the captain and Henry, exquisite fantasies of her imagination as she lays her head on her pillow at night. That suits her fine, for these pleasures of the mind bring her great inner contentment. These fantasies spring up to pacify her during the doldrums and sorrows that life inevitably brings.

Of course, Henry is aware of the intense bond he shares with

Catherine and their growing affection for one other, and tries to constrain his outright love for her.

"Catherine, Adam and I have a verra special bond. We've ayeweys looked out for one anither's wellbeing. I would kill to protect me brither from hurt," says Henry.

"Ah, Henry, Adam's indeed a very special individual whom we must protect from getting hurt by life, as I fear he often doesn't understand all the intricacies o' the human condition as we do. His feet and his mind are planted entirely on solid ground, as opposed to us, whose minds are flittering about at higher elevations, tryin' to catch hold o' the magical flavors that we sense are out there in the universe."

"Aye, I suppose ye could call us fanciful lunatics a' the mercy o' the moon and stars," says Henry jocularly.

Because of his temptation in regards to Catherine, Henry has looked elsewhere for the company of women. He has been stepping out with a young and very attractive teacher, Miss Carol Anne Goodman, whom he met in town at the mining office when she brought her class to view the mineral and gem display, housed in the glass cases in the large anteroom of the building. Henry is enjoying her company immensely. Catherine can tell this by the lilt in his voice when he describes their dining at Virginia City's finest restaurants two or three times per week, and to the opera or a play every weekend at Piper's Opera House.

He confides to Catherine about his association. "Miss Goodman's a verra sweet, bonnie, and intelligent young lassie. We've had a lot o' good times thegither. She's an unaffected young woman without a shred o' vanity, just pure kindness, unadulterated goodness."

Catherine hides her jealousy as she listens to Henry's raving about another woman, which is lessened by her remembrance that Henry periodically has indicated that "no one will iver live up to me love for Annie," which she construes to mean that Miss Goodman will never snatch his heart away completely. Catherine wants to view Miss Goodman as being no different than any of the many other flirtatious women in Henry's sphere, indeed a nice young woman, but one using every feminine charm in the book to catch this desirable man.

The number of young women interested in Henry keeps multiplying. Once it was discovered that Henry had begun a job at the mining office, storeowners noticed an influx of young ladies coming to town to shop, first making their way to the mining office to say hello to Henry. Henry has a talent for making the young women feel special, not consciously on his part, but in his way of treating each with great esteem. Attempts to ensnare Henry's heart are pursued with unquenchable enthusiasm, even though in some cases there are extenuating circumstances making Henry completely ineligible – Henry is too old in many instances; a number of the young woman are engaged to be married; several are of the Catholic faith and forbidden to marry a Protestant Scot. Flirting with Henry is a worthwhile pursuit for any eligible (or ineligible) young woman, as she spends hours after her encounter with Henry basking in rosy dreams of romance.

After hearing amusing vignettes from Henry of his social life, Catherine can no longer deny her true feelings of frustration and jealousy over his dating women. She consciously admits to herself that she loves Henry, but in a very different way than Adam. The brothers are so unalike, and yet they each offer so much to love as individuals. Catherine has matured enough in her pragmatism of what love for the opposite sex comprises, and is aware of the different types of love that exist, especially in her firsthand dealings with the captain. The many women she's come across in Virginia City that have shown an affinity for Henry are exhibiting the very same kind and degree of affection as women had for the captain in St. John's. The very thought of so many loving Henry has called on her pragmatic mind to stop romanticizing him. Why should she love someone that everyone wants? That kind of love is not practical or true love.

Her attachment to Henry, she decides, is warped by her romantic imaginings, just as her love for the captain had been. She decides she loved the captain, and now Henry, because both represent charismatic, god-like aspects of the male gender. She wonders why she's been drawn to two such dynamic types, not completely satisfied with the good man she has in Adam, who is so kind and down-to-earth in his love, providing for her a family and seeing to her every need and comfort in life. *Perhaps*, she muses, *it is just part of growing up and maturing into a good wife and mother. Ah... to have passion to look back on, 'tis not all that wrong!*

I'll cherish my passionate memories o' these men and tuck them away in my heart like I tuck away dried roses in sachets, taking them out when I need a lift from everyday ordinariness, when I feel less than pretty and desirable, especially when I'm verra auld, she thinks.

Despite her best intentions at keeping her mind from straying to thoughts of Henry, at particular times, mostly when she's frustrated and feeling neglected by Adam, Catherine wonders what it would have been like to have been engaged to Henry, and reflects on what would have happened if she and Henry had crossed paths in Scotland before their voyages to America. What if Jean Baird had thought of Henry, not of Adam, to be a perfect match for her, and logically so because he lived in Scotland? It would have been so easy for them to come together in Helensburgh or Bridge of Allan. Catherine would have been able to live close to her mother. Maybe her mother wouldn't have died knowing Catherine would be staying in Scotland, not traipsing to the other side of the world. Perhaps it was the thought of a long sea voyage that had destroyed her health? *Henry and I would have made a most perfect bonding of kindred spirits.*

She consciously pulls herself away from fantastical dreams of Henry. *'Tis but a dream*, she reflects. *I love Adam wi' all my heart, and I'd never have had my beloved Belle and this wonderful life in*

Virginia City if I'd stayed in Scotland.

On one of her daily walks with Henry and Belle, Catherine can't help herself but to bring up the subject to Henry of what it would have been like if he had courted her while they were both in Scotland, after Adam had left for America.

"Henry, do ye suppose we would've been a decent couple? We could have married and be presently living in Scotland and raising children. I could have helped ye raise Mary Alice. We would've been passionately in love."

"Aye, Catherine, I'm madly in love wi' ye now and foriver, daena ye ken? Ye must ken that our love's a rare kind that'll transcend all time, and 'tis true, we would've made a fine couple. But the word 'madly' describes our kinda love all too well. 'Tis sheer madness acause 'tis unreachable; 'tis at a star's distance right now, so far away in all rationality."

"Henry, no matter how insane – and 'tis – this doesn't sound like me at all, but sometimes I think we should act on our love, maybe in secret, just once. Adam is blind. He'd never guess, and we'd be so happy to share that kind o' special love, even for a short time. What I'm tryin' to convey to ye is that it might help us both be more grounded in other parts o' our lives. People who share the kind o' magic we do can have its effects spill o'er to ither aspects of their lives, and make life so much merrier. I know I'd get along better wi' Adam if I had your love just once to give me a burst o' heavenly happiness."

Henry walks closer to Catherine and kisses her fully on the lips for the first time. It is a magical kiss that conveys to them how well paired they are physically and spiritually. To Catherine, it seems as though she has entered heaven on earth, but it scares her a bit to have something so perfect and blissful in her life. This kind of love doesn't fit into day-to-day domestic life and motherhood, the life that has provided her stability and peace of mind in this new land. After being ensconced in Henry's blissful supernatural love, something akin to being touched by the glow of a heavenly angel, Catherine is made wise to the fact that the solidity of her life with Adam would be inevitably destroyed by an affair with Henry. *'Tis silly and foolish o' me to think I could share my love for Henry just once.*

Through much internal, emotion-harrowing debate on both sides, Henry and Catherine face the harsh reality that they must stay close friends and keep their fiery love tempered, for it would only grow as fires do, brilliantly and unstoppably. Their deep and profound love must not be acted on fully, and eventually be let go of entirely.

For that reason and a few more, one being Miss Goodman's anticipation of a marriage proposal, another being a good job prospect, Henry decides it's best to leave Virginia City and head for a new life in California. He fears that Adam will eventually pick up on the way he and Catherine feel about one another, even if they don't act on their love. Neither of them wants to betray Adam, and Adam might sense there is more than brotherly/sisterly camaraderie between them. This would cause Adam to clam up, withdraw, and ignore them both. Henry would greatly despair at the loss of Adam as his best friend and confidant in this faraway land, and Catherine would lose the closeness she has managed to achieve with her husband.

Catherine is the first to find out that Henry is making plans to leave Virginia City. She has picked up on Henry's unsettled mood in regards to his life in the city for a time. Though always the happy-go-lucky person, underneath the façade is a man who is aching for more than a desk job in a mining office. On one of their walks, Catherine brings up the topic of his possible dissatisfaction.

"Henry, I sense that ye're not as happy here as ye've been before. Mebbe ye're contemplating departin' Virginia City? I desire for ye to find your own life, but ye can certainly do it here wi' yer family."

"Aye, ye've read me mind so well, me dear lassie. Ye ken I canna hide me thoughts from ye. 'Tis time for me to take leave o' this fair mountainous region. I've been offered a position as a manager on the Matsons' ranch in the San Joaquin Valley o' California, wi' a verra good salary offer, enough to some day purchase me own land. Ye read me like a book, Catherine! Wi' a saddened heart, I must leave Virginia City and me beloved family."

Catherine swallows hard to hide her dismay in hearing what she has already sensed. She understands clearly Henry's desire to buy land of his own and make a good living ranching, as working the land is his true forte. She's also in tune with his need to earn a good living to support Mary Alice and the rest of his family in Scotland. Working as an accountant in the mining office does little for his savings. Also, there is Miss Goodman. Catherine is gratified that he does not love Miss Goodman in the way he loved his Annie, and in the way he loves her.

"I know ye've Mary Alice to support. Perhaps bring her to America? I'd be selfish in tryin' to make ye stay, although my life is richer and merrier wi' ye in it."

"Ye ken so much o' what goes on in me mind, Catherine!"

"I'll miss ye greatly, Henry, but 'tis time for me to devote myself to Adam and my family. I haven't told Adam yet, but I'm expectin' anither child. We must make a good life thegither in this wild, rugged land, try to make our little city a better place to live, a place where people aren't gettin' killed right and left for no other reason than religion or ethnicity. Adam truly needs me."

"Ah, Catherine, anither beautiful bairn. What could be better? I promise I'll come back to see me new niece or nephew."

"Ye just better come back often or I'll come after ye, Henry! I'll need to see ye every so often, or my heart will break into a thousand pieces!"

"Aye," replies Henry, "I'll miss ye terribly. 'Tis true, ye're a stronger person than my brither in many ways. Adam deals differently wi' issues and people that cause problems – he becomes verra rigid. He tends to follow laws to the hilt acause he's verra skeptical o' the synchrony o' the universe and what truly keeps the world balanced.

'Tis just Adam's nature! He's a fine man."

"We're different in our perspectives, ye and I from Adam," says Catherine. "I'm not certain as to why. We see an underlyin' balance in the universe that has a rhythm, is smooth and flowing, wherein by lookin' to the heart o' the matter and seeing what is preventing continuity, conflict can be resolved. Rules and laws need not always be followed precisely, like in the case o' interferin' in Paiute tradition." Catherine says this with conviction. "'Tis a practical matter o' savin' a life! Mary shouldn't have died acause she's a Paiute. There could've been a better outcome. All people, no what matter color or creed, must come thegither and prevent these terrible things from happenin'. One cannot turn away acause they're not your people. The wise elders o' Mary's tribe would've come to that conclusion if it had been brought to their attention that a bonnie young squaw was being abused and would die at the hands o' her wrathful husband. Adam would not listen to me on this acause he didn't think it right to get involved. I have to forgive him for his overly-cautious and limited scope."

"The world'll eventually change, but gradually," says Henry. "People are evolvin' and laws are evolvin'. Someday, there'll be more compassion and understandin' o' ithers and a desire to help those o' different races to have decent lives."

BOOK NINE

HENRY

Chapter One

I. Henry Leaves for the San Joaquin Valley — June 1876

Six years after Henry's arrival in Virginia City, Henry moves to the San Joaquin Valley of central California with Dr. Matson and his family (originally of Bridge of Allan and very good friends the Baird brothers), where the doctor has purchased 100 acres of land as an investment. Dr. Matson plans to continue his medical practice in Fresno and have Henry manage his ranch, which is located in the small town of Armona about thirty-six miles from Fresno.

Before finally accepting Dr. Matson's offer, Henry had been conflicted as to whether it was a good decision to move to California. He'd considered the alternative of going back to his family in Bridge of Allan. Another idea he had broached was to travel to Scotland to bring his daughter Mary Alice back with him to Armona. When he wrote of this possibility to his parents, they had responded that Mary was very happy in the Baird household with her siblings, and thriving in the local one-room schoolhouse taught by Miss Carroway. The senior Bairds encouraged Henry to accept the lucrative opportunity in California to make money for his and his daughter's futures, and when Mary was a little more mature and not so emotionally dependent on them, perhaps she would desire to join him in America. Henry hopes to accumulate enough wealth to build a house on his own land someday, and eventually send for Mary Alice to live with him in California, if she chooses to when she is older.

Punt has matured during his Virginia City adventures and decides to go home to his family clan in Bridge of Allan. Chief Elor desperately needs Punt's technological expertise on a full-time basis, as Punt is the mastermind behind all the clan's state-of-the-art computers and monitoring devices. Punt has been able to help his clan of Wee People from afar, but has not been able to carry out all the technological and scientific applications that his father is passing down to him.

There is a festive bon voyage soiree at the Delta Saloon in Virginia City for Henry. He is leaving with the Matson family in two days for Armona, and Punt, atop Henry's shoulder, dressed to the nines in a snazzy kilt, will be zipping off to Scotland on the same day that Henry departs. Miss Goodman, whose hopes for marriage with Henry have been dashed, is too upset to attend, but Henry visits her and presents her with a heartwarming gift – a locket of silver with a small ruby at its center.

Catherine and Adam, who have become more involved in community functions in recent years, host the party for Henry, inviting the many close friends that Adam and Henry have made from the Caledonia mines, as well as good friends from the Virginia City Presbyterian Church, Catherine's Sierra Women's Hiking Club, Friends of the Paiutes Women's Club, and Virginia City Women's Book Club, as well as Adam's fellow Masons. In all, the party consists of over seventy-five people. Catherine's Friends of the Paiutes Women's Club consists of like-minded women who work endlessly to aid in the preservation of the Paiute way of life and welfare of the tribe. Catherine was elected president. The women spend many hours each week baking and selling goods at bazaars and to the local stores. The funds are used to help feed the starving Paiutes at Pyramid Lake as well as the encampment in town. The tribe is still being deprived of their promised food, seeds for farming, and tool allotments from the government, as they are being taken by unscrupulous Indian agents who sell the goods for their own profit.

Catherine has remarked to Adam on a number of occasions that she finds herself becoming more and more like her mother, who loved to participate in her many Helensburgh clubs. Catherine admits that she is enjoying the social life of newfound friends. Adrian's wife, Elise, Catherine's first friend in the city, is the elected president of the book club, and Catherine is vice president.

Catherine informed Adam she is with child again, right after she had told Henry, and he is beaming with happiness and pride about his growing family. There is sadness on both of their parts in Henry's departure, as he has filled their life with much laughter from his charismatic and fun-loving persona, with never a dull moment. Catherine will miss the spritely spirit of Punt as well.

With Catherine's life very active with her growing family and social life, and Henry's move to the San Joaquin Valley, Catherine very rarely thinks about Captain Noble, and has not had any correspondence from him in years. Only when she is idle, which is not often, does she reflect on the titillating romance on the open sea and in snow-laced city of St. John's, Newfoundland. In looking back, she is astonished that this episode of romance and peril on the high seas actually happened. That she had been smitten with the handsome Captain Noble gives her much satisfaction in future years to come, something to reminisce on when she is a more mature woman and her children grown up.

II. Henry Bids Farewell to Punt with Great Sadness

"Goodbye, wee man, I'll be seein' ye in me dreams," whispers Henry, almost in tears.

"Ye'll be seein' me more oft than ye ken, I'm pleased to inform ye," responds Punt assuredly.

"How so?" inquires Henry, leery of Punt's response.

"I'm comin' to visit yer wee lassie bairn, for certain," responds the sprite, as if it should be quite obvious to Henry. And then he brings his hand to his mouth and says, "Whoops! I wasn't supposed to tell ye this."

"What wee lassie?" Henry inquires. "Ye mean Mary Alice? Aye, mebbe Wee Mary will come to live wi' me in the future," he says. "That would be grand."

"Not Wee Mary. Ye'll see," replies Punt cryptically. "'Tis me ye're talkin' to. I've glimpses o' the future. 'Tis one o' me many talents!"

"Ye mean to imply I'll hiv anither bairn?"

"Just wait and see," replies Punt, winking his beautiful blue eye comically. "The future holds a lot o' surprises for ye!"

As Punt is a notorious jokester, Henry does not take his banter seriously, but it gives him something to reflect on, to wonder if there's something to look forward to in his life in the San Joaquin Valley of California. He thinks back to his youth, especially when he first met Annie. How can he explain Annie's existence in his life but as an act of heavenly grace, an act from a higher power? And, of course, there have been many other mysteries in his life. How else can he explain the existence of his wee sprite friend, whom he's been privileged to know his entire life? The fact that many can't see Punt is another great universal mystery. *Why am I friends wi' this extraordinary creature?*

"Henry," says Punt, "we'll be lookin' efter ye from afar. Just ken that we're wi ye always to protect ye. I bid ye farewell for now."

With that remark, Punt flies straight up into the air and heads north. From a distance he looks like the smallest of hummingbirds.

Henry waves a fond farewell with both sadness and excitement in his heart, for he is anticipating a momentous journey to the heartland of California and the beginning of his new life in ranching. At the back of his mind, he's given a lift by the possibility that future events might bring him a family of his own, as Catherine and Adam have. 'Tis somethin' to dream aboot! He often daydreams about bringing his wee Mary Alice from Scotland to America to live with him in California. Is that actually possible? Perhaps a wee sister or brother to play wi' Mary when she arrives would be an added delight.

III. Catherine's Life Minus the Spark of Henry

After Henry's departure for the San Joaquin Valley, life in Virginia City becomes commonplace and uneventful, except for occasional stirrings of the Paiutes, and periodic brawls and murders by the unruliest white citizens, the brawls often occurring in saloons, and the murders usually of Paiutes trespassing on private lands or killed by vengeful vigilantes. A young Paiute buck was innocently going about his business when he was shot down on a major thoroughfare. Catherine finds out about these events from her club friends, never from Adam.

For Henry, Adam, and Catherine, there had existed a bond of great camaraderie as they explored the beautiful Sierra country and California, compounded by laughter and adventurous fun. She misses that. The two brothers together in her life created a perfect arrangement: Adam, her rock, offering a home, a child, and security; Henry and his engaging sidekick, Punt, offering laughter and friendship with someone second-sighted as herself. With Henry out of their lives, Catherine feared her marriage to Adam would reach an all-time low, that she and Adam would find themselves in a quandary, an unexciting relationship that would segue to inevitable doldrums. This did not happen. There is too much to do in the running of a house and tending to wee Belle, as well as the many club activities she is participating in.

Catherine's domestic life, particularly cooking, baking, and canning for her household, and cooking to sell at bazaars for the Paiutes and her other clubs, is an engrossing, enjoyable occupation that keeps her busy. She surprises herself by adjusting quickly to Henry's absence, as she anticipates excitedly another child on the way, and prepares for the baby's arrival by knitting sweaters and caps and gathering up Belle's old baby clothes. Motherhood, she has found, is the one thrill in life she hadn't counted on. *Why hadn't Mum explained to me what it means to be a mother?*

Catherine has come to understand why her mother was so worried for her safety. Every time Belle is out of her sight she becomes anxious. When Belle reaches a milestone, Catherine finds the experience magical. Since becoming pregnant for the second time, her estimation of Adam has changed as well. Catherine finds that Adam is less absorbed in his books and more caring towards his family, especially in regards to her health. Occasionally, he expresses openly how much he adores his family, albeit in his awkward way with words. She takes his comments to heart as an endearing way for him to express his love and concern for her, although some of his expressions could be misconstrued.

"Catherine," he had said to her as he hugged her on the way out the door to the mine, "take care o' yersel'. Daena work yersel' to death – Belle and I need ye to keep us healthy."

IV. Henry in Armona — June 1876

Henry arrives in the quaint little town of Armona in the San Joaquin Valley of central California with the Matson family in 1876. He is to manage 100 acres of prune and peach orchards that Dr. Matson purchased while the good doctor takes over the practice of an elderly doctor. The income from the farm is necessary for a rural doctor, who is often paid in food and gifts, as many of the doctor's patients are seasonal farm workers with little income. Henry falls in love with the beauty of the valley, and enjoys managing the Matson ranch. He works hard and it pays off. In just a few years' time, he is able to buy a forty-acre peach orchard of his own in Armona, and another thirty-acre ranch near Visalia in Tulare, while continuing to make a good income from the Matson ranch. In ten years' time, he has extra cash to invest in oil stocks. In twenty years' time, Henry is a wealthy man and very generous with his money. His life since coming to the San Joaquin Valley has been busy, and he has been quite content living the life of a bachelor, sending more and more money home to his daughter, Mary Alice, and helping his siblings in Scotland with their higher educations. He also enjoys spending time with the Matson family, or staying out on his Tulare ranch in the small cabin he built, about an hour from Armona. There, he fishes in the streams running through his property.

V. Telford and Malkie Receive an Offer from Henry

Postmaster Dean Macleod of Bridge of Allan directs his postman, Birdie Dowd, to deliver a coveted letter from one of their favorite past citizens, Henry Baird, to the Drumdruils ranch. After his delivery, Birdie waits patiently for information regarding the letter's contents in order that he can spread word of Henry's goings-on to neighbors as he heads back down the hill. The letter is inviting Malkie and Telford to join Henry in Armona to help him with three ranches: the

100-acre peach and pear orchards he manages for the Matson family; the thirty-acre vineyard he owns near Visalia; and his forty-acre ranch in Armona. Birdie is given the lowdown by Malkie, and he happily goes on his merry way back down to the Henderson Street post office, all the while spreading the exciting news.

Dear brothers,
I'm very much in need o' extra help wi' the ranches, and in the position to pay a very good wage. I desire to give ye laddies a first offer and money to travel, if yer wanderlust still abides wi' ye. I fondly remember our adolescent dreams o' voyaging to lands afar. Believe me when I endorse the merits o' travel. 'Tis very much worth the effort o' a long ship voyage and land crossing to view this glorious country.
Affectionately,
Your loving brother Henry

Dr. Matson of Armona is in his late sixties, and plans on retirement from his in-town medical practice this year. He is selling his ranch to Henry at that time. With the help of at least of one extra ranch hand, preferably one of his highly experienced brothers who can take over some of the managerial and financial operations, Henry will be freed up to spend more time at his Tulare vineyard. Henry's ranching duties require that he stay over a couple of nights of the week out in Tulare, and for many consecutive days during harvest. He has a very small two-room house built on his vineyard in Tulare, where a very reliable Korean couple has been hired to manage and live. Henry is very fond of the Kims, and they often feed him a hearty breakfast and dinner. He occasionally stays a couple of nights in town, especially if working late into the evenings during harvest. He stays in a boarding house in Tulare to be closer to his poker club friends, where the food is very good and his fellow poker players congregate after supper. When harvest is over he is free to stay at his small cabin and fish for a couple of days.

Henry doesn't plan on Malkie taking him up on his offer, cognizant of the fact that his younger brother is wed, body and soul, to the land of Drumdruils. This is all for the betterment of the family, as far as Henry is concerned, as it is necessary for one of his brothers to stay at Drumdruils to supervise Wee Mary and Susan. Both lasses have voiced their strong desire to remain at Drumdruils after college, the only home they've ever known. The lassies are enrolled at the University of Edinburgh, but come home almost every weekend. The Drumdruils ranch generates a comfortable source of income for Mary and Susan's major living expenses. Henry supplements the rest of their support, sending the girls an allowance every month for college expenses, clothes, music and dance lessons, doctors, dentists, and other necessary sundries that might arise. With the advice of Emma, who now is married and has never lost her love for clothes, Henry often sends all of the lassies gowns from fashionable stores in Fresno whenever he learns of a special occasion for which they will be dressing up. Although Malkie and Susan, and Wee Mary, have made the Drumdruils ranch their permanent home, Henry nevertheless graciously extends the invitation to both Telford and Malkie to avoid hurt feelings.

VI. Farewell to Telford — Departure for America from Glasgow — April 1882

Malkie, Wee Mary, Susan, Janet, and Emma traveled with Telford to Glasgow when he left for America in 1882. They watched his steamer as it made its way far out to sea, and gave him a festive fanfare for his send-off. Telford is to travel by train once in New

York to meet up with Henry in Fresno. Aunt Ethie, Wee Mary's great-aunt, who helped deliver Mary, accompanied the family to the docks. The siblings stay at Ethie's house, as she is always glad to see the Bairds, and Wee Mary spends many weekends with her.

Thirty-two-year-old Telford Baird is beyond excited as he steams away for America. The travel bug that he developed as a child alongside his older brothers during their enchanting bedtime discourses on America was never completely lost – it just lay dormant as his responsibilities at the Drumdruils ranch increased. Telford had always planned to follow his brothers to America. Regrettably, his childhood dream of experiencing the exciting adventures and explorations that Adam and Henry had described in their letters became an abstract notion as day-to-day ranching life took hold and the years passed by quickly. Telford, the eldest Baird brother to remain on the ranch, had initially stayed on with Malkie out of a sense of responsibility to his family. His parents were aging and needed help with household finances, and Wee Mary and Susan needed supervision.

Telford became responsible for the ranch bookkeeping and supervision of the ranch hands after Henry's departure. The senior Bairds died when Susan and Wee Mary were teenagers, still attending class at the small school in Bridge of Allan, and so Telford and Malkie took on parental roles. In the early years, when Henry first left, Malkie was too young to manage the ranch alone, and as the years progressed, Telford had settled on the idea that he'd probably never leave Drumdruils. This realization didn't vex him greatly, as he was content in his childhood home and ranch he was raised on, and had a close relationship with his remaining siblings in Scotland – that is, until Henry made a generous offer to pay for his voyage and all travel expenses along the way, as well money upfront to put down on a small rental cottage in Armona.

With a great offer from Henry to tempt him, and more maturity and confidence under his belt, Telford decided to accept Henry's offer and travel to America. Steamships are now making it across the Atlantic in less than three weeks and the intercontinental railways made traveling across America faster and more comfortable.

Malkie is now quite capable of handling the ranch with the help of the ranch hands. A couple of years earlier, Telford had instructed Malkie in all matters pertaining to the bookkeeping of the ranch as well as the home finances. Surprisingly, to those aware of Malkie's less than sparkling academic performance, he excelled at numbers and came to enjoy the financial part of his job.

Susan and Wee Mary are now young adults and away at the University of Edinburgh part of the year, with Wee Mary now eighteen and Susan twenty-one years of age. When they are home for the summer and holidays, Malkie, who adores them, is overjoyed they are back to keep him company. Housekeeper Violet, though getting on in years, is still an integral part of the family. Since the Senior Bairds' deaths, she has taken over the role of mothering the lassies and tending to their needs. Mrs. Cook still creates all the meals, though her husband died very near the time that the senior Bairds had passed on.

Telford's plan is to travel to America to broaden his horizons beyond the limited confines of his small farming community, but only help Henry out on a temporary basis. At thirty-two, he has grown into an intelligent, pragmatic young man, similar to his brother Adam in character, temperament, and outlook on life, though less shy, and like Adam has a hidden ambition to become an urbane, scholarly man with experience and knowledge of the world at large. He also has a penchant for expressing himself in writing that he desires to develop. When Telford accepts Henry's offer, he has it in mind to ranch for several years with Henry and then try his luck in the mines – he read that gold and silver is still to be found in Nevada and California, though it's now much harder to come by. After a few years of investigating lucrative mines that haven't been developed, his plan is to come back to Drumdruils.

Telford has a lot of ideas for his life back in Scotland. Eventually, he desires to bear some sort of a leadership role in the community of Bridge of Allan, as their father once bore, to possibly run for office on the Bridge of Allan City Council, and to work on a newspaper as a nature and travel columnist.

Telford arrives in Armona and becomes an integral part of life on Henry's ranches. Henry loves to have Telford around, and Telford is an enthusiastic partner who has gained much skill as a rancher at Drumdruils. The two brothers develop the same type of camaraderie that Henry and Adam had in Virginia City. It is a time in both of their lives that they enjoy themselves immensely in the outdoors. Telford and Henry spend time fishing and hunting together on the land that Henry owns in Tulare, about twenty miles from Armona. The two brothers spend time camping in the mountains, and often travel up to view the beautiful sequoia trees in the southern Sierra Mountains.

Telford continues his writing as a pastime and begins contributing nature articles to the *Armona Star Gazette*. His stories about his hikes through the beautiful countryside and the sequoias are tremendously popular among readers. He has a large following every Sunday in the nature column that he writes in the evening after ranching. Telford shows such an interest in writing that Henry decides to send him to a small college in Fresno to hone his writing skills. After working on the ranch for approximately five years, Telford is offered a job at the newspaper as a full-time writer and assistant editor, hired by Sam Fairway, the senior editor and manager of the *Armona Star Gazette*. Telford's plan to move on to a mining endeavor in Nevada never reaches fruition.

Chapter Two

I. Henry Meets Sarah Weir at a Picnic — Summer 1896

Henry arrives at a picnic hosted by the Matsons by himself. As he walks across the parkland to join his group of friends, he observes a woman sitting in the hot valley sun at a picnic table all alone, writing in her notebook at a frenetic pace. He looks to this very handsome woman with great curiosity. *At least she's covered with a hat*, thinks Henry. She is so intent on her task that she doesn't notice Henry approaching her to introduce himself. He wonders, with great interest, why this lovely lady is not with the rest of the picnickers, who are sitting at another table in the shade of a large oak tree, taking in the cool river breeze, drinking ale, and laughing at one another's humorous yarns. The Matsons see Henry approaching, and call him over, not seeming perturbed by the singular woman out in the sun at a table fifty feet away. Henry thinks that perhaps she is not part of the picnic group at all, but just happens to be seated close by. He decides to invite her to join their group, so she'll be out of the sun, as there is only one large tree in the vicinity to take cover under. Henry waves back to the picnickers, and goes over to the woman's table first.

"Hallo," says Henry gallantly. "I pray I'm na disturbin' ye. Ye're involved in somethin' verra important, I can tell by yer mad scrawlin'. I only pray ye're na overcome by the might o' the sun. A lovely pearly skin ye've been blessed wi'." Sarah jumps with a start, laughing gaily when she becomes aware of Henry's presence.

"Oh, my Lord, you startled me! Not all that important what I'm doing. Oh, dear, I must look like I've been ostracized from the rest of the party for bad table manners. I'm only over here for a few short minutes, as I had a great idea for the *Armona Star Gazette*, and had to jot my thoughts down before I forgot. Had to get away from those wild people to concentrate," she adds, as she raises her eyes in feigned disapproval, looking over to the table where raucous laughter abounds.

"Ah, then ye work for the newspaper?" inquires Henry with interest. "I've niver met a woman wi' a profession o' writin'. Ye might be familiar wi' me brither, Telford Baird, who works on the paper as well."

"You're Telford's brother? Oh, my goodness, I should have known that by the looks and the accent. Just didn't put two and two together. I know Telford well; in fact, he is one of my bosses. I'm not truly employed by the paper, but I contribute to the community affairs column once a week. The article is due tomorrow, so I didn't want to dillydally, as inspiration comes to me only on a whim. Creative ideas don't flow that often, and I must take advantage of what comes to my mind. I came up with an idea about the care of Armona's parks, and the need for the city to plant more trees. Case in point – there's only one shade tree for picnickers. They have planted beautiful Italian cypress in the cemetery over there" – she points to the entrance gates – "but not out here where we sit baking like turnovers in the oven. I'm writing in my column about how I've experienced firsthand the wrath of the sun from my table."

"Och, I daena desire to hamper yer creative streak," voices Henry politely but with humor.

"Not at all. I've completed my column, thank heavens. Hope the folks of Armona take some interest in my idea to make this park more enjoyable for everyone. It's a place that the farm workers' families enjoy on their Sundays, after working long and hard hours in the fields all week, a wonderful place where their children can cool off in the river."

"Aye, 'tis a noble idea. Let me introduce mysel'. I'm Henry Baird, come down from Virginia City, Nevada, o'er twenty-five years ago. Originally from Bridge o' Allan, Scotland, o' the Drumdruils Ranch."

"Well, so very glad to meet you, Mr. Henry Baird. My name is Sarah Weir Tuxbre. I'm a widow from a small town near Kansas City, Missouri, from a ranch as well," replies Sarah in her beautiful voice and perfect enunciation. "I've been out here only for only six months myself. That's my brother, John Weir, with the Matsons over at the table, and my daughter Clara is the little blonde girl playing with the other kids."

"Ah, ye're a member o' our party," says Henry with relief. "Heavens, I kent mebbe ye're a figment o' me wild imagination." He looks over to the cemetery plots adjacent to the park and winks. "One can niver can be too careful. I've a knack for attractin' unusual creatures – na that ye're onything but a lovely human creature, really na that unusual, but na ordinary in yer habits."

Sarah laughs heartily. "Oh, my heavens, I must appear quite ridiculous out here all by myself. You thought maybe I was a valley phantom risen up from the graveyard soil? I'm so glad you were brave enough to come over," she jokes. "Thought you'd never have the nerve, as I saw you walking towards my table and veering away when others called. Was disappointed that you'd given up on saving a damsel in distress from withering away in the sun. Let's go over and I'll introduce you to my brother, if you haven't met him yet. Indeed, it's time to get out of the sun. I'll be freckled and as wrinkled as an ol' prune."

"On the contrary – a touch o' the sun has blessed ye wi' a golden radiance," replies Henry gallantly, and with his consummate wit, adds, "and prunes are quite sweet and delectable. By the way, I've been friends wi' yer brither John for o'er twenty years. Heard he'd a sister out visitin', but hiv niver had the pleasure to lay me eyes on ye afore. Ye hiv remained well hidden from me, like a forbidden goddess creature o' the valley."

Sarah and Henry take to each other immediately, as they both possess intellect and wit and charismatic personalities that are quite synchronous. Together they rustle up a lot of laughter and jest for their own amusement, and for others at the picnic. Sarah steals Henry's heart away with her beautiful porcelain skin and fine features, her quick, inquiring mind, and her strong-willed, independent-minded demeanor. He finds her a compelling woman, appealing in her wholesomeness, a very handsome woman, not daintily pretty, but with a rare aura of spontaneity and lightness, sparking comfort and confidence in any individual by her presence.

Henry and Sarah have a whirlwind courtship, and together enjoy a renewed sense of their long-lost youths, broken up by years of hard work and the tragedies they've endured in their lives. The coming together of Sarah and Henry is indeed a joyous occasion, one that Henry recalls was predicted by Punt.

Ah, Punt, Henry thinks, looking up to the sky on his wedding day, *ye're richt. There's another lassie in this grand universe that suits me just fine. I'm sure Annie would approve.*

Sarah and Henry are married three years later in 1899, and their beautiful daughter, Katherine, is born five years later in 1904.

II. In Armona — The Incomparable Sarah Weir Baird, Henry's Second Wife

Sarah Baird is propped up against the white-pine headboard, as she has been for the last two months, due to complications from the birth of Baby Katherine eight months ago. Her bed and the bookshelf next to her bed are laden with an assortment of books, most that she has read before. She has pens and a stationery set on the other bedside table for writing her column in the town's newspaper, the *Armona Star Gazette*. Her favorite authors are Tolstoy and Dickens, but she is ensconced presently in Jane Austen, dreaming of visiting the beautiful city of Bath, England, where Jane spent her young adulthood amongst the gentry, entertaining themselves with lavish balls, daytime socials, and theater events. The mineral waters in Bath have special healing properties, and people in Jane's era had come from afar to bathe in the spas and drink the special curative waters. Sarah dreams of visiting the Meeting Square with the healing springs, where the wealthy had socialized every day. She would relish sinking into the therapeutic hot baths, the waters absorbing her pain, filtering out like a sieve those pesky invaders wreaking havoc on her body. *Perhaps the waters would heal me entirely of my malady*, she thinks.

At her request, Sarah's bed was moved to the eastern window, which enables her a view of the sunny countryside in the morning. She gazes longingly at the old sycamores and elms that line the long drive to the farmhouse, wishing she could walk out under their green camouflaging boughs and relish in their canopy of soft, muted shade. She used to spend many afternoons walking below them. Looking off in the distance to the east, she sees the Sierras rising majestically to the heavens. When she first arrived in the valley, she had ridden with her brother in a buggy up the switchback dirt roads into the mountains to view the magnificent forests of giant sequoias some sixty miles to the east, sacred ancient redwood trees, some older than Christ. Henry had taken her up there also on one of their early dates before their marriage.

Sarah studies the light coming in through the beveled glass window, the way it fans out into colors on the windowsill and dances on the walls in spectral prism patterns. She is on a first-name basis with all the birds that live in the tall, narrow Italian cypress trees lining the side of the house, especially the high-strung vociferous jays that flitter and fuss like gossipy old ladies, promulgating excited warnings to her about the approach of neighboring wildlife. They are so agitated at times lately that she wonders if they have a prescience of doomsday coming.

They must know something's up, she thinks. *I wonder who informed those gossipy creatures of my illness?*

Sarah loves the dry, arid climate of the San Joaquin Valley, with its torrid summers, wherein the rich black loam smells to her like a mix of an expensive tobacco and dried cow dung. Much to her surprise, she has come to love the nostril-filling dung scent from the cows, its rich earthiness an awakening of the senses. The scents coming from the sugar beet refineries in the valley also remind her of cow smells, but with more sweetness. Sarah and her first husband had cattle on their dairy farm in Missouri, but the scents were completely different, kind of gaseous smelling. She speculates the difference is because of the type of soil and that they had Guernseys for milking.

The days in the San Joaquin Valley are so hot that the cattle seek refuge under the cottonwood and poplar trees by the stream, but the evenings are gloriously warm, alive, and refreshing after the day's heat, and socked full of the many critter sounds of the valley. She had never seen such colorful sunsets before she came out West. With each setting of the sun comes a work of art that she can't get enough of, transfixed by the magenta, lavender, yellow, and salmon swirls of color.

In the winter the tule fog lies low across the valley, visibility reaching no further than one's outstretched arm. Sarah can feel and smell the absolute freshness of the damp, tangy air that has a life of its own as it creeps across the valley floor, sweeping across the mineral-rich, living spirit of the land. It hovers overhead for days on end during the winter, thick as pea soup. The winters are cold and wonderfully tranquil, and lend to a sense of coziness and sereneness, like being ensconced in a protective cocoon.

With the coming of summer, the heat bakes the rich, fertile soil until it is parched and cracking. One can feel the sheer energy of the land that has absorbed the hot sun into the far reaches of its infinite layers of richness. On this summer morning, she listens to the woebegone coos of the morning doves, their beautiful reedy voices a dominant part of the San Joaquin Valley's morning vocals, though she thinks they start their chorus much too early, at a time when the flat wide valley is just being tinged the color of red clay by the rising sun.

Eight years ago, when she came to live on her brother John's farm in the rural town of Armona, after her husband Ben had died tragically of pneumonia, she never thought she'd be happy again, being left entirely destitute with her seven-year-old child, Clara, to bring up alone. Sarah never would have imagined a life in the West, being that she stems from a long-established Midwestern family, her grandfather having come over from Scotland in the 1700s before the American Revolution to settle in Kentucky.

Her father had moved the family to a small Missouri town near Kansas City when she was small. Sarah is now madly in love with everything in the West, so different than anything she'd ever known in the Midwest. She was in dire straits after her husband's death, without relations nearby or any means of support. The farm had gone bankrupt and was repossessed by the bank. The harsh reality of widowhood had weighed down upon her with a nightmarish feeling of having come to a dead end with nowhere to go, and the thought of giving up Clara to someone who could feed and clothe her was a painful possibility. When her brother graciously invited her West to stay with him and his wife on his California farm in their large house, there was no other choice but to accept what she considered a charitable offer. Sarah was unsure about taking up space in his house, no matter how large. In California, she didn't know if she could provide Clara with a good life, but John had a small girl, Gladys, who could be Clara's companion. Then, out of the blue, before she'd had a chance to accept living in his home, John offered her a foreman's cottage rent-free that had just been vacated. It had one small bedroom and a small living area/kitchen area.

Sarah hadn't expected she'd like it so much in the California's San Joaquin Valley, for she had heard of the hellish weather, the hot summers and thick, soupy fog of the winters. She expected that her life would consist of raising her child with dignified acceptance of a being a poor and sedate middle-aged widow, but much to her surprise a new, exciting chapter in her life materialized at the ripe old age of thirty-seven.

Six months after her arrival in Armona, when Henry Baird introduced himself to her at the picnic hosted by her friends, the Matsons, it was like a breath of fresh air had come over her rather staid, though content life. Clara was settled happily at her school and had made good friends, and Sarah was happily writing her column for the local town newspaper, and had also made some good friends at the paper and amongst the farmers' wives. She had enough money to survive on thanks to John's rent-free cottage and an abundance of food from the vegetable garden, and the small payments from each column she wrote.

Sarah had become very impressed with Henry after they had walked over to join the picnickers at the main table. Three or four children came over to climb on him as if he was a large rock, and Henry played with them as if they were his own. Sarah concluded that children are good judges of character, and these kids certainly were attracted to the handsome Scotsman, who lacked any arrogance.

Sarah and Henry hit it off splendidly thereafter. Both she and Henry are clever and witty, and very intelligent. Indeed, they have confided to each other since their marriage that their meeting must have been one mapped out in heaven. At the picnic, Henry was acting his usual outlandish, witty self, and his great sense of humor was evident, which put her at ease and brought out her own wit and sense of humor. His kindness was apparent in his gentle mannerisms and the intelligent look in his twinkling green-blue eyes. The soft lilt of his Scottish accent swept her away completely. Sarah was totally smitten by his charms, and she learned from further interactions that Henry was an extremely generous and kindhearted gentleman, and quite well off. He was helping to college educate his siblings in Scotland, as he had made quite a lot of money from oil well investments. He owned a vineyard with a house out of town, which was run by a Korean family, as well as a house in town – the house that Sarah came to live in with him. She learned he was also managing a large ranch for the Matson family, located several miles out of town, so Dr. Matson could pursue his medical practice.

Sarah married Henry three years after meeting him, and has spent the happiest days of her life with "my charming and amusing Henry," as she refers to him.

"My Henry is the wittiest and funniest man I have ever known," she writes her friends. "His presence is a godsend in my life. There is never a dull moment. I am truly blessed with a kind, splendid man."

Even now that Sarah's illness has made her sedentary, she is still a very happy woman due to Henry, Clara, and her Baby Katherine, though she is tired of lying in bed day and night. After Henry is gone off to the ranch in the early hours of the morn and Clara is off to school, the main light in her day is when their housekeeper, Ernestine, brings her beautiful sweet baby to her, whose peachy skin and wisps of auburn hair delight her to no end. Katherine looks like an expensive porcelain baby doll, and is an exceptional child already. Her personality is already well developed, with so many exuberant mannerisms for such a young soul. Katherine, Sarah can tell, is constantly thinking and absorbing new information. Her little lips try to copy the movement of Sarah's, and she calls her "Mamma." She smiles and laughs with Sarah, and is such a loving baby. Katherine pats her mother with her little hand while she is feeding her a bottle, and puts her face close up to her mother's cheek in a loving gesture when she is being held.

The rest of Sarah's day is spent looking out the window or reading, and fortunately she's a voracious reader, which is probably why her eyesight is so poor, so that her small, rounded frame eyeglasses have gotten thicker each year. She is no longer nursing because the doctor said she has some kind of infection, a complication of giving birth, but insists on feeding the baby bottles of breast milk offered from a friend who is nursing her own baby.

With the library of books at her bedside, and those strewn across the bed, she has kept busy, and her good humor has not dwindled in the two months of her illness, since the infection set in after the birth. The doctor had explained that some of the placenta may have not exited completely and is now festering. She must rest, Dr. Battle has said, to fight the infection off.

Sarah has been writing a weekly column for the *Armona Star Gazette* as a way to keep in touch with friends, relatives, and townspeople. She no longer writes the social column, as she is unable to get into town to gather the newsy bits of the goings-on in the community. She has found from comments turned in to the newspaper office and published each week by the editor, her friend Sam Fairway, that the townsfolk are truly interested in her being bed-bound and in her philosophical thoughts on life in general. This has given her a purpose while lying in bed. Sarah relays her day-to-day thoughts, which are revealing and heartfelt, and she has a great amount of time on her hands to ponder the many facets of life. Dr. Battle has advised that it would be wise not to have visitors while she is convalescing, as exposure to new germs might bring on a setback due to her condition.

"What condition is that?" she had inquired of the doctor when he had told her she could have no visitors.

Dr. Battle had hemmed and hawed, and had finally come up with the idea, which seemed like a far-fetched hypothesis to Sarah, that interaction with the public might affect her already fragile state. "There is a risk of dire sickness with exposure to new germs due to your weakened immune system," he had told her.

Sarah sees neither rhyme nor reason for people not visiting her while she's lying in bed, expending little or no energy with little to do. What could people give her in the way of germs that she hasn't been exposed to by Henry, the baby, and others who care for her? Fortunately, her good friend Sadie Thompson, assistant editor at the *Armona Star Gazette*, typesets her column and makes it a regular feature in the community section. About 500 copies of the newspaper go out every week to townspeople and ranchers. She is able to keep her friends abreast of everything that is going on in her life, how wonderfully little Katherine is developing, and what she has been reading and thinking about.

One of Sarah's last weekly newsletters for the *Gazette*:
Dear family and friends of Armona,
I've just finished reading Dostoyevsky's *Anna Karenina* for the umpteenth time. She is a woman I can truly empathize with. What is a woman to do if the love of her life is gone and there is no way for her to live without him? Or vice versa. I'm thinking of my Henry when I'm gone. What is a man to do without his woman? My Henry is a survivor though.

As for my own life, the state of my body does not match the clarity of my mind. I can't fathom why the simple natural process of pregnancy can be so detrimental to a woman's body, but many women do die in childbirth or afterwards from complications. The human race does march on and will do fine without me.

Dr. Battle says that my body is not winning the battle against the infectious growths in my abdomen, and that it will it be a hard uphill battle to overcome the enemy. These are my descriptive "warring" words, of course. I look at this as much a battle as any battle of war. I have come to terms with my fate. If I fight off the enemy, I will go on with my life as it is; if I lose the battle, I'll have two beautiful daughters to leave behind to take my place in the world.

Signing off for now,

Sarah Weir Baird

III. Sarah Baird's Funeral Draws a Crowd — 1905

Sarah's funeral service is held on a crisp and clear autumn morning at the Armona Presbyterian Church on Main Street – a quaint, white clapboard structure with a classic wood church tower and tapering spire. Townspeople revered Sarah, regarded her as a remarkable positive influence on the community. Through her columns, they came to admire her indomitable spirit in the face of a life-threatening illness. The majority of the small town of Armona is present to pay their respects to a beloved member of the community – farmers have left their fields to lift their wives into wagons to head for town, storekeepers have closed up shop, neighbors have walked down the short blocks to the church; some folks have taken their children out of school to pay their respects to Sarah. Many have been devoted followers of Sarah's weekly letters, eagerly reading each entry like a novella installment, keeping tabs on the health of their friend and praying for the best outcome until there was no hope left. Everyone has planned for this day – Sarah had said that the day of her passing was imminent in her last column of two weeks ago, though her way of saying it was quite eloquent.

"Dear folks," she had written, "I will soon be soaring up and away, and reaching for the unknown, as I feel my time has come soon to meet my maker."

The townspeople flow solemnly into the church and take their seats on the polished hardwood pews. The church fills up to the brim, and a group of people stands in the back along the wall. On cue, as the organ begins to play, the sun streams in through a beautiful stained glass window behind the altar like a peacock spreading out its brilliant-colored tail, transfixing the church in a realm of sacred light.

Henry views this inspiring display of resplendent color as a fitting tribute to his wife as she takes a coveted place in the Kingdom o' the Almichty. He sits in the front row pew holding Clara's hand, who is gazing upward at the glass, mesmerized by the prism-patterns that bounce to the rhythm of Mrs. Baker's somber organ hymn. Henry thinks that this is not so bad, that Sarah would really like the service, and how nice it is to just sit and abandon despairing feelings for a wee bit and think of Sarah's spirit flying o'er another wonderful realm of existence. He glances across the aisle and forgets himself, smiling at some of the church ladies' hats, which seem to have taken on a life of their own, appearing to him as exotic jungle animals. *If Punt were here*, he thinks amusedly, *those ladies would be in trouble, sitting ducks for an audacious prank*. Henry is weary, his mind in a stupor from lack of sleep, but he is thankful for the mental fog that dulls his ability to dwell on the finality of death. He can feel the eyes of the congregation on the back of his head, causing his scalp to tingle. He clears his throat and sits up straighter. He is gratified that so many have come out to pay their respects for his dear Sarah, and turns his head around and smiles to everyone in a gesture of appreciation.

Henry looks behind him to see what Clara is looking at. Weir Smith, a distant relation of Sarah's, attired in navy-blue knickers and knee-highs, his hair plastered back from his forehead, is making a ghoulish face at Clara. She leans into Henry's side and hides her pained face in the folds of his suit coat.

Clara is hoping this is all one big mistake – her mother's death might not be real, only a bad dream that will be gone when she awakens. Her mother might reappear magically at their house after the service like a happy ending in one of her fairy tales. Sarah prepared Clara extensively for her death, and Clara assured her mother she understood that her mother was going to be gone for a very, very long time, but Clara is still holding out for a miracle. She is having a hard time distinguishing between fantasy and reality, especially now when it is easier to live in a daydream rather than accept the stark terms of death.

Wishes do come true, she reflects. *Mother told me that she'd be watching over me, would be keeping me safe, and wants me to be happy until we are together again. It would make me so very happy for her to come back now, although she said she'd be gone for a long time. If she knows how much I need her maybe she'll come back sooner.*

"My physical body is going away for good, dear Clara, but that doesn't mean I won't be with you in spirit," she had said. "Clear yourself of all thoughts, Clara, my dear, and think of me. You'll certainly sense that I'm there with you at your side."

Clara doesn't quite understand the concept of seeing her mother again in spiritual form. Today is the day Sarah said she could be seen in church. Her mother had instructed her to clear her mind for this special day, to think of her in spirit, to try hard to sense her presence in church at the special celebration of her life. Sarah had told her she wouldn't miss a church service in her honor for anything.

Clara gazes listlessly up at the resplendent stained glass window. Of course, her mother wouldn't miss her own "celebration of life," but she would prefer her to make her presence known after she's back at home, where she imagines everything will miraculously be back to normal. *Mother will certainly be waiting for us in the kitchen, preparing tea and scones, with raspberry jam and cream,* she ventures to dream.

Reverend Samuel Brody commences the sermon by asking everyone to rise. It is an effort for Henry to stand. The invariable emotional upheaval brought on by the death of his dear one has taken its toll, and his body is bone tired from lack of sleep. Reverend Brody instructs the congregation to recite with him the Lord's Prayer. Henry gets up and lifts Clara to her feet. She is still fixated on the stained glass window, the sun spraying a rainbow of colors onto the chancel and nave. Clara then senses her mother's presence and remains fixated in awe. Henry gazes up to see what she's looking at.

The sermon is a short but lovely tribute to Sarah by Reverend Brody, who duly praises Sarah's character – her considerable contributions to the community as a capable leader of many community events, her membership in the Eastern Star, her contributions to the *Armona Star Gazette*, her devotion as a wife and mother and, above all, her fearlessness in meeting a sickness head-on. The reverend captures the beauty of Sarah's short, remarkable life by equating her to "one who sparks other people into acts of duty and kindness, inspiring people to be their best to set a wonderful example." Sarah had picked out hymns for the choir to sing at her service: "Ave Maria," "Amazing Grace," and "The Lord's Prayer," and the choir leads the parishioners in a sing-along.

Sarah is buried in Armona Cemetery at the end of Main Street, in the town's only burial site, beside a beautiful row of robust Italian cypress.

BOOK TEN

THOSE REMAINING IN SCOTLAND

Chapter One

I. The Baird Siblings in Scotland and Housekeeper Violet

Henry has tried many times to get Wee Mary to come to America, but much to his dismay, his daughter has been adamant in her desire to stay with Susan and Malkie on the Drumdruils ranch. Despite the great expanse of ocean and landmass between them, Henry, fortunately, is not out of touch with Mary; in fact, he often communicates with her telepathically because both are endowed with second-sight. In this way, they can pick up on the day-to-day wellbeing of each other to ensure that all is well. Also, since Mary has gotten older (since high school and university years), with the help of the Wee People, technology has paved the way for the two to communicate even more effectively. With the expertise of Punt, Mary is able to view Henry with the advanced electronic equipment in Elor's lab. Mary is often taken down to the dun-shi for a session with Henry, to use a computer with real-time audio/video technology that was developed in the twenty-first century (but of course well known already to the brilliant wee time travelers). Henry, with the aid of Punt, installed the advanced technology in his Armona house as well.

Mary writes Henry to inform him of the date and hour (in his time zone) in which she would like to visit with him, and Henry responds back if this is a good time or not for him, and will suggest another time if it's not convenient. Henry is then able to sit down at his dining room table with a viewing screen at a designated date and time and have a real-time session with Mary. Henry often prepares, in advance, an entertaining discourse especially for Mary, usually a humorous rundown of life on the ranch, news of the family, and the latest milestones of his daughter Katherine. On many occasions after Sarah's death, when Katherine was still a bairn, Henry would have her on his lap, and so Mary was able to see her beautiful redheaded half-sister, who looks so much like their father.

Henry keeps up on Mary's school and social activities, and on the lives of his siblings, Susan and Malkie, as well as Housekeeper Violet. Mary and Henry correspond frequently by letter as well as exchange gifts and items of interest. Henry often writes down a list of books he's been reading, as both are avid readers, or sends clippings from newspapers of local events happening in the San Joaquin Valley; for instance, articles on the Tulare County Fair, occurring each September at the fairgrounds, or articles on fashion from the *Fresno Bee* that Mary and the other siblings like to keep up on. Mary will do the same, and oftentimes encloses pressed wildflowers from Scotland that Henry loves to receive. Through real-time virtual technology, Henry and Mary keep up with the social and civic goings-on Scotland and California.

II. Violet Goes Into the Dun-Shi

Violet takes her last walk on earth as Violet Shaw, the housekeeper of Drumdruils, and strolls down the woodsy paths that she and the Baird children habitually strolled for so many years; her intent is to meet up with Elor and Twixie for an epic journey. Over the years, Violet has aided in the development of all her Baird charges, and presently, at the ripe old age of eighty, is ready to move on to another realm of existence. Her stay at Drumdruils has suited her, as she has watched with pride the brood of Baird children grow up to be productive and successful adults. There are only three Baird siblings remaining in Scotland: Janet, Emma, and Malkie, plus Wee Mary, as they still call her, Henry's daughter. All of the children have now reached adulthood, with Mary and Susan at university in Edinburgh. The senior Bairds passed on over five years ago. Violet has missed their presence in the house greatly, for it was Jean and Adam Sr. who created such a harmonious environment on the ranch for their wonderful family, to which Violet, to this day, feels blessed to have been a part of.

Violet meets up with Elor and Twixie by a stream and nods in acquiescence as Elor greets her jovially with, "'Tis a very fine day to go to the dun-shi, dear Violet. Are ye ready for yer new home?"

Violet is more than ready to start her new way of being. This monumental journey will be a life changer for her. She will abide in the dun-shi as a bona fide semi-angel in training until she has earned the necessary credits to be a full-fledged Wee One. The dun-shi, where the Wee Ones dwell, is a vast subterranean world that opens up to infinite domains of reality. Infinite possibilities for her existence are available on infinite planes.

Violet has planned for this time, a retirement of sorts, all her life, and has looked forward to living in another realm where she might expand her mind and enjoy the thrilling novelty of experiencing new worlds, traveling from her home base of Scotland to multitudinous dimensions and times. She has no qualms about leaving, for once she has evolved into a Wee One, she will have the ability to fly over the earthly terrain with her glorious fairy wings, to communicate with Emma and Wee Mary, who, with their second-sight, can keep her informed about the rest of her far-away brood: the three Baird siblings now living in America. She is thrilled to have learned that although Punt is living in California and raising his family, he continues to fly in and out of the dun-shi at Drumdruils at will, keeping everyone informed about the lives of Henry, Adam, Telford, and Henry's daughter Katherine.

Violet will be able to keep in contact with Emma at University of Edinburgh, for Emma is in possession of very acute second-sight, and Emma will be visiting the Drumdruils farm on a regular basis to check up on her younger siblings. Violet will also eventually communicate with Malkie, though Malkie will keep on believing that Wee People don't exist, that Emma and Mary are playing make-believe games. "An imaginative bunch of dreamers, ye are," he tells them – that is, until a monumental happening occurs in his life. All the same, until then, he listens with rapt ears to what Violet and his second-sighted sisters communicate to him about the goings-on of his family in America.

Chapter Two

I. Janet and Emma Baird, All Grown Up

Emma and Janet are college graduates, both with advanced degrees financed with the help of primarily Henry, and are presently living in Edinburgh. Emma is a professor at the University of Edinburgh, soon to be married to another professor, and Janet is a wealthy housewife, socialite, and philanthropist devoted to many just causes, such as the wretched slum conditions of the poor in Edinburgh. She has played an integral part in the cleanup of the tenements in the city, where there have been outbreaks of cholera, diphtheria, and tuberculosis because of the horrid living conditions.

Susan and Wee Mary (not so wee anymore), in their late teens and attending classes at the University of Edinburgh, are of a mind to stay on the ranch at Drumdruils with their brother Malkie, whom they have deemed needs their protective influence, as Malkie has always been a very sensitive soul in need of emotional support. The lassies guide their brother through the rigors and upheavals of life to ensure that he is happy, well adjusted, and a successful rancher. Of all the Baird children, Violet had surmised that Susan, Wee Mary, and Malkie were meant to be together at Drumdruils, as they are all in many ways emotionally wed to the beautiful Scottish terrain and to the blissful life that this bucolic land of Wee Ones offers. They have always been close to one another, being the youngest three siblings.

One day, late in the summer, Malkie walks out to his fields with his head held high and shoulders back, feeling content and safe, very proud to be tending to his land on his beloved Drumdruils ranch. Malkie's perspective totally changes on that day when a miraculous event occurs – he falls into a dun-shi!

II. Lo and Behold, Malkie Develops Second-Sight

As at the glimpse of morning pale,
The lance-fly spreads his silken sail,
And gleams with blendings soft and bright,
Till lost in shade of fading night;
So rise from earth the lovely Fay,
So vanished far in heaven away

– Joseph Rodman Drake's "Culprit Fay"

Malkie is thirty years old, unmarried, and quite content to tend to the land he loves. Over the past several years, his older sisters, Emma and Janet, have brought quite a few of their single women friends to the Drumdruils ranch for weekend retreats, with the intent of making a match for Malkie. Thus far, he has not been enamored of any of the lassies, nor they of him. Malkie is a nice-looking young man, but his reticent, standoffish nature evokes some doubt among his female guests as to the normalcy of this man. Those who don't know Malkie wonder if he is "quite richt in the heid." He seems more interested in communicating with farm animals than with people, and when guests stay at Drumdruils and meet Malkie, they find him an awkward, obtuse conversationalist. Malkie often says nothing and stares at the others for long bouts, which makes visitors uncomfortable, as they have conveyed to Emma and Janet. Contrariwise, Susan and Mary are quite charming, and guests are generally impressed by their good looks, intelligence, and wit, which makes up for their brother's oddity. When Malkie does communicate it is slow, truncated talk, each sentence an uphill endeavor, to the point that guests, as if playing charades, help him out by filling in the words for him. His subject matter pertains mostly to animal husbandry, berry crops, or the weather, which the visiting city lassies find quite dull.

It doesn't bother Malkie that he hasn't found a suitable mate, for he is quite happy living with Wee Mary and Susan, and is never lonely at all with the two of them coming back from university on the weekends. They are lively and fun to be around, and have always been good companions to Malkie and kept him in good humor. The lasses maintain the vegetable and flower gardens that Violet left behind, and take long walks with their brother on the paths they took as children. After Violet went into the dun-shi, Malkie hired a woman to live in Violet's cottage to do the housekeeping and cooking, a Mrs. Ruth Smith. She is a middle-aged woman who is shy and speaks little, and reminds him to his satisfaction of their old cook, Mrs. Cook, who lived with them for so long. Susan and Wee Mary, attending university, are kept busy studying and are involved in many activities in town on weekend evenings such as concerts and dances, and an occasional walking out with a male companion. Malkie wants everything to remain the same as it has always been, as this is his nature, to have no marked changes to disturb the status quo of his life. The lassies have promised to come back to teach school in Bridge of Allan after college.

Malkie is quite content having stayed in Bridge of Allan, and never has been sorry about not joining his siblings in America. The brothers write to him often and continually try to persuade him to visit them in America, as the continent is so full of exotic wonders, but the invitations never entice him to even consider attempting the long boat journey across the Atlantic and a long train trip across the nation. *Quite a monumental and dangerous venture*, he thinks, though he misses his three brothers. *Mebbe 'tis fear*, he reflects. *I daedna want to die in a strange land on a visit, as I'm foriver attached to this part o' the world.*

Of all the Baird siblings, Malkie is the most sensitive, especially to death. Ever since his best friend, Cammie, died by falling off the bridge into the roiling River Allan, and Janet's best friend, Mary MacLaine, froze in a sheep pasture, he hasn't trusted his fate on earth. And then, his little sister, Wee Mary, the namesake of Mary MacLaine, almost succumbed to pneumonia. *It is a dangerous world out there*, he decides. He doesn't want to tempt fate. He sees death around every corner and desires to stay at home to die. *It's a hit or miss thing*, he thinks. *Why take chances wi' life far away in a savage land that is verra dangerous, whaur ye hiv a great chance o' dyin' a' ony moment!* Besides, he rationalizes, someone has to stay and look after the ranch and take care of Mary and Susan. This is not quite logical, as he has enough ranch hands to take over entirely, and his sisters can take care of themselves. He feels protective of his older sisters, Janet and Emma, as well, though they are both grown women in their twenties, Janet married and Emma to be married soon. *The weaker sex needs protection and supervision*, he has always thought, and he's the only brother left to do this.

Henry and Adam, particularly Henry, supported the lasses with their educations, and Emma has become a well-respected professor at the University of Edinburgh. Janet attained her diploma in social services. Malkie's older brothers offered to send him to college as well, but he declined. His place is on the land, working the rich soil to produce some of the best berries in Scotland, and raising livestock for milk and meat as well as profit.

When the sisters come up from Edinburgh and visit with Malkie on the weekends, Janet's husband, Maxwell Meredith, comes up as well. Most of the time, Janet stays at Drumdruils with her siblings and visiting friends while her husband stays a mile away on their country estate in neighboring Dunblane, and participates in golfing at his club. The entire family all come to together for special holidays at the large country home of Janet and Maxwell, or at Drumdruils.

One day in late August, as Malkie walks the land, he gazes down from the hills to the light blue cast of the River Allan, which appears to him like a slithering snake cutting through the village, dividing it into halves. He looks over the tops of the red-tiled roofs of the village, where he can just barely make out the high-rising tower clock of the bank, which he loves to hear chime the hour. He finds himself standing near the edge of the hilly green mounds that rise up in the pastureland, the dun-shis that his sisters have always called the home territory of the Wee Ones. He looks out to the distant town again, and then brings his eyes to his present location. For the first time since he was a wee lad under seven years of age, he is startled to see a swarm of large dragonflies buzzing around the hill next to him. They fly close and then fly off, and can be seen from his vantage point landing o'er some hilly mounds just a furlong away. Extraordinarily, as they land, they appear to become larger, and now appear to him to be more like stand-up stick figures. Malkie assumes the aberration is because the high sun is playing tricks on his eyes. He concludes that he is looking at little trees in the distance that look like stand-up figures, though they do move, which is probably brought about by the breeze. Near him, he views more dragonflies swarming o'er some of the grassy mounds. He continues to gaze out in the distance at the sight of the small trees that look like a group of children, and adamantly tries to convince himself that they are merely trees. In his continuance of looking out into the distance, one of the trees is definitely changing position, and he's trying to figure out why a tree is moving. He takes a couple of steps forward, not taking notice of where he is stepping. He inadvertently finds himself atop a dun-shi mound, which he has always shied away from getting too close to before, as his sisters have warned him against stepping on them. After only seconds of his feet touching the mound, he falls down, down, down into the bowels of the earth, landing on a bed of silk comforters. To his astonishment, he is greeted by Violet, who breaks into tears at the sight of her dear laddie. She knew he'd make it down sometime, though. "It was just a matter of time," she tells him. Malkie is so glad to see Violet that he forgets what has just happened to him and the oddity of where he is.

The Wee People are delighted to see Malkie, and bring out food, drink, and their pipes, and the merriment begins with fiddles and jig dancing. The Wee Ones are well aware that Malkie needs to learn how to enjoy himself, as he has always been quite a dour young laddie his entire his life. Malkie stays with the Wee Ones for what seems to be a few hours, but time is distorted in the dun-shi, for he's entered a plane of existence where time is condensed. Though he seems to be in the dun-shi for a week, when he comes back out, he finds only a few hours have passed in the day, by the position of the sun in the sky. It is the same day, as the cows he left in the pasture are still there, and back at the house Wee Mary and Susan don't seem to have missed him, as if he were just out in the pasture for a short time. When he was down below in the dun-shi, Malkie is entertained to the hilt. He learns to jig, drinks a special magical drink to make him laugh uproariously like he's never laughed before, and is entertained with a couple of fantasy journeys to other dimensions. Malkie comes back a changed man. When he gets back outside to the present time, he sees Wee People flying as dragonflies and landing as three-foot wee creatures o'er his land.

Och, he thinks, *they've been there aw o' the time, only I couldna see them. What a fool I've been!*

Every day as he goes out on his land, he accepts the fact that these special creatures, as he calls them now, are an integral part of his life. He tells Mary that he can see them, and he finds them quite lovely, as they care about the land as much as he does. She is not surprised.

"Ye're so much part o' this land, it resonates through yer spirit. 'Tis a wee wonder ye'd no been sensitive to everything livin' o'er this land afore. I'll ask Elor why ye've developed second-sight verra late in life."

"No need to ask him," replies Malkie proudly. "I've spent many days wi' them and learned aw 'bout Wee Ones."

Malkie understands now why Emma has always lived in her head, with her lively imagination. He envies her for being so productive with creative thoughts flowing from her continuously. That is why she excelled in philosophy at the university, and is to this day well known for her books of verse. Emma is a renowned poetry scholar as well as a philosophy professor. Her published books are well known throughout England and Scotland. She even had a chance to meet Robert Burns, which was a great highlight in her life. All of her works are related to the beauty of Drumdruils and the goings-on of the land.

Malkie thinks of Emma and her upcoming nuptials to Dean Rutherford, Ph.D. The couple will live in the Edinburgh and both teach at the university. She won't be far away, thinks Malkie. He is thankful that Susan and Mary are content to live with him on the land he loves.

III. Soon-To-Be Mrs. Emma Baird Rutherford

Emma walks along the woodsy path to visit Twixie, Violet, and Elor. It is Emma's last day before her nuptials, and then she'll be off to her honeymoon on the Isle of Skye. Twixie helped to design her wedding dress. The wedding is to take place on the lawn at

Drumdruils, with a reception on the porch and lawn. Tomorrow, she is marrying Professor Dean Rutherford of the University of Edinburgh, a professor of medical law. The Rutherfords are a wealthy family with an estate not far from Bridge of Allan in neighboring Dunblane. Emma and her new husband will spend many weekends near Drumdruils, so Emma plans to drop in on her siblings quite often, and live weekdays in Edinburgh in a terraced eighteenth-century manner house on Princess Street.

She walks slowly down the trail to the small stream that lies next to the Wee One's dun-shi, reminiscing about all the fine times she had as a child at Drumdruils. She savors the vivid beauty of the trees and foliage that are just changing to their yellow, orange, and red autumn colors. It is a walk she and her siblings took so often with Violet when they met up with the Wee Ones as children, a walk she has written poetry about.

Emma has become a professor of epistemology at the University of Edinburgh, a branch of philosophy that deals with the nature of knowledge and how it relates to the concepts of truth, belief, and justification. Her mentor and advisor has been the renowned professor James Frederick Ferrier, a metaphysical writer who coined the word epistemology, though he passed away in the last year of her studies. Emma was his prized protégé, and he found in her an enthusiastic, receptive, and brilliant student to pass on the research theories he had developed over his career. Emma's siblings never quite grasp what epistemology is, so she usually says she is a professor of philosophy. With her insight into what is coming in the world of technology and medicine, Emma is able to gear her lectures towards environmental and health issues brought on with the advent of new technologies, as well as ethics from voluntary consciousness in regards to medical law, industrial law, and public heath issues, as proposed by Ferrier. Also, the world is changing in women's equality, and the philosophical implications of this are touched on in Emma's lectures to her students.

Elor and Twixie have called on Emma to visit them, and she strolls along the wooden bridge going over the little stream to talk to the Wee Ones. She's thinking that they are probably going to give her some advice on marriage. *I'll be glad to have some*, she reflects, *as I hiv no idea what it will be like to be married, work, and raise children aw at one time.*

Elor and Twixie fly out o'er the bridge as Emma looks down into the murky water, and they soon land before her in their larger, child-like sizes. Elor hands her a package, and she assumes it is a wedding gift.

"Thank ye for the gift. Shall I open it now?"

"Aye, indeed. I want to explain it to ye," replies Elor.

She opens up the package to find a thick, brown leather-bound book with gold lettering that she will need to carefully translate with the help of the Wee Ones. Elor explains it is the ancient sacred covenants of the Wee People. "Aw o' our ethics a' laws," he says. "This book will be useful in yer lectures," explains Elor, "for it relates to many o' the problematic ethical issues o' today, and those that'll arise in the future as yer world becomes more technologically advanced."

Emma is extremely grateful for this treasure, and relishes the chance to educate her students so that as the advances in civilization occur, there'll be educated folk to take the lead and advance laws for the wellbeing of Scotland and the world at large.

IV. Emma's Wedding

The next morning, at eleven o'clock sharp, Emma walks down the path of blue hydrangeas, arranged in large urns, to the music from Susan's organ, brought out from the sitting room. The organist from the Presbyterian church in town begins with Mendelssohn's "Wedding March."

The weather is superb for early October, and guests have all have taken their seats on the lawn chairs provided by a restaurant in town. Janet is Emma's matron of honor, and Susan and Wee Mary are her bridesmaids. The esteemed Reverend Michael Anders from Edinburgh, who is pastor of Emma's church in the city, officiates the service.

Emma looks out to see the Wee Ones dressed in their finery off in the distance, and as the sermon starts they fly o'er the lawn in dragonfly formation, landing on bushes and shrubs around the pulpit so they can get a bird's-eye view of the ceremony.

The handsome, sandy-haired groom, Dr. Dean Rutherford, looks dapper in his tuxedo as he strolls down the aisle with his mother, Mrs. Winifred Rutherford. He seats her in the front row and takes his place at the front of the pulpit before the reverend. Malkie walks Emma down the red-carpeted aisle lined by blue and white flowers. She wears a beautiful cream silk, iridescent gown of a Grecian style, with an empire waist and translucent lace sleeves designed by Twixie. The bodice is embedded with tiny iridescent freshwater pearls. There are twenty tiny, satin-covered buttons running down the back of the dress. Emma wears a translucent veil draping down to her shoulders, held by a tiara of white baby's-breath flowers on her head.

Malkie is dressed to the nines in a tuxedo, which lends him quite a different image than his country persona. The maidens in their seats from Emma's university look perplexed, as they've never seen Malkie look so handsome. *Mebbe,* thinks Emma, before she walks down the aisle to the tune of the wedding march, *Malkie will find a fine match at my wedding. Wouldn't that be wonderful?* She waves to the Wee Ones as she comes down the aisle, and the guests assume she is waving at them, as they all wave back. She senses Violet is there, but cannot tell where she is, but knows she'd never miss her wedding. Violet is one of the tiny dragonflies flying out on the grass, creating an aerial spectacle of glorious light, color, and motion, with masterful aerodynamic showmanship.

The sermon is short but lovely, expressing the sanctity and joys of marriage, and words of wisdom from an ancient Hebrew text about honoring and cherishing one's partner in life. The bride and groom exchange rings, and the young couple is officially wed in holy matrimony. After the ceremony, a grand feast is served on the front porch, and umbrella-shaded tables with white lace tablecloths are spread out over the front lawn, the meal catered by a local Bridge of Allan restaurant. The highlights are smoked salmon, eel, pheasant, and quail, as well as baked ham. There is Drambuie ginger ale punch, Laphroaig scotch from the Isle of Islay, spiced honey punch and ginger ale for the children.

V. Malkie Meets His Match

Emma invited her student, Allison Wren, to her wedding, in the hopes of making a match with Malkie. She is a Ph.D. student of Emma's, terribly nearsighted and endearingly awkward, but a very intelligent and lovely young woman. Allison stands out to Emma as being a little different than the other young lassies in her class, appearing to have less concern in her appearance and coming across in her conversations and mannerisms as having much less ego than her peers. Emma admires Allison for her natural effect. When Emma first met Allison, she had thought of Malkie immediately. Something in their natures is the same. They both tend to focus on things that ordinary people don't focus on, sort of having an oblique mode of operation in the world.

Malkie spots Allison as soon as she arrives and asks Emma who she is. The moment he first lays eyes on her she is down on her hands and knees on the grass, poking a baby frog. Malkie loves frogs and this endears her to him.

Malkie falls in love with Allison, and after receiving her degree, she moves to Bridge of Allan and marries Malkie. Susan and Mary love Allison and she becomes a best friend to them. The three women and Malkie now hold down the fort at Drumdruils.

EPILOGUE

ADAM, HENRY, AND CATHERINE IN FRESNO — LATER YEARS

Catherine and Adam continue to live in Nevada until 1887. During this time, Adam works at the Caledonia, Savage, and Belcher mines in Virginia City and Gold Hill, with one summer spent at Lake Tahoe. Catherine has five more children to keep her busy – Jean, Will, Margaret, Ethel, and Mary. In later years, they move to Fresno in the San Joaquin Valley, not far from Henry in Armona, and remain close to the twice-widowed Henry and his daughter Katherine. Henry never marries again.

I. Twilight Years of Catherine, Henry, and Adam

Catherine came to enjoy her life in Virginia City after Henry left for California. Her marriage to Adam gave her the stability and love she needed after the death of her parents and sister. Her six children lend her much joy, and when she looks back she can't imagine life without any of them, each child so different and yet cherished by her and Adam. Catherine is grateful for the difficult choice she had made in coming to America to marry Adam and not staying in Newfoundland with the captain. Now a middle-aged woman living in Fresno, with Henry living close by, an added sense of satisfaction in life has been lent to her. Catherine and Henry relish one another's company without any of the sexual tension that existed when they were young. They enjoy the camaraderie that comes from being second-sighted, and have great fun with Punt and his family. Punt's kids are as wild as he was when he was younger, even a tad more so, and as they laughingly conclude "Punt got what he deserves." Punt's lads have been known to pull some hilarious pranks on their father. Henry laughs in reminiscing with Catherine and Henry what they have come to call "The Bird and the Wasp Episode" – the time the wee laddies stuck a small bird to Punt's shoulder with honey while he napped. What a spectacle it was when Punt awoke and tried to swat the bird away. The bird was hopelessly stuck, digging its claws into Punt's shoulder while trying to free itself. The crisis escalated as wasps in the area came storming in torrents, and poor Punt was getting stung. His only recourse was to run and jump into the cow pond, whereby the bird and the wasps took flight.

When Punt, looking for pity, told Henry of what his lads had done, Henry responded laughingly, "Punt, ye were an excellent teacher!"

In the years following their reunion in the San Joaquin Valley, after Henry is semi-retired from ranch work, Catherine, Adam, and Henry spend much time together reminiscing over their past years in Virginia City, enjoying each other's families, and most of all sharing their special connection of being Scots from a mystical, paradisiacal country. Henry and Adam often reminisce on their youths growing up on the ranch in Drumdruils.

Henry asks, "Recall when we were in Scotland as lads and told bedtime stories o' what the West would be like? Did it live up to yer expectations, Adam?"

"Aye, it lived up to and went beyond me imagination," replies Adam. "The West is more beautiful than we could iver hiv imagined, even when we embellished greatly on its magnificence."

Henry lives only a couple hours by buggy ride from his brother and sister-in-law, and rejoices in seeing their six children, whom he adores, as well as being able to spend more time with his own daughter, Katherine, who moved to Fresno to live with Adam and Catherine to attend high school. Henry travels to Fresno on the weekends to visit every chance he gets.

The threesome, Adam, Catherine, and Henry, travel often to the beautiful Sierra Mountains, with their glorious ancient redwood trees and beautiful rivers, and picnic or camp together in

Sherman Meadows.

Being the generous man that he is, and quite wealthy, Henry has taken it upon himself to fund the educations of all Adam and Catherine's children. Catherine stills loves Henry and Henry adores Catherine, and they both love Adam, so the comfort of being together as a trio is quite a fine recipe for a happy life in their golden years.

II. Henry Reflects on His Life

As a mature man in his late sixties, Henry looks back on his life, from youth to present day, and accepts with humble gratitude the memorable singular events, good and bad, that occurred in each decade. He is grateful for the days of just plain living, day-to-day aliveness – enjoyment in breathing fresh air, savoring plentiful food, soul-calming, meaningful work on his bucolic land, being in the midst and at the mercy of nature in its glory of showy seasons, with awe-inspiring heavenly skies and rich, aromatic earth, multicolored flora and fauna, and the innate mystical purity of water. Above all, his raison d'être for being born, he thinks, is hobnobbing with the motley representations of humanity, getting in tune with the dichotomy of frailty and strength possessed by the human spirit, in all forms of good and evil. He is gratified for the privilege of having known so many individuals, each one whom he equates to singular stars in the sky, for they have filled and educated his soul with a vast tapestry of light – glowing beings orchestrated by the universe, in their infinite variations and complexities. He has concluded that each person he has encountered in life is a smidgeon of the Oneness of All. Henry concedes that the bounties in his life have been great – pleasures offsetting the pain of his personal losses, but not lessening the tragedy and heartache. Yet some unknown force has kept him treading onward with his feet solidly planted on the ground, his mind fixed on the splendor of life. Life, he has concluded, is of such a short duration that one must be grateful and take advantage of all of life's gifts while they last.

Living through almost seven decades has endowed Henry with great insight and acknowledgement that his soul has expanded because of his experiences. He is philosophical about the good and the bad occurrences of his life, especially when considering the pain he endured with the deaths of his two wives, but with maturity he has come away with a soothing insight. The past pains have lessened with time, and he has come to understand that these experiences have reaffirmed his belief in the everlasting human spirit.

Henry, as a more mature man in his late sixties, recognizes that his deceased second wife, Sarah, had something in common with Annie MacGivens, his first wife, and with Mary MacLaine, the wee friend of his sister Janet who froze to death in the sheep pasture when he was a young laddie at Drumdruils. All three graced the world with their sweetness and vibrancy but were destined for shorter stays on earth than most, leaving a lasting remembrance of goodness that outshines everything else in the world, counteracting the bitterness and ugliness in life that pops up again and again like pesky flies. These dear human souls were like warm summer breezes wafting o'er pristine lochs. The lassies were a touch of spice and honey, a touch of magic, a touch of heaven on earth. Henry accepts knowingly that these rare beautiful creatures touched him deeply, that they provided him ever-flowing reminders of the beauty of the human spirit.

Being gifted with second-sightedness, and sharing his gift with Catherine, has given him insight to the grand complexity of a magical universe, and appreciation that what he has lived through in this fast and fleeting lifetime is only one page in the book of his soul's existence – there are so many more chapters for him to experience outside the earthly realm. In his maturity, he has gratitude for the bountiful gifts in life that he's been blessed with – Adam and Catherine; his daughter Katherine; his wives, Annie and Sarah; his daughter Mary and his large Drumdruils family; and, above all, his Wee Ones. As he sits serenely on his porch, smoking his pipe, taking in the sweet scents and sounds of the night – perfumes of jasmine and honeysuckle; birds and insects chirpings; the rustling of trees in a warm, velvety night breeze; the rich aromatic soil of the valley – he reflects that it will be a very fine experience, indeed, when the mysterious workings of his life are revealed to him when he enters another realm after death. He will then have perfect peace.

III. Adam Reflects on His Life

In middle age, Adam looks back at his long life with awe and with pride in what he has experienced and accomplished. Who would have thought that a shy, tongue-twisted, young laddie from Scotland would have made it across a wild and unsettled American continent to begin a new life in the West, and make acquaintances with handsome and clever indigenous people and people from all over the world? That he married a beautiful young woman, Catherine, a childhood friend from Scotland, is a blessing he never takes lightly, nor the added blessing of his five daughters and son. He acknowledges that Catherine, with her vital spirit and beautiful essence, has filled his soul with much joy and meaning. With Catherine at his side, he's had his share of a cornucopia of life's gifts, and its trials and tribulations – sadness and anger, elation and happiness, and everything in between, in an endearing, long-enduring relationship with his family. Adam reflects on the fact that as a result of having had so much going on in his life, he has inadvertently and with ease shed his armor of shyness. Through the years, particularly in Fresno, he experienced the association of many people through his work in the mines and his civic duties, and was able to exert his personality and share his views. He became liked and respected by many citizens in Virginia City. He was seen as a gentleman of intellect and sound judgment.

Now in middle age, Adam has developed a closer and more compatible relationship with Catherine, especially since the children have left home, and has come to regard her as his intellectual equal. Circumstances have eased since the time he was working in the mine when he had little energy left in the evening but to be alone with a good book. The couple has spent many evenings discussing world affairs as well as local civic and political events. Mornings bring on new topics of conversation as they peruse the newspaper together over coffee. To Catherine's satisfaction, they often have discussions about books they have both read. She, less busy with children, eagerly picks up Adam's books when he is done and reads them in their entirety.

Catherine is politically more liberal than Adam, and occasionally they get into heated discussions and have spats, but they both acknowledge to themselves that this kind of interaction is invigorating and healthy for their relationship. Catherine feels less closed off from her husband than she did early in their marriage, when Adam was ensconced in his own protective, private world.

Adam's life changed in Virginia City when he left the bone-tiring work in the mines and became a builder. His workdays were adjusted to an eight-hour schedule, enabling him to be at home for supper with his family by early evening. In many ways, this physical easing of his workload transformed his perspective and lent him time to see the rapid transitions that were taking place with his family and life in general, the flux of days that had to be appreciated and enjoyed before they got away. Adam looks back with pride at his work in the mines, as well as his craft of building lovely homes in Virginia City.

In Fresno, Adam became part owner of a hardware store that gave him a chance to chat and be personable with customers only when he desired, as he wasn't tied him down to the daily running of the store. In the summer months, he greatly enjoyed being out on the land helping Henry with the harvesting, bringing to fruition the beautiful peach, grape, date, almond, and pear crops.

A constant in Adam's life has been his charismatic brother Henry. Adam's life would not have been the same without the dynamic spirit of Henry, so different than himself, but very necessary for his growth as a human being. Henry in being Henry taught him to have the courage to set out on his own, to fulfill his dream to travel to America. Adam reflects that it was the contagion of Henry's glowing optimism, his humor, his wit, and his surety that life is to learn from and take pleasure in. This created the stage for an introverted Adam to view the world as a hospitable, giving place, a place to explore, spread one's wings, and cherish with exuberance.

In later life, Adam became brazen enough to discuss with Catherine the subject of her earlier romantic attachments with the captain and Henry. Catherine was totally taken aback when she learned that Adam had thought about the close relationship she shared with Henry. She had assumed he had not been bothered by it, for he'd always appeared oblivious to anything going on between them. As for the captain, she'd never discussed that relationship with her husband, and so wondered how he had known, other than to have surmised that she had been smitten.

"Catherine, did ye love the captain? It seems he was blown away by your beauty and personality, and would hiv married ye if he'd had the chance." Catherine looks up and blushes, which Adam finds very attractive.

"I read a letter the captain sent ye that was under the bed. I picked it up by accident," he confesses guiltily. "The letter was chock full o' this man's love for ye."

"Aye, Adam, the captain was a magical fairy tale of my youth. He sparked my spirit with light, and actually gave me a very fine gift to carry into my life's journey with ye, a present o' joyful memories o' youth. 'Tis what he blessed me wi'. What could be more enjoyable than for a dowdy, overweight, middle-aged mother of six to reflect on a fantasy romance on the high seas? 'Tis far more real and entertaining than reading one o' my romance novels."

Adam clears his throat and gets his nerve up to dig deeper.

"What about me brither, Henry? Did ye iver consider him a better match than me? I often wonder if he would've been more suitable to ye." Adam coughs and laughs with mild embarrassment, aware of the irony of a husband asking his wife about a better choice than himself after years and years of marriage. "Ye hiv been close to Henry, are more alike to him than me, and understand him probably far better than I do," he adds.

"Aye, Adam, Henry and I have been close acause o' being kindred spirits. We're cut from the same mold wi' our second-sightedness and our outlook on life is the same, but Henry was niver the man I was intended to marry. If matches are made in heaven, my dear husband, you're the one made 'specially for me." Adam looks gratified.

"Henry's verra desirable. All me life I've seen how the lassies flocked to him," Adam responds.

"Aye, yer brither's an outstandin' specimen o' a man. I've always thought that he was a wee bit like the captain acause they both hiv that innate ability to spark a flame in the spirits o' women. They've a unique quality the lassies are drawn to like fireflies to light. Otherworldly men are like fine wine to be entertained by, have one's heart and soul lifted by, but not the best to marry."

With that comment, Catherine drops into a dreamy reflection of the role that these two men played her life. The memories that reel through her mind like fairy tale romances in movies will be brought to light in times when she feels the need to remember that she was once an adventurous, beautiful, and desirable young woman. These memories are linked intricately with her need to keep her heart and spirit in touch with her basic essence – who she is apart from being a wife, mother, and aging woman – for day-to-day living often leaves one out of touch with the amazing knowledge of the orchestrated synchrony of one's life. Her sea voyage, a pleasurable slice of a golden time to revisit reminds her that she was once young and vigorous, that she experienced the total exhilarating aliveness of being caught in splendorous magic, a play staged with all the right components – a handsome man, the blissful sea, celestial skies leading to infinite heavens, a friendly lantern-like moon, and a young girl eager to take on the world.

IV. Catherine Muses on Her Life

Catherine, in late middle age, revisits her youth, now and again, with a perspective brought on by maturity and a heart full of gratitude for what transpired through the cascading years. Her only regret is that the years have passed by so swiftly, one on top of the other, coalescing into blocks of time that singularly can't be deciphered into day-to-day happenings, ordinary days that can't be remembered for any particular relevance or meaning, only days of ordinary living, waking-up-mornings and going-to-bed nights, all gone by like money being spent. Within these chunks of days piled on top of each other are highlights: her marriage to Adam, the birth of her six children, her life in Virginia City with many friends, Paiutes and white folks, her close friendship with Henry, and her unforgettable romance on the high seas with Captain Noble. She concedes, though, that the major highlights in her life have been within the realm of her marriage to Adam, her rock-solid companion of a lifetime, whom she treasures more than words can describe, and her six witty and beautiful children, who have given her everything to live for. She sees her lack of vision in youth to even question Adam not being the perfect partner for her. He has been a godsend.

And, of course, there is Henry. Oh, thank the Almichty for Henry! What she can she say about Henry's part in her life but that he has graced it with a touch of magic from the heavens. With Henry, she took a step into the mystical unknown and was blessed with knowledge that there is much more to the senses than humans are capable of perceiving. They shared the enchantment of Wee Ones, whose very presence has been synonymous with the mystical realm of the universe, incomprehensible but in existence without any doubt, and all the other mysteries on the fringe of one's perception.

Yes, Catherine was able to experience so much in her life, the excitement of traveling to America when young, living in Virginia City amongst Paiute friends and club friends alike, the romantic adventures with the captain, the intense, soulful love for Henry, and the steadfast, all-enduring love she has had for Adam and her children. This has added to the fabric of her spirit and the growth of her soul. In looking back, she sees a predetermined destiny played out its hand in her life. If not for her childhood friendship with Adam in Scotland and the death of sister Ruthie and her parents, she would never have come to America at Adam's request. Had it not been for this chain of events, Catherine never would have met the captain, never would have had a friendship with Henry, and, above all, would never have married Adam and been blessed with her six children. Catherine is very much satisfied with so much richness having encompassed her on this planet. She can see her soul's growth in all of her earthly experiences.

V. Deaths of Catherine, Adam, and Henry

Catherine and Henry both died in their late seventies, Henry in

1925 and Catherine in 1926. Adam moved to Oakland after the death of Catherine to be near his daughters, Ethel Baird Eccleston and Jean Baird, in Oakland, and Margaret Baird White in Piedmont. He lived into his late eighties. In Oakland, he spent time lawn bowling along the shores of Lake Merritt, and lived with his daughter Jean, a single woman and librarian for the Alameda County Library. His youngest daughter, Mary, lived east of Oakland in the small rural town of Brentwood on a ranch with her husband, Andrew Bonnickson, about forty miles away, and he visited her often. His second oldest daughter, Margaret, lived in Piedmont and died of breast cancer. Belle, their firstborn daughter, died in childbirth. Ethel Baird Eccleston lived to the age 92 in the Oakland Hills, the author's paternal grandmother.

Review Requested:
We'd like to know if you enjoyed the book. Please consider leaving a review on the platform from which you purchased the book.

CPSIA information can be obtained
at www.ICGtesting.com
Printed in the USA
BVHW031454080322
630899BV00001B/23

9 781682 354858